Father's day   June 1996

Dear Jerome

Happy Father's Day

I love you ♡

Gloria

LINES OF FATE

Lines of Fate

a Novel

MARK KHARITONOV

TRANSLATED FROM THE RUSSIAN
BY HELENA GOSCILO

THE NEW PRESS
NEW YORK

ORIGINALLY PUBLISHED IN FRANCE BY LIBRARIE ARTHÈME FAYARD.
ALL RIGHTS RESERVED. NO PART OF THIS BOOK MAY BE REPRODUCED IN
ANY FORM WITHOUT WRITTEN PERMISSION FROM THE PUBLISHER.

LIBRARY OF CONGRESS CATALOGING-IN-PUBLICATION DATA

Kharitonov, Mark.
      [Linii sud'by, ili, Sunduchok Milashevicha. English]
      Lines of fate, or, Milashevich's little trunk: a novel / Mark Kharitonov;
      translated by Helena Goscilo.
          p.   cm.
      ISBN 1-56584-230-8
      I. Goscilo, Helena. II. Title.
PG3482.6.H2654L5613   1996
891.73'44—dc20   95-21819 CIP

PUBLISHED IN THE UNITED STATES BY THE NEW PRESS, NEW YORK
DISTRIBUTED BY W. W. NORTON & COMPANY, INC., NEW YORK

Established in 1990 as a major alternative to the large, commercial publishing
houses, The New Press is a full-scale nonprofit American book publisher outside of the university presses. The Press is operated editorially in the public
interest, rather than for private gain; it is committed to publishing in innova-
tive ways works of educational, cultural, and community value that, despite
their intellectual merits, might not normally be commercially viable. The New
Press's editorial offices are located at the City University of New York.

Book design by Hall Smyth and Gordon Whiteside of BAD
Production management by Kim Waymer

Printed in the United States of America

9 8 7 6 5 4 3 2 1

INTRODUCTION

When Mark Kharitonov's *Lines of Fate* won the prestigious Booker Prize for the best Russian novel of 1992, the dominant reaction of Western specialists in Russian literature was intrigued puzzlement. Who was Mark Kharitonov? A proverbial dark horse, for even Moscow's normally informed readers had, at best, only nodding acquaintance with his prose.

Known principally for his translations of Elias Canetti, Hermann Hesse, Franz Kafka, Thomas Mann, and Stefan Zweig, Kharitonov (born in Ukraine at the height of Stalin's terror, in 1937) had worked as a secondary school teacher, a journalist, and an editor for a publishing house before settling on a freelance career as a translator (1969). Although he devoted considerable energy to his own fiction during the 1970s, after the publication of his first story in 1976, in the liberal journal *New World*, he waited twelve years before seeing his next book, *A Day in February*, in print.

Kharitonov's major literary achievement is the trilogy *A Provincial Philosophy*, comprising *Prokhor Menshutin* (wr. 1971, pd. 1988), *Lines of Fate* (wr. 1985, pd. 1992), and *A Provincial Philosophy* (wr. 1977, pd. 1993). Translations of his selected prose have appeared in Germany, Holland, Japan, Portugal, Sweden, and the Czech Republic; the French publisher Fayard plans to issue his complete fiction to date.

A mystery novel populated with artists, criminals, drug addicts, sorcerers, suicides, and half-wits, *Lines of Fate* combines a love story with a spiritual voyage. It contains slogans, poems, songs, aphorisms, stream-of-consciousness meditation, and extracts from a writer's notebook. Its cast of characters includes approximately fifty individuals. And it is profoundly concerned with Russia's past and present. In short, this (the second) volume of the trilogy that occupied

1

Kharitonov almost two decades, is Russia's *Doctor Zhivago* for the 1980s. Like Nobel laureate Boris Pasternak's novel, *Lines of Fate* charts the spiritual path of Russia's destiny through the creative philosophy of its outwardly hapless but inwardly inspired protagonists. Perhaps the critical difference between the two ambitious works, which observe the Russian tradition of seeking answers to "eternal questions" against the backdrop of a turbulent era, is the lesser degree of exaltation in Kharitonov's more self-consciously modern text.

Like its celebrated predecessor, *Lines of Fate* acknowledges the heady anticipation of Russia's historical upheavals, especially the October Revolution of 1917. Its focus, however, emphasizes the crippling effects of Soviet power—on the nation as a whole and on the psyches of its individual representatives. The chaos ushered in by the Soviet regime expressed itself in what Kharitonov calls the persistent "melody of destruction and loss"—bloodshed, hunger, separations, clandestine organizations and incarcerations, the wholesale demolition of an entire way of life, and the threatened disintegration not only of personal identity but also of continuity between generations. The tragic disparity between motivations and actions, theory and practice, hopes and consequences runs throughout the novel.

Kharitonov shows how the personal lives of people with profound vision become mangled in the meat grinder of Soviet planning, how the utopian dream of a "bright future" transforms Russia into a giant orphanage. Yet the weight of the novel falls on the redemptive potential of creativity and the human impulse to restore form and meaning in the midst of mayhem. Like Pasternak, Kharitonov has faith in secular miracles. That is why the coincidences that disturbed some readers of Pasternak's lyrical novel proliferate in the chance encounters, startling repetitions, and crisscrossing of fates in Kharitonov's complex narrative. Apparent coincidences are central to Kharitonov's understanding of history.

Lines of Fate embraces the Tolstoyan concept of history as a process that cannot be captured. Indeed, history is synonymous with mystery. In retrospect it can only be posited, collated from scraps by individuals with investigative passions. Subjectivity directs our bent for establishing coherent connections: we try "to glue together the grains of knowledge with the saliva of conjecture," and "after the fact even a misunderstanding looks like an inevitability." Insight into human psychology takes precedence over empirical verification of "what happened," or, to use Kharitonov's own formulation, "for history and life, so-called myths are often more realistic than so-called facts." Not unlike Freudians, we tend to find what we seek; we become the narratives we read, which in turn reflect us. This symbiosis is not error, but necessity, for "we understand ourselves through others (that's what both books and people are for)." If the self constructs the world in its own image, that self inevitably changes in the process.

Lines of Fate recalls several *glasnost* and post-*glasnost* publications, notably Mikhail Kuraev's novella *Captain Dikshtein,* which similarly stresses the prosaic minutiae of "swarm" life while deconstructing history as metanarrative. In dramatizing the process of assembling a continuous story line from disparate, often contradictory fragments, both works approximate verbally what cinema does effortlessly—to convey simultaneity through crosscutting and narrativize it via montage. Indeed, cinematic and musical techniques to a large degree determine the tempo and texture of Kharitonov's prose.

To simulate the fragmentation of life narratives, Kharitonov plays a variation on the age-old device of the discovered manuscript. In this case, the text from the past must be assembled from bits and pieces of candy wrapper sheets (*fantiki*), which during the early Soviet era of shortages substituted for regular paper. The scholar Lizavin's efforts to "piece together" the biography of the provincial writer Milashevich from the loose *fantiki* covered with the latter's ruminations serve as an organizing metaphor for the novel. That metaphor captures Milashevich's struggles to connect his own youth with his maturity, other characters' insistence on grasping the link between seemingly discrete aspects of their own or others' life experiences, and, ultimately, our desire as readers to "make sense" of *Lines of Fate.* The novel repeatedly stresses meaningful connection— between individuals, moments, eras, bodies, lands, buildings, and, for the immediate purposes of plot, between the enigmatic ideas

3

recorded on the numerous uncollated *fantiki*. If "the time is out of joint," then random insights may "set it right" only if they themselves cohere, become integrated into a "philosophy."

Both the suspect and the sublime power of the creative word enables that connection, achieved across space and especially time between the novel's twinned key figures: the writer-philosopher Simeon Milashevich, who presumably perished in the late 1920's, and the young dissertator Anton Lizavin, who approximately half a century later researches local literati of the postrevolutionary era. The two engage in a dialogue about life, history, and fate. Boundaries between decades, between imagined and empirically verifiable matter, between Milashevich and Lizavin, blur and periodically vanish in the novel's aleatory but insistent movement toward a perceived truth about human existence.

That truth resides not in the country's political center, but in "real Russia," in the provinces where Kharitonov elaborates his "provincial philosophy." It rests on a hard-won balance between the reassuring coziness of provincial life and the crushing boredom of its sedative rhythms, which breed a restless desire for change. That split in the human psyche recalls the dualism of entropy and energy depicted in Yevgenii Zamiatin's dystopian novel *We* (1926) and the eternal battle within the "heart of man" that Dostoyevski dramatized in *The Brothers Karamazov* (1880). Indeed, *Lines of Fate* reexamines the major preoccupations of the Russian novelistic tradition, to conclude that the banality of the everyday is the inevitable stuff of life, while creativity is the ultimate reconciler.

Kharitonov conveys his sense of timeless truths and of life's cyclic patterns through the related devices of repetition, echo, overlap, and doubling. Characters appear in multiple and mysterious incarnations: Milashevich's beloved Aleksandra Paradizova "returns" as Lizavin's Zoia; Milashevich himself becomes "resurrected" through Lizavin's passion for his writings; the painter Bosoi the Flyer returns from military combat as the poet Iona Sverbeyev, later to become the founder of a children's orphanage; the religious figure of Makarii splinters into two or three selves, and so forth. Moreover, Kharitonov's reliance on musical leitmotifs not only creates the illusion of eternal "basic principles," but also reinforces the symbolic significance of such recurrent objects as mirrors, plants, suitcases, clocks, angels, sweets, and paper.

Contradiction and paradox, according to Kharitonov, are inseparable from human psychology and the course of Russia's past. His own ironic, subtly shaded sense of the world complicates the task of locating him in contemporary Russian culture. For instance, in contrast to such transparently sardonic labels as Karl (Marx), Phenomenov, Printsip, and Kaif (meaning "a high") in *Lines of Fate*, names such as Angel, Paradizova, Ahasuerus, and Iona evoke cultural associations that have led at least one critic to call Kharitonov a "mystical atheist." That oxymoron provides a valuable orientation point for Kharitonov's readers.

While exploring the unknowability of human life and history, the novel affirms the necessity of seeking out their significance. In the final analysis, individual responsibility for one's own fate—provisionally equated with "the feeling of connection"—follows from the novel's central existential revelation: "There is no meaning besides that which you yourself create." Artistically the richest, as well as the most intricate and challenging, of the novels comprising Kharitonov's trilogy, *Lines of Fate* offers readers an opportunity to participate in the creation of meaning.

Helena Goscilo

I. IN THE DARK

"As I floated up to the wicket, I suddenly felt a strange pang of displacement, the kind you experience when you're only half-awake and
can't figure out where you are. It's as if you find yourself transported
to an alien planet: a clear ringing in your ears, a gray light in the air,
the smell of vinegar…The local creatures are hiding from the damp
in box-shaped wooden shells, emitting the smoke of their inner lives
through a tube on their foreheads, and in their eye sockets there are
flowerpots, in pairs, aimed through the watery glass surface at what's
opposite, at the splinter-colored fences bearing traces of chalk marks:
they're not unlike the Latin letters x and y, but then instead of z
there's God knows what…you can't understand a thing."

Thus begins one of Simeon Milashevich's strangest stories,
"Revelation," to the interesting fate of which Anton Andreyevich
Lizavin devoted the most crucial pages of his M.A. dissertation on
his fellow literati of the twenties. Actually, this was a prelude to his
topic: the story had appeared back in 1912, in the first and only issue
of the Petersburg almanac *Distances,* but it explains a lot about what
follows, and that's why it's also convenient for us to start with it. Its
fragmented episodes aren't connected by transitions or explanations,
so that at first the reader is somewhat confused, and only after the
fact realizes along what delirious waters the narrator is floating up to
his home, as if along a Venice canal. He's actually only talking about
a puddle, which in spring and fall in the town of Stolbenets would
flood below the rows of market stalls at the intersection of Swan,
Hound, and Soldier Streets, coming all the way up to the fences and
covering the planked footpaths. The puddle didn't completely dry up

even in summer; it seemed as eternal and natural a part of the land-scape as the nearby Stolbenets Lake. To get from this side to the stalls and Market Square during the spring flood, one had to make a big detour across the Pharmacy hillock, until it occurred to some enter-prising boys to ferry across on a homemade raft anyone who wanted transport for a five-kopek piece. Milashevich once published a humorous sketch of the journey in the capital's journal *Cricket,* and a boy with a barge pole also lurks invisibly behind the floating nar-rator in "Revelation."

3

And, in the next episode, the pang of vague anxiety, a kind of pre-sentiment, gets explained: an unexpected guest was waiting for the narrator in the house, a friend from former years, a fellow university student who was passing through and happened to be in town. They drink tea. On the ottoman in the corner, a brown Rumanian shawl wrapped for warmth around her shoulders, the host's wife, Shurochka*, sat in cross-legged silence. The guest was introduced not by his name, but by his student nickname, Ahasuerus—which, however, could also be considered a conspiratorial name. (A refined, mocking face, with a nervous cut to his nostrils, excitedly flashing eyes, an unshaven traveler's stubble). Certain hints led Lizavin to suppose that the man was traveling from some remote place of exile to the Stolbenets railway station. He had a small trunk, so precious that he didn't even entrust it to the entrance hall, keeping it on the floor beside his chair the whole time. That significant small trunk kept catching our eye: it was about the size of a Singer sewing-machine case, only worse, described in Milashevich's manner, down to its frayed edges, wooden handle, and brass nails turned green—no wonder its sizable appearance would be imprinted in Anton Andreyevich's memory. That's how montage sometimes is handled in the movies, the frame growing larger and larger, while the clock keeps ticking, evoking a time bomb, or at least intimating that some-thing vital is hidden in the ticking object. But in the movies such an

---

* SHUROCHKA is an affectionate diminutive for Aleksandra.

object has to explode sooner or later or at least be discovered, having delighted the spectator's soul with its musical solution, with the realization of his conjecture. Alas, Milashevich does not provide such a natural pleasure.

4

The small trunk, however, will play its part. In the course of the story it becomes clear that the newcomer is sick; the romantic glitter in his eyes happens to be the real fever of a high temperature, he can't go any farther, no matter how hard he tries to convince himself otherwise (they're expecting the small trunk somewhere), and, to reassure him, his former companion volunteers to deliver the impatient burden himself to its destination. He experiences a rather funny feeling of relief at this unexpected turn—until that moment, he'd kept waiting without knowing what anxiety this intrusion would bring. The thing is that all three heroes, as we discover little by little, are linked with this old story. A visiting student once incited a young girl to leave her parents' home for Moscow, but he soon vanished, entrusting the runaway to a friend's care. Now, after a long absence, he found both of them on the shores of Stolbenets, and the brand-new husband was worried, with good cause, about the woman's peace of mind. Since Ahasuerus spreads a mood of embarrassing, mocking soberness around him, he causes the leaves of the fading geranium to shrivel on the windowsill, mold to appear in the corners, one look says it all...But a retelling won't give much; better read Milashevich instead. The vital element in his prose is not the plot (you could say that's already been fully expounded), but, rather, that very "pang of displaced sentiment" that prompts someone to decipher a Latin inscription on a fence, while simultaneously laughing at himself; what's vital is the dry shadow behind the people sitting there, the light of the oil lamp, the play of sprung-up shadows, queer thoughts: the shifting air of narration. The whole motif of uncertainty, anxiety, and doubt in the values of a warmed life, and maybe of secret rivalry, a motif more musical than literary, is conveyed by means of turning to a slipper with a crumpled pom-pom, the sole pouting like a lip; like a touching, fearful little animal, it peers

8

out from behind the bed (where the edge of the overhanging bed-spread happens to be dirty and frayed, even the fringe), charmed and embarrassed by the presence of a stranger, by the proximity of an elegant—in spite of its dirtiness—shoe (the dirtiness even emphasizes the elegance), by the mysteriousness of the small trunk that was longing to get away, to the bad weather under the chilly skies. "It's okay, it's okay…," from time to time the hero reassures the shy creature with a glance. We know what we know, they know what they know. They certainly don't know more than we do. The smell of vinegar comes from anguish; I'll save you from it. I won't leave all of you poor things, I'll explain you to yourselves. Utterly vulnerable beneath the naked heavens—it's so hard, so frightening! You've only just started to get warm; where to now? You'll want to come back, wherever you are, I already know, but not everyone has the same kind of strength, you know… It's amusing that we don't actually hear any conversation out loud, some argument (which seems to have started earlier) is waging as if of its own accord. Let's at least take the incident where the hero addresses—as if to his mental arguments—his childhood feelings, "when we could dwell amidst household objects, as in the wilds of the universe, between the legs of tables and chairs, in the dusty cave under the bed, behind the blanket cover, behind the fortress wall of pillows." But something is happening to those dear objects before our eyes; the contents of the dwelling begin to fill the space, are swelling, depriving our breath of air; a samovar is burning inside our forehead, the down is poking with its quills through the chintz of the bedsheets, crowding its way into your throat; something is ticking in your temples, in the little trunk, in the air… We're infected with the fever of a man who's falling sick, and we're no longer concerned now with arguments; we should do something humane to ease the general state of things.

5

He leaves the house, in boots and galoshes, an umbrella in one hand and the trunk in the other. In the entrance hall, the mirror accompanies him with a mocking reflection. For the first and only time, we see this person from the sidelines: "the sad face of a monkey in a pince-nez, with feathery hair around his enlarged lips." Toward night-fall it grew lighter, and the emerging moon illuminated the puddle and the raft abandoned by the shore. Our absurd traveler tries to find a sure footing on the raft, placing the trunk between the logs so that it won't slide off. He takes the barge pole and floats along in the reflection of the stars and illuminated windows, floats for a long time, as if in a dream. The shores are washed away, the walls of the houses dissolve in the darkness. There, in the precious shining halos around the lamps, people are sitting by their samovars, scooping raspberry jam on their spoons, breaking up the bluish sugar on the wooden table with a knife, their lips protruding as they sip tea from saucers. There a drunken housepainter lying on a low trestle bed has set a lamp on the floor, and, with his varicolored oil paint, brushes the cock-roaches that have crawled out into the light, so that (after giving each one of them a name and even a patronymic) he can observe the mean-ing and events of their bustling life, their movements and encounters. There a newcomer, a member of the mysterious sect of Dyromoly,* who has drilled an opening in the partition and, perhaps using the empty peephole in the pattern of the wood, is praying in a whisper, his words carrying in the open air: "O hole of mine, hut of mine, save me!" My God, thinks the man floating on the raft, how much faith, spiritual strength, and thought one needs for such a prayer, which receives no support from the miraculous art of the icon, psalm music, or luxurious church adornments! Inner conviction suffices to endow a peephole with divine hearing. On a bed illuminated by the stove's crimson glow, a woman simply can't give birth; they've already given her soapy water to drink and stuffed her sweaty hair in her mouth, to accelerate her contractions through vomiting; in an animal-like state of exhaustion, she herself can't feel the great thing that's happening to a simple peasant woman like her—or, rather, through her, thinks the floating traveler. For we are all divine; no one is simple, but you can't understand that from the sidelines—that's the crux of the mat-ter. "From these alien, foreign heights how can you see, say, for

---

* DYROMOLY (lit. "those who hole pray") A religious sect that believed any open space was occupied by God.

instance, the madness of Cleopatra's lovers? Some being puts one extremity of its body into another body's aperture, to rub against it, after which it loses its head, and along with it the vital signs of life. From within, love, shock, anguish, and death; from the heights, a swarming of insects..." "I understand, I've suddenly understood it all...," mumbles the narrator. "The whole philosophy. But you can't put it into words right away. That's all right. You wait. I'll come back, we'll have some tea, go to the shore. I'll explain."

6

The critic Phenomenov (the only person who deemed this new writer worthy of mention in his monthly review) has noted, not without justification, a vagueness in this story that has pretensions to great significance. What sort of person the hero is, how and why he ended up in this remote place after his stint at the university, what he's doing there, and where, for crying out loud, does he have to bring the trunk so urgently, and what's in it anyway? It's useless to ask such practical questions. Everything here is hints, evasions, a fashionable withholding of information, the decadent movement of patches, and murky symbolism—of course, this trunk and the slippers with pom-poms aren't so much real objects as symbols, invoked to express the idea of the story: the clash of certain life forces or points of view. But, then again, should one seriously consider as an idea this apologia for a wretched and sluggish but nonetheless dear vegetative existence, as opposed to a striving to finish with it, to change and improve life, even by destroying something in the process or causing someone harm? Everything here is subject to doubt. However, certain details testify to the author's indisputable talent. Maybe that's why, independently of his intentions, this very vagueness, this at times almost delirious viscosity, these ill-defined thoughts and forms reflect, as if in an unintentional mirror, the not-so-fortuitous signs of the time. Then follows Phenomenov's discussion of the symptoms of problems— and not so much literary problems related to a lack of strictness, both spiritual and external, as the manifestation of a disintegration, the temptation of self-destruction, the pull of a modern consciousness away from civilization toward a more turbid, feminine, swamplike spontaneity. The story seemed to afford the clever critic an opportunity to express his favorite thoughts, and, incidentally, very profound ones, only they perhaps gave too much credit to Simeon Kondratyevich.

7

Everything appeared in a much more ordinary light when *Russian Morning* published a feuilleton by the well-known critic Korionskii, "Literary Resales," where, with a selection of quotations and entire passages, he conclusively proved that Milashevich simply stole the plot from the provincial writer Bogdanov. Bogdanov's story was titled "The Newcomer" and had been published three years earlier in Ganshin's printing house in the little-known town of Nechaisk, in a small edition of only twenty copies. Under these circumstances, a plagiarist (let's not be coy—in Russian we'd say "a thief") could hope that he wouldn't get caught. This seems even more likely, since, as people of this sort usually do, he took pains to change some words and surface details: he changed the title, slipped the newcomer a suspicious small trunk instead of a suitcase of foreign make, cut down and rearranged some sections of the story, omitted some things, and added some of his own material, particularly the philosophical ruminations. In Bogdanov's story, everything sounds more realistic, serious, and simple, and a certain reticence and unclear hints could very well be explained by a familiar sort of cautiousness. The student hero, who never completed his studies, left Moscow, carrying off the woman he loved (here her name is Verochka) so as to give her refuge, at least for a short while, from the dangers and worries that once again intrude on the house along with an ailing guest. What linked them was not simple acquaintance, but something that smacked pretty blatantly of illegality. In this kaleidoscope of mental images, there flashed the hero's recollection of a street fight: on the bridge there's a student's green cap and a small hat belonging to a woman whose hairpins have fallen out, releasing her light hair, but the near-sighted hero sees nothing, since his glasses have been knocked off. He gets up, groping his way, and supporting himself against the wall, only to find a policeman's overcoat right in front of his face...And the motif of agitated jealous uncertainty is much more distinct here, as are the doubts about his ability to make his beloved truly happy. But, most important, his rush to help his weakened friend betrays, quite apart from everything else, a sense of reawakened duty, and perhaps also an attempt at a new self-assertion in his beloved's eyes. Let's take just one small detail: the hero sees his reflection—with an enlarged area around his lips—not in the mirror, but in the mocking samovar. Such a portrait does look different, doesn't it?

8

But anyone who wants to know about all the details, including the characteristic corrections in language, can look at Lizavin's dissertation, which explained a great deal in this story. Mainly, he established that there was actually no plagiarism; what we have is the author's reworking of his own story. Bogdanov was Milashevich's real surname, a commonplace surname of illegitimate children (in these cases they're given their godfathers' patronymics, but priests from the sticks like to register more unusual first names—whence we get Simeon instead of Semyon). He seems to have first used his fictitious name when he was arrested, and then kept it as a pseudonym. Yes, he'd been arrested once; Lizavin even managed to find his criminal dossier in a Moscow archive: "On an Assassination Conspiracy at the Railway Station." Indeed, this incident appeared to pertain to some other unexpected person—unless we remember the circumstances of the ill-fated story. There was mention of an ambush at a secret meeting place discovered in Moscow and a suitcase with a double bottom (a suitcase, at any rate), which contained, besides a revolver and some documents from an illegal center, an explosive mechanism (at any rate, it was ticking). During his arrest, Simeon Kondratyich, who didn't have his documents on him at the time, called himself Milashevich and was registered under that name, "from the petty bourgeoisie of the Penza district," born 16 May 1884. For almost a week he kept repeating that someone had accidentally switched suitcases in the snack bar of the Nikolaevsky railway station. In response to the question how he came with this suitcase precisely to that address and even gave the password, he invented something totally unconvincing about a conversation he'd overheard at an adjacent table and supposedly thought he'd find the owner of the suitcase at that address. They considered him such an important suspect that they put him in solitary, with the window painted over with discolored whitewash, where they kept particularly dangerous terrorists. Simeon Kondratyevich later recalled this room. On the sixth day, he produced a confession of guilt written in his own hand, which could be considered the first draft of the story about the unexpected guest; the only difference is that the affair transpired in Moscow's Ilyin Hotel, no woman was mentioned, and, instead of the guest, we find his ailing neighbor, whose request had to be honored because of involuntary human sympathy. He used his real last name and explained his denial as motivated partly by fear and partly by foolish romantic fantasies. This story apparently enjoyed some success, at least temporarily, because Bogdanov's stay in the hotel was confirmed and his passport was even found there. A record of the interrogation that followed reminded Lizavin of a game familiar from his experience as a literary critic. The investigator tried to uncover the details, knowing all too well precisely which details he wanted, and the keen prisoner readily supplied them. He gradually recollected his lodger's appearance, with a small mustache and a goatee; in answering the question whether his lodger had had a birthmark or mole above the bridge of his nose, he remembered the birthmark as well. That volume of the investigation's dossier came to an abrupt end with that interrogation; for some reason, in the next volume Milashevich-Bogdanov wasn't mentioned. Possibly, he was singled out for a separate dossier that they didn't manage to locate, so we learned about his sentence only indirectly, from Simeon Kondratyich himself. What he was charged with is unknown, but it cost him three years of exile in Nechaisk, Lizavin's hometown, where Bogdanov's story was published in 1909. He then moved closer to the railway station, to Stolbenets, which has already been mentioned.

9

A comparison of these circumstances with the story certainly stimulated the imagination, of which Anton Andreyevich was not, we should mention, devoid. He asked himself, for example, the question: Did the five-day denial mean that for exactly this period of time the would-be doctor calculatedly waited for the ailing man to feel better and vanish from his room? Some other thoughts occurred in passing; perhaps we shall have occasion to mention them later. But, returning to the literary issues, we find another thing puzzling: Why didn't Simeon Kondratyich rush to explain the misunderstanding that took place? Nobody in the capital could or was obliged to know his circumstances. He'd only moved there after his exile, supported himself by publishing feuilletons, genre portraits, and "provincial fantasies" in journals of different sorts. What prevented him, though, from showing his prosecutors his real face, from which, judging by the only photograph that we have (a frontal view taken in prison; for some reason there's no profile shot of him in his dossier), his mocking reflection was copied quite accurately. (In his original attempt to attribute this to his samovar, there's a kind of sad self-defense, which later the author proudly denied.) In the meantime, a scandal, it seems, seriously undermined his ability to earn a living from literature; as far as we know, the doors of many publishing houses were closed to this shady character. Having no other means of making a living, Milashevich was in dire straits for some time. That very year, in fact, he got an ulcer, which he vividly described in a later story of his, with considerable knowledge of the subject. The hero of the story, a cashier, is suspected of embezzlement because he makes a careless, misinterpreted joke; he is dismissed from his job for a trial period and never gets rehired. His acquaintances turn away from him; servants talk to him only from the other side of a door chain, and the hero pawns his things and treats his ulcer, but doesn't wish to declare his innocence, partly because of his pride and partly because of his swamplike feeling—as in a dream—that it's simpler to change life to make it correspond to a word that's been spoken than to repudiate that word. Moreover, he even experiences the anecdotal satisfaction of a joker who's succeeded in playing a trick on everyone.

10

It goes without saying that fiction is not a document; only with obvious qualifications can one use it as a basis for making judgments about the author. The trouble is that we have practically no reliable documents on Milashevich. One can judge his whole life only on the basis of indirect data. Let's take his criminal dossier. That's a document, you'd think, but how much useful information can one glean from it? No more than from the story. Fine; we've found a photograph confirming the authenticity of his reflected portrait, but doesn't the lens play around with the samovar's effect? After all, the lens is concave as well. Like an eye, by the way. Particularly an artist's eye. Until he started his work, all of Anton Andreyevich's data on Milashevich consisted only of testimonies in the form of memoirs (we shall speak about them later) and an incomplete autobiographical outline of 1926. Well, this document was worth as much as the testimonies in his dossier. Even the birthdate indicated was different: 14 May 1886. Were the numbers confused by mistake, and if Milashevich lied intentionally, then where did he lie? We can only guess. Yes, it's possible he himself didn't know. On the subject of his illegitimate origins and homeless childhood, the author only drops a phrase in passing about his sense of kinship to all those people "who'd lost contact, dropped out of the community, and felt themselves outsiders everywhere." Then, following no chronological order, but according to the random flow of his thoughts, he indicates that for a short while he studied at Moscow University, first in the natural sciences division and then in the medical school. Milashevich explains his attraction to the natural sciences by a memory of a childhood miracle: a magnifying glass and a hazy dream about a microscope. At this juncture, autobiography turns into a eulogy of sorts to optical equipment. "After all, it not only enlarges the subject, but singles it out from its undifferentiated environment and focuses on it. Usually we don't perceive life when it's very close to us, just as we sometimes don't understand a text, though we follow it with our eyes. And suddenly there's a fly's hairy belly in the middle of a flower, its large, many-faceted, coaly eyes, small specks of pollen on the sculptured framework of the stamen, leading into the depths of a sweet fairy tale." Further on, however, we read about his disappointment with the microscope, which confused his view rather than enlarging it. One might think that the author didn't even finish his second year of studies because of this disappointment, and not

16

because of his participation in student strikes. "I became more and more convinced that the whole point is to single out, not to enlarge." Then, after a digression, which Milashevich favors, an unexpected episode appears in the form of a description of a strange tree with a web-footed trunk and grassy leaves; resembling a plant in a prehistoric swamp, it sways in the wind. If you look, uninterrupted, you can see how it grows and enjoys the damp, how it cringes from the cold and winces at a shadow cast upon it as at some inner feelings, how the body of a flying monster shakes it, causing the trunk to bend. Only when his patience is exhausted does the observer prefer to recognize the creature as a horsefly and the tree as a small blade of grass that's sprouted on the windowsill in front of a chink, or, rather, a scratch in a small painted window. We finally realize that Simeon Kondratyevich is describing his impressions in solitary confinement; this is an important lesson provided by a view that is singled out, indeed, has no need of a microscope and even contrasts with the world of the exact sciences and positive knowledge. For this view, something else is more important. "In a meadow you wouldn't notice this small blade of grass. You could even pass the meadow without having noticed it..." As for the story itself, it's passed over rapidly in a subordinate clause, "when I was there on trial for political assassination." At the very end, just as rapidly again, he mentions his exile to Nechaisk: "That's how I came for the first time in my life to the place my wife, Aleksandra Flegontovna, is from. It was destined to gradually become my second native area, too. Here, after the separation, I was reunited for good with my life's companion. Here I write these lines, listening to her breathing behind the curtain." By the way, her name and patronymic are the only things we know about this woman; about the rest we can only conjecture, based on his stories, where Shurochka's wordless presence is felt not so much directly as in her various pieces of needlework, napkins, chair pillows, and her jam making, Shrovetide pancakes, and the other joys of a provincial existence that Milashevich so lovingly incorporates into his descriptions.

Here, incidentally, is what seems curious: the heroine of the story, which is hardly devoid of autobiographical significance, turns out to have the same name as his beloved's in real life. Of course, the wives of artists, as they say, are a special phenomenon; they usually play the role of an artist's model, yet, you know, it's not that simple. Just as the autobiographical aspect of Milashevich's story is not that simple either. One of his stories contains his ruminations on literature as a way to speak the profound truth about oneself without baring oneself before one's audience. Sometimes we get the impression that Simeon Kondratyevich himself is above all trying not to reveal something really private about himself. That's why he plays games, fabricates things (not unlike his conversations with the investigator), and moves into the realm of complete and utter fantasy. And you can't always tell when he's speaking the truth. Moreover, he constantly throws you off track by his propensity for narration in the first person. One of his miniature sketches is engaging—a humorous study of a man who kept five diaries simultaneously, from five different points of view, and each diary was about him. Or let's take the concept of the "figurative eye," as Milashevich called it. It deals with the impulse to perceive the world from within other beings, permeated with their inner truths—as, for example, in his story about a poplar cut so that it wouldn't block the light falling on a rubber plant on the windowsill. Rather, the story is about a rubber plant whose light was blocked by the tree; the most important thing is the rubber plant's point of view. Without prior knowledge here, you can't understand who's complaining, who's asking for sympathy, who's depressed and full of reproach...and suddenly draws a deep breath, feels the exhilaration of freedom: long live the sun, long live light, long live wealth, long live the joy of life! The street with the brotherly burdocks on it is visible now; a dog approaches a fence and raises its leg. At the end, the rubber plant even begins to express itself in verse: "Freedom, bliss, and distant expanses are ours!"

No, there's something in the trick with the real name which is unusual for Milashevich. (Furthermore, it's in the story that describes the urge to free oneself of the oppression of harsh reality.) However you explain it, thought Lizavin, Milashevich could allow himself such a thing only in the completely alien city of Petersburg. In Nechaisk or in Stolbenets, where he'd be recognized, Simeon Kondratyich tried to shield his family life from immodest glances; all the more so because Aleksandra Flegontovna was from somewhere around that area. But there's something else interesting here. It turns out that Milashevich first came to Stolbenets only after the events described in his story. Before his arrest, he had been living in Moscow. Consequently, the provincial dimension was inserted into the text after the fact, and, moreover, it sounds really provocative only in the Petersburg version. Obviously, it was precisely then that the features of what Lizavin called Milashevich's provincial philosophy were being formulated. These ideas aren't expounded systematically anywhere, but are attributed to various characters in his fiction. This philosophy is completely alien to any system and requires no proofs. Its truth lies in the ability to guarantee inner harmony and vouchsafe a feeling of happiness independent of life's outer structure. It has no pretensions to grandeur; indeed, its strength lies in its general accessibility. "All philosophies," muses one of his characters, "are created for us by great people—by whom else?—according to their own criteria. This is the beginning of an incompatibility. These great people may be genuinely concerned about us and summon us to the truth they envision, but they'll never abandon their criteria. This is the source of disillusionment, anguish, and restlessness." It's important to emphasize right away the fact that Milashevich's province is not a geographical notion but a spiritual one, a way of existence; it has its roots in the human soul, independent of the place where he lives. Yet in this poetry of unpretentious philistine coziness, the warmth of the stove, the summer dust, the spring dirt, the evening foot washing, the tea drinking in the garden under the small apple tree... too much is connected with the worlds of Nechaisk and Stolbenets. When its singer attempts to establish himself in the capital as a writer, that, you'll agree, lends a certain abstract hue to the promise to return allegedly declared in "Revelation." Lizavin allowed himself some psychological conjectures on the subject. It's possible that precisely this Petersburg episode put an end to Milashevich's hesitation. Just imagine this thoroughgoing provincial: nearsighted, incoherent, ungainly, in a white summer hat, hot dusty boots, and sweaty peasant shirt... No, he couldn't feel at home among the members of society in the capital in their pressed suits. Perhaps he interpreted the literary misunderstanding as a hint, a sort of slap from fate that gave him direction, convinced him to overcome his cowardly temptation to return, proudly and vainly, to Stolbenets, where, without taking the tastes of others into account, he could build around himself a wall of unpretentious happiness and genius, as accessible as in childhood.

13

Of course, conjectures are nothing but conjectures, and we can legitimately ask the question: Didn't Anton Andreyevich partly try to make the author fit into his own understanding, an author for whom from the very outset he felt a kind of spiritual affinity that bordered on the closeness one feels to a relative? We won't instantly start denying this in indignation. Don't we all do something similar when we interpret a book, each according to his own point of view? The book, after all, tells us what we are already predisposed or inclined to hear. In his heart of hearts, Lizavin wasn't alienated even from fiction writing. Sometimes something wildly risky would occur to him. For example, that Milashevich's forced separation from Shurochka proved to be longer for Milashevich than he lets us believe; that a note of jealous rivalry, particularly in the first version of the story, betrays wounded feelings, although the Petersburg version already testifies to a new self-assertion; and that the authentic name of the woman who is found again is inserted as a sign of triumph secretly projected somewhere into space... But this, so to speak, is out and out literature. Let's just note that it's no accident, evidently, that in Milashevich's humorous philosophical flights the idea of fate that is incarnated in the most improbable chance occurrences occupies such an important place. How whimsically the man's own life unfolded until then (as far as we can judge); the optional studies, hazy, experimental enthusiasms, and suddenly one day the unexpected guest, his illness, his forced departure from home, the extended absence against his will, his exile and return, and the misunderstanding about plagiarism, which seems to have been thought up on purpose—and as a result he comes to that very thing for which, as it now appears, he was predestined by virtue of the makeup of his mind and soul.

14

Be that as it may, after a short absence, forced to find a way of supporting himself outside of literature, Milashevich once again turned up (voluntarily now) in his former place of exile. Lizavin knew Stolbenets well. For some unknown reason, the railroad tracks had been laid down about a mile and a half from the town, and that's where the station was located. Milashevich describes an amusing scene in which a somewhat tipsy passenger, getting off at Stolbenets and not finding the outskirts of the city, is afraid that he got off at the wrong place. Over the years the city and the station had tried to get closer to each other; the streets spread lengthwise in fluid structures—like amoebas, one might say—drawing their outgrowths ever closer, until they were joined as one. It's a good thing that the place wasn't steep, and provided a lot of space, unlike in Nechaisk. Stolbenets lay flat, almost even with the lake; the climate here was considered unhealthy, especially when it got hot, when the water became covered with lichen. On the other hand, on the silt of the lake floor and on the lyve (earth from rotted water plants) grew rare harvests of famous "white-forehead" cucumbers. Its proximity to the railroad made Stolbenets the center of urban civilization by comparison with Nechaisk. Electricity appeared earlier here; there was even a movie theater, the electrically operated theater Visions (now called Progress), and, among the industry that was normal for small towns (that is, leather tanning, brick firing, and lime boiling), the Ganshin caramel factory stood out, supplying the whole province with its sweets.

In a local book about Stolbenets, printed in 1922, there's a photograph of the town at that time: a cluster of gray buildings, like little barns (calling to mind Milashevich's *color of splinters*), along a spot of the same gray color that's the lake. This dreariness, of course, must be partly attributed to the poor printing; the same Milashevich testifies to the fact that the better houses, in any case, had at one time been painted in fashionable "edible" colors—more precisely, the color chocolate, *crème brulé*, or ice cream. And the tops of the three churches visible in the snapshot most likely were more attractively decorated (only one survives intact to this day), and the lake reflected the skies, and during the fertile season the greenery flourished. One can believe, of course, that leaves and especially flowers, like poetic words, conceal and embellish life's meager foundation; but who said there's more truth in a naked landscape? Judging from all this, the local picture was taken from a hill where the remains of an ancient settlement with earthen banks were preserved. The site was called *stolpie*, and from this the city took its name. At one time the banks were a favorite place for walks, filled, in Lizavin's memory, with potato gardens and vegetable patches that stretched as far as the statue of a soldier, a monument to those killed in the last war. The soldier was made from plaster and painted silver, the color of provincial monuments. Its foundation was a granite stone that had grown out of the ground; on it, smeared over with cement, were stylized Slavic letters: "To a Hero of the Fatherland—The Grateful Citizens of Stolbenets." The inscription was suitable in its contents, but was obviously not intended for a soldier. Lizavin also found on the stone a leader with a bronze mustache, in boots of the same material, but even he merely occupied a place that had become empty. The person to whom the inscription was dedicated was preserved only in an unclear silhouette in the left corner of the old photograph. It was the Stolbenets merchant Stepan Koltunov, who, so they say, rivaled the well-known Ivan Susanin in his exploits.

It would be worthwhile to divert our attention briefly to this story, to show once again how complicated the relationship between the truth and documentary evidence is. In 1912 the local zealot of antiquities, the teacher Semiglazov, found among the documents of the Voskresenskii [Resurrection] Monastery a petition of Koltunov's son-in-law "Ivashka Kvasha with the children Ignashka and Fomka." The petition, dated March 7128 (that is, 1620 A.D.), told of the martyr's death of Koltunov at the hands of Poles seven years earlier, in the winter of 1613, when the merchant was carting off the potash in the Kostroma neighborhood and was captured and used as a guide by the detachment looking for the adolescent czar, Mikhail Romanov. The petition consisted only of a request to release the heirs of the deceased from excessive taxes, in honor of his exploit. The authenticity of the document didn't arouse any doubts, but for some reason it didn't reach Moscow, and because of this the hero's name remained forgotten for almost three hundred years. Its discovery fortunately coincided with the impending anniversary of the Romanov dynasty and rumors about the possible arrival of the sovereign in Stolbenets; finally, the very stone that probably had been used way back by the pagans for their sacrifices had been begging for many years to have a monument erected above it. A collection for the monument was announced immediately, but while the cast-iron statue of the merchant was being made in Saratov, an argument got started about his exploit. The Kostroma historian Pogorelov, manifestly irritated by the appearance of a rival to his fellow countryman, published an article in which he mentioned that the petition, even if not a forgery, wasn't indicative of anything except an attempt by the merchant's relatives to obtain some benefits. How do we know that he was killed by the Poles and not by highway robbers, who were so numerous on the roads at that time? Semiglazov had an immediate response: Hadn't the various Solovievs and Kostomarovs expressed precisely the same doubts about Susanin's own exploits? They demanded proof that the Poles had even reached the environs of Kostroma. But one should accept these things with one's soul, just as the czaritsa Martha accepted the petition of Susanin's relatives. Pogorelov, growing more and more angry, replied that a rumor about the petition's success was possibly what two years later prompted Kvasha to attempt the role of impostor, that a local peasant was one thing, while a traveling merchant who didn't know the local forests and, since we're on the subject, might have gotten lost, without any heroic purpose, was another... In the meantime, the monument was erected, but the sovereign didn't make it to Stolbenets, and after several years the scholarly argument lost its meaning because of the events that unexpectedly ensued.

17

Milashevich remembered this lively episode of provincial intellectual activity at a time when the ancient stone was once again empty, and definitely not because Koltunov's rival succeeded in proving his exceptional rights. No, for a while the rival himself wavered, as if in a shifting mirage; both Susanin and Koltunov appeared superfluous for the revised story, in which the czar's salvation was no longer regarded as a positive achievement—even the reverse. The two of them virtually dissolved, melting into thin air, Koltunov dissolving more irremediably, one might say, without producing any definite legend—with verses or operas—and in addition burdened with unfortunate merchant origins. So when history once again became interested in the spirit of state patriotism, only one of them, to whom history had become more accustomed, came back into being. After all, he was quite sufficient. In Milashevich's story, various characters philosophize about this point. The idea is what matters, says one, and one way or another the image will take its form from it, using for its embodiment any material that's appropriate; it will find a name, features, lofty speech, and even cast-iron weight. Gradually it will cease to need proofs of authenticity—on the contrary, it will itself be the most important and sufficient proof. Another character declares that a mere fact is in no way closer to the truth than a vague feeling, a rumor, or a vision. We know better than anyone else how common talk and a dream can be transformed into the dense—and very weighty!—substance of life. The facts may be present in the rumors and versions, like pebbles in liquid clay, but when they dry together they have a shared solidity. If we don't subject this solidity to extraordinary tests, perhaps in the end we can do with just the clay; it's easier to mold an image from clay. We can live on music, but not on Euclidean geometry—a third person offers his view. Perhaps the provinces in their understanding in general anticipated the Weltanschauung of the age, out of which a new art, a new morality, and even a new concept of reality and a new theology arose. In the final episode, we hear what sounds like the groan of the vanishing Koltunov: "Help me! Let me exist for a while!" And the stone that has become empty is already striving for a new weight, already senses it above itself, feels the itch out of which the new weight will take form.

18

(Later in Milashevich's papers, Lizavin found a strange, touching note:

*What happened to me while I lived? I don't remember.
That is death.*

A draft version, a development of Koltunov's topic? Who knows?)

19

Yes, it's not always been that easy with historical evidence either. What about the seventeenth century? In the same local booklet, Anton Andreyevich came across the name of one A. N. Ganshin, a local socialist and propagandist. In his house, wrote the author, revolutionaries from the places of exile in that area held secret meetings; fugitives found asylum there. Nine pages earlier there's a reference to another Ganshin without initials, a notorious local factory owner, landowner and benefactor, an offspring of the princely Nogtev-Zvenigorod line. The coincidence must have been of interest to Lizavin, also because Milashevich knew the factory owner; his first story, we recall, was published in Ganshin's publishing house in Nechaisk; his other works written before the revolution had been published in the Stolbenets publishing house. But only after he began to study the topic in detail did Anton realize what no one else who read the booklet—perhaps even the author himself—would know: that the owner of both publishing houses and, at the same time, of the caramel factory and the electrotheater Visions, the landowner zealously destroying the inherited forests, and the socialist preaching revolution were one and the same person—Angel Nikolayevich Ganshin. The illegal meetings took place on his estate, about eight miles from Stolbenets. As we know, that chance occurrence is far from exceptional for Russia.

20

In Simeon Kondratyevich's later prose, there appears under different names a heavy athlete, his cheeks covered with a curly beard: *The beard gave the impression of being broad and thick, whereas in fact it was his cheeks that were broad and thick. Somewhere inside them was concealed another face—thin and nervous. It looked as if a dynamic, lively man were coated with a shaking wet layer and had to overcome his heaviness when he moved.* This description, which is better than the photograph mentioned earlier, lets us see this tired offspring of the aristocracy and the eccentric factory owner. He wanders through Milashevich's pages with the tread of a sick elephant, in the thickets of wildly overgrown lilacs with five petals. His little eyes are swollen, the inflamed rims below the whites show red; a leather fencing armor on straps draws tight the left side of his chest and his fat shoulder, and his pants hang loose on his behind. In a tub with patterned hoops, a genealogical tree grows without leaves, a multitude of desiccated branches. He's painfully oppressed by immobility, particularly in the summer; he's in anguish because there can be nothing fundamentally new. From year to year the furniture in his house either grows bigger, hoping to impress the owner's withered feelings with its grandness, or is replaced by the simple equipment that was specially invented by some genius, so that the construction might be dismantled and reassembled differently. Ganshin's estate is undergoing reconstruction all the time; moveable mirrors for a brief period renew the space, and in the garden there's a grotto with an echo that doesn't repeat sounds but lives its own independent capricious life; transparent figures made of wire and filaments swirl around in the wind, changing their appearance in the process and causing superstitious fear among the population in the nearby area; and in the greenhouse plant seeds are sown whose names the owner doesn't even want to know, in the hopes of a surprise.

21

Milashevich lived on the estate for a long time either as a friend or as a sponger-entertainer; but, then again, he occupied the position of gardener, puttered about in Ganshin's greenhouse, and also thought up candy wrappers, or *fantiki*, as children called them, for the caramel factory. Ganshin built the factory as if without planning ahead, without worrying about its distance from raw sugar supplies. However, an engineer-director summoned from Vilnius, a German called Fige, organized a very profitable business exceeding all expectations, by using the local potato syrup. Milashevich attributed the success of the business in part to the popularity of the *fantiki*. These little pieces of paper fascinated him as a phenomenon of provincial culture, as a means of enlightening and influencing people's minds. Besides a drawing (in two or three colors) and the name, they had useful advice printed on them, recommendations in agriculture, wise sayings, weather predictions, and forecasts for the year. There was a caramel called Fortune, whose wrapper bore a picture of the card suits: "An ace of diamonds means that you're dreaming of an honest, noble woman. It foretells a change in life for the better." There was a caramel called Hangover, with the additive of a secret grass extract and exhortatory verses for the drinker. The caramel Name day came in various names, mostly women's, with a picture of a blonde or black-haired beauty (and exactly the same face, by the way), with a note explaining the name, and sometimes with a verse expressing best wishes. It's difficult to suppose that every type of *fantik* corresponded to the type of product; too many of them came out. After the revolution, when the factory was closed for a long time, it turned out that they had been printed several years in advance. There was a time when the blank side of these uncut sheets was the only paper left in the area. They were used for letters, flyers, warrants, and ration cards. In 1920 they used the big sheets to print several issues of the Stolbenets newspaper *Guide* (in the legend to the right of the title, a muscular worker in an apron led a peasant by the hand toward the rising sun, the peasant's head thrown back like a blind man's). Lizavin even had in his possession some money bonds made from *fantiki.*

22

"Provincial tastes can change," a man who calls himself a "picture inventor" preaches to a rich benefactor in one of Milashevich's stories. "But throughout the ages, the majority of people from birth will know by heart Pushkin's tale 'The Priest Had a Dog,' and this dog will occupy a place in their heart next to Pushkin. There's no point feeling superior and looking down on this, otherwise we won't understand the inner life of the new social stratum of orphans, which increasingly is replacing the former peasantry; we won't understand the people of the future who triumph during times of momentous/historical change. We won't understand, finally, something vital in ourselves." "Is it right to be ashamed of commonplaces?" he continues some time later. "There's sense and charm in discovering the things that were known even to the ancient Egyptians. Music expresses what cannot be expressed in words. What a profound, what a wonderful observation! Did you think of it yourself? The point is that you were, indeed, the first to think of it, and it doesn't mean anything that it's already been said a thousand times before you. Believe me. Like love, a discovery is an act of genius each time an individual once again is certain that, until him, nothing like this ever existed before in the history of man. Millions have also died before us, but you're going to die for the first and only time; feel that." And elsewhere: "It's precisely the foundations of life that are banal. In art a person yearns to recognize what he already knows: himself—and that's precisely why he appreciates men of genius. What an accurate insight, gentlemen! That's my experience, too, and I've been through all of this. We appreciate men of genius for the same thing, in essence, that we appreciate in gypsy romances: a soul that coincides with our own, and the realization of our expectations—though revitalized, of course, by the harmony and even the elegance of expression that aren't always accessible to us."

The constant revitalization of feelings is our character's main concern. All mechanical devices, which are changed by means of springs and the wind, seem ridiculous to him; he offers his own prescriptions. The sick benefactor in *Fairy Tales for Angel* is prepared to renounce refined tastes, his habitual values, and French books; he buys painted rugs from the local artist Bosoi, who earlier was an unsuccessful housepainter, and hangs them on his walls; he collects handicrafts, and the inspired narrator offers him all sorts of new things for his museum: a slanting ray of the sun in a foggy forest, the warbling of a bird, a sigh on a bench, an accordian playing "Separation" at the Stolbenets railway station, a catalog of self-validating moments, seized out of time and history. "Happiness is more accessible to people without a genealogy, unburdened by the guilt of ancestors or even the feeling of original sin." "Yes, away with it all," the listener responds impatiently. "To forget about oneself, to renounce everything. Let me do it their way." He even agrees to have lice, even to perish, just let it happen quickly. Ganshin clearly sometimes lapsed into his own distinctive and by then already old-fashioned populism, but his revolutionary anguish, clearly, sprang not so much from ideas as from the same psychological need for change. He wrote a treatise, "The Lost Garden, or On the Inevitability of Revolutions," and offered money and weapons to the conspirators who visited him, so they could declare a social republic in two nearby districts, without waiting for the capitals. Even in the case of failure, the godforsakenness and remoteness of the region would let them hold out for a long time. (After only a few years, like an epitaph on his grave, the short-lived and mysterious Nechaisk republic emerged.) He was prepared to turn his own estate into a fortress and had already begun surrounding it with a stone wall, but the part that was already built suddenly collapsed into the ground, where they discovered hollow areas: the remains of vaults or of underground tunnels built by one of the ancestors. The collapse occurred on the day of Angel Nikolayevich's death; both events were noted in one and the same issue of the newspaper *Stolbenets Citizen,* 1 July 1914.

24

The announcement of Ganshin's death was titled in the spirit of provincial sensationalism: SUICIDE, HOMICIDE, OR ACCIDENT? The body was discovered on 28 June in the greenhouse with broken glass and wilted plants. A bullet was missing from the revolver that had fallen out of his hand; the mystery, however, was that no bullet was found either in the body or nearby. There was a black-and-blue mark as big as a kopek on his temple, but neither the weapon that dealt the fatal blow nor anyone else's tracks were found. The revolver made us think of a contemplated (and, as it were, realized!) suicide. Especially since a note turned up on his desk which could be considered a suicide note: "The will is in a drawer"—but nothing else was cleared up. If other details existed, the clumsy provincial investigators had trampled on them, or maybe the journalists got carried away and lied about these details, and it's not a literary critic's business, after all, to investigate the mystery that they'd let slip by. But, for Anton, one puzzling hint—an unfinished note among Simeon Kondratyevich's papers—proved to be connected with the subject.

25

This occurred not only on the same day, but at exactly the same hour as Gavrila Printsip's shot. What can I blame myself for? It's senseless to see a cause and connection in everything. It's mere coincidence: an intensification of a crisis, a forced absence, fruits ripening, a collapse. Yet nonetheless, nonetheless…Someone could have understood and sensed it right away. I didn't pick up on it. It was a harmless impromptu, a variation on the usual theme. Sometimes it would shake him up. One no longer "goes to the people," they say, but how do you feel about "bringing the people" to your home? See what a wonderful orphan I've brought? How about offering him shelter for a while? I waited, expecting the smell to make him wince, I even had a joke ready. But no, he didn't even notice anything. And how could one not admire the little boy, those curls, that angelic face? Everything went so well that I didn't rush to explain. The only unfortunate opportunity simply eluded my understanding. I had to explain, and that was that. But that trembling smile, those suffering eyes…

What is this? An outline of an ordinary plot? The mention of the shot in the shed directly linked the note with the date of Ganshin's death, only to make sense of it was absolutely impossible. Later Anton Andreyevich had occasion to turn his thoughts again to the hints that appear here. His imagination began seeing something, but these fantasies were so arbitrary that it's not even worth mentioning them. We don't know anything else about this period of Simeon Kondratyevich's life; in between it's still comparatively clear. From 1914 to 1926 there's almost a complete blank. We only know that before the revolution he served as a letter carrier in the Stolbenets council, and then for a short time was a curator in the Museum of Prerevolutionary Life, which they built on the former Ganshin estate. The estate later burned down; we've only got photographs of it. During Lizavin's childhood they called its former environs the "forbidden zone," and to this day Anton Andreyevich, who knows the area pretty well, hasn't been in those spots where that ill-fated "child who's grown heavy" (as Milashevich lovingly called him) used to escape from his depression. Almost all the stories of the Ganshin cycle were preserved in manuscripts, and between February and October of 1917 only two were published. They were, as always, slim booklets published only for the elect, printed on crackly *fantik* paper with *fantik* designs in the middle of the white cover; on one of the booklets there was a beautiful woman with a watering can, on another a boy with curls and an angelic face (just as Anton involuntarily imagined the little boy mentioned in the fragment; however, the woman had exactly the same face—which could be attributed either to taste or to the inability of the local artist to draw any other way). These two pictures, like a symbol of home production, appeared on all the booklets published by Milashevich, evidently in the Stolbenets publishing house. "Evidently" because neither the publishing house nor the place of publication was indicated. Simeon Kondratyevich could hardly have suspected that in time his elegant booklets would become a book collector's rarity. Collectors later called these "Candy editions." It was precisely these collectors, and not the literary critics, who helped to preserve Milashevich's memory.

It so happens that our attempt to maintain some sort of chronological consistency in this story only now allows us to mention the memoir, promised long ago, in which Anton Andreyevich personally first discovered Milashevich's existence. In Moscow in 1965 appeared the memoirs of the famous bibliophile Vasilii Platonovich Semeka, by then already deceased. He began as a critic before the revolution; right before that February he founded the publishing house Domino, which lasted nine years, and when it was later merged into the state association, he stayed there, occupying the indeterminate post of "consultant." But he'd been better known for his collection of books. Especially famous were his rare books; he was one of those collectors who, the more obscure a book, the more he was attracted to it. No one in Moscow had had more books of the kind that bibliophiles call "Idiotika," although, as a former editor and, moreover, as a literary critic, he was far from indifferent to literature. The combination of two such fundamental passions in one person gave rise to various rumors; malicious gossip claimed, for example, that Semeka turned out other strange things in his own publishing house, printing only one copy of some of them when necessary and searching the provinces for works by unknown eccentrics, and that it was precisely the income from selling rare and used books that made up for his publishing expenses. The photographs in the book showed a round face with an actor's full lips, a blob of a mustache beneath his nose, and a merchant's hair part; it smells of brilliantine, fresh laundry, the words "open-topped pastry" and "smoked sturgeon." He tells appetizing stories, too, perhaps embroidering them a little bit—actually, embroidering them for sure, and not just a little bit; entire pages of dialogue come out of his memory suspiciously fresh. What we read is a prose that isn't devoid of talent, but one cannot make exaggerated claims as to its reliability. So one of the chapters from his *Notes of a Book Collector* tells how Milashevich's "Candy" booklets found their way into his collection. Semeka came to Stolbenets having heard about the apocrypha that allegedly were seen around a crumbling local monastery. Concentrating on these hopes, he somehow didn't even think about Milashevich; only after the fact did he realize why those shouts of the women selling goods at the station ("Here's smoked bream, well done! Have some fried pike, sir, it's still hot!"), the dusty road to the city going past the low-built warehouses, and the sunken mounds of earth, even the puddle that rippled strongly, like a lake, seemed so familiar to him. It was as if he'd already been there before and seen it all. However, doesn't one get a similar feeling when one visits any provincial town? Only after he'd become convinced that somebody had beaten him to the apocrypha did the appearance of the head of the local reading room remind him of Milashevich, who'd inspired the undiscouraged bibliophile with the possibility of another success along the way.

28

We ought to give Vasilii Platonych some credit; he describes this character vividly, as if he just stepped out of pages that are familiar to us: a pince-nez, tied together at the bridge of the nose with dirty thread, a freshly washed Tolstoy shirt, with armpits that got soiled later, a wicker cord instead of a tie, an iron end of a pencil, its graphite intact, sticking out of a bulging breast pocket, and grayish feathers around a big mouth. We appreciate all these details: bare walls covered in violet inky spots, a boy with cropped hair—the only visitor leafing through issues of *The Red Newspaper*—and an iron cistern for boiled water with a mug on a chain. Semeka always dropped into libraries and reading rooms; they often sold books there, and conversations about books, of course, already sprang up of their own accord. At first he mentioned Milashevich's name just to break the ice: you know, this area also had its own poet at one time—but he realized instantly that at these words something quivered behind the sparkling lenses of the pince-nez, although his addressee didn't pick up on the topic. The book collector's instinct had taught Semeka not to disclose his real interest; he merely recalled, apropos, one or two plots from Milashevich's stories—and one can believe him in this—with good taste; he not only had several booklets in his collection, but had read and appreciated them. So we see the librarian listening to him, tense and distrustful, his head bowed, staring up at him from beneath his glasses, before he removed his pince-nez to wipe it, and his defenseless eyes with puffy reddish eyelids proved lost and helpless. "It's strange," he blurted out and coughed. "Strange to suddenly see your own reader." Semeka renders his mute reaction with three exclamation points, followed by the librarian's explanation: "You see, *I* am Milashevich."

29

"He said this, lowering his voice and for some reason casting a sideways glance at the boy in the corner, as if fearing witnesses to such an admission," Vasilii Platonych notes, not without humor. The trustfulness of his voice (as if to say, this is just between us; don't tell anyone) and the feverish look for a second created the impression that he'd said, "*I* am Napoleon." Psychologically one can understand why he heard the words distorted; by 1926 Semeka no longer thought of the author of "candy" booklets as still alive. Why had he vanished? Didn't he publish any new books? This question now sounded natural and disinterested. No, no booklets have come out for many years now. "You really aren't writing anymore?" "Of course I am!" He smiled ironically, and for some reason patted his bulging pocket with the pencil with the metal end. "All the time, every day. I can't live without it." And right then Semeka found (or, if one is to believe rumor, once again made use of) that turn in the conversation that in part gave rise to ambiguous interpretations: he started to talk about the necessity of trying to publish his collection in Moscow, maybe a collection combining his old and new works (the mention of "old," of course, hinted at the "candy" booklets as well), and he gave to understand that he also belonged to the world of publishing. They agreed to meet after six in a tearoom—Simeon Kondratyich apologizing in embarrassment that he couldn't invite Semeka to his home, citing his wife's ill health and the general mess in the house. Oh, how annoying for us! We really would have liked to get a look at Aleksandra Flegontovna and at his household setup from an outsider's perspective. Alas, we'll have to make do with what we have.

30

Let's note the details of the conversation in the tearoom with the same great attention: the stale air filled with smoke, the rather soiled tablecloths, but the balalaika player on the raised stand is wearing a Russian shirt, and they serve the famous local carp in sour cream, and prewar vodka, eighty proof, and there's even cognac—it's the NEP period.* We greedily examine Simeon Kondratyevich, who has appeared in a white cap, polished boots, and, in honor of the new meeting, changed his wicker cord for a short tie with a patch. This patch, we must admit, puts one on guard, and somehow the beggarly meticulousness of this provincial is improbably demonstrated here; if Semeka didn't invent this detail, the question arises whether Milashevich wasn't engaging in a bit of role playing with him. Incidentally, he refused not only an offer of drink, but also of sausage and even fish, confirming the authenticity of the vegetarianism that he proclaimed in his prose. But more important than anything for Semeka was, of course, the newspaper parcel, tied with string, that Simeon Kondratyich had brought with him. Besides two manuscript notebooks, there were ten booklets inside, among them six that no one in Moscow was familiar with; yet, to the collector's surprise, the author didn't have many of the well-known ones. Moreover, the author couldn't always understand which ones Semeka had in mind, and when the latter reminded him of the title and even of the contents of some of them, he was genuinely surprised: Did I really write something about that? Semeka recalled, for example, a story about a man who, at the peak of happiness, took the hands off a clock and didn't put them back, though he continued to wind the clock regularly: "It's difficult to relate the charm of this metaphysical joke." Among Simeon Kondratyevich's books, Lizavin never managed to find such a story. Is it possible that Semeka confused something, attributing someone else's plot to Simeon Kondratyevich? Simeon Kondratyich himself seemed inclined to think so. He seemed to have stopped thinking about publications and readers a long time ago. "Those that existed no longer do!" "But you said that you write all the time," Semeka reminded him. "For whom?" "There's someone to write for." Milashevich livened up with that answer and even repeated it, raising his finger significantly: "Of course there's someone. I don't write for myself." Somewhere after this point we begin to sense that

* NEP (also p.189) Acronym for New Economic Policy, devised by Lenin in 1921. It allowed for modified private enterprise, which was curtailed by the First Five-Year Plan of 1928-32.

the visitor from the capital was a bit disappointed by the personality in which was incarnated, so to speak, the name that was much more attractive on a printed cover, and so treated his companion rather condescendingly. Especially since the immediate goal has been achieved: the booklets he wanted are in his hands. (Semeka's sincerity here is beyond doubt; the small collection of *Provincial Fantasies* most likely came out in Moscow as a result of his efforts; moreover, with his short foreword, possibly even lowering the price of this book collectors' novelty, although, with a circulation of 180 copies, not by very much.) He notes now that the aborigine's cap can be called white only relatively, that the smell of his freshly washed Tolstoy shirt isn't really all that fresh, that his fingers are coarse and black from digging in the ground, that his speech is full of pseudosignificant hints, which provincials especially love as an intuitive method of self-assertion; as if to say, "We, too, aren't so simple; in our libraries we even keep up with world problems." Although if you begin to consider carefully what's behind these hints you'll just shake your head. "So what *do* you write?" Vasilii Platonych continued to show interest, already more out of politeness. "Probably something big?" "I don't know how to put it. It keeps growing by itself, like a living thing, in different directions. I just follow." "But to write without getting into print, without a wide readership—it's unnatural, after all." "That's true if you're thinking about literature. But I don't write for literature," answered Simeon Kondratyich, and one could think that he was showing false modesty (meaning, "As if I could!") had he not given us to understand here that he knew something about himself more important than getting into print. "There are times when you just think of a word, and it already exists, and how!" True, Semeka admits here that he'd managed to splash a little cognac stealthily into his companion's tea—to liven up the conversation; maybe it had already had an effect. Now he started a thoroughly suspicious diatribe about scientific experiments on the perception of thought, then about the sensitivity of plants, about the Indian scientist Boze, who while transplanting a sapling put it to sleep with chloroform, as one does people or animals, so that it would come to life painlessly, and even about whether the properties of manure used for fertilizing depend upon the properties of horses. Only when

Simeon Kondratyich started to talk about the Brazilian Sikeiros, who'd thought up the idea of feeding cows with the leaves of coffee trees, so as to get coffee with milk right away, Semeka grew suspicious and had the sense to laugh. Satisfied, his companion laughed with him. How well Lizavin knew this amusing though ambiguous embarrassment, which Milashevich could summon at the most unexpected moment in the most artless way. This ambivalent feeling, bordering on embarrassment, that welled up when you closed the last page or, like Semeka, parted with him. "We left, and it was still light outside. In front of a fence plastered with announcements stood a she-goat. The edge of one sheet of paper had come unstuck, but she didn't think of chewing it as she gazed at it attentively for a long time. 'She's found something,' said Simeon Kondratyich. I laughed and went up to the fence; the goat moved aside, to let me read the sign too: 'Goats and small livestock are to be inoculated by Saturday under penalty of a fine.'"

31

Lizavin chanced upon Semeka's memoirs when he was already writing his dissertation about his fellow countrymen, men of letters from the province and the oblast, without suspecting Milashevich's existence. It is worth mentioning that he immediately rushed to find not only *Provincial Fantasies* by an author whom he hadn't known before, and all Milashevich's prerevolutionary booklets, which by then had been transferred from Vasilii Platonych's collection to the library, but also consulted the Moscow literary archives and the holdings of the deceased Semeka. There he discovered, intact, the manuscripts of several more unpublished Milashevich stories (among them almost all of the *Fairy Tales for Angel*), and, on top of that, the unpublished draft that we've already mentioned. The draft and two or three more texts had been sent later at Semeka's request; the publisher wanted to preface the collection with information about the author, but apparently that, too, wasn't suitable for printing. That meeting with Milashevich was the only one; he heard no more about the man, writes Vasilii Platonych. He didn't even respond to receipt of the books that had come out; he must have died, concludes the author. He had no time to ascertain this in greater detail. Lizavin, sad to say, suspected that Semeka didn't actually try very hard to find out; by this time the absence of a response was an unpleasant sign. Anton Andreyevich managed to find out somewhat more. He dug up some journal publications of Milashevich's, among them the ill-fated "Discovery" and, finally, the investigation file, which contained the only portrait of Milashevich, the very same frontal view, a copy of which thereafter stood in a wooden frame on Lizavin's desk. And that was the sum of his findings. To Lizavin's embarrassment, it turned out that after all his efforts, semiaccidental successes, and even triumphs, he still didn't know whole periods in the life of the writer whom he was interpreting—even the date and circumstances of his death. The homemade booklets of that period weren't preserved, and he didn't succeed in discovering either Milashevich or Simeon Kondratyich Bogdanov in the civic archives or the cemetery records. He'd contrived not to get into print in any long-lasting papers. His quiet name didn't crop up even in the local papers, which, admittedly, weren't preserved in full. The local archives had suffered many losses, especially from various postrevolutionary abolitions, not to mention that in both Stolbenets and to a lesser degree in Nechaisk they'd burned at least twice in great city fires—the second time simultaneously in both towns, in the drought-afflicted summer of 1928, and this simultaneity gave rise to a notorious, somewhat mysterious trial for arson. Smaller-scale fires occurred here almost every year; both towns could produce a whole collection. "A wooden country," Anton Andreyevich often thought in melancholy gloom, "is an unreliable memory. In any European stone monastery one could restore every day of one's life over several centuries according to documents; who lived there and who visited, what they bought and sold, what they ate and drank, with whom they corresponded and had lawsuits, what they discussed and quarreled about during disputes, how much lime, stone, and gilding were invested in the church...but what's the point of going on! The Ascension monastery in Stolbenets, by the way, was also made of stone and didn't suffer from fires, but here there were other devastations. And in the not so distant past...however, those times are sometimes worse than those of long ago."

But we can still buttonhole living witnesses, ask questions—someone's quick to suggest. You needn't have any doubt on that score; Anton Andreyevich didn't miss this opportunity either, but his enthusiasm for such quests didn't last long. To begin with, only a few old residents remained in Stolbenets and Nechaisk, and these were usually people who didn't belong to that group who might have read Milashevich during prerevolutionary times. They perished; the former high school students moved somewhere else; their parents and teachers, the jealous historian Semiglazov—the first to attempt to create a local museum in Stolbenets—and the children's doctor Levinson, who'd founded the famous local orphanage-boarding school with a progressive method of self-education, disappeared; former assessors evaporated without a trace, as did excise tax collectors, telegraph operators, inspectors, and public prosecutors, to say nothing of members of a religious calling, monks, nuns, and so forth. If any of them could be found, then it was most likely in the capitals. The new population had come to the towns mostly from the country; Anton's mother, in fact, was among them. And to ask the longtime locals questions didn't make much sense either. The trouble wasn't that these old folks wrinkled their foreheads and shook their heads when they were told about Bogdanov or Milashevich, the local writer, gardener, and vegetarian. It was worse if they suddenly began to remember—as once the one-armed Khvorostinin, a former stovetender, did. "Kondratyich, eh? Yeah, I knew him. Sure! They used to call him a sorcerer." "Why a sorcerer?" "Well, he was from somewhere around Sareyevo, knew how to do something like that. You know Sareyevo? A while back, half the village was considered sorcerers—now, too. Ours was the most superstitious area, an old-style district. Sorcerers, sectarians. He lived there, near the cemetery, in the priest's old house. The priest also turned out to be unfrocked, grew tobacco." "Wait a minute. Near which cemetery?" asked Anton, already despairing in advance. And, indeed, it became clear that Khvorostinin was talking about Nechaisk and not about Stolbenets. But Milashevich certainly didn't live in Nechaisk after the revolution; the stovetender was confusing him with someone. "Then later they said he was connected with the Makarites." "With whom?" "The Makarites. Some sect that lived in the woods. People say they built a whole town out of mud; they found them from a plane. And this Makarii, the priest—that is, unfrocked priest—he was their leader. When there was a famine, when everything was burning here, what do you think they did? They'd meet at the cemetery, tear the corpses that were still fresh out of their graves, cook them like meat, and then go crazy from this food—well, you know, drunk, and they'd start dancing, do all sorts of outrageous things, until they fell down dead themselves. It was savage…And the priest, they say, fled to America. He's still broadcasting over the radio even now."

33

No, it's not worth reproaching Lizavin for the fact that he didn't take too many pains with these attempts. Really. He dug a bit and continued to dig little by little where he could, not because he was inclined to such archival searches, but just out of good conscience. The archivist's passion was just what he lacked; by nature he preferred to fabricate things, and for a while he'd even intended to become a storyteller. In his mind there formed the image of a provincial self-taught philosopher, preaching simple harmony, appreciating fantasy, humor, indulgence, and kindness, and this image contained so much that was close and pleasant to him, that if this were to fly, he didn't actually feel like complicating and confusing it with additional and, most likely, unnecessary details. He'd even shudder whenever he came across the name Bogdanov (already not such a rare name) on the printed page or in a document, and once he was sure that it wasn't Milashevich, he'd feel relieved. Once Milashevich-Bogdanov appeared posthumously, the two together, and in what a context! Lizavin saw this double last name (true, without initials) in the Stolbenets newspaper *The Way Forward*, 2 November 1930, which he'd been looking at by chance, for something else he needed; his heart missed a beat at the coincidence. And it was good if this was just a coincidence. The article was signed "K. Dialectical" and was called "The Claws of Puankare in the Forest on the Left Bank of the Volga." It talked about the intensification of the class struggle in the district, recalling the condemned arsonists of 1928, Sverbeyev and Fige, as well as "those who, with the help of a religious drug, tried to sabotage the great struggle to liquidate the kulaks as a class." And among them was Milashevich-Bogdanov. No, of course, it was a coincidence (but a double one, for heaven's sake!). In the first place, religious issues had never interested him seriously; here (as in many other things) he was distanced from the fashionable enthusiasms of the epoch. Second, it wasn't possible even to imagine how Simeon Kondratyich could have had anything to do with village affairs. Although Stolbenets was surrounded by villages, and life in it, especially in the large settlements, was semi-villagelike, the peasant question was alien to Milashevich as a matter of principle. In the third place... that means the third place also had nothing to do with it. It wasn't even worth thinking about. Except to check, to look through the pertinent cases. But to get to them was a bit more complicated than getting to police trial records. Lizavin didn't even try. To be honest, after that article he completely abandoned all zeal in searching for anything new. Better not. It wasn't necessary. We're not educated in a monastery's history. We'll make peace with the fact that there are no more documents as a fact of life. We don't know to this day who, say, Shakespeare was, although this problem feeds a whole army of researchers. And it's no big deal. He basically had enough for a dissertation; even the stuff that he'd found was, frankly, sufficient to quiet a scholarly conscience. Ultimately, his dissertation wasn't only about Milashevich, as we've already said. Moreover, Milashevich occupied a deservedly modest place there; other local natives and figures were incomparably more famous. That out of all of them Milashevich proved to be as close to Anton Andreyevich as a relative is another matter. Although, as they say in scholarly jargon, he was not a very dissertationable figure; if Anton were to dig up a revolutionary episode in his biography, it would be worthwhile leaving it out entirely. On the other hand, he wasn't an ordinary topic for a dissertation, one of those which, after the degree is granted, aren't read anymore, for they've become instant soporifics. Others were like fellow travelers in a train compartment; you spend some time with them, as pleasant and useful as can be, yet not obligatory. Simeon

Kondratyevich had struck a chord in Lizavin's soul. A certain lack of clarity in Milashevich's image not only didn't bother him, but appealed to his imagination. Maybe our story, too, will appeal to people in the same way? thought Anton Andreyevich once. In other stories, petrified and preserved, everything is too clearly defined, all you need to do is copy it out, and your interest in them is different. Our story hasn't become outdated; its failures are provocative even today.

34

It had to happen, of course; when the dissertation was practically ready, Lizavin managed to find in a regional archive—among papers certified for their lack of value and predestined, it would seem, to be burned, or, more likely, to be pulped—a small trunk filled with Milashevich's papers, or, to be more precise, with scraps; a messy collection of those same *fantiki* used on the back side. He could spend more than a year going through them—just put off his defense. It's no longer shameful now to admit that in the first second Lizavin felt, besides the joy of a discoverer, confusion and annoyance and a strange alarm. These contradictory feelings were aggravated by the doubtful circumstances under which the *fantiki* had fallen into his possession. No matter how you explain it and twist it, he, to put it mildly, had stolen them from the repository—but it's better to speak about this separately. However, even on first examination it was already clear that the sheets of paper couldn't add any significant information to his dissertation. They were basically various rough-draft notes, outlines, and even individual words, thoughts, excerpts, and such like, not always intelligible odds and ends, but not a single document. One could consider them a special topic that was worth studying in real earnest later, but now there wasn't time. So that's what he did. And then, the further he got, the more the fuss with the *fantiki* began to force out his other scholarly projects. And the more he dug in the heap of wrapping paper, the less he understood Milashevich. And the main thing was, the further he went, the more a feeling of at first vague anxiety, of some inner unease, grew in him. True, there were reasons for Lizavin's spiritual distress apart from those connected with his scholarly work; however, at times it seemed to him that the course of this work and the circumstances of his own life were linked by a kind of dependence that wasn't accidental.

35

And maybe this anxiety was born of the several strange notes that Lizavin kept coming across during his investigation; unintelligible and vague, one day they yielded up an unexpected connection in his hands—the words suddenly stabbed him, as if addressed to him:

What happened to me while I lived? I don't remember.
That is death.

a change of memory

The seeing, detailed fingers of a blind man feel around in the dark, defining contours in it

you're already close, any second now. I feel it, I hear. God!
Every step echoes in me, makes me tremble

it draws together, brings together from various corners, closer and closer…Oh, if only it doesn't pass by!

how much waiting, silently, without stirring

It's so painful, so hard. You really can't hear? But I'm here, here!
You're touching the substance of my soul, of my mind,
with your fingers.

don't look around, God, it's I speaking to you!

II. The Lines of Fate, or Milashevich's Little Trunk

How well you put it, somewhere, Simeon Kondratyevich: we people who write are needlessly embarrassed at coincidences, which may seem contrived and overly significant. We immediately start to justify ourselves, citing life, where in fact there are many more such coincidences—and more frequent. Moreover, we don't pay attention to all of them, and they don't mean anything to us, they make no sense, while in literature the intention and purpose are clear. But, of course, if we turn to lived experience, we also can discover some pattern in the interweaving of fates, designed as everything is designed in live and inert nature, which makes us think: Don't ideas about meaning and beauty that are accessible to us meet at a single primordial common point? Whether it really exists, this pattern, is another question. "That depends on the person," some would answer. Perhaps coincidence rewards the ability to make out among the world's noises a voice addressed to you, even if you yourself haven't grasped it? After all, we're often geniuses in love, when a single word or even movement generates an inexplicable response; but if that doesn't occur, it means the word hasn't been guessed and there is no love—it's dispersed in the air. To be granted a relationship with fate, one perhaps has to believe in it. And if a tram has left from under your nose, pay attention: you'll be given the next one, not without purpose; it's good if the soul proves sensitive and primed at the right moment. By the way, that's good with any tram, only one lacks the strength to be sensitive all the time. And then with a sober smile we admit that in general we see the significance and purpose only after the fact, that life's plot and its connections are but a trick of a cowardly mind, just a collection of scraps, really, and a woman whom you didn't notice in a split second isn't waiting for you—why? Is it really worth looking for the sense, the reason, the blame, retracing your steps along a chain of absurdities and coincidences that changed your life, maybe even then, when you pushed your way in through the wrong door by mistake and came across the trunk, condensed from a literary dream?

2

Anton Andreyevich had been looking in the district archive for something entirely different: information about Stolbenets's self-taught poet Iona Sverbeyev, a figure from the Nechaisk republic. Lizavin knew nothing about this republic, besides its name, but in a catalog he chanced upon a mention of the file with documents pertaining to it: he wanted to have a look at it, and for some reason they wouldn't give it to him right away. The main thing was that they could at least have given a sensible reason for doing so; but no, as always, there had to be a meaningful evasiveness, as if to say, wait, there's something we have to clear up first. And here's what else is interesting: Anton Andreyevich could have done very well without the file; it really didn't have a direct relevance to his topic. But go on, he kept insisting, although every inch of his skin already sensed the unpleasant guardedness of the curator of the local historical raw material toward any stranger who for some reason took it into his head to touch in person the unprocessed deposits that were possibly harmful to one's health. What for? For what purpose? Wouldn't it be simpler to turn to the already extracted, neutralized, and even wholesome products on the topic in question—products supplied by professionals who have a proven immunity to working with raw materials? But maybe he only imagined all this. Anton Andreyevich's education, alas, began in the years when libraries didn't give out even old newspapers right away, demanding explanations and written confirmations. And although Anton now had something to show them—an official form reinforced by stamps and signatures—they gave him the runaround for a month and a half with the last file, and he still couldn't bring himself to

demand clearer explanations. Demand, hell! Lizavin felt an inexplicable shyness in that building. It had started in the hall of the former
private apartment with the plywood wall between shabby columns,
where a female police officer with a frightening grenadier's build
perpetually stood guard. That is, not one policewoman, of course;
several of them took turns, maybe a platoon of caryatids, but all of
them choice, the same article, with powerful busts beneath the blue
cloth of their uniforms, sergeant's stripes on padded shoulders,
bright lips painted in a common color. This sameness of type and
lipstick, sword knot harness, and the shine of chrome boots for some
reason brought to mind the thought of barracks in the architectural
style of Empire stables. He felt ashamed of this vision, which wasn't
substantiated by anything, but their perfume smelled of horse sweat,
and all of them had hair arranged in nets, in the style of the forties,
as if they had borne their unfeminine watch from that time on, not
getting older or having children, only growing plump and expanding.
A stuffy smell enveloped him as he showed his pass and opened
his folder to be checked; he didn't pass through, but squeezed by,
somehow getting smaller, shrinking, feeling as if the giantess could
crush him completely if necessary, size him up and, for the present,
only scorn him as a nonentity.

3

Whoever wants to, of course, is free to laugh at the timorous imagination of a provincial reared for modest and unpretentious pastimes.
In his defense, Lizavin could have said that he didn't experience similar feelings in other archives. From ourselves we will add that timo-
rousness of this sort is related to the imagination; it is born of it and
encourages it, and, so, sometimes, timidity can turn into an artistic
advantage. But, in general, what can one say! Anton belonged to the
category of people who, having knocked at the door, and even lightly
but unsuccessfully pushed it, turn around or look for another way
in—especially if any kind of strict schedule is hanging on the door.
Although you had simply to pull the door toward you—and maybe
they'd hung the schedule temporarily God knows when, and then
hadn't bothered to take it down. It was like a fossilized inscription,

warning bogatyrs* about a path that was forbidden and therefore
seductive. As if it suddenly were really hot; that, of course, is what
was interesting. In any case, the matter at hand was the dissertation,
the master's degree, and that meant his daily bread; so he got himself
fired up, despising his own weakness, and this stimulation of embarrassment, perhaps more than doubtful arguments about bread, contributed to what came later. In a word, he finally shouldered open
the servants' door bearing the tablet with the forbidden sacred text
that had been pointed out to him; he either really made a mistake or
didn't hear all the explanations that followed, for he found himself
not in an office, but in an unidentified corridor or dressing room out
of which led two other doors. He knocked on the left one. It turned
out to be locked. He opened the right one, and out of inertia went
down three steps...At this point he should have turned back, of
course, and asked again, but he went on; and when he decided to
turn back, behind him, as far as he remembers now, three doors
appeared simultaneously, and he wasn't certain through which he'd
better go. Oh, how awkward it turned out, how annoying and bad! He
had only one concern now—to get out—but seeing the figure of the
local worker on the horizon, he was too embarrassed to call him, not
wanting to explain how he'd gotten there; and it wasn't worth attract-
ing the ear of the caryatids. Somehow he himself could...here they
were, the three steps going up...

4

*You're already close, any second now. I feel it, I hear. God! Every step
echoes in me, makes me tremble...it draws together, brings together
from various corners, closer and closer...oh, if only it doesn't pass by!*

5

Well, yes, Simeon Kondratyich, now when you know ahead of time
that you've found each other, you actually imagine how the eye with
raw red veins that you praised follows the wanderings of an awkward

---

* BOGATYR (also p.231) Preternaturally strong, larger-than-life heroes of Russia's
ancient epics and tales.

figure through the neglected labyrinth; so he almost ended up in the wrong place... but no, he turned back... a little bit more, Anton Andreyevich, getting warmer, warmer... and even the door, springing back with a rather crude familiarity, kept pushing the hesitant wanderer in the back; moving along the cramped official interiors, he made his way into the depths. Dirty windows at brow level merge with the asphalt, the drops swell on the exposed hoses, on the heating units. Crumbled lime crunches underfoot. He had such an intelligent, independent look that although someone may even have noticed him, he didn't pay any attention. A jacket, tie, small beard, a folder in his hands... No, we remember, there was no folder. But hadn't he left it in the reading room? He hadn't left anything; nothing of his was lost there. But he couldn't have come without a folder. Or could he? Look here, Simeon Kondratyevich, just try to judge the reliability of other people's testimony, if after only several years you yourself can't say for sure whether you had a folder in your hands then. And I don't think you had a beard yet, either... but that we can verify by the dates. And the feeling is fresh. The sensation of a sticky cobweb is unpleasant to the face—it was eerie, like the local air, and was spreading right there and then behind his back. Deposits of folders, flattened skulls. Suddenly he stumbled over a small washbasin placed on the floor under a drip. Now all he had to do was take a few more uncertain steps to see right in front of his nose the same sort of basin in a bear's clawed paws and to hear a dissatisfied voice: "He's finally here!"

6

The bear stood on its hind paws, shabby, looking like a janitor, a sharp-peaked cloth helmet on his head and a goat's foot in his maw; he held the washbasin before him, like a dish of ancient hospitality. The windows in the semicircular hall were sealed a third of the way up with plywood. Behind the bear towered a huge hollow wardrobe with a sign pinned to its door: "Magic lantern. An evening of amazing sensations and illusions in natural dimensions." One could see the said lantern on the wardrobe as well as a dusty glass cylinder with the handwritten inscription: "Human brain in alcohol." Neither the one nor the other, however, was in the jar; only a withered lump adhered

48

to the glass. The remaining space was crowded with piles of papers, files, and newspapers, tied together with string and heaped one on top of another right on the floor. Pressed by its own weight, this layered substance had stuck together into an indivisible primitive mass; in places it sagged like dough. Transparent wood lice licked off traces of the pressed ink of names of undistinguished earthly inhabitants, of whom not even the voices remained now; corpse worms swarmed inside, turning into the dust of rotten wood the remains of lives and the riddles of deaths, the whispers of denunciations, declarations of love—all vanished without a trace, as not even people's bodies vanish, but more like a mushroom, without leaving behind even a little bone. It smelled of putrefied time here, of moldy spoiled memory, of mouse droppings and the soggy residual odor of vodka. Weren't these the smells that Ecclesiastes smelled when speaking of earthly vanity?

7

But all this we sense later, when we recover a bit. At first Anton saw only the badly shaven sickly face of a government worker in a gray work smock.

"Why are you alone?" the latter asked. His red eyes were shrouded with the turbid film of servile madness. Lizavin opened his mouth to answer, but an uncontrollable sneeze suddenly came over the servant. Somewhere in the distance a caryatid pricked up her ears. "Ach-ch-ch-chooo!" The servant shook his head, rid of the latest attack, and wiped his nose with the edge of his smock. "Same thing every time. As you like, begin alone for now, there's no time to wait. And there are only a few here."

Before Lizavin could make sense of his words, he showed the future doctoral candidate the entire monumental simplicity of the situation. Without any key, he opened the tall door leading straight into the courtyard like an anal aperture, which, of course the caryatids have, too, together with an undozing sculptured pupil. Flush against the doors stood a cart. The driver indifferently waited for the loading.

"Here, take them from that corner," said the worker, and Lizavin— if you can imagine—set about carrying the packets, replacing or delaying an explanation with this easy help, and did so with a silly feeling verging on gratitude that this work somehow justified his venturing into forbidden places and would be taken into account in the event of something.

8

How did he espy his little trunk among those landslides? It's impossible to recall now what drew him in that direction. He himself didn't even realize at first that he'd recognized the Singer sewing-machine case, though it was flatter, the nails and brass corners green with mold, as if glimpsed in a dream, in forgetful infancy, or even before birth—a false recollection of what he'd never seen. There was no lock on the little trunk, and the wooden handle was half ripped off. The sides were spotted with black—scorched. From under the cover a smell preserved for God knows how many years was released; the smell of lamp kerosene, char, bedbugs, the smell of disease, rot, of dry but already rotten grasses—a sample of air that had chanced here, stored like a sigh of vanished times, and maybe even a part of the breath of the one who had bent over the trunk for the last time, closing it tightly... If only it were possible to be prepared in advance, to catch the smell in a test tube, so as to later grasp its contents, which can tell the soul a great deal... Surely the imagination didn't add this, too, afterward? Common sense demanded that one assume that the little trunk had already been opened; it must have been opened, if only to decide the fate of the contents. But either common sense was inappropriate here, or the remains of the smell nevertheless persisted, just as a languishing gray spiderweb persisted in the corner, bearing the weightless mummies of two little spiders, guardians of discounted treasures, faithful to the end. A few *fantiki* were turned over, their backs showing, and the handwriting caused Lizavin's heart to shudder.

9

When he turned his bewildered gaze to the official, the latter was drinking medicine from a medical measuring glass divided into sections.

"What'd you find?" The darting rabbit eyes finally registered Anton. He took a little cigar from his bear's mouth, sucked on it a bit without lighting it, and put it back. The smell of alcohol, which must have evaporated from the cylinder and already turned into residual alcohol, gradually overcame everything else. Aggravated by the dampness, the waft of alcohol tickled his nostrils, and Lizavin didn't have time to answer when a sneeze suddenly attacked him. "What's this trunk?" The fellow bent over the lid. Inside, it was also pasted over with multicolored *fantiki.* "No inventory number? Well, don't touch it for now, leave it. Although it's burned on the side..."

"A-a"—Lizavin helplessly pointed inside at the contents, but finished just as helplessly—"a-a-choo!"

"You collect them?" the servant understood without words and picked up a few *fantiki* with his fingers. "But, see, they're ruined. On the back."

"A-a," Anton Andreyevich continued in agony, and, *mirabile dictu,* his companion understood this language of his even better than articulate speech; he understood it as his own, penetrating, in spite of words, not so much into Anton's thoughts (Anton wasn't even thinking about such a thing), but into his unconscious.

"Well, take it if you need it. Take it out here, then. They might not let you out with it there. But leave the trunk for now. You have your own box?"

"A-a," began Lizavin, but, from surprise or something else, he didn't finish. The sneezing attack passed just as it had begun...What kind of box could he have in a sanctuary where it was forbidden to bring in even a briefcase? Anton remembered, however, the net bag that he always carried in his pocket in case he'd find something in a store. The *fantiki,* coming free, rose like leavened dough. Together Lizavin and the official stuffed them in, concentratedly wheezing residual alcohol in each other's face, banging their foreheads together. (Ah, who doesn't know this ability to get drunk from someone else's binge and get infected with someone else's madness! With some people it can be taken to the point of absurdity.) Under the *fantiki* they found a poster folded four times; it was very suitable for wrapping, for the small pieces of paper sagged in the mesh netting. With a tearful sound, time dripped into the basin; in the distant stable they didn't feel any alarm yet, but the melancholy of adventure into which Lizavin was being dragged, by heaven knows whom and what for, sucked at him. He could have suggested leaving the stuff there, and later working on it right there... But, on the other hand, who besides him would find it valuable? They'll burn it. No one knows whose junk it is. If they ask, I'll tell them how it was... I'll say I got lost, he asked, and I couldn't refuse... God! You can fabricate something more probable, whereas this resembles a plot of Simeon Kondratyich's. Not good. Let's say something else would be better...

10

The door slammed behind him. A big puddle had melted in the middle of the courtyard. By the barn lay the remains of piles of logs that had been used over the winter. A horse clattered along the cobblestones. On the fence by the tilted gates fluttered half-torn announcements that had got caked together, a poster with headlines in thin-legged letters with heavy black galoshes, in keeping with the fashion at the beginning of the century.

11

MASS MEETING OF 1923

It will begin at 12:00 midnight, at the signal of a deafening explosion of a device loaded with dynamite and a firework burning brightly over the city.

On Freedom Square (formerly Trade Square), a wagon is moving, decorated in dark colors and black flags, with slogans of the most important events of 1922. A figure representing a decrepit old man (the old year) sits in the wagon. In a loud voice, the figure declaims the past events of 1922. The masses who are taking part accompany the figure with loud ovations. A funeral note sounds: three volleys of gunfire. After the salute from the Red Hero Comrade Peresheikin Club, a car brightly adorned with red flags and slogans of the important upcoming events of 1923 moves slowly ahead. On it stands the luminous figure of a young boy. In a loud voice the figure announces events scheduled for 1923. Those gathered there receive him with ovations and cries of 'Hurrah!'

OBLIGATORY DECREE

*With the aim of regulating the housing question to grant all citizens
living in privately owned homes the right to voluntarily give up part
of their dwelling space before 15 April this year, so that every lodger
would have no more than 16 square arshins.**

*Seeing that the hung placards, proclamations, and announcements
are being ruthlessly torn down and destroyed by both counterrevolutionary elements and unthinking ruffians alike, I am issuing a warning that those guilty will be arrested and brought to trial.*

—Chief of Police Arrestov

12

The poster and several announcements, hardened by dirty glue, pieces
of them torn in places, testified to the collector's passion. Several *fantiki* forced us to think about this self-sacrificing passion as well. About
ten of them, for example, bore the signet of money coupons, or,
rather, moneyless ones, and that's what they were called: "Coupons
for moneyless issue"—of bread (five, ten, and twenty pounds), wood,
kerosene, rye, each with its own drawing; the children's coupons for
treacle (the toffee Angel's Day, with the picture of a familiar cherub)
were separate. To leave the coupon in the collection, someone possibly had had to deny himself food. Here, perhaps, was another spiritual
splash: the candy *fantik* costing a thousand rubles bore the gift
inscription "*To dear Roksana, as a keepsake for many years to come.*"
On the other side was a black-haired beauty with a watering can, from
a popular song of bygone years:

> *But next morning there she was, smiling,*
> *Beneath her little window, as of old,*
> *And her hand was tenderly beguiling,*
> *As from the can the water flowed.*

We'll also mention the *fantik* ticket banged out on the typewriter,
"For listening to the radio for two minutes, price: 1,500 rubles," the
fantik mandate "Of the Nechaisk Sanitary Dictator," and, among
papers of a different sort, a scrap of someone's commemorative list,

---

* ARSHIN An antiquated Russian unit of linear measure equal to 28 inches.

with the words: *"On the recovery of the slave of God Euphemia, on the marriage of Stepanida, for Melania on the resolution of sterility, for Fyodor Ivanych on the defense from oppression (and a new boiler)"* and a quarter-sheet from a notepad inscribed with the owner's name, with a vignette in the form of a palette and brush (clearly, they couldn't find anything else in the printer's supply), read only:

> *Governor*
> *Comrade Karl*
> *plenipotentiary*
> *in battle*

On the other side an unknown hand had written four peasant names in a column *(Merinov Fedot, Zagrebelnyi Ivan, Gubanov Ilya, Vikulov Prov)*. In general all the clean backs of the sheets were covered with Simeon Kondratyevich's handwriting, sometimes carrying over onto the side with the drawing. Obviously, at some time he'd picked up the pieces of paper not only out of a collector's interest, but out of a pauper's need as well.

What also attested to this need was the merchant Basalayev's old, almost disembowelled warehouse book: in essence, there were only four sheets left, and these were ripped. The first still contained the end of an old list, which began with "rye" and ended with "Dalmatian (antibedbug) powder." Here also, at the end of the page in Milashevich's hand, several headings were written out relating to God knows what—possibly a list of unrealized plans: "On Words, or The Beginning of a New Faith," "The Mind of a Flower, or An Attempt at Happiness," "Fyodor Ivanovich and Gertrude," "The Ark, or A Rock Will Yet Be of Use," "The Lost Garden, or God's Cleverness," and so on (Simeon Kondratyich loved old-fashioned double titles). The last heading, by the way, resonated with the title of the Ganshin treatise mentioned earlier, but it's not clear what relationship it had to it. Even less clear is what is meant by the same "Lost Garden" in another list on the next page. In spite of the beginning, which had been torn off, it was clear that Milashevich was compiling a draft list of objects kept at the ruined Ganshin estate until they established a museum there (a Flemish study, decorated with a turtle shell on foil, a carved Danzig mirror frame, and so on—right down to some sort of ruler with a notch). Objects that Simeon Kondratyevich managed to find throughout the villages were added to this list, in different inks and, clearly, at different times; among them a phonograph, Pathé brand, and also a small device for shuffling playing cards, a flycatcher with a watch mechanism, and, finally, that very same "Lost Garden," with a note in parentheses: "3 pieces." Those "3 pieces" were utterly confusing; well, never mind them. Barely intelligible notes of cursory observations on gardening took up half a page in the book: "27 April no. 2 cotyledons. no. 4 no sprouts," and so on. There was nothing of particular interest in the book, and Lizavin fairly quickly set it aside.

13

We'll also mention someone's letter on four sheets of good paper, covered on both sides with small, even handwriting. There was no beginning or end to indicate the addressee and the signature, but by the contents one could deduce that a man was writing to a woman whom he'd met unexpectedly after a twenty years' separation; at one time they'd been involved in a complicated, evidently romantic relationship, but he subsequently married someone else, and she also got married— the letter sounds like a belated explanation *"in pursuit, after the farewell." ("During the meeting we contrived not even to ask each other the questions that hung in the air").* The very situation of the meeting was curious: the woman, as we understand it, changed her name when she married, and when he came to see her (it must have been on business) he had no idea whom he would see: *"I evidently was confused, simply unprepared for such a meeting. I didn't connect the surname, which I knew only on paper, in any way with you. Accept my belated congratulations, incidentally, for all those years at one go. I omitted to offer them."* It looks as if, even after twenty years, the meeting aroused in him a partly comic panic *("Why didn't I stay for the night, at least?").* He considers it necessary to justify himself and calls his own behaviour "flight." From the letter emerges the picture of a tired, weakened, but once clearly remarkable person, a prerevolutionary émigré who'd not found a niche in the new order; he tells of his not too happy and rather shortlived marriage—everything was over, life hadn't panned out, his former wife and son now are God knows where, but he doesn't blame anyone, doesn't have any regrets. And so on, in this vein. Lizavin tried to make this letter fit in this way and that: Wasn't it addressed to Aleksandra Flegontovna? No, that didn't fit. Possibly, Milashevich had kept it, planning somehow to use it for literary purposes; it's difficult to say. It clearly had no relevance to any known aspect of his life and, therefore, alas, had to be relegated to the category of the peripheral.

14

To finish with the section of comparatively substantial papers, out of purely scholarly conscientiousness (we really don't know what to advise the person who gets bored with such a scholarly tendency; probably he should jump ahead immediately; but Lizavin couldn't allow himself that)—and, so, we'll also describe the creased and soiled notebook sewn together with white thread, in octavo, without a cover, once again without a beginning or an end. This one Milashevich must have picked up out of a love for curiosities. The handwriting was lopsided, as if drunk; the farther one read, the larger and less intelligible the letters; the ink was dirty and faint, in places almost invisible, and from the second page on was replaced by an indelible pencil, but was even dirtier (wherever saliva had been used, and where saliva hadn't been used, you could barely make anything out). A superficial glance at these lines, virtually devoid of punctuation, made one suppose that the person writing was not very literate, the reading suggested that he was, most likely—how can one put it more gently—not wholly intact mentally. *"If we draw a molecule, it is structured like the planetary system Or an atom I forgot Not important Let's imagine that invisible planets are swarming with life the way ours does…"* Some kind of local Tsiolkovsky. We'll add that the pages were dirty and stuck together with some kind of brown goo, which didn't smell, admittedly, but all the same, one could understand why Lizavin was squeamish even about ungluing them. And what for, in fact? With difficulty he deciphered the scrawl that broke off on the last page: *"emptiness between stars a pile of stones Energy needed all the time...*" He should have thrown it all out, but Lizavin didn't allow himself to do so—out of the aforementioned conscientiousness, still hoping to read it some day, to overcome his squeamishness. And maybe out of greed—he also loved curiosities.

15

Let's turn to the heap and rummage through it along with Anton Andreyevich—if only cursorily. What can we do? Without it we can't understand what follows. The unevenness and burrs from the scissors, which could be detected with the naked eye, testified that sometimes they cut the *fantiki* by hand or tore them off along the fold from big strips, like those on which *The Guide* was once printed. This confirmed the notion that Milashevich himself preferred, for certain purposes, the small format rather than using it out of necessity. The pages were covered with writing that sometimes was close and fine, in good ink, and, obviously, produced in the comfort of home, but sometimes was written any which way, on the go, and maybe even in a bumpy cart, in salivated indelible pencil, with handwriting to match; the entire record consisted of occasional fragmented half-phrases written for himself (all in lowercase letters and without periods) or even of a single unintelligible word. There were soiled papers, as if picked up from the ground, and a dry piece of what was unquestionably manure adhered to one of them. It contained, by the way, a mysterious and not very pleasant inscription in an unknown hand: "*From Trotsky.*" Quite a few sheets were creased; this made us recall the poet who kept his manuscripts in the famous pillowcase on which he slept. For sure Simeon Kondratyich preferred to sleep more comfortably, but several of his own passages incline one to draw such a comparison.

16

A thought caught unawares, an impression captured on the wing...
no, not captured—a little feather remained in the fingers, and a down
one, at that. If one is methodical, one can collect a whole pillowful
of them or even a feather bed—a choice one, feather to feather.
　　One can accumulate little feathers and create a scarecrow that
looks totally like something live.

The same thought underwent variations on another *fantik*: *No, there won't be any life in it.*

This sounded like philosophizing about a genre that was already famous enough—the genre of short fragments, of arrested and magnified moments. Simeon Kondratyich, with his predilection for the magnifying glass, clearly was a connoisseur of it. On the *fantiki* you'll also find a wasp in the hot bell of a flower, and tender pollen on the stamens, and the knock of a little spoon against a glass, the rustle of candy paper—the joys of provincial tea drinking; the hum of the stove, a wick on an earthen saucer, the little flame reflected in the glass migrating into outer space, as if hoping to warm its distant expanses. Everything acquires significance, is magnified: a gulp of hot liquid, a step on the street, home laundry, *clumps of lather in the basin,* and, on an even smaller scale, *the membranes of lather.* Several fragments of thought were on this very theme, like this one, for instance: *"Not a word, in fact, but an exclamation, an interjection, an attempt at a word. The Gospel scholars later put it together."* Or: *"You can accept everything, accommodate everything: the sky, grass, flower bed, and the radiating sun..."*—farther on a whole list, which we can leave out. But isn't all of this about the same thing—on the possibilities of a *fantik* genre?

However, far from all of the *fantiki* were susceptible to interpretation in the spirit of a conscious genre, to any interpretation at all. In part it was a kind of notebook, an instrument and document of multifaceted daily work, the fruit of literary reflection, when out of necessity or for future use you seize any trifle along the way. Sometimes Lizavin vividly imagined this librarian—in a pince-nez and a Tolstoy shirt with a cord instead of a tie—getting some boxes from his bulging bib pocket (or, say, a cigarette case) stuffed with *fantiki,* and, after separating one from the rest, copying out something from the newspaper; or, in galoshes and a white cap, the tin tip removed from his indelible pencil, stopping on the way by a fence, to rewrite some verses or an inscription in the cemetery: "Here lies God's former slave, now a free citizen of God, Nikita Fokin"; at the bazaar, at a meeting, while walking, lost in thought and forgetting to chase a fly off his sweaty forehead, jotting down on a piece of paper a fleeting thought, detail, word—the everyday trash of life—and what does he do with this later? Does he throw it into the little trunk when he comes home? Or does he use it somehow? Perhaps as material for the very book of which Semeka spoke?

On other *fantiki* you could clearly see preliminary sketches for topics unknown, and sometimes known—a detail made more precise, a turning point in the action, a characteristic response. Once again the vision of the memorable puddle appeared: *"The raft floated up, we climb onto it, and the helmsman waits for us. Careful, I say, don't stumble."* It was as if Milashevich were trying out a continuation, a solemn epilogue to the old story, with a return and a meeting that gets realized: *"Well, now, I said. Shall we have some more tea?"*—there's even that sort of line. By the way, we forgot again to mention the sheet of paper (not a *fantik*) with a note about Gavrila Printsip's shot and about the angelic-looking boy: so, a very similar kid appears several times on the *fantiki*, sometimes playing among flowers and grasses, sometimes in a little gray Levinson jacket, that is, in the uniform of the Stolbenets free boarding school; the saliva of curiosity and self-oblivious eagerness drools from his childish lip. Did Milashevich plan to develop this vague plot? It's impossible to say, just as it's impossible to determine whose is the first-person perspective imprinted on the *fantik*. Several phrases convey the feeling either of a child or simply of a short person: someone wearing little boots with inner, built-in heels, a tall hat that helps him seem almost of a height with others, someone stretching on tiptoe, tugging down on the door handle, toward himself, and succeeding in opening it with difficulty. *"At twilight, the knees of big people, an unfamiliar smell, gingerbread in a bare hand that comes closer, the sweetness of glazed bread crusts on the tongue, and through the door emerging once more from the cool semidarkness into the seething light."* What is this? A feeling from childhood, of course, a moment of incomprehensible happiness: a child came from outside into a room; they treated him to gingerbread, no one knows who, nor does one have to know; knowledge won't provide that radiant aura of a miracle. But who is this child? Simeon Kondratyevich himself? Or is this simply yet another experience of the "transported figurative eye?" We can assume that the illegitimate child has an orphaned childhood, not too happy. Isn't that why he prefers moments from a coherent story, taken out of the connected flow of events? In this arrested, static form they are more likely to convey the feeling he desires. The *fantiki*, apart from everything else, demonstrated this philosopher's strange but quite consistent relationship to time.

17

If one could only imagine a chronological order to these notes, then all one would have to do is look, and something like a moving picture would take shape of its own accord, and we would have some sense of the unity of this life in its development. But even the gardener's unintelligible notes in the barn book, which registered days and months, neglected to keep track of the year—so what can one expect from the scraps of paper? The very method of keeping this diary, if one may call it that, indicated precisely an artistically disorganized nature, not that of a precise scientist. Where dates were concerned, in some places one could judge only obliquely; for example, by the stamped message on the back of the *fantiki*. So, the message on Hangover—"Down with Drunken Stupor"—allowed us to date the note no earlier than the years of NEP. There were also oblique indications of a different type. Let's take, say, the beginning of a poem copied from somewhere: *"It's almost nine years / Since we acquired all freedoms."* (On the back of the caramel Jubilee.) It's clear that this was the year 1926. Well, what of it? No, this inattention to dates had its own system; several notes could even be grouped under a general heading.

ABOUT TIME

Temporal duration is created by the substance of life, by which time is filled up. For the soul and for memory, eternity is indistinguishable from an instant, in which everything exists simultaneously.

What if the way our mind is organized is not the only one possible, and the sequence of numbered dates is contingent?

I stretched out my hand—when was that?—and the palm of a hand rested against mine. But what filled the moments between the beginning of the movement and the end?

of our whole life—the four seasons, a child's carousel

Seven old rubles now count as millions. In the same way, translate God's seven days according to the new calculation.

The last note, by the way, lent itself to an oblique, even if approximate, dating. One could link it to another one, such as this: "*a time when you borrow five hundred rubles and within a week have to give back a million.*" Apart from everything else, it conveyed a sense of severed connections characteristic for Milashevich and redoubled by the revolution. One could select several more *fantiki* where time was described in terms of signs: "*a legendary time when a bottle sold for half a ruble in remote villages, even cheaper in the ones nearby*"; "*a time when new things weren't being produced, and one used the old ones, squandered, patched, and reconceived.*" Or such as this one: "*This was the year when Golgother started sewing purses once again.*" An epic beginning without a continuation: to find a place for it meant to understand it, such as, for instance, this image: "*the place of crime before its time.*" Or, even shorter: "*splashes of time.*" (By the way, wasn't this about the *fantiki* themselves? It's worth thinking about.) One series mentioned a clock without hands—something from a hypothetical story. Other lines gave Anton Andreyevich food for thought, so to speak. For example: "*there's no end, and to look for a beginning is senseless.*" One could compare this entry with another—"*along the chain of caused reasons you'll get to the foundation of the world, but you'll explain nothing anyway*"—and see here the conviction of a man who refuses to think about origins, connections, and history, to look there for the sources of the present, just as he refuses to think about death...But in the first phrase, one could see simply an observation about a notebook without a cover, and that's just what it was...

61

Anton Andreyevich got two dozen cardfile boxes, and one by one would shove the *fantiki* in them, sorting the scraps according to such categories as, for example, dialogues, sketches of landscapes (*"The air is extracted from winy fumes, just breathing makes one's head spin"*) or portrait sketches (among the last, incidentally, one encountered again the familiar reflection of a sad little monkeyish face, as if the author were too stingy to throw out something he'd once found and saved, together with the hot side of a samovar, for a new use), aphorisms (*"Someone else's saliva is spit"*), notes on gardening, including botanical omens and superstitions (*"If a century plant withers it means someone's death"*), and on vegetarianism. A special box was needed for all kinds of folklore, including recorded anecdotes and various small poems, from rhymed exhortations (*"To avoid cholera's pangs, wash often and well your hands"*) to a long prophecy (beginning with the lines: *"The moment is near, close at hand / An abyss of water all around"*). There was a section of literary notes (*"There it is. The same story, not for the first time. Either you squint, crack, and go blind, or acknowledge reality, damn it, reflect what is shown"*), there were obvious extracts and quotes copied out (*"Can one see a tree and not be happy?" "They lived happily and died on the same day"*). There was enough on smells for a whole separate box: *"He smelled of the cream Holofernes"* (like a memory prod, such as the one used by the Indians of some tribe, who affixed to their belts a selection of objects that smelled, and sniffed them whenever they had to remember something; many years afterwards the smell allowed them to reconstruct the fullness of the event in its entirety)—or here's one that's familiar:

The smell of vinegar, a touch of melancholy, which chills the souls dwelling somewhere between heaven and hell, but not yet in purgatory, on the threshold of a life that's not yet begun, or perhaps of a death that's not taken place.

the ability to pull out of the air what is inaccessible to others

A tax collector, a village constable—smells foul, doesn't it? So here: an inspector of finances, a policeman.

The last *fantik*, however, could be placed in a different assortment, about words (*"little she-goat words and little ewe words"* or even *"words from pain"*)—there was such a category. The section on names formed a separate category. Besides a collection of various details and curiosities it also contained general thoughts:

Meaningful names are not an invention of classicism. Did they derive from nicknames, which are given, after all, for a reason and bespeak traits that become consolidated in inherited matter? Or do they exert an influence afterwards, making one justify one's expectations?

It's possible that in some mysterious way hitherto unknown to science a name has an impact on one's actual bodily makeup and even on bodily emissions.

All that would be fine, but the name is careless! And with such a height! But you can't go back on your word. That's the trouble, Lord!

One must admit that something not very comprehensible began here. Or, let's say, elsewhere: *"You won't mention such a name out loud on the street, brandishing a whip, and swearing to boot."* Almost every section contained such strange entries, referring to God knows what. What does *"yours are the waves, the manure is ours"* mean? Or this one here: *"one needs a Finn to remind one of happiness"*? One could only rack one's brains at that—if, of course, one had decided that it made any sense. Some comparatively substantial entries, which clearly didn't fit onto a single *fantik* and carried over onto another—sometimes one could find the carryovers, but that only added to the bewilderment. For instance, we've already mentioned the list beginning with the words *"You can accommodate everything: the sky, grass..."*—the last word appeared on the very edge of the sheet *"a riding gig without wheels"*—and on another sheet the list resumed with the words *"with a rooster on the coachman's seat."* The ink, the handwriting—everything confirmed that this had been written in a single breath; well, and what next?

19

Among the portrait sketches by Milashevich were separate outlines of eyes, noses, and brows; one really wanted to put them together. And not just them. One group of *fantiki* Lizavin even titled "Halves of Comparisons." They began immediately with "as if": *"as if you placed your chess pieces on the board and suddenly noticed that your opponent had laid out checkers"*; *"as if they chose him, rusted for lack of use, like a part in an unneeded mechanism, wiped with kerosene and put back in its previous place."* Here, if you please, is another: *"so the ice floes of the strewn field try to coincide, to join together once more with their jagged edges"*; or: *"thus the unexpected, as yet unexplained world is born beneath an infant's spread fingers"*; or: *"it's like the charge of electricity in a cloud, even if there's no lightning."* It sometimes seemed to Anton that he knew what this was about and he could find the half that was lacking, or, at any rate, could link the comparison with a personal feeling. In *"Amusements at the Soirées of the Public Meeting,"* Milashevich as if confirmed such a possibility, *"holding half of a cut card in his hand, to find in the dancing crowd a person with the other half—most likely he's also looking, rushing about pointlessly, and can't put the whole together: 'Everyone wants something, but it's not to be had.'"* Simeon Kondratyevich, evidently, had an interest in similar amusements. In one story of his, children amuse themselves with a well-known game: they take turns drawing on folded pieces of paper, one of them the head, another the trunk, a third the extremities, without seeing what the others have drawn, so that as a result awkward monsters emerge, either with a bird's beak, a shaggy belly, and a fish tail, or the other way around, with a fish head and wings, but with human feet in slippers—the accidental grotesques of which life is full, exercises on a theme as ancient as the world. Much of Milashevich's work calls such grotesques to mind: suddenly, a horned face with human teeth peers out from the *fantiki*; the bell-like mouth of a phonograph rises above a flower bed, like a flower. Sometimes it seemed to Lizavin that there was some kind of game behind this, not necessarily even intentional, at times capable of surprising and puzzling the writer himself. Anton Andreyevich thought about this once when he was standing in line for mayonnaise; it was no longer so big, really just to the corner, but for some reason it wasn't moving at all, and several times he tried to leave, chuckling at his culinary weakness, but every time he regretted the time he'd already lost, and so he went on losing more and more of it; and then it turned out that there was no longer any mayonnaise for sale, and it seems there hadn't been, they'd only promised to sell some—and suddenly all of this was linked to the phrase *"The place of crime before its time."* Like the solution to a riddle. Just as if it had been thought up for this. If there was, indeed, a game here, then it wasn't clear with whom and for what it had been invented. But maybe it happened accidently, and it wasn't worth looking for a more profound connection, sometimes going so far as to suspect a code. With the same success (and sense) one could pick out the coincidences in the unevenness and the burrs on the cut sections, as if assembling a fossilized vase from fragments. So the question, then, is: Was there a vase? and didn't Milashevich himself warn against imitating a scarecrow? By the way, the entries about a scarecrow and a feather bed also didn't pair off right away, not of their own accord—just try, like Lizavin, to pick them out from the pile, which, once it was free from its container, expanded and grew so much bigger than the container that the scraps could barely fit back in.

20

"Can you stick any nose to any chin?" Anton once wrote on a small sheet of paper. "And if such a nose has already been joined to such a chin, then this determines the arrangement of the larynx, and maybe even the esophagus, teeth, and stomach." By the way, he started to carry small sheets of paper with him in his pocket, in case on the way he'd have a fleeting thought and observation. Did Milashevich's example influence him (as it influenced the style and the construction of his phrases, which is natural and even inevitable with close contact over many years)? Anton Andreyevich didn't lose any thought over the question until he himself discovered this new manner of his while looking over his incomplete notes:

> Frosty flowers on the glass, it turns out, aren't at all arbitrary. They spread along directional scratches invisible to

6 5

the eye, and the laws of composition of icy crystals are calculated mathematically.

What can we say about another person who's not distanced from us by time, space, and conditions—no, about anyone who lives at our side? To us, only the surface on view is accessible, only the external facts, and we interpret them to the extent of our ability and predisposition. If we find the time to interpret at all.

What's more, how reliable is our own self-knowledge? And why do we look around in bewilderment when we discover what's happened to us?

This was written on another sheet, with a different color pen, and, clearly, at a different time, but obviously in connection with the previous note, although since then he'd managed to forget both entries—as he did this one:

> We flounder in the stream, sensing neither its substance nor its direction. Does it really exist, direction?

Anton Andreyevich never entered any dates, but he could guarantee that some of the entries would be separated according to months. Why, however, hadn't he troubled about the dates? Maybe without realizing it himself, he'd repeated Milashevich here, too—and now he was convinced that everything could be laid out in sequence, as if it had been planned that way. One of his notes actually spoke of this:

> A connection can be established by itself. You turn
> around, and it seems that life nonetheless has a unity
> and direction that you yourself didn't suspect. Year in
> and year out you return to the same thing, inadvertently
> make more precise and develop the same old under-
> standing—or the same old bewilderment.

After selecting five pages of Milashevich's most effective and self-sufficient fragments—thoughts, sketches, humorous aphorisms—and furnishing them with a foreword about their author, Anton Andreyevich submitted them for publication to a journal; the reception he encountered there embarrassed him. What can you do? A collection of feathers, he explained to himself, doesn't make an impression on strangers. Each of us is capable of producing a little thought or saying, sometimes no worse than those of a celebrity. You look, and images come to mind, metaphors and similes, as many as you'd care to publish! And whoever can, does so, printing pages from his notebooks and diaries during his lifetime; you read them—ah, they don't sound good. It's no worse than the stuff of the greats, yet it doesn't sound good. One has to be a bird for feathers to start fluttering. And for whom did a bird like Simeon Kondratyich exist? He sometimes sat over those scattered sheets as one does over a game of patience in which the deck can't be encompassed and the cards are of unintelligible suits; in order to put them together you have to know something about Milashevich's life—but an opposite feeling gnawed away at him, too: one could understand something about Milashevich after one put together the sheets of paper. What did this column of strange pairs mean: *"Man and woman, name and person, candy and fantik, voice and echo, conception and history?"* What did this exclamation of the irrepressible mystifier refer to: *"They cheated the fool for all he was worth!"*? What's this groan of pain and exclamation of bliss about? And the question *"Do we really give birth just to a body?"*; and the incantation *"Just a little more, just a bit, and it'll come together, come to pass, be resolved"*? Who laughed so long on one sheet, lacking the strength to stop? Whose is this fantastic diagnosis: *"There must have been a defect inside the body. A cavity, a crack. Most likely, in the head. Then it spread farther. From spring on the water accumulated and poured from the armpit"*? Who was this square being with crooked little legs and lumps on his forehead? *"Hammer and sickle has grown menacing, better have nothing to do with it."* A pang of displacement, a displaced language that one must understand. *"It enters with a tickle through the pores, penetrates us with the wind from the earthy dung, flows into the little hairs."* "*No hair left at all, however"*—a chance, senseless continuation was tacked on, clearly not about the same thing; but another time a different connection offered itself, this time more like it: "*V. V., now, lived till eighty and didn't have a single gray hair..."* Amusing, to be sure. One could keep turning it endlessly, trying out the combinations, sometimes constructing whole chains, but a cautious instinct suggested to Lizavin that nevertheless he shouldn't be too zealous here—it was senseless, useless, and the trifle already smacked of insanity. And, as if teasing, he came across something like this: "*Why go there? Is it really better there? But the hardness of transparent air draws and attracts you, and you strive to break through it with your mind, to penetrate beyond an inaccessible boundary, instead of feasting in the room where the jam still remains uneaten in the saucer."*

22

In memory the lines were confused, the sensation of liquid refuse mounted, of an incomprehensible life where swampy bubbles gurgled, where indiscernible beings were uncovered; in little enclosures behind temporary partitions live flesh stirred in abundance, flesh swayed, touching other flesh, tumbled out onto the street, grew, spread, withered, spoiled, aged, and ceased being warm; stems turned black right before your eyes, their charred husks curled up; the hero on the stone cried, a pale bud opened its eyelashes, the incomprehensible tower threw off its latticed shadow, broken glass tinkled, hills and white valleys shone, rivers from the clear breath of clouds stirred in the ravines, the steaming earth was soaked with milky juice; and in the moonlight someone was dancing on crooked legs, making music for himself, the phantoms of houses, branches, and trees faded from view, white roots ran into the ground, fear and exultation, pain and delight were mixed, as in a love union...Lizavin was submerged in this saturated solution, as if in the air of semislumber: something was stirring here, wandering about, and in that space there sounded a diffused, undiscovered voice... *Just a little more, just a bit...our whole life was an involuntary resistance to this ease and freedom...to find the words that are an equivalent of it at least for an instant...*

Incorporeal particles, freed from the power of heaviness, from intellectual explanations, were ready to freely try each other, as occurs in the inspired moments of sleep. Only a thread was lacking for the little crystals to start forming and arranging themselves around it. Sometimes it seemed to Anton as if he'd already guessed it; all he had to do was catch it and wrest it from the depths. But, after emerging on the surface and coming to himself, with a smile he'd recognize in his booty nothing more than the words of a catchy couplet:

But next morning there she was, smiling...

But in his breast there resounded something like the hum of an ending suddenly cut short: *It's so painful, so hard. You really can't hear? But, I'm here, here...*

23

After a long stint in Milashevich's atmosphere, Lizavin would return to the world around him feeling slightly dizzy. The room seemed not quite familiar, a shadow would make its way along the zigzags of space, not duplicating at all the movements of his hand or stopping still when he did, and the papers on the desk were far away and small from a distance. "Metal sawdust without a magnet." Anton Andreyevich wrote the passing thought down on a sheet of paper. He pulled a box toward him, to place this entry in it, and found another beneath his hand: "particles in high-tension space." He smiled at something, picked up his pen again, and added, making the feeling more precise: "The power field of time, the lines of Fate."

III. Children's Games

Thus wrote Anton Lizavin, sitting at a desk by a lamp. Its light makes it impossible to make out the conditions of the life around him, but, with unusual clarity, it sculpts the face bent over the papers. You really can't recognize him immediately. Either the shadows under his eyes enlarge them—unhealthy, even suffering?—and in such light the cheeks look sunken, or the beard is untrimmed, longer than usual, and has grown too long, perhaps; it's as if the supply of hair has gone into it, while the baldness has set in further, enlarging the prominent forehead. The wrinkles were scored more sharply, at the wings of the nose and especially between the brows—but, again, you couldn't tell right away whether it was a contrast of shadows or whether time had produced them.

How much time had passed, in fact, since, as acting associate professor in the district pedagogical institute, on the occasion of his thirtieth birthday, with an irony not devoid of pleasure, he had appraised (as one does questionnaire items) the plastic perfection of his situation and the obviousness of what lay ahead of him? One could calculate it, of course, strain one's arithmetical faculties, subtract figures from figures. Not from us, but from him that would, indeed, demand a special high-tension effort. The time one has experienced in general thickens unevenly where memory's concerned; there are voids that are indifferent and therefore seem to fall out of the calculation—it's not a matter of arithmetic—and here, undoubtedly, mental fatigue from many months of what likely was not completely harmless work took its toll: you suddenly start talking aloud with a nonexistent interlocutor, and the feeling of the simultaneity of life, which Milashevich referred to, becomes too familiar. Visions emerging from letters, lines, dreams, and the play of an inflamed imagination occupied a place in it more intimate than the phantoms of the institute era or even the current library work. To set out in a row the chain of events that had tossed him from one condition to another—this turned out not to be so simple. Indeed, there didn't seem to *be* any chain. There was rotation, confusion after his father's sudden funeral, coincidence. There were many days of insomnia— fog, cobwebs, a murky suspension instead of thoughts and feelings. Next door, in the apartment of the old woman who was his neigh- bor—a distant relative of the Lizavins—lived a woman barely known in Nechaisk. Anton had picked her up at the Stolbenets railroad sta- tion, confused, at a crossroads in her life; she'd left her husband, carrying only a frivolous little suitcase, fleeing not to him, he knew that, but he grabbed her, settled her in next door to him for a while, as if he could explain why and how he'd be with her later on...No, of course, a search for original causes would have to begin even fur- ther back, when he and Maksim Sivers, a visiting guest, a chance Moscow acquaintance, dropped in at the house of Kostia Andronov, a specialist in radios from Nechaisk. It was there that for the first time they both saw this Zoia, Kostia's wife. That is, Anton had known her when she was still just a girl, but there he saw her for the first time as a woman, strange in her sickly beauty. In Nechaisk they know that this former librarian stopped speaking soon after her marriage; something happened to her after she had the flu, most likely some- thing to do with nerves, although some rejected that opinion, insist- ing that they'd heard her at the bazaar asking in her own voice how much the garlic was. In any event, her muteness was strange: the whole time Anton had the feeling that she really could start speaking if she had to, simply the need for her to do so never arose; in her presence others became talkative on their own and her behalf, even excessively so, especially Kostia, a simple-hearted lazybones in a tracksuit, stomach already bloated, a decent fellow whom something had possessed to fall in love with an incomprehensible and, in essence, inaccessible woman, although she was considered his wife. Anton saw her, then, the one evening. He left Nechaisk before Sivers, and he could only speculate as to what happened there, but he didn't even need to know; after all, he later met Zoia at the railroad station not completely by chance—he was going to see her in Nechaisk and then looked for her in Stolbenets, although he wasn't prepared to admit this to himself right away. It was awkward, irresponsible, if you please—after a single meeting—after all, his marriage to a completely different woman was ripening in its natural course; it was only a question of time. And here it all came together in a few days; it suddenly fell through, was suddenly snatched away, as his father was by death, with which it all coincided and intertwined. Anton's situation at that time could, of course, have been called abnormal; all the same, it wasn't in his nature to seek adventure, to reach for the stars; the joys of stable life were more than sufficient for him. Certain actions of his, movements, even his immobility could, indeed, arouse bewilderment; at times he was capable of dispassionately realizing that, and at those moments he'd see himself as a fool, and her as a sick, speechless fool, whose beauty, moreover, he had clearly exaggerated. True, here he'd had the help of some prompting; these words were once uttered in his stead by the woman who, say what you will, had been hurt by the sudden, ridiculous unfaithfulness of a lover who'd seemed so reliable and tame. But this ridiculousness even made an impartial understanding and a certainty of her own superiority easier for her.

"Well, dear," Tonia smiled during their chance meeting. "I knew that men could be blind, but you...You poor, poor thing."

What could Anton say to her in response? That her saying things like that was pointless? That it had been nothing but a mental eclipse (look, it's temporary)? That he doesn't understand himself? No, he couldn't put it into words. He only averted his gaze, like a naughty but stubborn puppy who was making no promises to reform.

"And, you know, it's not like you." Tonia pursed her sharp lips. "You'll come to a bad end."

Her lipstick was dark, her lids painted blue according to the fashion in the capital, but the skin on her face was no longer young. Anton saw that for the first time, and to him her whole smart figure seemed to express vulnerability. "We're all poor, poor things." With that he could sincerely agree.

2

For all that, he shouldn't have considered other, everyday and work-related things, as trifles and misunderstandings. In that he was wrong. Death and all those feelings—they're, what can one say... there's nothing *to* say; one can only respectfully bow one's head. But the report on the department's fulfillment of its social duties through improving its level also demanded respect. The unclear story with the woman whom he'd settled in with him (even if she was next door—even, to be more exact, across the hall) almost instantly prompted an anonymous letter, sent to the institute. On the one hand, it was the dregs again, not worth talking about. But, on the other hand, the department just happened to be expecting an inspection committee, and there's no denying that signals like that spoiled the picture, demanded some kind of response. He could have understood that himself. No one planned even to touch him—what of it, that Klara Stupak stared specifically at him as she quoted his namesake classic?—"Everything in a person should be beautiful"—as if Anton Andreyevich answered personally to Anton Pavlovich for fulfilling these ticklish points.* "The face, too," Klara Stupak, the chair of the local trade-union committee, reminded him after a stiff pause, and Lizavin, still unaware that this was directed at him, looked at his colleagues with the dull-witted confusion that marked all his behaviour at that time. The pale, dusty light lent the air the glassiness of a magnifying lens, but, as usual, their faces managed to hide everything that could be illuminated in them from within, below the surface of the opaque flesh. Only great pores on a damp landscape, the juice of fatty secretions, ravines and creases in the alluvium of sweaty cosmetics, little hairs, precisely separated twigs, and not every mouth, alas, a pearl, perhaps gold—but who on earth is to blame, Lord? Who's to blame for the fact that the blind butt end of a wall outside blocked out the sky and earth, that one's lifetime vegetates at meetings and in lines for vegetable oil? It's not fair... One shouldn't do that to us. "And clothes, too," Klara Stupak added, moving on to the next point in the list of duties. Here Lizavin was obviously inferior

* The reference is to a statement by Anton Pavlovich Chekhov.

to others, and there was no need to inspect himself; but, after all, this was something one either could obtain or not. With this, maybe, it was even more difficult. It was fine for Klara; she herself sewed, although she might have made her dresses a bit longer, so as to cover her old-maid knees, which were as prominent as knee pads. Yet he had no reason to fix such a heavy, senseless gaze on those knees, which made her suddenly stop short and, as if gasping, for a solid minute be incapable of recalling the next point.

"And the soul," prompted Anton Andreyevich. From the most sympathetic motives—really! And still with the same distracted pensiveness, one could say. But once again it would have been better had he kept quiet, as he himself realized immediately upon seeing the spasm that wracked her; and everyone else was left with the impression of a hint, of some obscenity or challenge.

"Yes!" Klara flowed and dissolved in hysterics. "Yes, Anton Andreyevich, and thought, both moral and moral-political, Comrade Lizavin!..."

3

A cobweb, a belch of kvass, a hole in an empty place. During the break, the department head, Spartak Afanasyevich Golub , said in surprise, "You smoke?" and grasped him soothingly under the elbow and led him down the hall between the men's toilet and the department. But he kept throwing him guarded sideways glances, looking searchingly at this newfound smoker: Could he be hiding more surprises under his belt? Electric clocks hung above the doors of the department and the toilet. The toilet clocks were twenty minutes fast, whereas the department ones, at a given moment, showed the exact time, but by pure coincidence, for they'd completely stopped. In a strange way the tone and even the vocabulary of the conversation changed as they drew near one of those geographical poles. "Nerves? Nerves have nothing to do with it," Golub grumbled good-naturedly by the toilet doors. "What are we talking about? Treat it humorously." "We'll raise the level of humor during the five-year plan," Lizavin said, trying to match Golub's tone. "If it's possible to make the moral level obligatory..." "What are you, against social duties?" "Why?"

Lizavin became confused; he felt that something wasn't right; the proximity of the department was already having an effect. "You voted for it yourself." "Of course I did." "And what if it suddenly touched you personally, immediately." "That is...what does 'personally' have to do with it?" But they'd reached the turn already, the toilet was already on the horizon, and Golub unfastened the button under his tie, easing his swollen Adam's apple. What were they really talking about? Only about this, about coincidence and reflex; about playing at password and giving the response, the idea of which was: stability, self-preservation, a peaceful commonality with everyone. "What, do you consider yourself better than other people?" Golub finally asked, squinting. "Why better?" Lizavin tried to find as modest an answer as possible, one that was disarming and soothing; after all, he also wanted to remove the vague but perceptibly expanding threat. "I'm simply different. Special," he added for the sake of humor. And, with the melancholy feeling that instead of humor he was making it worse, he hurried to correct himself: "Like any person."

4

Yes, that was really quite pointless. Why had he uttered those words? Anton didn't inject any profound subtext into them. But suddenly, on the way home, he realized that not so long ago he'd never have expressed it that way by chance. Something was happening to him. That's the way naked tree trunks in the middle of spring were surrounded by a membrane of condensed, revived warmth, its pulsating tension ready to pull the leaves from the buds to their full length. He sensed this membrane like the tightness of skin, from behind which he knocked over objects without touching them, as if he took up more room than he'd thought, and he summoned a relationship there where earlier he'd slid by smoothly, no worse than others. He wanted to move his shoulder blades to chase away the uncomfortable shivers. *The roofs and bell tower shivered with chill. The ravens beneath the turbulent heavens were a parody of a tragic chorus...* there seemed to be music in the air, but it vanished before one had time to recognize it. The river carried garbage and mud, chips, a film of gasoline, and porous clouds. Between the roots, the previous year's fallen foliage was rotting through, seeping into the ground for good. The foliage replenished the very concept of trees—without them, you could say the tree as a whole didn't exist, just a trunk and branches. Moreover, it doesn't exist without this membrane of warmth, without this readiness and anxiety, similar to joy, wouldn't you say? The pages of dry newspapers rustle, the wind carries the animated trash over the earth. *No one chased us, we were running ourselves, suffering from soreness of the mouth*...A flock of noisy boys disturbed the peace with a shout, carried it farther off, and quite some time passed before the overactivated air calmed down.

5

The road through the children's playground. The little girls have interrupted their game of hopscotch to argue about the rules that were broken: "It's not true, it's not like that! The fifth is cursed, the sixth is gold!" Two little tots are listening carefully from afar, imbibing wisdom and the rules of the life into which they're dying to enter; the smaller one has golden droplets in her ears. The kids scamper about in the quivering moisture, nimble delicate flesh, swelling little shoots, impatience and promise. Porridge from light blue sand in canning pots, hard rocks of potatoes weighed out on a swinging board in a store. The rich owner of a bicycle establishes a ranking order of favors. A builder defends his tower of stone and sand from attempted attacks, snarls, repels the attackers, heaps a little more on top, a little more, as much as it'll take, so as to finally tug at the cord tied to the foundation rock and destroy everything with a magnificent explosion: *Boom-baroom-baroom, boom-rat-tat-tat!* "Mister, me too! Watch and see how I can do it! Watch me, mister!" Vanity and rivalry, the shame of defeat, jealousy, inequality—don't we go through this school when we're no longer equal in age, and that means also not in height, strength, and power? Everything that comes later only adds experience, and Mister smiles from above at their passions: to him they're all the same. *By touch, at random, in the resounding emptiness, with surprise and without understanding the whole, with anxiety and curiosity.* We bustle about in the shadows of the adult world, touch the air, explain, afraid to mistake someone for someone else, and choke at the bottom of a pile of small bodies; pull it apart, buddy, stretch your hand down from the heavens, your lungs still remember the horror of the drowned boy, a first-year student, you yourself, squashed by a mass of bodies! Flowers of joy on fresh grass, a delicate thin layer, little fingers spread to catch a ball, eyes shining with happiness and delight. A huge human cub lovingly chokes the body of a cabbage butterfly with his fingers, babbling, "Sweet butterfly, my pretty butterfly!" And the word *cruelty* hasn't yet been invented by mankind. God, how many possibilities on a simple road, strewn with rocks and bottle glass! You can go from one end of it to the other, stepping only on the bricks, and not on the ground, you can collect beer bottle caps for a game or, let's say, stamps, and then, after getting rich, you can even buy for a million the stamp of the island Mauritius, whose entire value consists of a misprint made by the engraver—this misprint has prompted crimes, forged wills, and who can say that this possession makes less sense than any others? The asphalt in the far end of the playground had been destroyed by recent construction work. That's where the ruts and last year's wild grass began; there, also, the testers of nature were melting tin in a tin can on the fire, and on the railroad embankment behind the sickly saplings girls were collecting a bouquet of coltsfoot, the first sorry flowers, not yet covered with oily dust and the town's char, their yellowness growing thicker toward the center, as if flowing there— oh, Simeon Kondratyich, you'd have appreciated this, you'd have understood me. *What do you need such...*Anton didn't have time to complete the thought when a wire bullet from a wooden weapon stung him on the cheek. Good thing it wasn't in the eye. He looked around: the wild grass was dense and empty, life there went on at a level inaccessible to the adult gaze, under the crowns of last year's grasses, in the carved golden thickets where the chubby horseman gallops on a beast with a red mouth, brandishing a toy saber, proud of his movement; the eyes of the porcelain cherub stare senselessly. A breeze rustled the crowns from above as it sailed farther on. In the flickering haze on the horizon, the factory funnels loomed tall, the town's ravines heaved like mountains, and above them the round clouds appeared white.

6

In those days, Anton tried to run into his neighbors as little as possible. He even boiled water for his tea not in the kitchen, but in an electric teapot in his room. But he constantly kept running if not actually into them, then into their glances, as physically tangible as hunters'. In his abstraction the doctoral candidate didn't even suspect that they'd already laid siege to him, had lain in wait for him, and were looking for a way to eliminate him from the ranks of claimants to his neighbor-relative's living space. Vera Emelyanovna hadn't left her room for a long time, couldn't walk at all, spent the whole time lying down, and how much longer she had to live no one knew—but he didn't even think of waiting it out; the arch-manipulator was way ahead of everyone. He didn't even have a wall in common with the old woman's room, and so he settled his girl in there; now she was looking after the sick woman, pushing out the others who had longstanding rights to bring her semolina porridge in the mornings and to carry out the pots, not to mention the fact that at one time their rooms had formed a common living space with the old woman's. Well, dealing with the girl was no problem: for the time being she was afraid even to poke her nose out the door, and when she did, she kept quiet, no matter what they said to her back; he, however, could produce evidence of a distant relationship through his mother, and also the little book corroborating his status as a doctoral candidate—and maybe some other trump card? The main thing is that no one had expected such agility from him. Clearly, he'd sensed that it would happen soon, and it was even likely that *she* would speed it up. That's the kind of tension that was building up around Anton Andreyevich, and he could consider it an illusion as much as he wanted. As if to say, since he never dreamed of anything like that, it means it didn't really exist. A philosopher. One might even say an idealist. It was precisely his incredible simplicity that seemed particularly clever. Meanwhile, at the Titkos' the suite of Finnish make for the anticipated room had already materialized— you could touch it; the Titkos' own mental work was in full swing. The furniture cluttered up the corridor and jutted out into the kitchen. Wrapped in paper and covered with polyethylene covers, it had the look of modernist sculpture. The ready collections of works were already ripening in the belly of the bookcase.

7

The layer covering the furniture glittered with a vivid slime, turning the corridor into something resembling winding intestines, the kitchen into a stomach, the pantry into an appendix, and all the insides of the house into sections of some body or other; as in medieval anatomical descriptions, each had a life of its own, and the parts that were perfected had to be vomited up, freeing up space. Sitting curled up beside Vera Emelyanovna, who was isolated from the neighbors' poisons only by the thin walls, was Zoia, not a member of the family, but a chance, temporary grain of sand. The unexpected role of nurse justified her staying there; it didn't even allow her to move on, for she couldn't leave the sick woman. They also adjusted to heating up their food on a stove in the room; they didn't need much. A sticky coolness would blow in through the ventilation window, interrupting the smell of sickness, the odor of bodily secretions. The room was cramped, with scanty old-fashioned furniture and objects. The wall opposite the bed was hung with photographs of various quality in little frames—the faces of the foster children who'd passed through Vera Emelyanovna's hands in the various institutions where she'd worked; two more plump albums in rose plush lay on the bureau, on napkins with lace embroidery, a gift from someone. The table was covered with the same sort of napkins, and so were the little pillows on the sagging couch, where at various times the orphans she'd chosen and brought right to her home had slept, and where now, legs drawn up, sat Zoia, who in her muteness delighted the old woman with her ability to listen.

8

Anton's arrival always interrupted her telling of one and the same story, it seemed: about one of those children on the wall, who since then had had time to get older, die, and leave behind new dullards, who were increasingly confused in her memory. The illness deprived her of movement; the once bony body had fallen apart, but in her

confused mind the stubborn energy of those times still hadn't mel-
lowed—times that might have allowed her to organize her life once
and for all, had circumstances not interfered and the children who'd
reached an unsuccessful adulthood not lost their way. In the story, the
world of orphanages, communes, prisons, and children's homes
seemed more sensible and safe than the life around them; here justice
and a regular portion of bread were in more reliable supply, and the
main thing was that one could always get involved and defend something if need be, set it to rights. The helplessness started when the
children left that care, grown up only in appearance, but having an
adult's capacity and means for all sorts of idiocies, injustices,
and hurts, for criminal acts and wars. Aunt Vera grieved over this as
if it were her own shortcoming in fulfilling her duties to the end.
She seemed to be rambling more and more, and sometimes she mistook Zoia for someone else, suddenly demanding corroboration:
"Remember? You knew him." But Anton's fear of any awkwardness
was uncalled for: Zoia would nod seriously, and Aunt Vera couldn't
stop. It was apparently important for her to explain something, to
finish saying something to her unexpected, grateful audience; the only
difficulty was that any trifle turned out to be too implicated in, and
confused with, other things, and she couldn't pull free any unifying
thought from under the pile of faces, circumstances, and stories.

"Just a second, just a second," she said to Anton as he came in
that day, returning after the departmental meeting, as if he'd come
just to hurry her and she were justifying her delay.

"Do go on," Lizavin made a magnanimous gesture; only later, in
recollection, did those words and that intonation grate on him. Vera
Emelyanovna was finishing some story about a fire in the orphanage,
about a cruel trick the little boys had played, locking the director in
his office.

"Yes, he barely got out alive... But he didn't try to find out who
did it. He loved them so much and spoiled them! He always carried a
caramel for the boys in a little bag. But you shouldn't have only boys
together in the house, I told him..." Lizavin listened distractedly,
visions of the children's playground still in his mind's eye, while life
simultaneously went on in the children's home, which blossomed

more beautifully than earlier ones in the province's capital, in the restored and washed police chief's private residence. "You know, it's that one opposite the *European*, across from the hotel." That's where soon after Vera Emelyanovna had met Liudochka, her lips painted shamelessly, that same timorous little Liudochka who'd arrived with the special train of Leningrad nobles. It was so difficult to get her out of the habit of biting her nails. She had two little fatherless children with her, it turned out, so she got the brainwave of going to the *European*. "My God, what is this, I said!" Anton noticed that Aunt Vera was already very tired, it was becoming difficult for her to get her tongue around the words. "Just a second, just a second," she anticipated his soothing movement, and he realized by Zoia's glance that it was better to listen through to the end. Something crucial was still left unsaid and didn't allow Vera Emelyanovna to calm down. The needle kept jumping on grooves that were too compressed, the faces kept crowding in, as they had at the railroad station, where the crazy woman had tried to breastfeed, her breast empty without her child, the unfamiliar Petunia Sirotin, his head covered with green scabs. The same life kept gazing out from all the photographs, the same record went on turning, and she had to take the unhearing, stupid, and helpless by the hand, so that they wouldn't grow wild, wouldn't get overgrown with the dirt of orphaned neglect, but they bit that very hand—see the scar that's still there....

Her hand didn't move, she only thought she was showing it, and Lizavin finally realized that she was now delirious; Aunt Vera only thought she was explaining something that was important to them, who'd soon be left without her.

"You know I always tell them what I want; I ask them to stand in pairs and hold hands more tighly, if they don't understand, my dears. But no, in the evening they opened the damper. Only Sashulia woke up. He had a cough from charcoal poisoning, until the war. He's this one here in the middle. Got a prize not long ago. A certificate and this ...tape recorder. Fighting and winning...with songs. Can't tell what kind of music it is. And at such a speed. Why, it's nothing but a mouse squeaking. Not the right way. He set up experiments with mice, but I couldn't watch, I felt so sorry for them. He left them spinning around. Faster, faster. Speed on ahead. A stop at the commune... No, it didn't work out. The red-eyed little mice twitched and died. A girl flew up on a swing, dappled by the sun shining through the leaves. Maybe that's it." The faces of those sitting by the bed became transparent, like curtains. "So bright... right in the eyes. Just a second, just a second. Only to die."

9

As if in answer to that wish, the lamp twitched, once, twice, then began to shine dimly. The old woman's chin grew weak, pulling open her black mouth, but she could still re-collect herself and tightened her lips. Her face grew stern, the elongated profile of a Don Quixote turned to the ceiling, a tear slid down her wrinkled skin. A fly had settled beside her nostril, gathering momentum for flight. Anton carefully brushed it off. Vera Emelyanovna didn't flinch, and fear stabbed Anton. It was fear at the thought that Aunt Vera had already died, and if not yet, then she could die any second now, not just some time, but then and there, as he watched, just like that, after muttering something unintelligible. Amidst a bad smell a particle of life will break off, vanish with its care, impatience, madness, and love; only a fly will reign over a stranger's dead skin. And what did you think? Only that and nothing more. But he still caught himself looking greedily, without tearing his eyes away; he'd never seen anyone die before—this alien, impermissible little thought redoubled his fear; something more horrifying than death itself crept in after it. The moment lasted an instant; he noticed that Aunt Vera had simply fallen asleep. He got up; his knees were shaking with fatigue, as if he'd helped roll a great weight up a mountain. Outside, the darkness had thickened. For some reason he avoided looking at Zoia as he said good-bye in a whisper. He wanted to smoke. The slime of the labyrinth glistened whitely in the half-darkness. The furniture shifted impatiently: if only this temporary languor would end quicker, no matter whether it was early or late; things were ready to flow by themselves through the cracks into the space that was still occupied by a person; they understood better than people the indifference of life, which went on. God, God, what is this?—this wasn't Lizavin's thought, but his groan about something.

10

Later he stood on the porch. The wings of the house fenced the yard in from the street. The ropes stretched between the balusters and the poplar in front of the outhouse crossed out the luminescent air; the source of light existed invisibly. Whom do we feel sorrier for, he thought, the person dying or ourselves, who are left to grieve and suffer? Better slip away as fast as possible, so as not to probe your own feelings. She still remembered even his parents from those years—from the times of Milashevich—and she had tried to trace some kind of connection with them, but kept letting the opportunity slip by. The same effort. Just a little more, a tiny bit more...There was even something behind her delirium; he felt it, only couldn't catch it. And maybe he didn't have to try, he shouldn't, it was impermissible, forbidden—just try and grasp with your mind everything that was ripening then, every instant, in that cold lush radiance, while people tossed in their sleep, tried to hide in each other or simply breathed, opening their mouths, from which you could smell the remains of the day's food, the sweet milk of childhood, youthful freshness or rot. A worm made a creaking sound as it burrowed with its head into the wood. The little tongues of glossy leaves moved as they sprouted forth. Little bubbles of black moisture jostled each other, swelled, and burst in the huge belly of space—myriad blind lives existed in it simultaneously, happily incapable of intelligently sensing and fearing the unique moment. In the square of a window a woman was suckling a silent infant, one moment walking up to the synthetic transparent curtain in the light of the night lamp, then disappearing in the depths the next. The small signal-like flame of his cigarette glowed hot, then slowly died out. The air was filled with an audible tremor, and Anton didn't hear the steps approaching from behind.

11

"Is it you? Oh, my God!...Has anything...? I thought, 'She's fallen asleep, and you should, too...' No, that's not it, I simply didn't feel right. I don't know...Everything all at once. And I left you there, I thought...No, again that's not it. It's good you don't answer—can't or don't want to." He mumbled, trying to suppress the shivering that grew stronger; then he noticed that she too was shivering—she'd come out in only a dressing gown, and he didn't have a jacket to throw over her. They should have gone into the house, put the tea kettle on, and gotten warm, but they both kept standing on the porch, and he put an arm around her shoulders, so that she'd at least warm up a bit, and he talked and talked, so as to subdue the shivering. The words helped; they came without effort, by themselves. *Words from pain*—does that mean they're born of it? Or can they cast a spell against it? *To compare with oneself this muteness spilled in the air...* The summer lightning flared up; something showed clearly again, but was immediately extinguished. "For some reason I've recalled how, when I was little, I was afraid alone in the empty house; I thought, 'No one will come to get me now.' The fear of loss. And you know what I also just caught myself thinking? That I want to understand life, want to feel something in it, grasp it, but I'm afraid to put it to the test. Till now I always hoped to get around something by indirection... through humor, intelligence, the imagination. This also has its own truth. There was this fellow—he explained that you have to leave certain things to the professionals. The slaughter of cattle, for example. Or taking care of corpses. Their feelings have adjusted to those things; it's nothing to them." Why did Simeon Kondratyevich suddenly come to mind? Everything seemed connected then: the night, Aunt Vera, her unspoken anxiety or unshakable worry, the flashes of summer lightning, and Milashevich's sheets of paper in the room where they finally went, unable to stand the icy cold. The tea kettle stood on the lit stove, but, given the level of heat, it could hardly start boiling soon. The walls shivered feverishly, and he and she nestled closer to each other, and he kept saying that she shouldn't vanish, without noticing precisely when he started mumbling to himself, no longer out loud: it was all accomplished by itself, with them, but not owing to their effort. "There, you see, it's easier together, for you, too, isn't it? For you, too." People reach out to each other, so as to lessen their fear of loss. To hide, nestle close, press together. Oh, yes, it's frightful, but we look for feelings as a way of finding some calm. We reach out for that calming effect, as for a finish, and the lamp goes out by itself, unneeded, and time diffuses like the moon's juice, spills out like music, like gratitude and rapture, the tenderness of a violin and the tenderness of a bow... That's how it is. How easy everything is now—even strange. What vision seemed to flash there in the light of the summer lightning? What troubled the soul? Now everything is genuine, with genuine cares and problems, of course, but that's all right. We'll cope with that somehow. Now you have to think about and then arrange a realistic life with this real woman, a stranger, in essence, whom you caught and carried off when she wasn't looking for you—what now, then? She's utterly still, no longer shivering, doesn't even move—a woman who so far hasn't said a word to you, so that everything amazing and unusual that you dreamed was merely the product of your feelings?...

12

And the light that flared up instantly—as if hurtling out into the emptiness, where instead of music the drip from the tap thundered *boom! boom!*—into merciless sobriety, like the sight of empty clothes on the chair or the floor, as agonizing as a hoop squeezing one's head. The corridor was empty, resonant, and frightening. In Vera Emelyanovna's room, on the table that had been moved to the side, the coffin decorated with paper flowers loomed, and two garlands with funeral ribbons leaned against the legs of the table, covering them. Aunt Vera lay with arms folded on her stomach. Long black hair had had time to grow on her chin and under her nose, completing her resemblance to a decrepit and hideous hidalgo. Under the closed left eyelid a strip of dead eye showed white, with the final vision frozen in the pupil: a crowd of tiny capsized children, orphaned along an endless road. The bed had already been carried out, and in the wall to the left, a rolling door that had always existed secretly under the wallpaper was now open, clumps of wallpaper hanging from the frame. Through the opening the Titko couple were helping to squeeze in the sideboard, as yet without dishes, but already crammed with souvenirs from the countries they'd visited or were planning to visit. Elfrida Potapovna, in dressing gown and hair rollers, was plying her energy from behind, while her spouse lifted the bottom of the sideboard over the threshold.

He wore pajama bottoms and a uniform jacket with official state medals and ribbons. His striped behind stuck out, the surplus of flesh, malignant like a tumor, swaying; their mouths were open, but the grunts from their efforts were produced silently. Silently. A wall also yawned wide on the right; the former actress Kamenetskaia had been slow and couldn't drag in the three-leaved-wardrobe pier glass on her own. It got stuck in the passageway, grown larger on account of the parts that had swung open. Anton could go and help the old woman, but it was terrifying to make a move and thus attract neighbors' glances and appear naked in front of them. The light burned brighter and brighter, to an unbearable whiteness; it was impossible to understand how the lamps could hold out, and Zoia already has her little suitcase and the winter coat lined with fish skin over her arm; the light pierces her, she dissolves in it, ready to vanish, and there's no stopping her, as in a dream, when the daylight sun is already penetrating one's eyelids. Makeup ran down Elfrida Potapovna's face; the face grew swollen, losing its outlines, and for lack of fat Kamenetskaia was drying out completely into a tiny old woman. Finally the sideboard tumbled in over the threshold, the retired colonel's rear end collided with the artist's skinny behind—and the light movement sufficed for the rival to lose her balance. She sat on the floor next to her recalcitrant pier glass, like a doll, her legs helplessly sprawled as her fist smeared the helpless tears blended with mascara all over her cheeks. Like a human monster, the dachshund, Dolly, whined in tune with her.

13

Why did she disappear without saying a word, without even leaving a note of explanation? She disappeared while he was running around taking care of the papers for the funeral, but she left her things—that is, the little suitcase and the coat—in her room (where the smell of the burned, melted tea kettle, out of which the water had boiled, still lingered). He'd asked her not to go out anywhere, even to lock herself in, if she wanted to. Everything had seemed already decided without words, and had to do only with practical everyday problems, which were his worry, and if even for an instant he'd felt embarrassment, he'd certainly not expressed it. She couldn't have heard his random thoughts—and random is just what they were, pushing in uninvited, and no one can shut his ears to them, one simply has to ignore them. What happened? What had he done wrong? Something had been half-discovered—or did it just seem so?—and once again there was the agonizing impossibility of restoring a dream or remembering a word, as had happened before the deposit of *fantiki*, and the familiar bewilderment of the funeral, intensified to an extreme, when you know that your soul isn't stretched far enough to grasp the significance of what's happening. The waters have closed in, and the sun sparkles on the surface. Something wasn't right; all the time something wasn't right. Anton experienced this feeling on behalf of the many people who came to bid Aunt Vera farewell and saw, instead of a familiar face, a stranger's, changed by death.

He probably couldn't call himself sober even before he came in, disheveled, past the mirror to the mist-filled air of the funeral reception, which had been arranged God knows where and by whom. He thought that at the cemetery someone whom he barely knew brought him, as a relative, a little cut-glass tumbler, and he drank, without even realizing that he was drinking. Afterward he rode along somewhere on a rickety funeral bus, and at first he seemed to have arrived at the wrong place. The crackle of branches, the dense, fragile snapping of faint conversations invaded Anton's ears and cheeks as he squeezed his way through. The orphans who were left without Aunt Vera milled around. At the table a fat woman was chewing concentratedly; the boy beside her was a smaller version of the woman, and you could surmise that inside her there was also a small being who, at one time or another, must have been starved enough to last a lifetime. You must eat when they treat you—who knows what there'll be later? A one-armed invalid was trying to inflate a balloon, but a drunken friend was getting in his way: stop it, stupid, it'll burst. They hadn't had time to play when they were the right age for it. At some point Lizavin noticed that he was sitting at a small table on a dangerously fragile child's chair. On the wall rug, a rooster with a scythe was going to chase a fox out of someone else's dwelling space.

"Something's not right," said Lizavin to his neighbor, and the latter nodded in agreement. People were starting to dance in the middle of the room, and there, finally, Anton suddenly saw a familiar face, definitely familiar, only he couldn't place it right away, much as he needed to. How did it go?...Just a second...that's it:

> *Side by side, hand in hand,*
> *Our tread will sound throughout the ages,*
> *We're spat out from the pods as shoots*
> *Of a new life in history's pages.*

Where did that come from? And was there something else he should have remembered? Why did this stranger's face with the over-bearing brows seem familiar? It aroused a vague unease, which also demanded a solution:

> *Thoughts swell our foreheads apace,*
> *Breath leaves our chests in a hoarse stream,*
> *Our minds, full of sorrow, race*
> *With impatience and a scream...*

Amidst the feast the orphans hung around with zealous frozen faces, creating music with their feet, voices, and palms; inside their bulky bodies languished swooning beings who demanded that something be remembered, and an infant with a chicken bone in his little pink fist skipped utterly fearlessly among the heavy legs of the men and women:

> *Here, among orphans in the ark,*
> *Your ascent to happiness will begin...*

Pyotr Gavrilovich! Lizavin suddenly recognized him at last: it was Pyotr Gavrilovich, Tonia's father, a big shot in town, whom Anton had previously seen only briefly; does that mean he's also Aunt Vera's Petunia? and he too was orphaned? This unexpected insight made him want to go over to him (a rubber hedgehog squeaked beneath his foot), take him by the shoulder, and explain how it all came about with Tonia: I didn't want to hurt her, you see, don't think that, but I was blown off course, carried away, there was no connection, who the hell knows what it was, it's all crazy, really, that even a word that's a thought already exists—how come?—it would be impossible to live like that, why like that?...and now with a chill down your back, understanding that once again you've taken a wrong turn, you've already broken loose and are flying off somewhere—but what flared up at the last instant, while your foot was slipping to the edge and you only shaded your eyes with your hand to protect them?...

1

For the time being, we'll have to hang around in a not overly fragrant spot, where the force of weight is canceled, the uncoordinated parts of the human body protrude from above, from below, and from the sides: toes in sticky hole-ridden socks, the dandruffy shoulder of a jacket, a wrist in a dirty cuff without cufflinks, a tattooed torso without a head, while the head, separately, feels like a watermelon, squeezed by hands that are testing it. And all this, it turns out, can be explained by the simple formula "Additive no. 3," because Kesha Babich, a man with one hundred and fourteen entries in his work record, personally was hitting the bottle with a chemist from the liqueur factory, who'd invented twelve additives to vodka.

"Additives?" we ask again.

"Means 'additions,' but in scientific talk, we say 'additives.' Each one has a special effect on a person. Additive number one: you become talkative, like a slut. No holds barred; consider yourself a real find for the first spy you meet. Number two: completely the opposite effect. Can't squeeze a word out of you, even if they hang you by the balls. You're as silent as a Hero of the Soviet Union under interrogation.* They can get the star ready in advance. Posthumously. Moving on, additive number three: you won't remember a thing for six, ten, or twelve hours, depending on the dose."

"Why?...What do additives have to do with anything?" Anton tried to recall any reason that wasn't local lore, and even shook his head slightly, so as to gather his scattered thoughts. "Different doses

---

* HERO OF THE SOVIET UNION From 1934 on, an honorary title conferred by the Soviet state upon those in politics, industry, culture, the armed forces, etc., who purportedly achieved heroic success in advancing the state's interests.

simply work differently on different people. It also depends on their condition." But it was pointless to look around for sympathy and support... There was only someone's face, covered in dirty sweat, lowered from the plank bed, down to the center of conversation. No, by local standards it was precisely the underground, secret possibilities of life that were reliable.

"I talked with him in person, like I'm doing with you. He used to be a big shot. For these additives they made him a colonel and even gave him a prize. The kind they used to give then, the Stalin Prize." Kesha's thumb indicated somewhere behind his dandruffy shoulder, in the past, while the movement of his eyebrow reminded one that the prize awarded then had no equivalent nowadays, like a heavy, old-issue coin. "You gotta understand, it had an official state significance. They treat you, give you stuff to drink, and the next day they say, 'Yesterday, at such-and-such an hour, you killed a man.' And that's it. They've got you. You can't disprove anything, because you don't remember a thing. What were you doing where at that time? Maybe you did kill someone. A blank."

2

A chord or vein throbbed in his stomach, below the heart. There was nothing to hold on to, and to look back was useless—behind him there was emptiness, a blind spot. If he really exerted himself he could make out a yellowy-white toenail, like a disfigured being, separated from him, in an even halo of electric light, the slime of tiles at his cheek, peering into some people's faces with a greedy sense of shame, as into a mirror. Could this pretty woman his own age, with ruby earrings, really be a judge? She kept on writing something, the sweet thing, head bent and zealous little forehead puckered, as the fat house policeman dictated information to her about the ticketless tram passenger, his uncensored insults, and even physical resistance. Interesting... Whom is this about? Second question: How do you write "ticketless," hyphenated or not? Question understood. It's you, you probably knew, you even did it with joy—at least it's becoming clear what happened. But it's unreliable—oh, was it ever unreliable to try to fill up the hole of your life on the basis of what others said;

the policeman proved to be the wrong man, the tram had to be exchanged for an apartment, but nonetheless, with physical resistance and even broken glass (my God, my God!)—cut it short right there! After all, the report's already filled out, so well, too, without any grammatical mistakes; maybe it's not worth copying it? Five full days, nonetheless, and you can pay for the mirror so easily. On my part I'm always ready. If I can be of use in some way. I should ask—one favor for another—so as not to have it advertised at my place of work. Then to wake up, as if nothing's happened... O Lord!

3

But there was something else: the chill of freedom blowing on his unprotected head, a cowardly and despairing sinking of his heart, the forbidden delight of weightlessness, the fear of novelty, which you yourself would never have decided on, except in irresponsible visions, when you try out something like that, unlawful (as if you could!). Now there was nothing to decide. The possibility of choice remained in a different life, where there was a high and a low. When will you come crashing down again? But maybe it'll pass you by somehow, maybe you'll control the fall, like flying, and you'll end up getting carried not downward, but somewhere into the distance. (*It's empty, clean, and cold in the sky, the body's weight is disappearing...* the touch of scarcely audible music.) What happened was incredible, terrible, shameful. If only he could get out of there as fast as possible, as if from a nightmare; but if he were to be honest to the end, what awaited him there during his waking hours, after awakening, seemed even more terrible. He wanted to delay the inevitability, not think about it—and to hell with it; his curiosity was already recovering, too, making him listen attentively, greedily take in the cloudy little window with bars across it, the piles of cigarette stubs under the plank beds, "The Moral Code" in a little frame on the wall, the hazy air around the ever-lit naked lamp—and in the morning, in the sunshine, the chaotic martian scenery: a crazy structure of pipes, crowned with a snow white pissoir, and a colorful sign on the fence ("Alternate Intellectual and Physical Labor") and another sign, a bit smaller ("Neva Brand Brake Fluid Is Poison"); wrinkled, disheveled figures with spades, stretchers, and wheelbarrows among ruts and pits. They carted their equipment there to level out the ground and set up a square for some celebrations at which they were expecting a high-placed guest from the capital; the structure of pipes turned out to be the frame for a future platform for the foremost personages, and the pissoir, it turns out, was an essential accessory—what did you think? Without it you couldn't stand there so long waving your hand, especially at an age when the organism has lost its powers of endurance. They finally explained this to the slow-witted doctoral candidate, and for the first time, from a perspective previously inaccessible to him, he appreciated why the rigors and honors of leadership were more within men's power than women's. There was so much he hadn't known before, it turns out! He hadn't heard about additives, couldn't imagine where one could possibly get a hangover in the middle of work in a closed police establishment, hadn't suspected that Jews at the local factory had mixed toilet paper into the cooked Polish sausage to increase the weight—why, of course, there was a trial recently, they said in the newspaper that's why there wasn't any paper and why it was impossible to eat Polish sausage. And was it worth quickly rebutting that there was no increase in the weight of sausage, while the newspaper seemed to be saying something else, that all this was . . . how can one put it more delicately?— a myth, or what? As if you didn't know that you need to read newspapers with a special skill, not word for word, as if the very nature of your studies hadn't convinced you that, for history and life, so-called myths are often more realistic than so-called facts. It's strange that Kesha Babich needed to remind *you*, an interpreter of *fantiki*, of such things. No, it was right to try to persuade a mind that was trusting, inadequate, and weakened, to become a member of a general religion. Woe to the apostate, unchristened among the christened, to the sober among those who have managed to get a hangover, for they won't get any rewards.

"So, why are you standing there like a pederast? Here, take it, drink."

4

Music wheezed from the loudspeaker. We have no obstacles either at sea or on dry land.* The cultured workers from the poster above the fence‡ looked into the distance, somewhere above the dubious earth diggers, who had settled in, in the shade of a pile of earth—but the eyes of the poster people gazed down somewhat askance at the bottle with the small glass that made its rounds, at the newspaper that lay spread out with a loaf of bread on it, salt in a matchbox, scallions, pickles, and that Polish sausage made from toilet paper. Neither ice nor overcast skies frighten us. Lizavin felt stupider than everyone else there; he was ashamed of his inability to use obscene language, and he listened without butting in to amazing conversations about the technology of transforming shellac and polish into a drink, about the local authorities and those far away, about life's mysterious phenomena, about woman's perfidy, and about stunning tricks involving earnings and thievery. "But I have no reason to steal," someone remarked haughtily. "My old lady makes ten honest ones a day in the supermarket, on wrapping paper alone." "Everyone steals," asserted one of those who were displeased with such arrogant overfastidiousness, creating a stir. "What about you? And you—do you steal?" It was an unpleasant moment: the candidate of sciences finally grasped that the question was addressed to him and shrugged his shoulders in embarrassment. "There's nothing for me *to* steal," he mumbled uncomfortably. Except paper clips from the department, and sometimes paper, he immediately hastened to recall, so as to justify himself afterward. God, what trifles!…Allow me, please! And Milashevich's *fantiki*? He'd carried off the whole pile of papers from the state archives, if you please. There's also that, you know. He should have said…But while he agonized, the fire of the conversation shifted to other matters. Yes, thought the doctoral candidate, listening intently to the growing hum inside him, as if a long-ripening understanding

* A quote from a kitschy Soviet propaganda song, "The Enthusiasts' March," with music by Dunayevskii.

‡ A typical Soviet poster of idealized workers.

was ready to reveal itself to him at that very moment. He had to examine things with a different mind. What's truth and what is the opposite? That's not the point at all. Then what is? It's the muddle of life, that's what. First he had to get to the level of the general temperature, become part of the genius of intoxication, the most accessible sort. (It's no accident that there isn't a single actor who couldn't play drunk brilliantly. Where do the grotesque, the wit and accuracy come from?). The only thing that's bad is that this genius doesn't lead to any discovery, but turns immediately into chaotic disintegration.

5

They sat and lay around, leaning on their elbows, like ancient Greeks—a locksmith and a gas fitter-assembler, a driver, a funeral parlor worker, fingers covered with plain and stone-studded rings, a pensioner, a stevedore, a furniture store salesman—while Kesha Babich, with a hundred and fourteen entries on his work record, told them what good money he'd made in the movies playing Germans whom Soviet soldiers and especially intelligence agents beat on the head with rifle butts. They had beaten him on the head in twelve films. He'd lost his teeth at that job, but on the other hand he was considered irreplaceable, was awarded the title of distinguished actor, had a Moscow apartment, lived with artists, and dined every day in a restaurant. The conversation kept returning to the topic of food and drink, someone remembered about a duck hunt in the town park: "Pfoo, they're not afraid of anything now. They're tame ducks. You just grab them by the neck, and crack..." True, but when they plucked them and roasted them, the actual meat turned out to taste of gasoline, just like the water in which they swam, which they drank, and with which they were saturated down to their tiny cells. "And what happened?" "We polished them off, that's what. With vodka they weren't even that bad." "I didn't want to sleep with her," someone behind Lizavin said, pursuing a different topic, "so she raised a hullaballoo, the bitch. Scratched her own face..." Yes, yes—Lizavin tried to define the rapturous melody more precisely. "We don't know what we ourselves consist of. Yet we won't perish, no. We're a miracle of adaptation. Is it possible they're trying to frighten us with the future to no purpose? Microbes and insects are no longer affected by pesticides—they digest them like food. Does life really end in the water of the sewers? Perhaps it's reborn in new, unprecedented forms. Above all the lands and oceans." "Yes," the voices of the conversation behind him interrupted, "a woman doesn't give a damn about putting a guy away. Look here, I know one guy, a scientist from the institute, who changed his mind about getting married. And her daddy's a boss or something—he was also in charge of something in trade. He heard from his daughter that the guy had started up with another woman…" No, wait a minute—Lizavin tried to think his own idea through to the end. What was I thinking of? Yes… maybe some special intellect was bred recently in our altered genes, superior to the one before, and now we no longer want to leave here. We're afraid of another life. Our stomachs have already digested and assimilated this liquidy water-based paste, with pellets of uncooked grain; it seems that for our lungs they can serve as air, these fumes, these eruptions of dirty bodies, brewed on tobacco smoke and the smell of spoiled processed oil, and wild fantasies, old wives' tales, scraps of rumors, and phrases from newspapers are quite capable of substituting… "'I'll not only put you away, you bastard,' he says, 'but you'll be kicked out from work and won't get your fucking dissertation.'" "Whom are you talking about?" The doctoral candidate finally caved in and turned to face the fellows who were talking. They didn't answer him right away, clearly not very pleased about the interruption; then, finally, someone willing to include him among the audience explained, "He's telling us about how a dame got a scientist put away." "But what does the dissertation have to do with it?" With a heat that was perhaps out of place, Lizavin insisted on the specific point. "Well, he was already considered a Ph.D. candidate, or, I don't know, an associate professor." "I myself am a doctoral candidate," Anton Andreyevich bragged needlessly. "What does one thing have to do with the other? A dissertation is one thing, you know, and trade's another. So how's it possible to get the guy put away?" "And how did they get you?" was the response, and they all laughed readily. "First for five days." "And then?" Anton Andreyevich's curiosity was completely senseless now; he'd wanted to say something completely different, namely: "No one got me put away," and immediately realized that it was precisely this subtext that had grabbed him, made him butt into the conversation, which, of course, had nothing to do with him. "And then…" came the response, with something added in rhyme, but not reproducible, again to everyone's delight. Lizavin laughed together with the others at his own idiocy, at the stupid anxiety that had for no reason poisoned the ease he'd almost found and that despite all its absurdity had cost him a sleepless night.

6

Like the surface of dirt, the half-naked bodies bathed in black sweat reflected the festering light of the ever-lit lamp. With a wheeze, scream, cough, and asthmatic whistle, they gathered energy for tomorrow's life from any air they could, and little clouds of dreams appeared above them, like steam from some mysterious work.

"Eh, Simeon Kondratyich? What is this, really?" "What are you talking about?" "About all this. Just go and try to make judgments about someone's life from the distant past, when it turns out there's a gaping hole in your own yesterday, and maybe it can no longer be filled in with certainty. Did you hear them? It's as if they were offering me my own story, but in what a form! Delirium, nonsense." "So why go on about it." "On the other hand, I've just now remembered how Volchek, a local journalist I know, suddenly came up to me at the funeral and started asking how things were and was I interested in another job? It just so happened, he said, that some vacancies had opened that weren't bad, at the company I Want to Know Everything and at the district library, very decent. The positions weren't so easy to get, but, he said, he could help me, he had connections, and with my M.A. degree the loss in salary would be comparatively small and I could supplement the sum by giving paid lectures. It's complete nonsense, you understand. How could I change my job for such a position? And the main thing was, why? I thought he might be joking, and his tone was appropriate, yet it had that shade, I recall now. If anything happens, he says, keep it in mind. What did he suspect? Or know?" "It's interesting, Anton Andreyevich, interesting. Ask him when you get the chance. And, then, he knows Pyotr Gavrilovich, Tonia's father, that fellow, well—look how smoothly you've fitted it together. It wasn't for nothing that you practiced constructing all kinds of plots on the basis of my *fantiki*. Maybe you also ended up in that apartment not through your own?" "What nonsense we're speaking, Simeon Kondratyevich!" "It's my fault if something's amiss—I'm simply following your tone. So what were you talking about, then?" "About whether one can understand anything at all in life. Why does everything fall to pieces, everything come out wrong? Why did she leave anyway? How can I look for her? And should I?" "Yes, you're capable of understanding that now."

> *The umbilical cord snapped,*
> *The poison flowed out with the pus,*
> *There's no support underfoot,*
> *It's desolate, windy, and terrible.*

"You haven't recalled yet where it's from?" "What is it?" "It's not important. But the music, Anton Andreyevich! Do you hear it now? The melody of a life that's shaken, overturned. *Why like this? I didn't want this…Who's listening in on our wishes?…She came and captivated me…* Captivated…The melody of loss and the melody of return." "What does this have to do with it, Simeon Kondratyevich? I'm falling asleep. Don't. I want to sleep. I'm afraid that I'm not up to all this. Neither in strength nor in ability." "My God!" There was an audible unevenness in the philosopher's tone. "Just wait, will you? Have you really not understood yet, Anton Andreyevich: What happens to a man explains who he is. If something has happened to you, it means it's about you. Something like that didn't happen to you before for a reason." "But, Simeon Kondratyich! Does that mean that this is about me? This is what I'm worthy of?" "Don't, Anton Andreyevich. Don't pretend that you didn't understand. Especially now, please…"

7

If only they'd given him more time to think a bit, to get a hold on himself! No, he was only trying to remember, to recover the melody that had wafted by like the breeze and melted away when a savior appeared, that same Volchek the journalist, and on the second day he literally took him by the hand and led him away, shaking his head in concern, yet smiling, well-meaning, mysterious, and Lizavin didn't even ask where he'd found such opportunities, such connections, all the more so because he didn't expect to get the answer. He kept listening intently to something, while distractedly and indifferently filling out the application, according to what was dictated to him, for a transfer to a new job where no one would pay attention to a newcomer's cropped head, because no one would have known him earlier and so they could think that that's the way he always looked because of his whimsical taste. For a second he almost had a twinge of doubt as to whether he was in too much of a hurry and should arrange things some other way. No one was pushing him besides Volchek, who seemed to be guided by some sort of knowledge. But this doubt dissolved in the more general one: Where was choice operating, and where inevitability? *The fear of understanding... Why like this? I didn't want this...* He kept listening intently to the vague mumbling even after he returned to his former life, but as if from a different passage; he listened, spitting out from his lungs the nasty stuff that had accumulated over two days, examining the cards in the library and preparing tea for himself during the lunch break—but the chill of presentiment already touched his skin. *Like a breath of wind before the sun disappears behind the cloud...*

v. On Words, or The Beginning of a New Faith

like a breath of wind before the sun disappears behind the cloud
   the papers on the table scattered and the inkwell fell
   with an ear pressed to the ground, to the wall, to a tree trunk
   you're already close, any second now. I feel it, I hear. God!
Every step echoes in me, makes me tremble
   The raft floated up, we climb onto it, and the helmsman waits for
us. Careful, I say, don't stumble.
   I stretched out my hand—when was that—and the palm of a
hand rested against mine. But what filled the moments between the
beginning of the movement and the end?
   Temporal duration is created by the substance of life, by which
time is filled up. For the soul and for memory, eternity is indistinguishable from an instant, in which everything exists simultaneously.
   the middle is cut out, as in cinematographic film, the ends
glued together
   The little bones of the fingers show white through the stretched skin
that's already blue from chill. Without braids. And the coat isn't local,
it's light for our autumn
   it condensed, like a snowflake from the November wind
   She came and captivated me. I knew it would be like this. I
thought, I wanted, I tried.
   Who's listening in on our wishes? It's frightful to be misunderstood. Better not to want anything.

The little boy opened his mouth. The saliva of curiousity and self-oblivious zeal drooled from his pink lip. He didn't understand; he's the only of us who didn't understand anything.

The old people on the shore crowded together in a heap. Someone lifted a leg, trying to get it into a galosh that was stuck in the mud. The wind flutters the gray hairs. Ripples on the water.

the roofs and bell tower shivered with chill

the ravens beneath the turbulent heavens were a parody of a tragic chorus

2

Just a second, just a second, just let your heartbeat calm down... Even now he's not able to think about it calmly. How, from what collision of thoughts, vague voices, or feelings amidst the darkness, was the spark struck?—a spark so tiny at the beginning that Anton didn't immediately look in that direction. He kept trying to recall the author of the lines that stuck in his mind, and suddenly some slim booklet from long ago, about revolutionary events in Stolbenets, surfaced before his eyes; the name had worn off, but the old dirty script was clearly visible, as were the uneven lines, the brittle paper speckled with wood dust, even the place at the top of the first page, where finally a name blazed forth: Iona Sverbeyev, the same self-taught poet, the future public figure of the Nechaisk republic, in connection with whom Lizavin had searched the archive for details (without success), we recall, and so had to make do without them, without Sverbeyev altogether; but, it turns out, some lines stuck in passing. (Just a second, just a second. One doesn't want to miss the combination of circumstances here.) These were reminiscences from a collection that had been printed only three years after the events described therein, and still had not been proofread by an editor, which was typical in those times; they therefore retained the authenticity of half-literate speech and the immediate sense of chaos from which history was born. The author came to Stolbenets from Petrograd,* together with

* PETROGRAD (also p.269) The name given to St. Petersburg in 1914, changed to Leningrad in 1924, and, after desovietization, rechristened St. Petersburg.

Sverbeyev and also some woman, to speed up the seizure of power. The town had three local Bolsheviks in all, and although the revolution had already taken place in the capital, they were preparing for desperate battle in the meantime, recruiting supporters, waging a propaganda campaign in the barracks of Sheepsville, where a reserve regiment was quartered, and acquiring weapons from whoever passed through the station of deserters. For Lizavin the reminiscences were basically a storehouse of passing details, like the fact that in those days you could buy a Colt machine gun at the bazaar for three hundred rubles, or that, just before the train reached Stolbenets, the deserters aboard almost robbed Sverbeyev's travel companion, who gained time by removing her gold earrings and giving them to the men; while they were testing the gold with their teeth, the comrades arrived, in the nick of time. All the preparation of the local activists proved unnecessary, however; immediately upon learning of the arrival of the armed men from the capital, the regiment commander and his officers hid without any attempt at resistance. Perhaps they didn't understand that there were only three people arriving, and mistook for the armed detachment the entire crowd that tumbled out of the train at the station but had no plans to go into town. After the fact, even a misunderstanding looks like an inevitability, and in the world of such events strength and weakness aren't measured by the number of rifles. The leader of the Stolbenets cell, Fyodor Peresheikin, who, as history tells us, perished that very evening during the suppression of the counterrevolutionary sally, bequeathing his name to a town street and a worker's club, was so shocked by the ease of the coup that, on learning of the colonel's flight, he burst out laughing and laughed a full minute, another, and a third, until the author of the reminiscences had the good sense to lift a glass of water to his chattering teeth... Just a second, just a second... Anton hadn't even expected that so much would be retained; they say that our brain stores memories that we ourselves don't suspect, but to extract them we need some kind of electric shock at precisely the right juncture of nerves, at a point, as it were, in the backyard of our awareness. The author's name, that also evaporated; the man came to Stolbenets for all of three days, and then left by rail to create history further on. He mentioned several events from that time on the basis of others' statements; for example, how the town council, with the children's doctor Levinson at its head, was arrested during a meeting and sent to prison. Recalling this episode, Anton imagined for the first time the route taken by those arrested from the current executive committee to the prison at the end of former Soldier's Street, now Red Army Street—that is, most likely they walked through that same memorable puddle. The author also remembered being told that among those arrested was the husband of the woman who'd arrived and who hadn't seen him for many years—that's how they met again...

3

No, before thoughts and words there emerged, as though heard in sleep through the cawing of autumn ravens under the turbulent, transformed sky of a provincial November, the melody of melancholy and love, the melody of loss and renewed hope. *So the ice floes of the strewn field try to coincide, to join together once more with their jagged edges...* Having barely gotten out of a scrape, and not having yet put his affairs in order or having yet grasped how shaken he felt by his collision with reality, Anton Lizavin reached for the library catalog as if he'd moved to a new job precisely so as to find out as quickly as possible, to recall, whether the woman's surname was cited in the book. And so hasty was this idiotic impulse, which for the moment made more important things seem secondary, that fate probably decided not to be needlessly petty, not to delay the discovery at which he'd have arrived anyway sooner or later. The concession was trifling; fate had enough tricks in reserve. Lizavin managed to find the collection and to figure out its title almost immediately. The collection contained the article of a certain N. Sukhov; the woman's surname was mentioned, with initials, no less: A. F. Paradizova. But what of it! That wasn't what made it such a gift. Lizavin didn't even have to root around too much in further reference publications, although the surname he needed was located only in a single index to a prewar edition of the scholarly notes of his own (former) pedagogical institute. Heart quivering, he read: "Aleksandra Flegontovna Paradizova, participant in rev. events in town Stolbenets. In emigration until 1917." Question marks stood in place of the dates of birth and death.

4

Independently of any further searches, even precisely because they added so little, Anton Lizavin already knew that it wasn't simply a coincidence of the name with the rather rare patronymic (and she'd evidently kept her maiden name, the surname of a priest or seminarian). The guesswork that had condensed from emptiness (*a snowflake from the November air*) became overgrown with details and substantiations of its own accord. Simeon Kondratyevich had been working as a clerk in the council then and might have been seized for a short while with his superiors—Lizavin could see him half-rise behind his office desk, which was the color of wood stain, then rise, staring at the door; he could see the papers flying in the slow air and the spreading lake of ink; he could see the banks of the puddle, the wooden bridges pressed down into the dirt to such an extent that by the touch of your foot you could barely tell the treadworn track, the galosh stuck in the mud, the council elders in the wind, below the convoy, the bell tower on Trade Square, the raft made from old gates that couldn't hold more than three people; he held out his hand to her, to help her step up or down onto the shore—as he did sometime then, a moment ago, in the other reality, which was connected with the farewell story more intricately than one might imagine. For it wasn't just a question of what he'd left home for—as it turns out, for a long time—with someone else's little trunk (or suitcase, as the report insists, but the little trunk is more real for us, we saw it), leaving his wife with the sick man and then waiting it out for almost a week until he could give his name without endangering either of them. No, it was a question of her having left him, then or some time later, under circumstances unknown to us, and who remained on which side of the threshold has little significance now—as little as the number of years between their meetings had for Milashevich— now, when the beginning and the end of the film were glued together and the middle could be cut out and omitted. Crazy! He seemed to have been waiting for this, waiting confidently, neglecting the time in between, and having no doubts about the purposeful work of fate— as if even world events and catastrophes served to realize his personal intentions and family affairs, as if he considered himself the be-all and end-all of these events. An awkward, proud joker with a sad monkey face—anything can come of such a being. And even if for the moment something that wasn't completely appropriate had sneaked up and come together at random, one could still imagine how on that very day, finding himself in prison for a short spell, on the *fantiki* that happened to be in his pocket—precisely on them, they were handy for that—he tried with a pencil, and later, at home, with ink and a good pen, to capture the palpitation and moisture of the moments that still hadn't dried out, to make them stop, to make sense of them, for now everything was acquiring a value for him: the crackling voice of the wind over the chilled waters, the turbulent heavens, the evening journey home past the illuminated windows, the intoxicated scent of new times.

5

The air is extracted from winy fumes, just breathing makes one's head spin—perhaps it was that same evening when the soldiers, who had been left without a commander, dispersed through Stolbenets and together with the inhabitants soon started an attack on Sotnikov's wine shop and warehouses on Governor Street, where five thousand casks of wine and spirit, not counting the bottles, were stored. Thanks to the efforts of carters and soldiers, all winter for a radius of thirty-odd miles people drank spirit as if it were water. *A time when a bottle sold for half a ruble in remote villages, even cheaper in the ones nearby*—one could begin an account of the epoch from this recollection. The first night a few men with Peresheikin at their head tried to stop the pogrom; they broke bottles with their rifle butts, releasing the cold, dark, stupefying liquid from the casks into the waste gutters. *The night when people were up to their waists in wine and drank their fill from the puddle.* Someone, apparently, struck a match, perhaps attempting to smoke while drunk; later he couldn't explain more precisely anything of what happened, since he became the first log in the fire in which four people were burned alive, including comrade Peresheikin, and—not for the last time—the ill-fated archive also perished. If one wanted to, one could choose quite varied pictures on the subject of fire: black phantoms of houses, branches, and trees melted in a bright substance; someone smiling at the fire, like a bronze idol, with the flames reflected on his face, in a cotton cap with a ripped-off earflap... but there were certainly more fires in Stolbenets and around it. Maybe this is about another one. Or here, perhaps this is from that night: *The tinkle of broken glass. I jumped up, began to rummage around for matches by the bedside. Before I could light the lamp, two more shots rang out and something whistled right by my ear...*

6

thus the unexpected, as yet unexplained world is born beneath an infant's spread fingers
* from a blind man's touch, outlines and shapes emerge from the darkness*
*   the fragment of a torso, a smooth shoulder, frozen laughter, an impassive, incomprehensible complaint*
*   the seeing fingers of a lover*
*   by touch, at random, in the resounding emptiness, with surprise and without understanding the whole, with anxiety and curiosity*

7

Farther on, the road wasn't visible. The last smoldering pieces of wood from the night of revolution were burning down and smoking, the sour smell of charred ruins tickled our throats, and we barely had time to make out by a single flash of lightning a woman in a light coat—light for European weather—the small bones of her fingers white from cold or from tension (and what was in her fingers? surely not a weapon?—but you couldn't see). How did this meeting on a mythical raft in the middle of a puddle get transposed onto the other meeting, after which she stayed with him in his house? And stay she clearly did; we have no reason not to believe Simeon Kondratyevich. Of course, one can smirk at the cunning of the words in his autobiography about a "reunion after a separation"; this man really had, it seems, his own way of reckoning time, too; ultimately, he didn't sin so very much against truth. But *how* and *why* did such a woman return to him? After all, it is clear that up till now it was only our

106

own imagination that had placed her on a level with Milashevich—at his prompting, oh yes, although here, too, he could have been sincere in his own way, presenting her as vulnerable, weak, domestic, created for family joys, for the peace of the provinces, needing his protection. Ultimately! Ultimately! But to return under such circumstances after so many years, and what years! To stay for good with him, who remained unchanged, as if after a brief marital tiff? That is, not simply to stay with him, but to enter a new existence, as it were abandoning what had been her identity to such an extent that she didn't even cast her own shadow, didn't leave a trace of her own? For some reason the annals of local history had not preserved additional information about Aleksandra Flegontovna Paradizova. ("Oh, about her, too?" one can already hear a voice, derisive and mistrustful. Yes, about her, too. What can you do? Let's make peace with that at the outset, as a condition. Lizavin isn't to blame here.) But, if you want, precisely this in a paradoxical way confirmed that she's the one whom, in his autobiography years later, Milashevich will call his life companion. Why? Let's ponder it ourselves. If she'd died immediately, like Peresheikin, or if she'd continued along her particular course, which we discovered belatedly, then even if she'd suffered a not overly successful fate, she'd have left a distinct and firm trace worthy of a person of such merits; her inconspicuousness was more inexplicable than anything. The flash of light not only didn't illuminate anything around it, but only thickened the darkness, heightening the enigma or mystery, forcing one in retrospect to reexamine familiar data. Did she know when she went to Stolbenets that Milashevich was there? Was she going to him? Or was she simply sent there as a local who'd been born there, and did the meeting result by chance? Then all the more so, all the more! With what could he, this provincial philosopher and visionary with a cryptic smile on his enlarged lips, win her heart, captivate and convince her? So we still have to figure out who turned out to be whose captive on the raft among the parodic Stolbenets elements. And meanwhile we'll accept the following as fact: there was something in him, in this person for whom Lizavin and we simply felt a liking out of habit (because we are Lizavin, and you and we, now merging sometimes to the point of identification; it's probably time now to explain ourselves and, maybe, ask forgiveness of those who feel differently—but, after all, that's coauthorship, in which any reader is involved in certain moments that are related to love). Yes, there was something in him; it demanded yet again that we get the feel of the soul and thoughts of this strange person, still unidentified, and it was necessary to shift from one timeframe to another and to reinterpret the many *fantiki* on the bliss of a life *à deux*—not simply from literary interest now, oh no, but to slake the anguish, more and more vital, of our own soul.

8

From the very beginning it seemed to Anton, at first vaguely, as if he'd already read a very similar story somewhere about a woman revolutionary taking part in the arrest of her own husband. This resembled a false recollection, but Lizavin managed to get to its sources and was convinced that the subject had actually been used in literature, namely, by the local writer Ispolatov. Moreover, it turned out to be by no means a chance coincidence: the author of the novella *The Meeting* was inspired by the same episode from N. Sukhov's reminiscences. Later, in his book of literary musings, Ispolatov recounted how Sukhov's story had made an impact on him: "It emanated the breath of ancient tragedy"; how he'd unsuccessfully tried to find out further details about the heroine (oh, Lizavin could understand him here, although the novella was written in 1932, when the trail was comparatively fresh); how he ascertained only that she perished a year after the events described, apparently from typhus (the self-assured haste, however, is pardonable—he didn't know Milashevich); how he tried to fill in the lacuna in people's knowledge about her, and, following the Tolstoyan canon regarding gossip about the fate of several real women, added a rebellious youth to her life in a family of religious fanatics (using material from the case of a sect that took a vow of silence, which had created a stir in the province at the beginning of the century), a trusting love for a student (and, after all, that's pretty close!), together with whom at one time she vowed to fight for a better future. "One day a cleansing storm will erupt, will clean this abomination, squalor, and dirt off the earth's body like the scab of a disease, and the cleansed sun will shine over the renewed earth!" Stronger than anything else in the novella is a scene in prison where the heroine reminds the man she once loved of this oath of theirs; now he's a grumbling intellectual, with no wish to understand the grandeur of what's happening. In general the whole drama is impressively portrayed, and something in the heroine's features recalled the woman whom Lizavin imagined; it's possible that a latent recollection of *The Meeting* even gave his own conjecture a push in a certain direction. The only flaw—but, for Anton, alas, a decisive one—was the fact that there was simply no way he could link all this with Simeon Kondratyevich.

9

One probably had to look for Aleksandra Flegontovna's tracks farther from Stolbenets, maybe even in the annals of émigré history, since her surname had finally surfaced. (But maybe at other times she'd had a different surname? That was also uncertain. Who was her traveling companion during the years hidden from us? Was it the man who turned up once on Milashevich's pages under the nickname of Ahasuerus?) Such a search, however, was possible only in Moscow; he had to wait until he had time off, and if he had to be perfectly honest, he somehow wasn't very drawn in that direction—into a world of political passions and intrigues, party struggle, epochal flourishes, programs, sacrifices, wars, and shocks. He's of our blood, is Anton Andreyevich, the peaceful blood of the provincial, and if someone's quick to reject such an equation—well then, for God's sake, we'll retract our words immediately and not insist on the point. Only first it would be worthwhile to examine our inner selves: Are we really so eager and impatient to venture forth under the cold skies into the tragic arena of history? In the sincerest depths of our being, don't we prefer material that is more in proportion?—that is, is it really true that the provinces have no power at all over our souls? Whatever happened to both, happened; with time it will possibly become clearer (if what needs to be clarified has survived), but right now Simeon Kondratyevich was living with his Shurochka in Stolbenets, which with all its inhabitants had made a transition, with great difficulty, into a new era of existence. Here's where one would want to look, above all—and Anton Lizavin, turning over the *fantiki*, tried to discern which of them were still imbued with a feeling of the events of those times. He no longer doubted that at least some entries were one and the same attempt to capture the stabs of a momentary feeling in the process, already transformed into the lines of a possible work— but he couldn't pick them out with any certainty. Here you could see the smoke from the smoldering bits of charred ruins, the black skeletons of ovens sticking out like evil mushrooms. In the smoky light of the new day, wrinkled, green, unshaven faces cautiously peered out from behind the gates, from behind the curtains that had been pulled aside. *The new word had already sounded, but what did it mean for the minds?* The council elders were ferried away on the raft across the eternal puddle, to the hooting and whistles from the shores covered in the sunflower husks that had been spat out, a woman who'd just arrived after a separation from her former husband met him, a soldier whom they'd thought dead returned from the war, and in the public wine store they broke bottles, drank from casks and puddles, and burned in the fire. The rest is words. Other words were added to the first, as was the music of the diminished orchestra of firemen, and a coffin covered with red canvas; but as always the town idiot Vas Vasich walks in front of the coffin, his quilted cap shoved under his jacket, and smiles with his habitual joy: as always, people were dying and kept on dying, but he, as always, was burying them, while he himself went on living. Even life's upheavals hadn't changed that law.

Yes, no matter what, the most important thing was the certainty, now strengthened, that the *fantiki* did indeed have a relationship to real events—even if not a complete relationship, even if he couldn't tell what kind of relationship and still had to figure that out. A way of thinking and perceiving the world, possibly connected with professional habit, was ingrained here; set aside, involuntarily undergoing a transformation, was the trifling litter of everyday life by which Milashevich measured the fullness of time and which to him was, simply, inherently closer and more accessible than epochal politics, programmed speeches, and the thunder of guns. When it was connected, this litter could outline the contours of what happened to him or around him, just as clinging seashells, say, outline the bottom of a ship: when it rots, they can give a sense of its form—if they themselves survive and don't disintegrate. It was necessary, of course, to glue together the grains of knowledge with the saliva of conjecture, but what do we know completely, exhaustively, even in the life that's close to us, accessible to our gaze? The only question is that of correlation. One has to enlarge, to accrue these grains. "The main thing for Schliemann was to believe, as one does a vision, in the reality of Homer's Troy," was written on one of Lizavin's sheets of paper, "so as to later, after digging, find the fragments of pottery, layers of ash, and half-rotted bits and pieces." It's difficult now to recall what Anton Andreyevich meant by this; if he had a comparison in mind, then it didn't completely fit, of course. He didn't have a poem, after all, instead of hexameters; he had fragmented scraps, shavings from an item whose existence was unknown. Moreover, fragments of pottery in fresh soil aren't as reliable as those deep down—you look closer and see that one's a substitute and another's a renovation. And, besides, there's too much ash. And yet, yet . . . Maybe that's not even the main thing. What, in essence, did Schliemann uncover for us? Was it really the Troy of Homer's hexameters? But, after all, it wasn't even the Troy of fragments of china pottery, of stone walls, buried utensils, or even golden ornaments. He uncovered—and firmly established in us—the awareness and the feeling of a connection between hexameter and fragments of pottery, of a profound, inexpressible, musiclike connection between us—who sorted out the fragments of pottery, today's earth diggers suffering from fever and bad water—and the eternal spirit of the human species.

10

What's this music about? Was it about the November wind, about the chill that pulled at the surface of the water, like skin, about the restless clouds and the cry of ravens, about a woman who'd vanished and returned, about tenderness and melancholy, about meeting and recognition, about sheets of paper with prophecies that the wind had blown out of a cave, so that an interpreter would collect them?

It's about what the November wind can say about melancholy and tenderness, and what the human soul can say about the raven's cry

111

and the restless clouds. It's about what makes us grieve over the loss
that occurred before we were born and see in a return of long ago a
small grain of new hope and a new understanding, about what connects the human soul with the whistling of the wind, connects melancholy and tenderness.

11

In his free time, and sometimes, if the truth be told, during working
hours, too, Anton would leaf through newspapers, books of reminiscences, and collections of documents, on the chance that the surname
of Paradizova (or what could her name be?) would turn up again somewhere by accident. It wasn't a very sensible activity, but it ensured and
filled out the solitude that drew Lizavin to be at home less, or in places
with a lot of people, not to meet old acquaintances, not to respond to
their questions, which were frivolously curious, indifferently sympathetic, even if sincere. He visited the Stolbenets archive, but only to be
convinced once again of the hopelessness of his search; the holdings
of those years had gone up in smoke. All the same, in the process
Lizavin found something of interest to him in this reading. He traced,
for example, how Peresheikin, a one-eyed clerk at the Ganshin factory,
was transferred after his death into the category of workers, and the
further one went, the more Peresheikin was enriched with biograph-
ical details, even with new photographs, from which his two bright
eyes gazed upon his descendants—unlike Iona Sverbeyev, his short-
lived comrade-in-arms and Aleksandra Flegontovna's fellow traveler,
who managed to live to the time when he turned up as one of the
accused in the case of the big Stolbenets fire (together with the former
manager of the Ganshin factory, the engineer Fige) and who, as a
result, vanished completely from history. The only things that
remained of him were a dozen verses printed at different times and
gloomy news about the Nechaisk republic; it seems he was then briefly
in charge of a children's home established on the former Ganshin
estate—that's all. In N. Sukhov's memoirs this man, whose name for
some reason continually appeared like a melodic accompaniment
together with the topic of Simeon Kondratyevich, was mentioned as a
local native, a soldier who'd suffered gas poisoning at the German

front—his family no longer waited for his return; they thought him dead, his mother even going so far as to arrange a requiem mass... Anton recalled how once, rereading this information, he'd suddenly felt that the lines seemed to be moving apart and he was falling through them, diving into a world from which he'd been about to be completely pushed out.

12

Among Milashevich's characters was the Stolbenets housepainter and painter (but above all drunkard) by the nickname of Bosoi the Flyer. The second part of the nickname hinted at Bosoi's special ability to fly without wings. That fame was derisive: it meant that he managed not to get smashed even when falling from the tallest Petersburg roofs—a circumstance that wasn't so rare with painters, especially those who drank. Bosoi, however, being incredibly combative, didn't allow jokes on this topic; he genuinely seemed to know something about himself, and in the midst of derisive comments someone was even prepared to declare, as if he'd once seen it himself, how Bosoi hung next to the drainpipe gutter and began a smooth descent. Bosoi was still a teenager then, one of those whom mothers sent off to study at a co-op of peasant seasonal workers: he got up at five in the morning to put on the samovar for the skilled craftsmen and apprentices, washed off the paints, cleaned the brushes, washed the dishes, ran to the druggist's shop for material and—secretly, so that the owner wouldn't find out—to the liquor store for vodka for the craftsmen; but, puny, trusting, and good-natured as he was, he didn't let himself be plied with drink. In winter, when the painters had no work, he went to study with a signpainter and was already starting to draw then, endlessly copying drawings from a book, where light, thin creatures with little childen's faces flitted among vast flowers and cut grass. Wasn't it this vision that took root in his mind and gave rise to the joke? Was that what presented itself before him when, in the midst of work, he suddenly froze, brush in hand, leaning forward a little, pupils dilated, and only a blow on the back of his head and the ensuing laughter brought him back to the matter at hand, and, maybe, averted a fall? In any case, the only flight authenticated by a witness turned out to be indirectly connected with this sight. That morning he discovered that all the drawings in his secret storage behind the stove were lewdly daubed over, body hair having been added to the soaring infants in every conceivable place, and something else besides. He launched himself blindly with his fists at the first person who turned up. They pulled the crazed fellow away with difficulty, and a few hours later he fell from the roof. This was on a hot day in July, when the white-hot tin baked one's bare heels, the paint was mixed with sweat, and the contractor, hiding in the shade of a pipe, looked at the sky and hurried them on for fear of rain. The witness qualified his statement, saying that at that moment his own head spun from the heat or the smell of paint, and, admitting half-seriously that the flight lasted some time, he added, now laughing freely, that all the same the fellow crashed from the height of the third floor. By the time they rushed down to him, he was already standing up, admittedly staggering and deathly pale, but without any trace of injury; he looked at everyone as if he didn't recognize them, as if the impact against the ground had shaken up something in his mind, and the next day he vanished from the workers' co-op house, contriving at the last to set fire to it. Just three years later he was pronounced done for in Stolbenets. At government expense they brought him with a group of prisoners under guard and transferred him to the district authorities—lanky, the worse for drink, barefoot, with a youthful, untidy beard: his shirt, covered in dried paint of various colors, had hardened like a coat of mail, and didn't rip, but broke. The most bitter disgrace he had to undergo was at children's hands. Other people who returned from Petersburg in boots and galoshes that creaked and shone were in the habit of bringing ginger cakes from the capital for the neighboring kids; he couldn't treat anyone, which is why he became famous throughout the village and town for his nickname of Bosoi (Barefoot). "Bosoi the Flyer!" the kids tagging along after him would yell. "Bosoi the Flyer, where'd you fly?" And Bosoi patiently, even somewhat guiltily, tolerated the children's ridicule—but only theirs—although thereafter he always tried to carry in his pocket something sweet as a treat or as ransom; it wasn't worth others' while to tease him.

Simeon Kondratyevich was convinced that in those seconds of the first fall or flight Bosoi really experienced or saw something about which he couldn't tell anyone later (especially since after that he was rarely sober when talking with anyone). These were moments, Milashevich explained, outside normal time; they couldn't be squeezed back into the seconds shared in common by all, and within them one could survey one's whole life, distinguishing or recalling vivid new details, clear and interfused with light and soundless music, moments where there was neither fear nor torment, but a sky of unprecedented blueness with unprecedented rainbow clouds, visions of a radiant life, and tender faces and flowers—incidentally, it's possible that pictures from books interfered here. The problem was that the feeling of connection as if disintegrated from his collision with the ground, and not once did he manage to recapture it subsequently. The one thing that Bosoi could convey fully with words was his revulsion at the faces that suddenly surrounded him—at their hair, pimples, wrinkles, breath, and smell. After what he'd experienced it was unbearable and offensive to see them; they seemed to invade and crowd out the vision, not leaving any room for it. At least that's how Milashevich translated into the language of his prose the drunkard's hardly intelligible words. That's how he himself explained why he drew only children's faces in his pictures. They turned out well, he had fans, and not being devoid of talent, instead of painting houses in Stolbenets he worked on commission drawing signboards and sometimes portraits. One of the stories mentions Ganshin himself among his customers. Reading Milashevich's descriptions of these pictures, Lizavin imagined some of the drawings on the *fantiki*—possibly Bosoi had something to do with them. For him children were the only acceptable and higher beings among the rest, who were already hopelessly poisoned by life. Like many who drank, he declared that life was poison, alcohol an accessible antidote, and he worked between his drinking bouts whenever his need for money recurred. He led a bachelor's life—who'd risk marrying him, after all?—and seemed to be always waiting for something on the verge of happening. Alas, at the beginning of the war Bosoi was taken into the army. Milashevich wrote about him as of someone who'd already perished at the German front—that's possibly why he allowed himself to write a story about a man whom readers knew in real life.

14

And Anton Lizavin now felt as certain that Bosoi really had existed as he was convinced that the man was still alive and had reappeared in his home town, so as to finally clean up his wretched past record— mourned as dead by his mother and resurrected in a barely recognizable form (could even be christened as a newborn), poisoned by German gas, and sobered forever if not after that experience, then after the devastation wrought by wine. Now his damaged hand clearly couldn't hold a brush, but to express the feelings that had fully ripened in him he resorted to a pencil or, maybe, a typewriter. In Iona Sverbeyev's verses one hears more strongly than anything a contempt for a world obsolete, poisoned, and damned. And the images sometimes encountered of hovering, weightless freedom and lightness, of shining clouds and the innocent happiness of children on a clean flowering earth no longer seemed figures of an abstract verbal utopia, one of the many to be born in that turbulent time seething with bubbles. Vital feeling pulsed here; impressions from the front, it seemed, once had helped Iona to live anew what he'd experienced in childhood and to finally find the words for it:

The umbilical cord snapped,
The poison flowed out with the pus,
There's no support underfoot,
It's desolate, windy, and terrible.

In these lines an explosion hurls the hero from a trench, raises him above the defiled, disordered land, above the piles of people, and behind the flash of fire, behind the flash of emptiness, the vision of a wondrous world suddenly opens to him—in the air infused with light he discerns the happy fellow brethren of the future, unaging and beautiful, for whom flight is natural, for their very bodies are free from their former foulness and weight.

15

Here only those whose cheeks are not befouled with hair, nor breath with tobacco, partake of delight—Anton Andreyevich suddenly added the *fantik* that had floated to the surface. It fitted accidently, but was just right, as if Milashevich had been translating some thought of Iona Sverbeyev's into prose or jotting down one of his own after a conversation with him. After all, he could very easily have met and talked with his old-time acquaintance after returning to Stolbenets, couldn't have avoided hearing him and reading him even if he'd wanted to. Probably other notes lying at the bottom of the pile were also capable of confirming this. Like this one here, say: *They're more complete than we; they have no bowels weighed down with dung, and that which we hide, like shame, is supremely beautiful and fragrant in their case.*

16

Hm, hm... well, let's allow that's so. Sometimes sheer momentum would carry Anton Andreyevich pretty far, one can't deny it; afterward he himself was convinced of that and readily chuckled at himself. But this was already the laughter of a man who can allow himself private mistakes and unsuccessful sallies, because he's certain of what's most important. And the most important thing was the growing feeling that the *fantik* pile nonetheless was connected simultaneously with the real world and with a world that Milashevich had created; moreover, for the first time he thought that maybe this wasn't at all the material for the book mentioned in his conversation with Semeka, though perhaps Simeon Kondratyevich saw in those very sheets of paper this far from obvious book growing of its own accord. It contained some of his unrevealed characters, like Iona Sverbeyev: he was Bosoi, a former housepainter and painter, a crippled soldier and poet, a representative of an unknown republic and a patron of children. Like a thread dropped into a solution, this name began to get overgrown with items, to be enriched with details and live features:

An apparition. In English boots with puttees. Pockmarked skin on drawn cheekbones—like grainy stone, slightly smoothed on top.

The blood didn't subside into a transparent substance in the eyes irritated by gasses to the state of raw meat. Such eyes neglect close objects, they look into the distance.

Nostrils pale, thin, quivering. Their sense of smell compensates for defective vision.

What's more important than a sense of smell at such times, when neither the mind nor knowledge gives support, when it's better not to rely on one's own eyes and ears?

the ability to pull out of the air what is inaccessible to others

A gift, without any scientific basis, for guessing from afar at whom to wag his tail and to whom to show his fangs if that person isn't quick to pay up.

17

So what if once again not everything fits inarguably. No problem, it'll get clearer somehow. That was the time Anton Andreyevich's excited thoughts flowed simultaneously in various directions, carried away by any hollow or excavation en route. *(Water will find its own way; it doesn't care through whom it flows*—Lizavin had lingered once on that not fully intelligible phrase; at one time he'd set aside this *fantik* in the category "About Fate and Chance," seeing here a thought about inevitability, which for its own realization in history can use any figure, simply the closest or most receptive one; but now he thought with a grin that it fit his search, too.) Without finding a direct approach to the riddle of the reunited husband and wife, he tried this way and that to peer in at least through the little window of their wooden Stolbenets house (most likely wooden and moreover one-storied, like the one he described in the visionary story, where he only tried out in his imagination how he could live, how he'd live some day precisely in this town with the woman who by then was no longer at his side), and through the chink of a shutter, in the closeness of the heated room, he discerned by the light—not of a kerosene lamp, but of an oil lamp—the familar face of the philosopher and gardener; he was using a teapot to water the shoots in long wooden boxes (how had he managed to save the household flowering paradise from the cold?), and somewhere behind him, not quite in the shadow nor in the twilight—in a blind spot—one could guess at, could almost assume, the presence of a barely discernible woman with a brown shawl around her shoulders. She must have been there without having completely cleared her lungs of the London or Paris air, but what was she doing?—feeding a log into the stove (one would like to think that at least they had enough firewood)? making linden tea according to Milashevich's recipe? darning?—you couldn't see, couldn't see. The small flame of the wick reflected in the glass was dying down, but from the darkness there gradually emerged the town, visible through the tender childlike dawn with the emptiness of its trellised fences and whitish pink switches of branches. The boats tucked their noses into the shore as into a mother's belly. The top of a burned house was dismantled into firewood. The shutters on the windows of the first floor were closed tight. On a brick wall was the faded slogan "Everyone to fight against the louse." The stone from under Koltunov stands empty on Stolpie, the shameful inscription laced with once red material; but the material wore out, with time the stone was planked with boards, on holidays they'd surround it with portraits, like a speaker's rostrum, and meanwhile *The Guide* discussed the question of how one is to understand the words "we'll destroy to its foundation"—inclusively or not? In the evenings the electrotheater Visions shows the film *The Heart Also Withers Like a Flower.* The snow is disappearing, there's a thick layer of manure and dirt on the streets. It's fine when it still freezes a little—there's someone in a decent coat and lambskin hat, probably one of the old-timers, hesitant about stepping off the planked footpath, carefully testing the road first with a stick, then with the sole of his rubber galoshes. Doctor Levinson still goes to see his patients, on foot; they requisitioned his wagon and horse, but all that would be nothing if it weren't for the dread dog by the nickname of Hammer and Sickle. Of course it was a dog. Some unidentified ruffians had burned this emblem into his short fur with a white-hot wire—whether from mischief, out of ideological zeal, or the opposite, in mockery, thinking to desecrate the symbol. In the last case they miscalculated. *How he jumped—fearful, baited, always the very last—how he sensed protection and his new position!* Lizavin added details to the subject. Hammer and Sickle became a threat; even for dogs it was better not to have anything to do with him. But dogs weren't what interested him. His strength consisted in the rare ability to determine from whom to demand a contribution in the form of food. A gift, without any scientific basis, for guessing from afar…

18

It's possible that in some mysterious way hitherto unknown to science a name has an impact on one's actual bodily makeup and even on bodily emissions—inspired, Lizavin tried a further fit, but again felt that there apparently was no way. *All that would be fine, but a name is careless. And with such a height!*…No, it was already clear, it wouldn't work. For an uncertain instant a dubious new character arose from the pile—and immediately dissolved in the damp mist of the Stolbenets streets. Lizavin would have followed, but he lost track of him. Once again he felt unsure, once again kept sliding on slippery ground and proved to be merely seated before a deposit of papers. Outside, instead of music, the racket of a motorcycle rent the air, and the fading sound still trembled and stretched like a cobweb.

19

Fingers sorted through the small pieces of paper in a box marked "Names." *Mylnikov is changing his surname to Melnikov. On words, or the Beginning of a new faith.* And how did that get here? Should it have been in the section "On Words." Or "On Religion"? Anton Andreyevich had such a section, too, one of the skimpiest and most dubious ones, by the way. *A new faith begins with new words.* Well, of course it fit in there.

Not a word, in fact, but an exclamation, an interjection, an attempt at a word. The Gospel scholars later put it together.

religion for the people

Believers in the disposition of stars perish from it, nonbelievers cope.

In any event, these were the notes of a person who didn't belong to the church. In the sphere of religion, too, Simeon Kondratyevich held aloof from the fashionable crazes of the time; in his prose he didn't display a special interest in this topic, and such a note, for example, as this one on a *fantik*—*"every day we do that over which, it seemed, power was given to the Lord alone"*—simply betrayed the proud feeling of a modern man. Incidentally, he also didn't always write the word *God* with a capital letter, as though at a certain point it had become for him, as for others, a question of spelling. Whether the thoughts, words, and half-phrases that he jotted down here were his own or originated with someone who hasn't been revealed yet was another question (as always). Inspired by his experience with Iona, Lizavin tried to match up a suitable figure also for the role of the character who carried the religious theme. In Milashevich's writings one encountered only a single clergyman somewhere in the background, who, moreover, interested the author more as a kitchen gardener and scholarly floriculturist—that is, a colleague of sorts. Even earlier this character had caused Anton Andreyevich to examine him more closely, for they called the father Makarii, like the leader of a later sect that the old-timers dimly remembered to this day. But this, of course, could only have been a coincidence; even if we assume that the literary hero had a prototype, he was doubtless called something else. Lizavin wasn't able to repeat the experience of inspiration in his case; he could only mechanically pick a few more scraps of paper on the topic. For example, an echo of a religious dispute about the possibility of creating the world in seven days (*Seven old rubles now count as millions. In the same way, translate God's seven days according to the new calculation*), a vague half-thought (*Within, it's like God. And chance comes from without*), a poetic prophesy and the familiar commemorative list: requests on various people's behalf, asking for recovery from sickness, for marriage, for a solution to sterility, and for protection from oppression. On several *fantiki*, by the way, disjointed impressions of a pilgrimage to some holy place were recorded, but, once again, whose and where isn't known.

20

A crystal shrine, transparent, all shining from inside. Only to stand there for a while with your feeling was impossible. Whatever you manage to mumble hastily has to do.

And even then the line was one and a half versts long. It's not that they came from every corner of the world, were drawn from different countries. Everyone needed something and would hurry the person ahead to go on.

it's one thing to appeal to a drawn image, another to see embodied the one to whom you appeal

Their bodies are fragrant even after death

One by one they let them by without pushing. You had to put your ear right up against it, which is why it seemed that something individual, special, was whispered to each one. So, what was said to you?—they tried to find out from those who came out into the courtyard of the monastery.

not to talk about it, but to say something about a cow or even manure in such way that it would be about it

21

Lizavin remembered holding just that *fantik* in his hand when something happened to him. He tried to understand why it had turned up among the religious notes. Was what he had in mind here that devout, chaste bashfulness that doesn't allow one to pronounce other words or names in vain, which is opposed to any theology—that is, to logical arguments about the divine? Or perhaps it had to do with an unwillingness to formulate a thought or feeling directly?—because there are thoughts and feelings that resist a direct naming; they begin to grimace like a child in embarrassment, and permit only an image, a likeness ... Yes, it's precisely where Milashevich's thought is expressed directly that one shouldn't particularly believe it; it's still uncertain what it will be connected with.

to compare with oneself this muteness spilled in the air

He sat there, still trying to make something fit, shifting it around, until he discovered that he was already thinking about something completely different, something that lent a significance to another person's words that they couldn't have because they were about someone else, after all, not about him, but now they couldn't be freed from this significance, just as if by the law of illusion he saw in a drawing a human face between two vases, and after that could see only the face, while the vases disappeared and couldn't be restored. In a word, he was no longer thinking about Milashevich; the delight of the first insight had exhausted itself, although Lizavin thought that it was for Simeon Kondratyevich's sake that he urgently had to go to Moscow, to the Moscow libraries, for his sake that he'd cleverly wheedled for himself the semi-business trip, the semileave that would be applied against his past and future compensatory leave. Man's good at playing tricks on himself; and what thought really drove him there, for whom he really planned to look, and why there, Anton fully admitted to himself only when he was already climbing the stairs of the old Moscow house.

VI. HISTORY
OF THE DISEASE

FACES

*a time when you could recognize a student not only by his
service cap and jacket, when there wasn't yet a mixing of types and
one could guess by a face to which class someone belonged*

*The breakdown of centuries gives birth to such faces; a time
that chose as its art subject Salomé, the fateful dancer, the kiss on
dead lips*

*pale, refined nostrils, the sweat of sickly cold on transparent
temples tinged with blue*

*the little face of a flower: the double hillock of a forehead,
little cheeks, chin*

an angel's features immune to time

1

There was no need to ring, the door to the apartment turned out to be
half-open. Behind the shining chink, voices swirled together with the
tobacco smoke—the bathhouse hum of a crowded gathering.
Someone with a sweaty bald head and beard took the bottle out of the
newcomer's hand in businesslike fashion.

"What, there was no vodka?" he asked, as if they'd earlier agreed on
vodka. Lizavin guiltily shrugged his shoulders as if to say, I brought
what I could. As if to say, I didn't think I'd find a gathering here, it was
by chance...But explanations were pointless; the bald head was
already floating away with the bottle into the interior of the apartment, to an unseen feast. Anton looked around uncertainly: Had he

come to the right place? Seemed like it, everything was similar. Yes, there was the host's portrait soaring in a cloud of tobacco smoke by the door, the narrow young face with an ironically smiling birthmark at the corner of his lips. From the kitchen a woman appeared with a pot of smoking potatoes, slid a worried, unseeing glance over Lizavin—and then, two steps later, realized who he was:

"Anton! Oh, Lord! Finally!" The joy in her voice was genuine; she even lifted her chin above the pot and raised her lips. Lizavin was slow to react and forced her to hold that difficult pose for a moment, but then, quickly bending down, he kissed her. What else could he do? "It's so good that you turned up. I didn't know any more what to think. Come on through."

With every minute the doctoral candidate felt more and more stupid. So she didn't know what to think, eh?...The only other time he'd been in this house, he'd only looked in, going by the address a chance acquaintance, one could say a Moscow street acquaintance, had left for him (precisely *street:* they'd met on the street in Moscow, got to talking by chance, and became interested in each other), but he didn't find Maksim Sivers in then and spent the evening in conversation with Maksim's wife, Ania, this bustling woman—a single evening, and now she says "Finally!" and raises her lips for a kiss.

2

The company at table greeted his appearance with lively noise, someone even yelled "Hooray!," some beautiful woman clapped her hands, and Lizavin bowed slightly in various directions, like a fool, because they were greeting not him, of course, but the potatoes that emerged from behind his back. Maksim didn't come out to meet him, and, hard as he looked, Anton couldn't find him among the multitude of faces. Those seated moved up, squeezing together, and freed a place, so he was soon settled in with a clean set of utensils in front of him, his ceramic glass filled.

"Well, let's drink to him."

"Lord, surely I didn't chance on a funeral banquet?" Anton Andreyevich suddenly grew cold. It all seemed to fit. His fear, of course, was foolish and short lived: the faces around him were animated (still, people also laugh at funeral banquets...). No, and then Ania...

"To Maksim..."

Well, of course, they don't drink like that at funeral banquets. They don't clink glasses.

"To the name-day celebrant..."

Relief. So that's what it was. A bit clearer. But where had the name-day celebrant disappeared to? Lost in the kitchen? It was time to make an appearance. But to ask would be sort of awkward, especially after that fear. Meanwhile Anton looked around. How interesting all the faces were. Well, how were they interesting? You couldn't say right away. Lots of bearded men, not what we've got. No, that wasn't the point, of course. But something in them was really special, something...how could he put it...Muscovite, that's it, the stamp of significance, of intelligence that at one time captivated the provincial in Maksim Sivers. And the women were somehow the same...And you couldn't understand the conversation right away.

"...the reason's simple. Since the Tatars knocked us off course, to this day we can't get back on course."

"Oh, yeah! Predestined for six hundred years..."

No, so as to absorb the conversation, one first had to be on a par with the temperature of the company at table, where the cigarette ash on the plates had already powdered the herring bones and the scraps in beet stains, where the mess of various kinds of dishes, bottles, and faces developed the topic of the long, once immaculate, tablecloth, where voices drifted up above the whitish smoke like isolated bubbles.

"...when all is said and done, there are historical accidents, the self-will of personalities, the interference of foreign powers."

"But don't you think that this eternal interference and self-will are also as if programmed? The means of realizing power reproduces itself. Remember how Maksim expressed it?"

"Maksim had something else in mind..."

Where was he, anyway? He should go to the kitchen to have a look, to ask. Otherwise there was the impression that they'd gathered without the name-day celebrant and were toasting him in absentia.

Uncomfortable and incomprehensible somehow. Anton hastily shoved another piece of food in his mouth and, after he finished chewing, started to leave the table.

3

Ania was smoking in the kitchen by the window, like a person taking a break. Another woman was smoking at the table, a third was washing dishes in the sink. Seeing Lizavin standing embarrassed by the door, Ania beckoned him in friendly fashion and tucked her arm in his, but didn't introduce him to those present, possibly because she hadn't finished speaking.

"...the thing is that now they're taking only five kilograms. And for him the main thing is tobacco. All five kilograms could be tobacco."

How she'd changed, noticed Anton. A completely different woman. Even smokes. No, how could he ask her now?...

"You definitely need lard. It doesn't spoil," said the woman sitting at the table, and at the same time she looked at Lizavin, as if seeking his authoritative male confirmation.

"Yes, lard doesn't spoil," confirmed Anton Andreyevich. For some reason he asked for a cigarette and lit it from Ania's.

"Is it really true that they came to Lifshits's yesterday?" the same woman asked. She turned to Anton again—either seeing that the hostess had drawn him close to her, or impressed by his authority.

"I don't know...I'm not up on things. I just arrived in Moscow," mumbled the doctoral candidate.

"They say they broadcast it over the radio."

"I don't have a radio. Mine broke," Lizavin said, seizing the chance to say the absolute truth, not discrediting himself and at the same time getting out of a slippery, incomprehensible spot. Fortunately, right then people from the other room came to get cups. The woman washing the dishes hurriedly wiped her hands and went to take care of them; the one sitting at the table extinguished her cigarette butt in the ashtray and also followed her. Ania remained for a few more drags.

"Are you surprised?" she glanced sideways at Anton.

"Not so as to...but I..."

"Yeah, so many people. I didn't expect it. I'm seeing half of them for the first time myself. Even most of them. They brought money, bought tons of everything themselves. Maksim's done so much for many of them, after all...You can see how they love him."

"Ah...and where is he now?" Anton finally used a convenient reason for showing interest.

"Still there," she said tiredly and sadly. She extinguished the butt and closed her eyes for a moment.

"Ania!" someone called from the room. "Ania, come here for a minute."

"I was really happy to see you," she said. "Won't you stay a little later, when everyone leaves?"

"I don't know...Somehow I..."

"Ania!" they yelled again.

"Coming!...Stay, if you can. I wanted to talk to you...to show you something."

4

That decided the matter. To tell the truth, Anton Andreyevich hadn't been opposed to slipping away. Not because he was feeling increasingly uncomfortable on account of the conjectures, which he didn't need to confirm, except to clarify details. But simply, what was there for him to do among strangers from the capital—he, a newly arrived provincial who had nothing to do with their unknown affairs? He really had nothing to do with them, as he could explain and prove, if need be. He stayed in the apartment mainly out of personal interest. However, he secured for himself the visible position of a stranger-observer: he didn't return to the table, to the crush, but stood at the lintel by the door, as if surveying the scene from a distance and trying to grasp again the point of the disorderly dispute.

"Just don't tell me that a nation is a collective personality. A collective personality is a song-and-dance ensemble."

"But a person can't exist independently..."

Like the *fantiki*, Lizavin suddenly thought with a grin. *Fantiki* everywhere. Looks as if I'll go crazy over them: a splinter of a conversation overheard, a fragment of someone's life out of context—the

128

same feeling dogs me, appears before me everywhere. And am I really so impatient to put them together? Maybe, I'm really just shy, like right now. Maybe sometimes I simply don't want to admit some connections and meanings into my consciousness...

Anton hadn't at all planned on spending the night there; however, the guests dispersed after midnight, and not even all of them. For the three who still remained, Ania, energetic, smiling, full of goodwill, began preparing a bed on the floor. How she'd blossomed and cheered up, noticed Lizavin. A wife acknowledged by her husband's friends. A like-minded woman. A devoted friend. He waited for her in the kitchen, tidying the remains of the dishes.

"Leave it, I'll do it myself," said Ania as she appeared. She lit up a cigarette again. "They're also from out of town," she explained, indicating with a movement of her head the wall behind which the guests were settling down for the night. They had to speak quietly, and this half-whisper created an aura of confidentiality. "Maksim constantly used to bring people to put up for the night. Now that he's away, I want it to be just the way it was with him here. I could tell you were surprised when I greeted you as I did in the doorway...It's inertia. That's their style when there's company, don't think anything of it." She didn't notice that she'd said "their style." Her liveliness and vivacity were vanishing from her face like a layer of make up, leaving tired skin, shadows under her eyes, and wrinkles in the corners of her lips. "Last time, too, I seemed talkative to you for no reason? I was...but, believe me, in general that's not the way I am. Only with you for some reason...and today, too, for some reason I wanted to talk to you."

"Because you and I are provincials among Muscovites," Anton eased her explanation.

"Yes, yes," she responded gratefully. "Probably. I've been in Moscow so many years, yet always feel lonely. So lonely!" She suddenly blew her nose in a handkerchief. "I really have no one left. You know, I especially wanted to tell you. This summer I was walking home once...Maksim was already gone. And in the little public garden opposite our entrance I see a girl sitting on the bench. Thin. It was only later I realized that this wasn't the first time I had seen her;

that morning she'd been sitting there too, with her little suitcase. It was an old suitcase, worn, and to me it suddenly explained, intimately, everything about her. It was as if I were seeing myself when I came to Moscow with exactly that kind of suitcase, to enroll at the university; I knew no one here, and not having a kopek or a dormitory, I walked about the streets, so hungry that I felt weightless, until Maksim picked me up. I go up to her, start talking, and feel that I've guessed it all. She just nods. You know no one in Moscow, I say? She nods. Hungry? She nods. I suddenly felt so close to her! I persuaded her to stop in, and on the way started talking about myself. Then things got strange. She came in and saw Maksim's portrait. You know, it hangs facing the doors? She stopped and looked at it. I even thought: Is it the face that interests her so much or the painting? But while I was dawdling around with something in the room, she suddenly vanished. I only heard her heels tapping on the staircase. I wanted to go after her, but didn't. So strange. For some reason the thought of robbery didn't occur to me for a second—there's nothing here to steal anyway. I was left feeling that I'd seen a vision. I hadn't even had time to find out her name, hadn't got a word out of her, it seems. She was beautiful." She paused until Anton finally met her gaze, and in that gaze she seemed to find just what she needed. "Very much so, in fact. Just too thin...But really, why am I telling you all this?...Maksim left a notebook. During our last conversation it's as if he had a premonition...yes, probably did have a premonition, and asked me to take the notebook to another house if something happened, to keep it safe. And, you know, for some reason he mentioned you. Well, you'll see yourself, you'll understand. As I understood it, he gave his permission for us to read it, he even wanted that. And now I don't know what to think. Maybe you'll explain it to me later." Again Anton met that same probing glance. "I think there's something incredible there...something terrible. I never knew him, basically. Or his affairs. He didn't relate to me seriously, didn't even talk about such things with me."

"He was probably sparing you."

Ania shook her head, dabbed at the corners of her eyes with her handkerchief, and blew her nose.

"I know he didn't need someone like me. I can understand that, too, you know. He was always raring to escape. Perhaps this is also a way of doing that."

"Come, now," Anton touched her shoulder, "he'll be back. Everything will be fine."

"If he'd only come back. He doesn't have to come back to me, I don't need anything. Although, no, I'm lying...But I wouldn't make any claims. Just to serve him, to fulfill his wishes, his whims...I'm afraid...I'm afraid he doesn't want to at all...Not just with me. To live at all. I mean, there already was...But what am I...Excuse me, Anton, I won't any more. Here's the notebook, read it. There's a bed made up for you over there, and a lamp, too."

5

And once again, as if from nowhere or from another time, Anton heard a voice, muffled, at times gasping, interrupted by a cough, the voice of a man who, it would seem, barely flashed through his life; but staying up all night to read the oilcloth-covered notebook that had seen better days, Lizavin increasingly felt that Maksim Sivers had entered—and continued to enter—deeper and more fundamentally into that life than he himself had imagined. The first page without any heading or preliminary explanation started with short, barely intelligible notes a line long: "18.10.70. Teacher on the train. Cough 3 mins." "22.2.71. With boss. Itch, not long." "6.11.70. TV ensemble. Asthma 2 mins." "3.4.71. In church. Rash, cough," and so on. Farther on, Lizavin came upon drafts of several tables where along the horizontal axis those same dates were accompanied by the letters C or B, and on the vertical axes were recorded the symptoms—cough, asthma, cold, itch, rash—with crosses at the intersection of the coordinates. In other diagrams the horizontal axis was divided into two large halves, "comm." and "boor.," each divided into somewhat smaller squares without any headings. There was also an attempt at a graph with cartesian axes: horizontally, the names of months; vertically, "no. of attacks." But evidently not a single diagram worked, everything ended up being consistently crossed out, and on the eighth page under the heading "History of the Disease" there began a continuous text. "For a scientific observation even of myself I'm afraid I lack many qualities, above all a systematic method. I'll try literature," wrote Maksim Sivers, a student who never completed his studies, who knew what anamnesis, aetiology, and pathogeny are, but didn't know how to approach his own strange ailment, a severe, capricious allergy of mysterious origin. The physicians who had finished their studies of his condition had long ago found themselves helpless in the face of it, he noted with a smile. Not one text or objective analysis yielded any results. It seems to have been one of those cases where the patient himself could sooner understand what was happening with him, but he remembered that belatedly, and only when it really got its clutches into him did he take it upon himself, after the fact, to recall and try to make sense of the stages in the disease, so as to get to the root and method of elimination. "In the beginning," he wrote, "the cause seemed simple: the bookshelves in my father's house, the smell of library dust—a classic allergy, forcing me at the age of eight to move to Aunt Ariadne's." As the years went on, however, it grew clearer and clearer that the heat, itching, and gasping could be triggered by irritants that weren't at all material and, indeed, more frequently weren't: so one time a simple combination of words like "the day's agenda" or "honorary presidium" provoked a full set of symptoms, allowing the student Sivers—to the envy of the other students—not to attend meetings. Sometimes he didn't even get to open a newspaper: either the smell of fresh paper and printer's ink or the sight of the headline "The Call Signs of the Labor Watch" precipitated an asthma attack. The disease developed and got more complicated; the short notes in the diagrams proved insufficient, Maksim now tried to decipher them from memory, reconstructing in detail the history of his attacks. Just try to understand what could have played a role: the smell of coal and the foul bedding in a railroad car, the taste of railroad tea, the landscape outside or his fellow traveler's conversation about summer holidays ("Sun, air, and water—there was everything. An assortment of meats," he recorded verbatim), and maybe it was her face, covered with a layer of powder, with red lips and rouge, that made him think of primitive painted toys. He also specified precisely that an ensemble on TV played "Moscow Nights" and that the carpets in the apartment were synthetic. At one time he'd been strongly suspicious of synthetics, especially when they simulated natural material—but no, in other cases it hadn't had any effect at all: he couldn't find a common denominator. Evidently the attempt to track separately his reaction to commonness and boorish-ness didn't work either, although it would seem that in the first case it elicited more disturbance in his breathing (spasms, cough), and in the second, in his skin (itching, rash to the point of blisters), and he could sometimes get rid of the latter when he put the boor in his place. On the page that mentioned this not too scientific hypothesis there followed an enumeration of several skirmishes, described in various degrees of detail, in different styles, at times even rather literarily, and obviously at different times, and also with references of sorts, small insertions in the margins, notes intelligible only to the author, arrows extending from one event to another and clearly intended to indicate a connection; but for an outsider to delve into all this was difficult, and the writer himself couldn't come to any final conclusion even *here*.

6

In general, from one page to the next the notes grew more and more fragmented and multilayered. Tracing the plots of skirmishes that brought relief, Sivers tried to separate out and group together other episodes after which the attacks passed. The first proved to be a section of the most diverse scuffles. Farther on, again in different inks, was written in small letters "Comp. Armenian," with an arrow extending somewhere, but Lizavin got only as far as a line placed sideways— "Almost all three Armenian years I breathed easily, as never before"— and didn't bother turning the page anymore, hoping to return to it later, when he'd begin to understand something more fully. He also leafed through the next confused page, beginning with the line "Breakup of relationship, departure, sudden change of place," and far-ther on again began to read, seduced by the continuous text and the legible handwriting, "But why did the rash and the hoarseness sud-denly vanish at one point in that same room of my father's with the smell of book dust and the windows barred against thieves? For some reason I rummaged in the desk drawer (looking for money? I don't remember; no, I sold his books for money) and found an old photograph of my father in a black jacket from revolutionary times, as yet without a mustache and beard. A thin sorrowful face with a nervous cut of nostrils. Aunt Ariadne thought that he destroyed Mother's life, but she treated him with her own brand of respect, as she might a dragon or a wizard who, say what you will, had succeeded in casting a spell and kidnapping the princess: to do that one had to be remarkable, nonetheless. In my opinion, she saw this remarkableness in the fact that he could sire a son at an age when few are still capable of it; she had absolutely no doubts about his paternity, just as she couldn't have had any about the mother. I remember him only as a little old man in children's sandals whom it was hard to call Dad, indifferent to everything except his passion for books. (Under his shirt he wore a cord around his neck with keys to the especially valuable bookcases.) And yet there had been a lot before that: socialist-revolutionary activity, flight from exile, emigration, then the revolution; he was saved, as I understand, by a miracle, because he soon abandoned everything and got involved in museum matters. When he got to know Mom, he was already over fifty, a different person. Before the revolution he'd already been married—even Aunt Ariadne didn't know anything about that. In general she talked about him reluctantly, only when the occasion called for it, and I wasn't interested and never asked him. We were strangers to one another. Only later did it start to feel like loneliness (one of my many lonelinesses). But what wafted to me from that photo? Some sort of *authenticity* of life, of passion—maybe that's the word?"

7

Although Anton had the night at his disposal, and moreover no one confined him, he began to leaf through the pages more and more cursorily, without abandoning his intention to return to them later: he wanted to understand as quickly as possible what was in this notebook, as Ania had hinted that it could have something to do with him; but he still traced the dotted line of thought as he read the most legible pieces. "I can't stand the same leather jackets in the movie theater:*

* Black leather jackets signaled Bolshevik commissars.

a story of stage props, operetta anarchists, masked passions, sham struggle. Let's allow that it's a matter of taste here; let's say that even a healthy person could get sick from the falseness. But I do watch films about Indians, at least, without batting an eye. (More precisely, I used to watch them; I haven't done so for a long time, but I'm not about to swear off them.) Perhaps they simply don't have anything to do with my experience and knowledge, just like science fiction about Mars?" Sivers continued to ruminate on the topic of authenticity and inauthenticity; the suspicions that synthetics had provoked at one time were now transferred to another, spiritual dimension. "An attack in church. Nothing of the sort ever happened to me before, I responded calmly to the smell of incense. Maybe because this time I went in with the guys and saw them cross themselves?" The writer categorically refused to try to connect and group his observations—it didn't work; what took precedence was the wish that Lizavin knew so well: to capture the momentary pinpricks of thought. "But the conviction of these people is unfeigned, I know; everything here is done in all seriousness and truthfulness, and they're ready to pay even with their lives, and I acknowledge their rightness. Why do I get short of breath even in the midst of our conversations, as if from talk about shortages of products?" "The disease is pushing me away from my loneliness, makes me sensitive to any misfortune I encounter, any need or untruth; it demands sharing, helping, interfering, otherwise not only would the skin itch—so would the insides, the intestines, the heart. And at the same time I'm invited to rely on myself alone, not on anything else." "Perhaps this disease is my connection with the world, my unfreedom and my blessing?" "Again I imagined a conversation with my dead father. Oh, how easy it is to show him, his generation, what it was worth! And what am I offering in opposition? A student's hopes and disappointments? Understanding, disease, the inability to live?" "A tipsy out-of-towner on the street expounded to me the philosophy of a universally accessible happiness..."

8

There—Lizavin's stomach fluttered—that's about me. After our meeting, still before arriving in Nechaisk, he said: "An amazing blue-eyedness,* not afraid of being funny. In general it doesn't get embarrassed by banality or even triteness, on the contrary, it's ready to found a stable universe on them. And rightly so. Some song or home-made item also speaks of life, only in a different way from *Faust*. Besides, what's accessible to all is *a priori* more likely to be universally significant. Something affected me in this turn of mind or in this person. An amusing coincidence with my own thoughts—but as if from the other side of the mirror." The next page was empty, and Lizavin, with bewilderment, even with a sense of insult, reread the lines relating to him, remembering a long conversation during a hangover on a Moscow street at night, to the accompaniment of a persistent cough, his companion's profile with the mole in the corner of his lips, which gave the impression of a grin, though he was in no way in the mood for laughter. It meant that this was how Maksim had understood him then, and he'd coughed terribly as he'd listened to the comments about Milashevich. What kind of coincidence with Simeon Kondratyevich's world philosophy did he perceive in his own flailing about, bred by his ailment? It seems he even went to Nechaisk to seek relief from it, met Zoia there, and fled once again. Is there something about her? There must be. Here, after the blank page, as if starting afresh:

"What did we see in each other? Wasn't it ourselves? We understand ourselves through others (that's what both books and people are for). Lord, how the charm of her gracefulness was revealed to me immediately, that ability to be a princess without caring about her outfit (something that doesn't depend on one's origins, but also can't be acquired by study), that innate distinctness of predilections, similar sometimes to unhealthy whims, that fantastic sensitivity to the genuine and present, 'one's own,' which she herself, it seems, doesn't realize—and, maybe, thank God, Nature cleverly took care of her, otherwise how could she have lived so many years in that house?" Yes, that's about Zoia; Lizavin was convinced of it, but how mysterious! Just try to figure it out...There was something improper, nevertheless, in reading someone else's notebook. Surely Maksim hadn't

* BLUE-EYEDNESS Guilelessness and naiveté, not unlike the qualities personified in Thomas Mann's fiction as "the blond and blue-eyed."

really given his permission for that? People write like that for themselves, not for a reader; they even fear an indiscreet eye, and an official one all the more: Who knows whose hands it might fall into? There was good reason for always using initials instead of names: farther on, Kostia Andronov was designated by the letter $\mathcal{K}$, and Anton himself by $\mathcal{A}$. Lizavin read on, recognizing by hints the memorable conversation at table at Kostia's, when the former friends succumbed to Armenian reminiscences in front of Zoia. However, Kostia spoke for both; the taciturn Maksim, as the notebook now made clear, was thinking then about some Marat or other (this name was given in full; he also, clearly, was one of the Armenian acquaintances). What did the Armenian friend have to do with it, once he'd already begun about Zoia? Here, again: "I recall deciding from the start that he was from the mountains in the Caucasus. No, a Kazakh from a simple family, who finished school. But where did he get this innate, aristocratic code of honor?" "When the class sense of shame connected with the duel vanishes," Sivers added, in the margins, "the only hope is in a personal sense of shame. Equality proves to be equality only before a fear of punishment, before the criminal code. Fear and shame regulate behavior. Or an inherited disease like mine." "'How can he write such beautiful letters to a girl,' Marat wondered, bewildered, 'and in the evening let down his pants for corporeal punishment? And if she were to find out? I'd shoot myself!...' I myself never imagined how serious this was. He saw me intercede for K., he believed that I knew how to act, that I wouldn't be afraid, that I'd go as far as the tribunal. Alas, I didn't get any farther than the hospital—he lay without me at the female sentry's place with three bullets in his back, but I sometimes see this scene very clearly and know that I'm to blame."

9

God knows, what a garbled mess! Anton shook his head. Cold air wafted in through the open ventilation window; he should have closed it, but he just pulled the blanket higher over his shoulders so that it wouldn't be so chilly. Had this Marat shot himself or what? No, the bullets were in his back. (But that's why he's named him in full, because he's no longer alive. And does he feel guilty for his death?

It was impossible to understand anything.) Why did Maksim end up in hospital? After some scuffle?... "Returnees don't like to talk about the service. Humiliating nightmares are displaced into the realm of dreams, altered humorously. Everything's fine, otherwise you can't live. Human life is impossible without passing over things in silence, without substitutions, self-deceptions, simplifications, untruths. Life can be built only on the universally accessible, shortened, kind, incomplete, and concealed, but not on truth—maximal, naked, and terrible, like the bodies of corpses (in the morgue, when for the first time the orderly turned on the light in my presence and I saw men and women of different ages lying side by side on the zinc tables; sex here meant less than in the delivery room, where newborn babies lie on their backs just like that—and breathing was easy, Lord! That's what surfaced as I recalled Marat. That's when everything connected, and I grasped that I was doomed.) Any beauty is only a part of chaos singled out by us for use. The maximal truth is forbidden; its air isn't suitable for normal breathing. All the vast culture of many centuries with its religion and conventions, costume and poetry is created by humankind, to fence itself in and defend itself from that truth. It's funny to have this sickness, but what can you do? I didn't choose it, and maybe my monstrosity, my fateful inability to be content with incompleteness, is needed for something in the world, too. An incomprehensible force higher than us drives us somewhere. If only I could talk about this with A.! I'm afraid the problem that his philosopher formulated is now more serious and hopeless than it seems." (This is about Milashevich, about our talk, Anton realized.) "There's probably one way out: for everyone to search and decide as much as he can to grasp his own incompleteness, to be drawn toward the opposite, which might complete you, and so to toss about non-stop—but to live. I also felt this desire. But some kind of synthesis or compromise, apparently, isn't allowed me. And that means I don't have the right to get anyone involved with me. My guilt concerning Ania is enough. Whatever I caused her, I hope nevertheless that she has enough strength to hold her ground. But how am I to protect this poor, amazing woman? She herself lived her whole life at the limit, on the edge. A. could sooner do it. How can I tell him; he'd understand, and I'd be calmer. One needs this ability to limit oneself in time, not strive beyond the limits. He thinks, in essence, about the same thing I do, but with opposite aspirations and therefore is more capable of seeing them through, and maybe, of even expressing something on others' behalf and giving support."

10

That's about me, Lizavin realized, that's already an almost direct apostrophe to me. And precisely this incomprehensible apostrophe reeked of threat, which Ania had sensed so correctly. She's right—for some reason he wanted me to read it because he himself had no hope or desire to return. "'All hope abandon, ye who enter here.' I think this is about submersion not in a symbolic hell, but inside oneself, in the abyss of conscience and understanding. Whoever clings to hope is less capable of going through it. Hope inclines one to feel sorry for oneself; it summons one to go back before it's too late. And rightly so, rightly so. It's not for nothing that sometimes one is so drawn to an open window at a high altitude. We fear freedom because at any moment we ourselves will disappear together with the prison." By now a distinct violent trembling had seized Anton—nonetheless, it was time to close the ventilation window. What was this?—and why was it again addressed to him?—as if he'd been chosen to inherit and interpret the languor of others who had gone. Nonsense, this fellow was still alive. This was an attack of depression, melancholy; of course, he was sick. He wasn't normal. But at any moment it would pass. Anton finally got up to close the window. It was allowing the black air, illuminated from beneath, into the room. The ventilation pane was large and located not too high, somewhere in the middle of the window. Anton thought that one could quite certainly stick out from it, and for that reason he did. In the depth was darkness, empty windows all around, a light emanating from somewhere—possibly from the lantern around the corner. The shadow of a huge animal cut the space—it was a cat—and Lizavin thought that it wasn't high at all here, two and a half floors up. Displacement of feelings, nothing more. Lizavin jumped from the windowsill. The tremor passed. He knew what to say to Ania in the morning.

VII. The Mind of a Flower, or An Attempt at Happiness

Lizavin himself later laughed at one of his mistakes: several *fantiki* that he'd been about to attach to the flickering characters proved to be simply extracts from the life of a certain elder Makarii, who at the beginning of the sixteenth century had set up a cell somewhere beyond the Nechaisk lake. This name flashed before Lizavin in the table of contents of works by the province's Commission for the Study of Early Texts for 1923, which he'd taken to leaf through in the Moscow library. At first simply the coincidence with the name of the episodic character in Milashevich's work (and, chiefly, once again with the name of the local sect) caught his attention; but reading it led him, strangely, to think that possibly there was more than a coincidence here. The apocrypha, as the author of the article showed, had been written a long time after Makarii's death, already during the schism and, obviously, had been on the list of writings of those condemned. The point was that Makarii considered unfortunate human nature as something remote from heavenly innocence and bliss. Beings who had the same name as people (but only the same name), insisted the elder, lived in heaven as flowers, not animals, without knowing suffering and so not needing movement, thought, or verbal speech. Makarii saw in a flower the primordial foundation of God's plan; he explained how "flowers" are parts of the human body: the face, palms, and even soles. But the comparison favored the beings who'd managed to preserve an ingrained peace. "They're more complete than we; they have no bowels weighed down with dung, and

140

that which we hide, like shame, is supremely beautiful, fragrant, and displayed like a face." "Their bodies are fragrant even after death," was said about simple hay. They shared with people the divine gift of live breathing, but they were much better at rejoicing at light, warmth, and moisture. But most remarkable of all, the commentator marveled, is that even the ability to distinguish good and evil, which for man was connected with expulsion from paradise, in Makarii's opinion, was by no means alien to plants. If we are to translate his discussions into modern language, this ability to react in various ways to good and bad, the pleasant and the unpleasant, in general distinguished the animate from the inanimate. The animate knew how to defend itself from the bad and look for the good, to remember past experience and to change under its influence, cultivating and mastering something like intellectual ideas. It's amazing, wrote the author, that the man discussing this was someone who not only hadn't heard anything about phagocytes or immunity, but not even about a cell, about the origin of species. As far as one could judge from the description, the philosophical part of the "Life" looked like an original poem on the nature of primordial happiness and the origin of reason in suffering. The embryo of a thought, taught the elder, is inseparable from the membrane of suffering, and whoever irritated the pain, disturbing the silent peace, awakened mental torment. The Lord punished those who'd lost paradise with this fateful melancholy, and for a lifetime of history the mutual heightening of mind and suffering led their descendants further and further from the original and longed-for bliss. As late as in recent books the story is told of how the flower *primula veris* sprouted up on the blood of Tatar horrors, a flower whose head had little lamb horns and which ate the grass around its root—a living example of a development captured *in medias res.* But for mankind the image of the flower and the memory of paradisaical peace remain the dream and goal in a search that promises transformation and bliss. "Wasn't this the bliss sought by the zealots who buried themselves up to the waist in the earth and lived like that, assuming that in this way they were seeking bodily torment?" asked the elder, who himself spent many years immobile in his cell, who attained such perfection that he no longer had to cope with bodily needs and his behind released rootlets into the bench. The fate and the current location of the apocrypha were unknown; however, it wasn't impossible that Milashevich knew it not only from the description—besides the obvious copyings, several unclear fragments that surfaced in Lizavin's memory could have related to it: in these, someone's body disappeared into the ground, someone stirred the sprouting roots, which opened up to the light and moisture as to music, someone tried to penetrate through the silence and was tormented by the awakening of a thought, like the rubber plant in the story of long ago.

2

the pale bud opened its eyelashes, on the stem of the stalk a seeing pansy unfurled

Do we really sense only foul weather, only a bodily prick or burn?

it enters with a tickle through the pores, penetrates us with the wind, flows into the little hairs

the juice rising in the veins becomes red and burning

the fear of understanding

a word from pain

It's so painful, so hard! You really can't hear? But I'm here, here! You're touching the substance of my soul, of my mind, with your fingers.

3

In the *fantiki* linked anew, if one wanted to, one could now, as if in the rustling of leaves, distinguish something like a fantasia on the theme of Makarii's apocrypha. Long before sensitive instruments confirmed the ability of plants to respond to harmful contact, someone's unaided hearing could detect their trembling and complaint; someone talked about how the flowers in a room and even in the garden had fallen ill together with their owner and had dried up on the day of his death...How can one describe the new swarm of ideas suddenly whirling in Lizavin's head? Like a swarm of tiny insects, like specks of dust, a chaotic turbulence, a dusty fog, from which worlds are born. Here were mixed, and for a while enmeshed, allusions to death and to the cemetery in which those who called themselves Makarites had behaved outrageously, and again some cemetery priest in Nechaisk, and once again the scholarly father-horticulturist who nevertheless can't have had the same name in Milashevich's work by accident. A sparse Mordovian beard, heavy peasant boots, a faded hat, gray cassock. When greeting someone, he'd hold out a big hand hardened with callouses from a shovel. One more note was unexpectedly added here. *A former father in his place. The work is a matter of habit for the hands, only the pits are deeper.* Did an already heated imagination need much more? The cemetery priest, who'd possibly lost his job after the revolution, came to Nechaisk when they closed the churches, and adapted to the work of a gravedigger. Let's say that's so, then what next? One could add some sketches here—say, grave inscriptions—but after several similar tests the cemetery line grew very thin and no longer seemed relevant; it was more tempting to collect around the same character *fantiki* that were not so much on religious as on gardening themes; Simeon Kondratyevich had a pile of these. Who was it who talked about the different food tastes of young and old plants, who tried to extend the youth of flowers with the help of tobacco extract, and tested the effect of alcohol on them, observing how the leaves started to rustle in blissful disorder? God knows who it was. Why not Milashevich himself? Wasn't he busy with nameless seeds in the Ganshin greenhouse? Aren't the numbers of the plots of land recorded in his handwriting, as well as the flower boxes (or types) in the reports on those unclear experiments where no. 2 outstripped others in height and no. 5 never sprouted? According to Semeka's testimony, his fingers were also black from digging in the earth, and the spot of manure on the paper with the twisted inscription "From Trotsky" was real, not prefabricated.

4

This strange and, frankly speaking, disturbing *fantik* jumped out again in passing, like a splinter, demanding to be understood. Curiously, a note that turned up in the newspaper had almost offered an explanation. The paragraph had reported the appearance in the district of a pretender calling himself Trotskii. This man had declared himself such in the countryside, illegally repealed taxes and assured people, by the way, that he and Comrade Lenin had personally sent three wagons of sugar, tobacco, and tea to the district, but the local powers had kept the goods for themselves. The piece also described the adventurer's distinguishing traits: a pointed beard, a large mouth, sometimes wears a pince-nez, limps on his right leg, and wears a short Astrakhan fur coat. His real name, as it was explained, was Uspenskii. It was also reported that measures had been taken to capture him. There was no information about further sightings, and for a brief moment there flashed in Lizavin's mind, as if patched from bits and pieces, a picture of a country hut with soot-covered log walls and a dim window. On a shelf in the corner for icons, beside an icon case, among the vials, spindles, and bottles was the lop-sided fragment of a mirror. In these sheets of paper Anton always saw the impact of the times when Milashevich went around the surrounding villages collecting for his museum things which had been pilfered from the Ganshin estate. Now he suddenly made out in the reflection of the mirror the face of a man in a leather jacket, with an imperial beard and the blob of a mustache beneath his nose—an incomprehensible foreign figure in such a context. Was Simeon Kondratyevich interested in news of the pretender? Did he try to sketch a portrait or plot about the adventurer, provocateur, or maybe genuine madman, one of those people thanks to whom history is so rich in legends and falsifications? But perhaps he really had known him and had even gotten something with an inserted paper?... The attempt to connect the manure *fantik* with this personality burst right here like a bubble; the chance to laugh at this idiosyncrasy also presented itself to Lizavin—in time another explanation suddenly came by itself.

Moscow allowed the doctoral candidate to discover something more important than the Makarii apocrypha. He'd already spent a large part of his dubious leave in the libraries, still hoping to encounter Aleksandra Flegontovna's name in reminiscences or publications about prerevolutionary emigrants, finding, as we've seen, something completely different along the way—when the name Semeka emerged as if sideways in his memory—which finally prompted him to glance once more in the memoirs of the deceased; not in the published book, however, but in the rough draft from the archive collection. He should have guessed earlier: somehow it hadn't immediately occurred to him that, of course, far from everything that had been written would end up in the printed text. Oh, Anton Andreyevich, Anton Andreyevich! That is, he even remembered that something similar to this thought had stirred in him once, but he hadn't stopped to consider it. Well, what can one say? Without exaggeration he knew the pages devoted to Milashevich by heart, and without any difficulty he began to find in the manuscript places that had been omitted or changed—in some places a few lines, in others a word, in yet others a whole page. The reasons for the condensations and corrections didn't always lend themselves to explanation. One could understand, for example, why the author's final regret about a man who'd disappeared from his orbit didn't make it into print: "I can't imagine whom that quiet dreamer, secluded in his own world, could have bothered." Did that mean he nevertheless had grounds to think that Milashevich hadn't simply died a natural death? But he preferred to avoid this touchy material. Yet why, for example, did a detail such as this one about Milashevich get crossed out?: "He didn't look too tall, but when he stood next to me he turned out to be no shorter than me. And according to the old measurements I'm two and a half arshins" (that is, about seventy-eight meters, Lizavin quickly translated). Also noting condensations, and sometimes insertions, too, or even simple word changes, he more and more clearly started grasping the direction of this editing. More likely on his own initiative than under someone's pressure, Semeka had tried to build an image more consistent, more integrated, and therefore also more authentic than he himself had put together from separate details. But don't we all really edit, consciously or unconsciously, our sincere recollections? It's even strange to suppose that they could have only one version!

6

Especially important were two condensed passages. Before leaving the tearoom both companions at one point had simultaneously taken out their watches; Milashevich's cheap onion bulb opened with a musical chime. "It was a quarter past nine. 'Yours is five minutes fast,' said Simeon Kondratyevich. I happened to glance sideways at the dial of his watch and didn't see hands on it." This was very similar to a literary reminiscence from the lost story that Milashevich himself didn't seem to remember. Semeka probably had felt that no one would believe him anyway, or maybe the editor tried to do something; this place wasn't crossed out in the manuscript. But the very literariness of the episode, paradoxical as it sounds, made it authentic to Anton—like the tie with the patch around the neck of this person, who was as if acting out his own pages in front of his companion. The second change was of a different type: instead of a reference to the Indian Boze's botanical experiments, there followed in the manuscript an entertaining conversation about the possibility of radio waves having an effect on living things. At first Simeon Kondratyevich was interested to learn whether it was true that the radio tower in Moscow had exploded—a typical question of a clever provincial boy whose contact with the real world came through rumors. Semeka authoritatively refuted this nonsense (as, by the way, at about the same time did the newspaper *Hammer and Plow*, formerly *The Guide*—the rumor clearly preoccupied the locals' imagination: for several days the Stolbenets station hadn't been receiving any signals from the capital); Vasilii Platonych rose to the occasion here, so his elimination of this episode didn't spring from any external threat. But his companion shook his head skeptically in response—also the habit of a provincial whom you can't put down so easily: we're shrewd, we read more than just the district newspapers in our library, and we know something even the capitals don't know.

For precisely during those few days that coincided with the broadcasting problems, the sprouts on his experimental plots were developing very strangely. But could this really have an influence? Semeka didn't understand, and Simeon Kondratyevich responded in like surprise: Could it really *not* have an influence? Just think. What if some invisible but material waves are now penetrating everyone. "Everyone, including you and me. Here we sit, drinking tea, and each moment they're penetrating us. Our brain, our cells. Our nerves. Hasn't it ever happened to you: words or thoughts suddenly start to sound in your head that couldn't have sprung up inside you by themselves? Where do they come from? If you analyze it sensibly?" "At this point," wrote Vasilii Platonych, "I had the sense to laugh." However, the phrase about laughter was crossed out, and opposite it in the margin was glued a separate sheet of paper with another fragment, but it was unclear to what place in the conversation it pertained: "We can't accommodate everything" (this, evidently, was Milashevich's reasoning). "Here you and I, let's say, perceive each other, this food, table, people, smoke, air—what else? And every instant, like now, inside us and around us life goes on without end, ungraspable. The blood's flowing inside, juices are dividing up, cells working, molecules moving, and around us is the whole universe, billions of people and beings; and inside our heads are memory and thoughts, and outside of us there's an incredible number of them, if you know how to listen carefully." Like everything earlier, this piece is crossed out with crosses on top of one another, and lower down it's clearly been replaced, in fine handwriting, with the beginning of yet another tale about the director of the horse yard in Nechaisk, who in his zeal removed from the stables the icons that had previously hung there of Frol and Lavr, patron saints of cattle, and in five stalls had hung plaques with the names of Moscow leaders in their stead. "Here I finally realized what was going on, and laughed"—Vasilii Platonych had transferred this phrase to a new place, and these were the only words on the whole page that hadn't been crossed out, because in exchange for the former a less offensive little subject, about the experiments of the Brazilian Sikeiros with the coffee leaves, had been transferred from a new page, so the concluding laughter and realization that it was a joke were completely appropriate and fit in. Ugh, how much the author had managed to say during one evening, probably yearning for a favorably disposed listener! Semeka couldn't have thought all this up; it was probably then that he made some rough notes so as to remember the episode, and now was only selecting, arranging, and connecting his rewritten drafts, as he worked on the image.

7

Because this manure, the manure "from Trotsky," really did exist. Anton Andreyevich not only saw traces of it with his very own eyes, but could even have smelled it with his very own nose if time hadn't dissipated the smell. It was as if, while developing his own plot, the naturalist got and checked the manure from that same stable, in portions from under each plaque indicating the new name of the stall's inhabitant. *You won't mention such a name out loud on the street, brandishing a whip*—indeed, and not necessarily just out loud; the point of the search was something else. *It's possible that in some mysterious way hitherto unknown to science a name has an impact on one's actual bodily makeup and even on bodily emissions.* Oh, my God! Five plots of land were fertilized each in its own way; seeds were sown from a Ganshin burlap sack without an inscription. No. 2 rapidly and prematurely outstripped the others; the fruit looked either like a pod the size of a cucumber, or like a cucumber with an end sharpened like a pod. An inexplicable fine grass, self-seeded, came up everywhere, flowers of changing hues recalled a rash, the rootlets intertwined in the soil. Something suddenly happened that couldn't be explained by inner development alone, the leaves writhed, the early fruit started to snap with a bang reminiscent of a gunshot. There was the sound of broken glass. The stems dried up and turned black. The covers of the pods curled up in charred spirals. Do we really feel only bad weather? Do waves, full of unheard words, really not permeate us— each of us—in their own way?

8

Proletarians of all countries, unite!

TICKET

for listening to the radio
for 2 min.

Price: 1,500 rub.
Plenipotentiary of Gublit no. 8

The equipment stood on the bell tower, a wire from it stretching to the big bell. An hourglass marked off the time.

It was square, its legs crooked, two lumps on its forehead, double tentacles from the crown of the head extended upward. And a sharp-pointed paper bag served as a musical bell or an ear.

One by one they let them by without pushing. The voice was soft, you had to put your ear right up against it, which is why it seemed that something individual, special, was whispered to each one. So, what was said to you?—they tried to find out from those who came out into the courtyard of the monastery.

Place your legs wider apart, he says, and bend down, he says, your right hand to your left foot, and your left hand to your right foot.

9

Courage, now, courage! Don't let the world that emerges from a fantastic combination of circumstances disturb us, a world captured or transformed around him by a perhaps still enigmatic vegetarian and gardener with a large mouth, pince-nez, boots, and Tolstoy peasant shirt with a bulging breast pocket. In height, too, he proved bigger here, as if he'd come closer; he didn't need to think of hidden inner heels so as to appear taller, and the anguish of being undersized was to be passed on to someone else. This philosopher of the simple life turned out not to be so simple himself and didn't live simply; in his little corner he listened carefully to the voices and influences of the big world, translating them into his own homemade language, which wasn't immediately comprehensible. In his tiny area, nestled behind the woods, the same elemental forces were reflected in their own way, the same waves that engulfed all the land and permeated the country passed through it, fanning over the life that fed off local manure, and at the crossroads were born unexpected fruits... So out of the haze appeared a distant monastery, the bells not yet removed from the bell tower, the grass growing between the stones of the stonework, and echoes of talk reach our ears about the crooked-legged equipment, in the bell of which you could not only hear words from a distant central source, but you could also whisper your own words there, to the source—only they didn't allow that. The little town turns cold in the twilight. The dirt has frozen slightly, the laundry rattles in the wind. From a cloud of moonlit dust, as in the act of creation, are born and harden the silhouettes of houses and the outlines of naked branches. The white walls of tradesmen's stalls shine transparently, figures wrapped in shawls hide in the shadows, press up to the gateways. But here a shadow has separated from the shadows, slipped to the closed doors of the former shoe shop, and immediately others run up to it silently, just like nocturnal creatures, forming an instantaneous incorporeal line. The day before they'd announced an allotment of galoshes for distribution throughout the district—there had been a rumor that starting in the morning they'd begin issuing them. "Disperse!" The voice of a military guard draws nearer. "Disperse, or I'll shoot!" And just as silently the shadows scatter, disappearing into the shadows. We see this, we hear this together with Lizavin more clearly than what surrounds us. (Does the person reading these lines really take in the voices and faces around him?) We feel much more at home in the atmosphere of someone else's life, among people who to us are more authentic and closer than, say, the passerby who just disappeared outside our window. The flame on the wick wavers, the broken shadows shudder. The oven hums, the red shimmer from the open door falling on someone else's sheets of paper, and once again everything's extinguished.

10

You can't make out the letters in the dark—but do you need light?
You could read this even as is, because you know everything
by heart, including the arrangement of lines on the page and the
inadvertent misprints.

    In the moonlight an ugly creature was dancing on crooked legs,
his rear thrust out behind him, making his own music for himself,
and somewhere in the earth's space those capable of hearing stirred in
rhythm, their brows and shoulders twitching intermittently in sleep.

11

What was this music about? About the moonlit night and the cries of those half-asleep? About the fading clouds, about pain overcome? About the dawn over the lake, about awakening from sleep, about hope and realization? It's about the anxieties of universal battles and everyday anxieties. It's about what a blade of grass and a drop can tell the human soul, about the hungry frost, about a sick person prostrated by fever, about a mattress filled with lice, and a thirst quenched with a blissful drink—tea from birch bark. It's about hunger and satiety, about sacrifice and execution. It's about new words and eternal passions, about the depths in which ambition and greed, thirst for power and possession are united by the impulse to secure for oneself the continuation of one's own life in posterity—but that is from where also come love and hopeless fidelity, and many years of waiting. In a blast it scatters the frayed tatters of human bodies, the small bell interrupts the orator, the world's borders shift with a creak. On the wall there's a live monogram of cockroaches around the kerosene lamp. The eternal provincial sky turns gray above the roofs, moss pushes up through the stones, the amazing dog Hammer and Sickle appears in the streets that have grown quiet. A small boat is sailing in the fog, the soul swoons, the petals of flowers, smoothed out, stretch blissfully. Repeated in a new time and in a new connection, the same voices change their sound, like the theme of a fugue repeated in a new tonality or new sequence, but the music is the same—only in the transitions there emerge from time to time seemingly accidental syncopation, sobs, and sometimes squeals, too, and then the heart is lacerated, as if something were bursting from the dark forbidden chasms where devils and madmen grimace.

12

An exclamation of loss and an exclamation of triumph, laughter and tears, were mixed on the sheets of paper, as in life, but what were this laughter and these tears about? Where was the loss and where the triumph? What came before and what after? Where, let's say, did this fat naked person under the apple tree come from, with a saucer on the five fingers of his hand? A woman with spots of blush pours strawberry jam onto pancakes. A little boy on a pot is eating a peach—a sculptured figure from the life that flows uninterruptedly. From where, excuse me, is the peach? From what period is the flour for the pancakes and the sugar for the jam, and this blush, and the cherub who's not grown yet? For several years Milashevich himself hadn't even been getting ration cards for bread; he was considered devoid of any standing—he obviously hadn't shown evidence of his prison and exile services, which in those years might have helped, however slightly, in getting food. He wasn't the intended recipient of the *fantiki* with coupons for free receipt of food (maybe it was Aleksandra Flegontovna); he got clever, like others; most likely, he dug up turnips in his own garden, beets, cabbage, carrots, and cucumbers, too, of course, the famous Stolbenets kind, and also tobacco, which was valuable for bartering; he himself didn't smoke, it seems. Did one need much beyond that?—kerosene, matches, and salt. Maybe he kept a goat? Unlikely. But what of it? This didn't change the main thing: the same music was heard. *Just a little more, just a bit, and it'll come together, come to pass, be resolved.* Here, can you appreciate the divine taste of pirozhki made from grated carrots? And can you understand happiness from an increase in soap rations?

13

Yes, historical upheavals that completely changed the surface of life seemed not to have changed or refuted anything in the depths of his philosophy; on the contrary, they had helped it be more consistent. What had looked like the comic fantasy of an idiosyncratic individual during Ganshin's time, when the inventor of pictures tried to establish the equal value, for a rapt soul, of Bohemian crystal and tin mugs, willy-nilly was becoming common property at a time when people would give away wedding rings for a loaf of rye bread, when they burned books to heat ovens, when one could dedicate an ode to galoshes, and their fortunate owner felt elevated above other mortals, when the booty of kerosene and firewood acquired significance, even a biblical solemnity, when, in the words of the poet, home goods once again became utensils—everyday life, indeed, was turning out to be Being. Life was ready to attach a new price to the wisdom of holy men like Makarii, who'd contrived to partake of the riches of the world without stepping over the threshold to the world outside, the wisdom of the destitute dervishes, who were indifferent to external details, but who'd found the source of light and joy within. That was the time it was just right to be filled with solitary greatness and the fullness of any instant—precisely the small *fantiki*, taken out of their context and time, consolidated that which in a connected plot would resemble a passing detail: here everything acquired an epic grandeur.

14

Half of a human body sticks out of a barrel. A smile of bliss on thick lips.

Did an emperor in a white marble pool with the fragrant petals of roses really enjoy himself more?

A wasp in the hot bell of a flower. Tender pollen on the stamen.

The transparent wings of a dragonfly with an accumulation of rust on its body

Can one see a tree and not be happy?

The air shines, made entirely from a substance that traces the slanting rays of the sun in the foggy forest.

light through an unwashed window—as through a bottle of badly refined home-distilled vodka.

clusters of foam

a samovar is the owner of non-Euclidean space

the tinkle of a spoon against a glass

the rustle of candy paper

Heavenly sweetness

A moment of life

A moment of life

A moment of life

A run of 1,500 cop.

And more, if you want

15

The *fantiki* seemed more than a notebook for Milashevich, a diary without dates, a manuscript of literary fantasies, a way of thinking over on paper the ideas of his philosophy. They themselves were an idea and a philosophy, a way of thinking and imagining the world as an eternal collection of moments cut very small and taken out of time. There was a catalog of material here from which the life of the great and the small, the fortunate and the unfortunate is made—that's how coal and diamonds are formed from identical atoms. Whose are these pale petals that form the likeness of a little human face: the uneven double forehead, the little eyes, the small chin? On whose sheets did the little hairs quiver and the pores breathe sweetly? Was it a hothouse orchid captured on paper or a trifle reminiscent of a rash? That's just what it was. If one didn't worry about a comparison of scale, about a connection, everything seemed equally significant: nuclei pure and simple, without protoplasm, without a joining element. Maybe he'd hoped to put together from them an endless, all-embracing moment, about which he'd spoken to Semeka in his incomprehensible language in the Stolbenets tearoom?—a moment that will accommodate the expanse of the universe and the tiny pinpricks of a feeling, the entire fullness of genius, beauty, and love. An attempt to make a fleeting condition intransient, to strengthen it, hold on to it—as he'd wanted to hold on to the woman at his side who for him had embodied the world, vulnerable, good, trusting in him. This wasn't simply a mental search for him now—perhaps his very life depended on it. Not for himself but for her he'd arranged a floral paradise at home, for her he'd removed the hands from his watch and the dates from his awareness. *Take shelter in the silence, even let your watch not tick. You can't run eternally. Our whole life has four seasons, a children's carousel.*

16

Perhaps, perhaps. But did he seriously think that he'd succeed where no one else had? Even if it were only because life stubbornly concerns itself with the whole and doesn't wish to change according to the hue of each routine moment. We usually don't register such moments, just as we don't register the life of our healthy body, the striking cosmos of its arrangement, where there are kidneys with retorts and vessels, where the crystalline lens of an eye and the branching out of nerves are not simply unimaginable and ungraspable. Here's where the contradiction lies: happy tranquillity doesn't let you sense anything; pain reminds you of feeling, and that pain was what Milashevich didn't want at all—he hoped to elude it. How? He knew, after all, what a heightened sensitivity to life meant. *The red stump of a cow on the scales.* His whole vegetarianism in essence developed from this feeling—an exaggerated imagination prevented him from eating the flesh of live beings. But man is born a carnivore; you can't remake him so easily. It didn't work out—fine. Simeon Kondratyevich didn't seem to vacillate in the main direction of his thought. (And in the end he did succeed in doing the main thing: he convinced the woman, kept her, even if we can't quite make her out; as before, there's a blind spot there—not a blot from which one could still make something out, but like a light-sensitive layer damaged on film: What can you develop from emptiness?) No, at times it even seemed to him that the direction of his thought coincided with the search for a great epoch, which, after all, had mad visions of the imminent end of a pre-liminary human history and the realization of earthly hopes. Except he translated this dream into his own homemade language.

17

One needs a Finn to be reminded of happiness—even this mysterious *fantik* got explained at one point, after it was joined with a newspaper report on the times when the Nechaisk republic had just been abol-ished by the central power, and Iona Bosoi-Sverbeyev had gotten the directorship of the home for orphaned children. The Greens were hid-ing in surrounding forests, avoiding mobilization; in the country and villages young fellows and heads of families used carbolic acid to make holes in their eardrums and stuck syringes with bonemeal oil into their legs to make them swell. Right under the drawing of the guide* they published a list of deserters conditionally sentenced to the ultimate degree of social protection; they gathered the older members of the family as hostages. "With profound pain in our hearts we have to pro-nounce the death penalty, against which we were the first to rise in protest. But a bloody battle in a fortress besieged by a universal enemy has no other laws. We don't punish, we're being punished. Choose the lesser of two evils." In the electrotheater Visions there was a lecture on how to use frozen potatoes. The greater part of Europe, as had just been discovered, was slowly sinking under the level of the world's ocean and within fifty years was supposed to vanish completely. There was a revolution in Bulgaria, riots had flared up in India, and at a non-Party meeting in the railway kitchen of the Stolbenets station the shouting prevented the speaker from talking about the events of the times. That's when an unidentified Finnish comrade took the floor. There were many Finns in the district, as there were Letts, all owners of rich farmsteads, descendants of exiles who'd ended up in the area after the suppression of various uprisings; but none of the locals knew

---

* The reference is to the illustrated local paper, *The Guide* (see pp. 32-33).

this fellow, he'd only just escaped from Finland, and could tell an excited audience about what he'd seen there with his only eye (as was the case with the deceased Peresheikin)—the second one, knocked out by his torturers, was covered with a dirty bandage. There, in Finland, he'd seen how hunger had mowed people down in thousands, how the victorious officers had drunk nonstop and raped in the cities; he'd seen ravines filled with the bodies of those shot, and women breast feeding the masters' pups. You can't value your life until you lose what we lost. Appreciate the freedom and power you have; even now you can live here, but imagine how it could be! They say that a carful of soap has just arrived, and they've increased the ration.

18

Did Simeon Kondratyevich himself experiment with the role of such a Finn? The provincial idea was becoming more specific and undergoing reinterpretation, assimilating new experiences. The ability to isolate oneself from connections in time and space, ways of making a comparison with others—all this had its own science, technology, and maybe even art, which seriously occupied Milashevich.

The science of happiness begins with a comparison.

Why should we envy them? They'll shoot this one before he reaches forty, that one they'll throw into penal servitude, and melancholy will chase that one from his house when he's already an old man.

Vas Vasich, now, has lived till the age of eighty, and not a single gray hair

For every place maybe its own genius, crowned with a local laurel, is enough. Let it not be a trait, but a profession or duty in the system of divided labor.

19

The whole time there remained the feeling that amidst the ironic smiles and grimaces Milashevich was hiding something that was far from a joking matter; after all, even in his conversation with Semeka he'd constantly been joking and pretending to be poorer than he really was, always playing a role—that's how a wily character in a fairy tale marks his neighbors' houses with fake crosses, so as to hide only one among them—his own—from threat. Perhaps he'd even given his stories to Vasilii Platonovich not just out of literary vanity, but to release into the world a minor double in his stead. There was one plot there about a provincial poet whom no one outside the town limits knew; to make up for it, however, he was really a symbol for the town, a mouthpiece for the soul—or maybe, on the contrary, his spiritual makeup and way of thinking told upon the system of life, the very character of its inhabitants, so that even standing in line for kerosene they argued with the same comic pathos; they even declared their love with lines from his poems. It was naive to seek in the personage of this fantasy the features of the author, a man who, at home in Stolbenets, was more worried about being recognized; one found nothing more here perhaps than a sad dream—but for all that, the heartfelt Russian conviction that literature is nevertheless not simply that; a word, no matter what you say, is capable of having an influence on one's life, of changing it and restructuring it, even if it's not written down, but is only pronounced. *I wrote this knowing that I would burn it, but for some reason I corrected a word, found something more precise. As if it makes any difference whether the paper burns with this word or another.* Did Milashevich have himself in mind? Did he earmark this speech for a character? There was something here redolent of a primitive feeling, of the magic of country wizards for whom in fact the district had at one time been notorious; there, in the countryside, even after the revolution they believed that you could bring about a wart and summon a fire with a word. These were places where they smeared sick children with dough and put them in the oven, "for the spirit"; where, to the agronomist's question as to why they didn't exterminate the gophers and mice, the peasants answered, after thinking a bit, "If there are a lot of mice it means they're for the harvest, and we save the gophers just in case: if there's a famine again, we'll feed off them, as we did in previous years of hunger." Milashevich's province lived at the intersection of urban literacy— by which those who'd left for Petersburg but returned could be distinguished—and pagan superstition; the stubborn philosopher continued to interpret what words meant for the provinces at a time when they were renewed daily together with the changing world. The names of the country and of streets were changed, people's last names were changed, and the church calendar was reinterpreted, and the stamps on candy *fantiki* increased: the caramel National became Popular, the simple Cockerel became Red Cockerel, and the name Hangover was covered up with the letters "Down with Drunken Stupor." Words proved not indifferent as regards taste, and they could change it. *A quarter of an oil cake, ground rye and grated potato—what does this sticky, heavy substance smell of? In a word, bread. It's not the brew that smells fragrant, but the word tea.* There existed little ewe words; one could reinterpret them, but also keep them; goat words got banished into outer darkness, somewhere there, whence hostile tribes of Curzons and Liberdans continued to threaten, where butchers and police, the death penalty and censorship remained.

A tax collector, a village constable—smells foul, doesn't it? So here: an inspector of finances, a policeman.

an official is a coworker

a jail is an arrhouse*

to change is to kill

disease no. 5 is typhus

hospital of the former Lord's Cross, now of the Red Cross

"So that means according to your system calico is now 66 kopeks an arshin?"

"Not an arshin but a meter—how many times do I have to tell you?"

"Fine. Go ahead and call an arshin "Fekla," then you can charge a ruble for it."

It used to be that you'd write: a man in a three-ruble cap, and it

---

* acronym for "house of arrest"

was clear what class he was, whether he was rich, what kind of taste he had. And here you borrow ten thousand—and in a week, if you please, give back a million.

A new faith begins with new words.

20

The words fanned one's head with an insensitive breeze, entered the body, and changed cells in the brain—the provincial thinker listened carefully to their effect. Words gave birth to elemental calamities, life was under the spell of words. With them, for example, one could completely alter the past—that which, it had seemed, power had been given to God alone to do, we do every day, changing the complexion of remembrance or transferring more of the negative things to the past, so as to better appreciate the present. Visions of the future blossomed in words. Provincial soil is nourishing for utopia—Milashevich already knew that. We produce dreamers who come with eyes irritated to the point of redness, with pupils fixed in the distance, it's our visions that roam over the country and the world, like troubled dreams. Others aren't in the mood for that; they're always busy with matters at hand. We think up for them how to surround the world with a huge magnet, so as to direct the clouds, ensuring forever the weather and the harvest; how to smooth out the surface of the earth, flattening the mountains and filling in the swamps; and how to cover the surface of the universe's waters with rafts and to found on them a convenient system of farming; we're the ones who envision light, happy creatures flying above the flowers. *The steamy earth flows with milky juice. Palms shrunk for convenient use grow in even cabbage rows.* But the main thing is that we, as distinct from others, don't stop at powerless visions, but rush to incarnate them without delay. And if people say to us that to do that we need to change human nature itself—well, so what?—someone in our midst is even ready to think of that. New people will appear earlier among us—one has to look around more attentively. We live crowded so close together that you don't have to look around long. After all, we still don't know how new universal waves affect us; maybe they're already equalizing everyone bit by bit, like a pebble on the shore, and are making us permeable to each other, saving us from loneliness; maybe this is no longer simply about the future—we, we have the shoots of all of future civilization breaking through the eggshell.

We are to Moscow what Jerusalem is to Rome.

Ten of those provinces could fit into any block of theirs. But in that closeness they stifle one another and lose a confident idea.

the waves are yours, the manure is ours

Since time immemorial we strived to fulfill a maximum role in the world. Maybe to fulfill the words about a time that will never be.

All roads lead to us.

Paris—is it far from us? Three thousand miles? My God, what a province!

VIII. THE VEGETARIAN

ON FATE

It's like God within. And chance comes from without.

In olden times they called him an angel. Maybe he didn't fly to you, but it was no accident that he touched you with his wing.

Life takes shape at the intersections.

1

On superstitions. "Cuckoo, cuckoo, how much longer shall I live?"—and we listen like idiots in the local forest, counting off our years without noticing the choir of those like us scattered behind the trees. A collective count. What, will a bomb fall on everyone at one and the same time? Not that you even believe in omens, but you guess the number of the bus ticket—nevertheless there's something in a number, a Pythagorean sense of the world order, maybe even of a law according to which any moment your well-earned good luck will finally be realized. If it won't be realized—well, you knew beforehand that it was all nonsense. Or let's say you're walking around Moscow, along an asphalt street where there aren't any trees or grass, and suddenly right in front of you on the sidewalk is a live chicken. Really and truly! No one knows where it came from, no one knows where it's rushing—lost, speckled, fat, shrewd, its head twitching, its eyes wild. A phenomenon of life. An unexplained *fantik*. But what if there's a specific reason behind it? What if it means something?... Oh, Lord, Lord! It was already time for Anton Andreyevich to leave the capital, his meager Moscow days were running out, he hadn't even gotten around to visiting the stores; instead of that he'd spent all of his free hours wandering among the crowds in the comic hope of outwitting the theory of probability, of meeting just like that, right on the corner. Although why was he convinced that *she* was here at all? An attempt to return to a dream will always result in ridicule, in overshooting or falling short. But, after all, it does happen: you desperately need a coin for a phone call, you look for it under people's feet, and if your desire turns out to be impassioned and patient enough, then something will shine in the dirt. Perhaps the passion of desire is a material energy, capable of moving something in the world in some way unknown to us? And then there's still the chicken. And the doctoral candidate unobtrusively squeezed three fingers on his right hand—like the three-fingered Christian sign, children's home magic, a shameful weakness. Then he hesitated, remembering how he'd trembled upon hearing his name. From the other side of the intersection, Associate Professor Nikolskii, his former official dissertation opponent, was looking at him through his thick square glasses.

"Well, Anton, who says there aren't any forces that direct us? I was just thinking about you: we really should see each other. A conference is about to take place and there's a possibility of inviting you. But the main thing is that yesterday for some reason I recalled Milashevich: well, with whom but Anton, I thought..."

2

It had happened. Lizavin had only a few acquaintances in Moscow, yet amidst a crowd of millions fate had slipped him precisely the person whom he'd not dreamed of seeing at all. In mockery, to bring him to his senses. Everyone wants something, but it's not to be had. He certainly didn't want to discuss his affairs with a paradoxical wiseguy who valued the study of literature more than literature itself, and people less than knowledge about them. To Anton's surprise, the associate professor didn't start asking him about anything; he expressed his knowledgeability with a single strange phrase: "I heard, I heard. Got a yen for genius, right?"—but didn't insist on an answer. He knew the answers himself. Oh, Associate Professor Nikolskii was a smart one, all right, although he loved to make himself out to be a man who always reduced the complexity of life to deliberately simplified formulas. He called the flings and impulses of youth "hormonal reconstruction," just as to an anatomist the breast is a "lacteal gland." "What, no woman for a while, I bet?"—he diagnosed Lizavin's troubled frame of mind. "Ideal visions and thoughts have gotten going, right? That's all just the sperm not going where it should. I don't mean anything bad by that, not at all. Sometimes elevated inspiration gets born this way." Of course, he was showing off a bit with these daring expressions, but actually, regarding women, damn it, he'd hit the nail on the head, and Anton really was experiencing the inspiration of different ideas then. And the main thing was that behind it all one sensed the unspoken words: I'm joking, but I seriously do know something about myself, only I won't give it away just like that. He was always too sober, and being, like Milashevich, a vegetarian, he could drink without getting drunk. No, this associate professor was really clever, but how naked a person could feel when confronting his mind! Behind everything, mechanisms opened up for which he could find a name and from which emerged any movement of the soul, any human type, an explanation of heaven and hell, religion and love. The sharp scalpel removed the covers; the timid fog that had hidden so much of Milashevich faded; male and female animals implemented the program implanted in them for the preservation of the species and the propagation of life, one by one and in the system of interconnections out of which cultures, and wars, and the mysterious impulses of peoples were born. Literature was interesting because it supplied graphic, in part lab-experiment, models for analysis, structural comparisons and mythological correspondences. The assistant professor was wearing a gray peaked cap, just like the one Lizavin had. For some reason, on first glance one noticed the rumpled, untidy, sweaty hair under this cap. His face in the light of dusk seemed flaccid; on his mealy cheeks were warty little islands of white bristle that he'd missed when shaving. But when he took his cap off in the hall, under the lamp shone a completely shaven man's skull. And although his face remained mealy nonetheless, the impression of flaccidity and even of spotty shaving almost disappeared, and the two or three light protuberances the color of skin really weren't worth considering warts.

3

After two divorces Nikolskii had developed a handy philosophy of day-to-day existence, the essence of which was quite fully contained in the maxim "A woman shouldn't live in." These non-live-in women usually were recruited from among graduate students, and sometimes students, too, which time and again gave rise to scandals of various magnitude and even official trouble; the cold-blooded and experienced associate professor, however, knew how to manage such things. The woman who opened the door to them this time was introduced as Larisa. Anton wouldn't have called her a beauty at all; but the main thing was that there was also a little boy, seven years of age, and in his presence the associate professor lost his self-assurance so strangely that it encouraged the absurd thought of the sort "he's got caught" or "he's come a cropper." Or, maybe, "he's met his match this time." They sat at the table, and the boy acted spoiled, didn't want to eat his soup.

"He's not eating." A nod in the associate professor's direction allowed him not to use his name or to reveal their relationship.

"I'm not eating because it's got meat in it," Nikolskii tried to explain. "That's different."

"Why different?"

"Because I don't eat meat at all."

"Why not?"

"Now is not the time to explain," the associate professor started to get a bit irritated, at the same time trying to preserve a tone of condescending humor. "I, how can I put it...I don't eat anything living."

"Meat's dead."

"It once was a cow."

"Chicken," corrected the woman.

"Cow or chicken—I didn't look." Nikolskii clearly didn't want to get drawn into primitive explanations. "The important thing is that it ran and breathed. In short, eat, listen to your mom."

The boy thought for a little while and thoughtfully took a sip from his spoon. But no more than that.

"But a potato's alive, too," he said. "And you eat that."

"What does 'alive' mean? It can't feel..."

"And it can't run away from you."

Lizavin barely masked his inappropriate burst of laughter with the cough of a person choking and, so as to silence suspicion, hurried to intercept the conversation:

"Do you know that there are ancient notions—Milashevich, apparently, was interested in them—that a plant in fact is able to feel, say, pain. And even a threat. I read here in the library about a supposedly actual incident when a flower remembered a person who'd hurt it. When it heard his steps..."

"Ahem," the associate professor uttered vaguely. His tone didn't express particular gratitude for the interruption, sooner the opposite. Again Lizavin had to smoothe something over.

"You know, I read a lot of interesting things this time. In South America they say there are plants that shoot."

"That shoot?" The boy became interested.

"Yes. With the seeds of ripened fruit. And they really hit hard."

"Can they kill people?"

"Well...if they hit the temple..." Anton didn't want to disappoint him, but for some reason he was faltering. Nikolskii was gloomily tapping on the tablecloth with his white nails. "But, anyway," Lizavin continued, finally remembering something more suitable, especially for Nikolskii, "Milashevich has some amusing stories about vegetarianism. For example, a short biography of a piglet by the name of Flick—didn't I show it to you?—from his early journal writings. Scenes from a piglet's childhood, innocent joys, playing in the grass, growing up—right up to his last bewildered glance at the beautiful blue heavens. Because this whole biography with the likable portrait of Flick was written, as it turns out, on a ham label..."

"Mmm, yes." Nikolskii didn't appreciate the support, and the boy turned away from the bowl altogether and seemed to grow pale. "What am I doing?" Lizavin suddenly thought. "And why do I always butt in to settle other people's relationships?..." Here Larisa brought in a pot of something like small meatballs or steamed cutlets, and it was unpleasant to look at them—to hell with it, he'd lost his appetite. Suddenly the doctoral candidate saw Nikolskii catch a piece with his fork and pop it into his mouth.

"He's watching," the associate professor remarked, having noticed Anton's glance, nudging the woman's elbow. "He thinks it's meat. You think it's meat, eh?"

"Well, isn't it?" Anton didn't start to deny it, although he didn't find it pleasant to end up looking idiotic once again.

"There's not a gram of meat in this! Imagine!" the host livened up. (Well, thank God, at least he's perked up.)

"It can't be!" Lizavin tried some in slightly exaggerated bewilderment.

"It's called fake rabbit," the woman smiled modestly. Nikolskii's upper lip curled up tensely, revealing two large white incisors.

"Personal recipe. She knows how! Especially for dear guests."

"Vadim, you know very well I wasn't expecting guests." For some reason she turned pale.

There you go, they use the formal "you." Anton pricked up his ears.

"You mean to say you're trying hard just for me?" Nikolskii bared his incisors even higher.

"You know very well, Vadim, that everything I do is for you."

"Oh, yes! I know even more than you'd like me to."

No, something's not right here. Lizavin got more and more frightened; he even mechanically clinked glasses with Nikolskii and downed a glass of fruit liqueur that he'd only just refused. Some sort of solidarity was needed again that he couldn't avoid. But ultimately he should have left, waiting for an appropriate moment after he'd enjoyed the hospitality. Fortunately, the boy wanted to go to sleep, and Larisa took him away to another room.

"And we'll go to the study," announced the host, getting up.

4

The associate professor's apartment had two rooms, and what he called a study was a corner by a large desk, partitioned by a bookcase. Once the overhead light was extinguished, one could feel rather isolated here. On the wall in a gilded frame hung a color reproduction: a portrait of a short-nosed man in a uniform with white close-fitting riding breeches, in the style of the century before last, with an off-center lock on his forehead and the mouth of a man who loves himself. A small decanter, bread, and raw vegetables had migrated to the study.

"Let's have a bit," said the associate professor. "Just a wee bit, heh? This is a special fruit liqueur, it's good for you. You started saying something about Simeon Kondratyevich? I've been looking over your little article; you express an interesting thought there in passing. That the very couplings of Milashevich's images can tell us more about his ideas then direct statements. That's more interesting than you yourself think. In general, bravo! Well, what are we waiting for? ...Here's to you!"

Alas, once again we have to admit that Anton Andreyevich didn't stand firm, but somehow we don't have the will to reproach him for his weakness. A person capable of seriously talking about Milashevich—and listening—was so rare that at times it really oppressed Lizavin, like loneliness. Fired by the praise, even if it wasn't completely comprehensible, he began to tell Nikolskii in brief and, where possible, with humor, about his latest conclusions and findings, about his preliminary hypotheses, about the elder Makarii, about Semeka's testimony—but for some reason he didn't mention the main thing, the new encounter with Aleksandra Flegontovna, as if there were something personal here, even intimate, which he didn't want to give away unnecessarily to the associate professor.

"Remarkable!" Nikolskii laughed at the joke about manure. "Both the radio and that elder, too. Oh, that Simeon Kondratyevich knew how to keep people guessing! And you can't even say that he did it on purpose: maybe it's simply his way of thinking, living, and explaining himself. Does it mean that suffering makes a plant like an animal, and an animal like a person? Stop the suffering and you'll be blessed?"

"Yes. But it turns out to mean—stop the thought. It turns out mankind ultimately owes its development to suffering."

"Bravo!" It wasn't clear whom the associate professor was praising. "I'm more and more convinced...I didn't even expect it from you."

"Why didn't you expect it?" Anton realized that he was being praised further, but again it was unclear for what, and it was even a bit insulting.

"Come, come!" said Nikolskii. "No, I've always seen something in you. But all the same...I remember at one time I found it rather amusing to be your opponent. You commented on this provincial philosophy in such an intimate way, so seriously...Don't be offended. And let's have one more. It won't hurt us, I assure you. ("Us...," nevertheless. As if this could be flattering.) Yes, Simeon Kondratyevich isn't simple, that's obvious. I hope you won't try convincing me of the opposite. He gives something to each of us according to ability. And, most important, according to need. Whatever you want, whatever you're ready to understand, you'll be satisfied with it. It's funny to complain about why contemporaries don't understand a genius. He outstripped them. Listening to you, I'm prepared to believe that until a certain time he perhaps didn't even want to be understood."

"Really?" Anton Andreyevich mumbled vaguely. Although with a touch of irony, too. He somehow still couldn't get oriented: Was it a hint that there was something he couldn't understand, or the other way around? And those words about genius...Milashevich used to poke fun precisely at geniuses; he contrasted himself and his ideas with them, even with an element of challenge. But for now he didn't start to dispute anything; there was something pleasant in this elevation of Simeon Kondratyevich. "What do you mean?"

"The formulation of an idea. As you recall, the beginning of the century had a nostalgia for the spirit of tragedy. Lofty minds were troubled by whether the idea of contentment, bourgeois banality, mediocrity, and philistinism was triumphing in the world. They, the best minds, made too much of the idea, as if of a discovery, that happiness certainly couldn't be the goal of mankind. A certain degree of contentment, of course, is desirable; without it the spirit would wither—this, as the saying goes, is the condition of a developed life. But only the condition. The goal is something higher. Truth or beauty. Or goodness. And happiness can only accompany this higher aspiration. But not necessarily and not for long. Happiness isn't the issue. God forbid that someday a happy ideal be realized—Dostoyevski refuted it in advance. Nietzsche spat at it in disgust. (And in their souls they suspected and hoped that it was impossible.) Better to be a dissatisfied Socrates than a satisfied pig. Virtue is akin to banality; it reduces the appetite, assumes limits to striving and passions for the sake of stability and peace. I believe I'm quoting, only I don't remember whom. It's interesting that precisely our idealists were particularly horrified at the triumph of the Western petty bourgeoisie after each of their routine revolutions. Commonplace happiness leads to the deterioration of humankind, the peaceful provision of public services and amenities heralds the fall of a people, a country, and finally humanity. What's sacrificed again? Freedom. Striving for freedom, like striving for truth and perfection, is inevitably tragic, just as inevitable death is tragic. But with this tragic element are connected all of the finest things in life, raising us above the mediocre and the banal. Without it there will be no progress, only stagnation; life will begin to decay. Well, and so on. It's a vicious circle. All literature is about this; you yourself know that."

"Let's say it's so," said the doctoral candidate. "But Milashevich made no claims to a general solution with his philosophy."

"What do you mean, made no claims?" Nikolskii was amazed. "Really, Anton, what are you saying? Of course, I don't know Milashevich the way you do, but I'm judging by your presentation, by your work. You yourself show what all of it leads to. As if you don't want to get out of your role. I think he understood everything."

"So you mean..." Lizavin became confused. (Was it irony? He didn't get it.)

"There's an old problem in Western religions," the associate professor didn't bother waiting for the formulation that got bogged down, "of whether to consider the mind and experience the source of truth. Or, on the contrary, did the Fall of mankind, which had pursued knowledge, sooner close the source of authentic truth off to us? If so, then refusing such a pursuit will lead people to atonement, free them from the horrors of life. What, in my view, does Milashevich do? If you really think about it, he leaves the ambiguous understanding of truth to those who for some reason can't live without it, but for the mass of others he declares it, in essence, not necessary. By no means everyone has to know it, and the main thing is that not everyone wants to. To every person is given the truth that he or she is capable of enduring."

"Yes, yes . . . it's amazing . . . as a matter of fact, these past few days I've had occasion to encounter almost word for word . . ." Lizavin mumbled, but immediately remembered not to say anything unnecessary. "But you yourself said just now that it's not so easy. It depends on the person . . . always to settle oneself in between incompatibilities. One of my acquaintances, you know, developed a strange allergy . . ."

"You're not talking about Sivers?"

"But you . . . How did you know?" Anton Andreyevich was almost frightened. It wasn't even clear of what: the coincidence of acquaintances, Maksim's unexpected fame? Or the mysterious perspicacity of this phantom with a dimly shining skull and mealy face? However, his fear was probably foolish; Muscovites have their own relationships. In the meantime he'd completely forgotten his recent intention to leave, as he'd also forgotten his annoyance at the senseless meeting.

"Were you by any chance at his birthday?" Oh, that squinting gaze, as if red eyed, from behind the thick square glasses spoke less of a mysterious perspicacity than of a knowledgeability that was no less mysterious, however. The associate professor enjoyed his guest's confusion for a while. "What do you need this company for, Anton? It's not for you. They're not serious people. They're doomed. But it's not even a question of a conflict with power. They only think that the flaws or mistakes of power don't suit them; in actuality they don't accept its essence and don't understand it. For them this concept is identified with people who sit in offices. They enter politics, while essentially having an aversion to it. And perhaps those who sit in offices themselves can't realize what forces move them. But this Milashevich, I think, did realize."

"Well, I don't know," Anton finally attempted to express his vague sense of resistance (with which was mixed, weakening it, an also vague but suspicious satisfaction). "Power and politics weren't subjects, I think, that interested Simeon Kondratyevich. True, his *fantiki* include several strange exclamations about the inscrutability of some forces . . ."

"You keep on digging, rummaging around. I don't mean the direct exclamations, but the combinations, as you yourself once expressed it, of images. I'm certain he thought about this more than it seems.

After all, what's the ideal goal of any power? To benefit the masses, precisely the fundamental mass of the population. The body, the stomach, the soul, and the brains. To guarantee safety, stability, and contentment. But great minds by definition can't be satisfied anyway. Life is always imperfect. For them. That's also understandable. Inequality, stupidity, deceit, and hierarchy have existed from the beginning of time, are natural and inevitable. Despise them, struggle, knock your brains out. I, by the way, don't dispute whether anyone's right. The danger of life's stagnation and rotting on all levels is also not the invention of great minds. It's existed eternally, and mechanisms admitting passions and blood have always sprung up. Foreign nations drew close, interests and groups clashed, free will intensified into resistance and superiority, passionate leaders emerged, and commanders and ideologues, wars and revolutions began—all for a purpose, all so that the human race wouldn't decline. But let's agree, pleasure is doubtful. And the main thing is that the further we get, the more doubtful it is. I think that Milashevich sensed earlier and better than many did the proximity of those times when these former, elemental mechanisms would become obsolete. They'd become exhausted. In this sense our civilization really sensed the dead end of former, that is historical, development. It looks as if the time is really approaching for organizing people once and for all. Without shocks, crises, wars, commanders, or heroes. Incidentally, that's the dream and guiding idea of any revolution. And the partly Russian, Christian dream of the end of history. But here's what Milashevich took into account: that the rightness of great minds shouldn't be applied to humanity. They mustn't proceed from the assumption that the mass of people yearns for the same thing they do. As if to say, just let humanity be imbued with their lofty ideas, and a likeness will shine forth there. The central question of any utopia is: Whom is it for? For people like me, a high-minded restless author? Or for others, not only unlike me, but not even seeing a special joy in such a likeness? Milashevich draws a conclusion: universal happiness is not only impossible, but it's also unnecessary and dangerous. It's possible that for the basic majority happiness is still necessary. And what you call the provincial idea might come in handy for it."

"Our conversation is turning out paradoxical," the doctoral candidate suddenly burst out laughing. "You're giving back to me familiar thoughts, practically in my own words. And I still don't understand what's causing me to resist."

"Maybe you simply haven't got it clear yet to whom you should belong, to the majority or the minority. Here I mean not the infantile minority, like Sivers and others, but the mature, conscious, if you please, secret minority, without which the happy stability of the majority is impossible."

"That is," Anton interjected, finally bringing together the frayed ends of a thought, "you mean that Milashevich conceived of himself as belonging to the majority?"

"With a mind like his? Just think. After all, just to conceive of a thought as suffering he needed a mind that took this torture upon itself. He, perhaps, is a tragic figure. And this means that he understood that Makarii and all the rest—as the saying goes, that was for the poor."

"And is the provincial idea for the poor?" reasoned Anton.

"Does the word disturb you? If you say for the fortunate, that'll be even more true. Others could never break through to this. A developed human being has to suffer, suffer. And with new details, using new historical material, they explained and proved why final universal happiness is nevertheless impossible. And what is charming in your Milashevich is this provincial imperturbability. For you, maybe, it's not possible, but we'll keep looking. Laugh if you like. What's true is that which is conducive to a happy state, personal and communal. You say that society's happiness can't be maintained for long on its own? That means that someone must direct it, constantly renew it, take upon himself responsibility for the idea, the movement for the sake of health. For freedom, by the way. That's to make sure that a happy person nevertheless considers himself free without realizing how predestined and directed all his choices were, all his tastes and movements. Here we also need the intervention of an artist, in the broad sense of a creator, that is, a helper and even a rival of the Divine Creator..."

"Wait a minute, where are you getting all this from? Milashevich says nothing of the kind."

"No, that means we haven't found it yet." Anton's confusion clearly gave Nikolskii pleasure. "Keep digging; consistency of thought should lead to this. I'm not talking about technology. Tsiolkovskii also provided an idea, an image, and wrote all sorts of rubbish in passing. But now other people are making rockets."

"But he doesn't have such images."

"I don't know. To me he himself is an image, if you will. I don't insist, however. Once again I repeat: we're not talking about truth. Truth can have value only for an individual personality. Someone can even be ready to die for its sake. It's happened. But the aggregate of people submit to laws of survival, of self-assertion. And for this lies may be necessary, and madness, forked mechanisms of influence— maybe even deliberate provocation. Doesn't it seem to you that Milashevich knew this well, too? What an experimenter! Keep on digging, keep on; I'm interested to see what you'll find in the stuff about him. Let's imagine that one can build happiness from a design, all you need do is clarify the rules. That's the job of professionals, of superior, richly informed, unsentimental ones."

"You're making him start to look like a sort of... superman," the doctoral candidate smiled wryly.

"It was called superhuman then," Nikolskii answered imperturbably and as if slightly amused. His face changed suddenly; he assumed a smile. "Shhh. To your health."

5

The overhead light came on. Larisa came in to clear away the dishes left on the table. From behind the cupboard, reclining in the armchair, glass in hand, Nikolskii followed her movements with a mask-like gaze. *Teeth bared in a grin that's not fully conscious*, Lizavin recalled, and he thought that this probably referred to just such a smile. At one time it must have meant, say: I show my teeth like a weapon laid down on the table, as a sign of trust and friendship. I wanted to note down some word on paper, so as not to forget it, thought Anton. The associate professor's shaven skull reflected the blue and red lights of an advertisement outside; tiny upturned people stirred in his glasses.

"Be careful around her," he suddenly leaned forward confidentially when the woman left, turning off the light. "I see through her, and she senses it."

"Careful?" Lizavin involuntarily withdrew. He noticed that Nikolskii had started to sweat profusely. The breath from his mouth was unpleasant. "In what sense? After all, I have nothing to worry about."

"Who knows," smiled the associate professor, straightening up. "Who knows from what angle they're looking at us. Who needs us. It hasn't reached us yet...You've got blue eyes. Naive healthy blood. That's good. That'll come in handy. Maybe we didn't meet today for nothing. We'll see...And little lights have already appeared in your eyes." He suddenly looked at Anton, pensively and sadly. "It would be pointless for you, eh? But you know they don't always ask. He'll hurt you—and just try to shout that it's a mistake. You don't understand what's happened to you, eh?" he unexpectedly switched to the informal "you." He took some greens from the plate and started to chew.

A person who's gotten high involuntarily begins to see his companion as being in the same state. Lizavin didn't immediately realize that the associate professor was indeed high.

"Hmm, hmm...Still, aren't you really attributing too much to Simeon Kondratyevich?" Anton carefully returned to the conversation (meanwhile feeling around in his pocket for a pencil and paper so as to jot down a word, without looking). "I doubt that he himself made such claims."

"Maybe he didn't," Nikolskii agreed with unexpected ease; he kept chewing on the stalk of the greens, pensively and almost distractedly. "Things happen without one's being aware of them. To prophets and madmen. But there's a reason that I sense something in him. I'm a vegetarian myself."

"Well, I don't completely understand vegetarianism as a whole." Lizavin was prepared not to make his embarrassed confusion more precise. "I'm not discussing the topic, don't think that, but it seems to me that something in his specific case doesn't quite tally—with his views on plants and with his imaginative capabilities. If you look at grass as a living creature capable of suffering, how can you eat it? And what can you live on in general? Do you happen to remember how in one place he describes a little pig on a dish: as the pale corpse of a child with squinting eyes, its little eyelashes stuck together? It even had an effect on me."

"Vegetarianism is different for different people." Nikolskii smiled, selected another stalk from the plate and, before putting it into his mouth, looked at it with a smile that Lizavin couldn't understand. "Just like Christianity. All sorts have taken it up! You can see it as a diet, a way to health, to pacifying animal instincts and passions. It's a very useful outlook. To modify the nature of man, who was created a consumer of flesh. To weaken his aggressiveness, his will to rivalry and power. To promote peace of mind. For the poor. Maybe it'll even come true soon. There's already not enough meat for everyone, after all."

"Ha, ha, ha," the doctoral candidate caught the topical joke. His thoughts nevertheless were in a muddle, in addition to his feeling once again as if he was now about to grasp something.

"But that's when it will also become clear that for others—for a few—the ability to restrain oneself is connected with sobriety, strength, and mental intrepidness. You call this imagination, but it's more correct to speak about the mind's readiness not to fear and not to mollify any conclusions, not to protect oneself from anything with soothing words. Soothing, calming words are for the poor. For those with weak nerves. It's also a method and principle of selection and distinction."

"I don't understand a thing," Anton admitted quite frankly.

"And there's no need. You'll understand when you need to." The associate professor again switched to the informal "you." He leaned back in the armchair. A little Napoleon in white breeches jutted out from the mirrorlike skull. "Don't listen . . . don't listen to me now," he said, suddenly leaning forward again, dousing Lizavin with the smell of rotten innards. "And forget what you've heard. I'm not myself. Never happened before. You've drunk with me, you tell me: Did anything like this ever happen with me before? She mixed some meat in that rabbit, I'm sure of it. Wants to tie me up. To sap my strength, as

Judith did Holofernes.* That's the kind they always send."

"Who?" Frightened now, Anton moved away from the malodorous mumbling; there was something in it that wasn't simply from drunkenness.

"Oh, there's someone! But right now, not a word about it...Don't let it show. It'll be clear later. You can bet they already have an eye on you—you know Milashevich. Keep on confusing them. I'll explain later. I'll explain everything. What witches they can be. Tits out to here. Shhh..."

6

Larisa returned. She turned on the light and, as on a lighted stage, sat in the armchair in the far corner, with an expression of complete indifference turned to the audience, but so that they still could see her. They didn't have to wait for the beginning long. Nikolskii got up, staggering, and left the study, on the way turning intimately to Lizavin as if inviting him to appreciate the show.

"I don't feel well, somehow, hmmm?" he touched the woman under her chin with his finger. She put up with it, like an inanimate doll, even allowing him to turn her head. Oh, something bad, unnatural, and sinister lurked behind the games of this pair. One of them is crazy, Anton thought with growing fear. Yes, definitely, Nikolskii hadn't simply suddenly got drunk. He's crazy—why didn't I realize that right away? "You didn't by any chance slip something into your rabbit? A very fake rabbit? Let's say...uh...a pale sheldrake?" For a split second the associate professor showed the audience two beaver incisors. He leaned down and from behind grabbed the woman under her breasts with his right hand. She was completely pale, but she responded quite sensibly:

"What point would there be in my poisoning you, Vadim? I need you alive." (No, of the two of them she's probably the normal one.)

"Ah, alive?"

"Yes, alive."

---

* HOLOFERNES The general of Nebuchadnezzar's Assyrian army, killed by Judith to save her people.

"Ordered to take me alive?"

"Get a hold of yourself, Vadim."

"Talk to me like that and I'll kick you."

"I'll be going now," the doctoral candidate blurted out, leaping to his feet.

"I'll kick you!" the associate professor repeated with a triumphant chuckle and winked at Lizavin, who'd already begun to flee.

"Just try," said the woman, still in the room, without paying any attention to the departing guest. He was already rummaging about in the hall, unable to find his coat. (No, she's crazy too. They're both psycho.) Nikolskii finally came out to see him off.

"Get it? Did you get everything? Not a word. Not to a soul. Because the whole thing smells of something deadly. Remember my words in the presence of witnesses."

"Okay, okay... lay off." The doctoral candidate tried to adopt the same familiarity. That's how people in their own way try to calm down excited drunks. He hurriedly pulled his cap over his eyes; his head was lost in it. Damn it, it proved to be Nikolskii's. They were totally alike. But what a head, nonetheless! What a skull! And what kind of brain must be hidden in a skull like that?

7

Well, let them all go to hell, those crazy psychos, thought Anton as he strode down the street and gradually started to calm down; he'd already sobered up in the elevator. What had he been spouting about poor Simeon Kondratyevich over there? As if even he were crazy. But maybe he was. I'm the only one who's normal. Or everyone's normal in his own way, only he shouldn't have contact with this Larisa—else he changes. How could she have yoked him? It was a mystery, an impenetrable mystery. What do we know about any person, even someone comparatively close? He opens up to us, like a little window, during the brief moments of a meeting, a conversation, a contact. And what's he like on other days, other nights, with other people, on his own, throughout the span of his life? We have access only to the *fantiki*; the rest you have to come up with yourself. We don't even know ourselves. I probably went too far from the unexpectedness of it.

His health simply isn't what it used to be; he drank too much and didn't even realize it himself. Strange as it sounds, it was precisely in this form: sickly, sweaty, vulnerable, and with a bad smell emanating from his mouth, that Nikolskii seemed humanly a bit more understandable to Anton Andreyevich. A rational irrationalist, he could know anything about love, passions, suffering, death, even about God, without being in direct touch with anything himself, removed from it all, dispassionate. But everyone has some rudimentary capabilities and feelings—even the person who calls love something completely different is involved in it. Until now, for Nikolskii understanding compensated for other things. His mind helped him to attach an artificial limb to the stump of a limb, a limb whose electrical impulse sufficed for it to function as if it were alive, to the point of deception or self-deception in a world where neither love nor God was necessary—everything was simpler and much more interesting there. But for the stump to be trapped, for the artificial limb to really fall ill, in defiance of his understanding! . . . How even in Milashevich he contrived to see a superman-experimenter in his own vein (and, one wonders, what—or whom—is this experiment on? Does it follow, on the one hand, the development of an idea, or, on the other, real-life fates? *Why is it like this? I didn't want this!* Also a turn of thought). After all, he doesn't know about Shurochka, who was lost and found, about tenderness and pain, about life for her sake. Good thing I didn't say anything; he would have tried to distort this too, spoil it. No, he's not normal, the poor, crazy fellow, however enormous his head may be. Let anyone who wants to imagine himself a genius and lose his mind. You hold onto your own. By the way, I'd like to know how you yourself looked when you were wandering through the streets with that senseless three-fingered sign? Perhaps the powers of irony decided to give your brains a good shake for some reason, but you're just not ready yet for another meeting. Perhaps there are some things a normal person such as you isn't meant to understand. Oh yes, by the way, what did I jot down there in my pocket?

The lantern on its tall pole was burning dimly, pink like a bud. Lizavin stopped under it and took out the piece of paper. He found it with difficulty and started to make sense of the pencil scratchings:

"con...constructor"? He couldn't understand the word. And he didn't remember the sense of it. A rowdy group of friends passed by: two fellows neighing with laughter were pulling a woman under her arms, fanning out to the sides and then coming together, like an accordion, all of them of the same height, shortlegged, and all of their faces—vast, flat, crimson, with kopeklike noses and small eyes—so alike that it seemed an illusion. Only the woman had brows made up like half-moons and a painted mouth. "What ugly mugs!" Lizavin shook his head. He watched them as they went along and saw that after a few steps all three looked at him and started neighing with laughter again.

"What an ugly mug!" he heard the woman exclaim.

IX. THE LOST GARDEN, OR GOD'S CUNNING

1

Our flat mind and glance are only a simplified splinter of full-fledged divine curvature.

a samovar, the proprietor of non-Euclidean space

You can accept everything, accommodate everything: the sky, grass, flowerbed, and the radiating sun, a huge crooked dish on the five fingers of a hand, and somewhere there a tiny face, incapable even of blushing from the sweltering heat, the black blob of a jacket, a riding gig without wheels

with a rooster on the coachman's seat, the curved corner of a study, a clock face with a zodiac sign, but without hands, the buildings of a household yard amidst greenery, the remains of a mirror in a slanting frame, and on a stack of firewood a piece of its own image.

Above the flowerbed, just like a flower, opened the bell of a gramophone.

One had to have mental recall of almost the whole trunk, so as to suddenly recognize in this crooked samovarlike collection the objects from the barn book: the Flemish study, the clock from the Danzig secretaire, the carved mirror frame (still with the remains of glass), and in addition the Pathé gramophone from the same inventory list—everything had been placed in the midst of the green courtyard under the bright sky. What for? For removal? For packing? And a piece of carpet or oilcloth with a picture of a samovar was laid out on the log pile like a doormat that needed to dry... but why a piece?

MARK KHARITONOV

Lizavin supposed that the piece of paper containing the inventory list enumerated objects that had been kept at the Ganshin estate after the crushing defeat of 1917 or had been selected from around the villages by Milashevich for the museum. The estate was among the last to be destroyed (not until September), although it had been standing without owners or security: a lawsuit was still dragging on among the heirs, the last sentry crew had fled, each seizing as much as he could, and the absurd walls, which had collapsed even as they were being built, only teased with their defenselessness. But something seemed to keep the neighboring peasants at a distance; for a while they chopped the forest and wasted the meadow, which were closer, and grew inspired only after the Chechens from the detachment that the retired colonel Brykin got for his protection caught a Sareyevo shepherd who'd driven his cows into the Brykin meadow, carved the calves of his legs and released him, covered in blood, to crawl to the village. They didn't dare settle accounts with the colonel—but Ganshin's peasants did unburden themselves. The rout was disinterested in its violence: they trampled on porcelain vases, they seized the corners of the Italian linen curtains and tore them, they wrecked countless mirrors with their sticks, they threw candelabras, armchairs, and books into the pond, but when someone tried to shove a box with silver plating inside the front of his jacket, they broke his nose with that same box. Only later did they start coming to the estate on foot or with carts to get what they could; but now singly, surreptitiously, and as if ashamed of one another, they picked out the debris from the ground. For a long time afterward all over the surrounding villages children played with the hammers and keys of a broken grand piano, and in the huts and courtyards Milashevich found a cavalier's spur, a bedroom slipper without backing, old-fashioned crinoline that had been used as a chicken cage, and leather plates from fencing armor which had been converted into blinders for a horse that turned the wheel in a saltworks.

*a marble-white hand with a finger pointing up rose above the
dried heap*

a bony strip of landscape with a cherry tree in the withered grass

These probably were also estate impressions: a fragment of sculpture, the plate of a Japanese fan—by nature a scrap of paper seemed
adapted precisely for such descriptions. Life winked at the philosopher, suggested or prompted an idea, making the subject material
smaller; closely, with interest, he examined these pieces, scraps, fragments, and he described on the *fantiki* even separate splinters of mirrors with reflections lost in them. That same samovar flashed in one
of them, and also someone foreign in a jacket, with an imperial beard
and a mustache; another could never leave the gloomy corner of the
study (an armchair with gilded carnations of upholstery is seen); yet
another showed something like the edge of a painting canvas without
a frame...

Suddenly it occurred to Lizavin that the canvas also could exist cut
up. The name of the picture was *The Lost Garden*; Milashevich had
managed to collect three of its pieces, which had been fastened down
in huts as doormats. And in light of that, why couldn't he assume that
Simeon Kondratyevich, as was his habit, had also registered these on
paper, describing each one separately? One could even try to guess
what they were. The painting's title undoubtedly alluded to the garden
that, in Russian translation, had at one time been called paradise. All
the *fantiki* with trees, flowers, and fruits—all images of happy
utopias—might correspond to such a picture. *Palm trees shrunk for
convenient use grow in even cabbage rows. The steamy earth flows with
milky juice.* And maybe even this one, too—Anton Andreyevich tried
it out anew—*a horned head with human teeth.* Is that the tempter
peering out from behind a trunk? *Pale nostrils of a refined cut, the
sweat of sickly cold on transparent temples tinged with blue...* No, this
way one could be carried away unnecessarily. And here's a naked fat
man behind the samovar under the apple tree; a tea saucer with the
words "These things please me" around its rim could certainly be

from here. If Milashevich had set out to imagine paradise—what else did he need? He could have done even without a garden. A warm room, the stove crackling, a little flame flickering on a wick. *What have you been given such happiness for? It's senseless to ask. For the capacity for happiness.* Yes, the samovar most likely was from here— a piece of canvas or oilcloth, a scrap of the painting *The Lost Garden* that hadn't been collected in its entirety lay on the log pile in the courtyard of the former Ganshin estate, reflected in a real samovar. The more Lizavin fantasized on the topics suggested by this title, the more the picture seemed to him to be one of those oilcloths that the art patron Ganshin had acquired for his whimsical collection from the local painter—except, perhaps, that it was of special dimensions (if it could be cut even more). Angel Nikolayevich had ordered from Bosoi-Sverbeyev a subject of his own composition that was close to his heart and for him was somehow connected with the inevitability of the revolution. And if Iona painted the picture, it would have depicted light beings with children's faces—for him, the inhabitants of heaven could only be children, as they'd been created from the beginning, among flowers and resembling flowers, until, tasting the fruit, they unfortunately let themselves become subject to the passage of time. The same golden-haired cherub fit in here; Ganshin wanted to see him depicted and Iona's taste coincided with the predilections of his customer—ah, not in vain, not in vain did Angel Nikolayevich harbor a weakness for his homemade work.

3

Two years after the unexplained death of the manufacturer, *The Stolbenetsian* mentioned the name of the deceased once again in connection with the fire on his deserted estate. Arson was suspected; perhaps one of the embittered heirs deprived of his share had been mixed up in it. The case was being administered in the law chambers of the province. A journalist hiding behind the initials *N. K.* savored the piquant details: the widow of the deceased turned up, from whom, as it turns out, he hadn't been formally divorced, although he hadn't lived with her for so long that no one here knew about her; she'd been residing permanently in Nice, from where she hurried to the province especially to contest his will; in a secret part of the will there apparently figured a certain young man or boy whose name had not been subjected to publicity, and here the grandiloquent N. K., with a significant smile, had warned against the too-hasty conclusions of those who wanted to assume that Ganshin had a morganatic son. No, something else was meant. Through this ambiguous grin one could glimpse a hint at a sphere so alien and physically incomprehensible to Anton Andreyevich that only upon rereading Milashevich's whole Ganshin cycle anew did he notice and appreciate for the first time the strange absence of women at this hurt and tormented personage's side, and the fleeting single mention of the book in his hands, a luxurious edition of Plato's *Symposium* in French. It seems that Milashevich himself didn't understand something right away, otherwise he wouldn't have started an impromptu with the orphan picked up God knows where. That is, maybe not an orphan at all, and not chosen—someone turned up by chance who fit the topic of a half-joking conversation not yet put into play, but poor Angel suddenly took such a fancy to him, he so badly wanted to have at least some short-lived joy!—even if at the price of a temporary omission, even cunning...No, Milashevich, of course, didn't suspect where the joke got him, where it could lead—*the only unhappy possibility eluded my understanding. . .*—the same one, the very same...My God...And maybe even Ganshin himself for a time didn't realize the nature of his sudden attachment to the prodigal boy, a forbidden, impermissible tenderness; he didn't understand yet that it was precisely the children's faces that captivated him on the oilcloths of the Stolbenets painter—the unhealthy offshoot of a degenerating tree (the lapel of his jacket sprinkled with cocaine powder as if with dandruff), a person who tried to enclose with a wall the ark of a possible joy, knowing in advance that he wouldn't be able to stay there long.

4

hills and white valleys shine there, rivers from the pure breath of clouds stir in the gorges

The air shines, made entirely from a substance that traces the slanting rays of the sun in a foggy forest.

the tinkle of a spoon against a glass

a fly in the jam

No one chased us; we ran by ourselves, tormented by dry mouths

Not for nothing had the apple been hung in full view. Cleverness, a trap staged in advance according to roles.

A plan needs someone to support it all the time, to move it along, without letting it cool and drudge on.

there's a name for soreness of the mouth: boredom

Here's what Angel Ganshin knew about himself, thoughts he perhaps tried to develop in the treatise that didn't reach us. What did his overly compassionate friend, the unreliable philosopher, want to substitute for this truth? Whom did he hope to refute? And how? With advice to isolate a piece of life, to cut himself off from comparisons and connections, from the guilt of his ancestors, from original sin?

To stay there, to stay and not want anything else. That's the pinnacle; that's bliss.

"I'd be glad to, I'd like to, but I can't."
"Then go. Do as you want."
"Can I really?"
It's so easy. Like leaving from a dream.
Hide in silence, not even letting the clocks tick. You can't run forever

just a little, more just a bit …

5

It didn't work out, something always didn't work out. The walls that had just been built collapsed into holes, passages, cavities, torn open by someone before us, the plans had been lost—it's funny, actually, to get to the original sources of what's happened along a chain of reasons. It's senseless and impossible. *The conception was perfect, but the elements interfered, and the material undermined it; it was joined imprecisely. It cracked on the third tier. The eternal story.* What's this about? About the construction of an ancient tower? About a catastrophe in Moscow? About chance, which wasn't possible to take into account? Which inexorably invades the best conception, turning it into mockery and disaster? The imprecision of the joints. Yet it already seemed that Angel had revived slightly, had cheered up; it seemed that it could even work out all right, to everyone's joy—if only it weren't for an ill-fated dirty trick, a freak of nature. Suddenly it became unambiguously clear. To the embarrassment and confusion of both, it seems. In his confusion, in his exaggerated embarrassment, it seems, Milashevich was too hasty in taking away from the estate the boy who'd come from God knows where—he suddenly saw himself in a dubious role. It's difficult to say exactly what happened there. Maybe there was something offensive in this haste. But perhaps it wasn't even a case of this particular instance; perhaps this was only the last occasion, the last disappointment, exacerbated by shame or deceit or ambiguity, and is it really that important what chance occurrence ultimately determined the bullet, having replaced it, as if for laughter, with another weapon?

6

It didn't work out. Indeed, in the *fantiki* one could see not just philosophical samples; they were themselves a philosophy, only not the kind that the writer, possibly, was thinking of when he invoked and tried to reduce the substance of life. We've already forgotten what was written on the sheets of paper thrown into the little trunk, what was conceived, what was meant—the words moved by themselves, took shape by themselves; white rootlets got enmeshed beneath the earth; the connections changed the meaning, they as if renewed it and created it anew: so a flower joins in different ways with a spring meadow and with a chink in a window smeared with gray paint, so music changes its sound, joining with different words, so people change, joining with a crowd or in intimate couplehood. *She joined her life with his. Exactly like that.* Bodies adapted to each other with every curve and exchanged juices:

> *man and woman*
> *name and person*
> *candy and* fantik
> *voice and echo*
> *conception and history*

—every enmeshing harbored something unpredictable to the mind. Everything was connected with everything else in a universe expanding from particles: the life of people who'd existed but had decayed long ago, and their thoughts, transformed on paper, the visions of the Stolbenets painter and the lines of newspaper print, Milashevich's literary fantasias and the confusion of the person who read them— it's as if you're moving along in your sleep, in a false, unreal space, and suddenly from another dimension something solid emerges and takes shape before you—and you bang into it and sense that this really is pain, this is indeed death.

7

At a loss, smiling at ourselves, we try out the possibilities of new unions, we exchange winks with an epoch when everything was made from the reconceived rags of secondhand stuff, when people wore pants made of church brocade and shoes of billiard canvas and they nailed the sign of a public cooperative to the gates of the town cathedral. The nonworking days of the calendar were May Day, Whitsunday, Easter, and the Day of the Paris Commune. The hotel prostitute Fena's room was pasted over with new newspapers, and the headlines disturbed the literate guests with the unexpected concept: "Who got whom?" Affixed to the stone on Stolpie was what turned out to be a short-lived memorial: three plaster figures of warrior-heroes; the one at the center evoked Peresheikin, who'd perished, but the commissioned sculptor had added to the other two figures, who flanked the first, a portrait resemblance to local officials, who, admittedly, were still alive. That's probably why they appeared

188

on the pedestal for such a short time that they hadn't even been captured in a photograph; there were only the lines of a poem no one knew in full: "*We share veins and a common breath, /And a common body temperature.*" However, perhaps this isn't even about them. A rumor was confirmed that silver and copper coins were coming back into use; the enterprising craftsman Golgofer had purses ready in time—not everyone had kept his old one. In the cooperative shop they sold icons and portraits of the leaders together with nails and tar, and the store called New World advertised books, fish, beer, and snacks, adding in conclusion: "We have a separate private room." Yes, the times were revitalized, the word *NEP** already sounded composite, inflated, truncated, just like the phenomenon it designated. On Monday, St. Thomas's Day, day laborers and proprietors gathered on the square across from the National House; they were hiring. Together with the authorities' announcements on the gates and curbside posts were the posters of dubious touring artists. In the Stolbenets tearoom the gourmet Vasilii Platonych Semeka has already helped himself to the famous local carp, and once again the production of sweets was resumed at the factory that hadn't yet burned down, formerly Ganshin, now the stock company Hero of Labor [*Geroi truda*], "Gertruda" for short. *Fyodor Ivanovich and Gertruda.* Hah! Well, the engineer Fige had popped up out of nowhere, the former founder of the factory; according to his papers his name was Fyodor Ivanovich Fige. As do other creatures in the winter's ice, he had a rough time in the period when his brainchild stood still, overgrown with grass, and the driving belts were separated and cut into a horse harness. Suddenly he came alive, spun around, as if they'd picked him, rusting without work, like a part in an unneeded mechanism, and rubbed him with kerosene, greased him, and put him back in his former place. Engineer Fige was yet another hero in the later arson trial; Milashevich, of course, knew him—and that means he didn't let him out of his sight and was already trying out the headings of a plot that so far had taken shape by itself. He was clearly similar! In a satin Tolstoy shirt to his knees, his bald head sweaty

* See note on p. 35.

under a white cap. His stomach was swollen not with fat but with the liquid of a disease. His short but nimble legs promised death on the double. From here, alas, we know his actual fate more exactly, but there, on paper, the comic fat little figure was still hurrying somewhere, whereas an unknown pilgrim entered in a list of rites for the deceased the name of Fyodor Ivanovich, for whom he'd decided to ask someone for a new boiler and protection from oppression. Maybe he'd actually managed to whisper something, even hastily—the necessary words before a crystal shrine. Here on a *fantik* is an exclamation of surprise about the results that surpassed expectations:

That the woman recovered, got married, or even bolted—we'll allow that's a natural thing. But that such a figure should leak and come down!

There must have been an inner defect inside the body, a cavity, a crack. Most likely, in the head. Then it spread farther. From spring on, the water accumulated and poured from the armpit, from the left.

If it had simply dripped, one could somehow have sealed it up. But it says: "a slope." Here you can't seal anything, you can only lop it off. Just as I'd guessed, as I'd warned in time!

8

The left "sloper" came down from his post, the figure lopped off from the pedestal; now two were left standing on the stone. On an indistinct dotted line, as if hiding from someone, Simeon Kondratyevich outlined the code of the plotline that was complete. *By touch, at random, in the resounding emptiness, with surprise and without understanding the whole, with anxiety and curiosity.* It's one thing to know from a later perspective what particular form history took; from inside it's all unknown, shadows, wandering, despair, and hope. In the thick mass of possibilities a drop eats through the only capricious course, the rest are forever fused with the darkness; they don't exist and seem never to have done so, but it only seems that way. *I knew it would be like that, I thought, I wanted, I tried…So, he said, shall we have some more tea?. . .* A frozen chess position can delight us by its intricate interrelatedness, regulated by the expediency of the pieces: each one supports another, defends it, blocks some moves and makes others necessary (try to put something like that together on purpose); it's achieved by a combination of moves controlled not just by you alone. And history doesn't have one or two creators; it's a mongrel of too many parents, so should one be surprised that it offends any independent taste? As if someone's combination of papers always leads us astray by mockery, throws us back onto the surface of events, doesn't allow us to attain a certain depth—and we don't have the strength to repudiate the conviction that it exists, this depth; we cannot repudiate ourselves—and we continue trying to penetrate through the surface, like a fly through a window.

Why go there? Is it really better there? But the hardness of transparent air draws and attracts, and you strive to break through it with your head, to penetrate beyond an imaginary limit to the tempting mystery, instead of feasting in the room where the jam still remains uneaten in the saucer.

9

The little face of a large-mouthed mournful monkey looked through a pince-nez from the samovar: little feathery hairs around enlarged lips...

(And who in the world could it be there—a second person behind the samovar, who'd not even taken off his black leather jacket in the heat, reflected in the remains of the mirror that had been carried out into the courtyard among other museum furniture? The soft yielding soil offered no stability, the heavy frame tilted, the glass, stubbornly preserving in its gloomy depths the memory of the study and chairs with the gilded tacks of the upholstery, reluctantly, as if with one eye open, with a fragment, agreed to accept the alien figure: an imperial beard, the blob of a mustache—the new ruler of their fates, a museum expert come to select the remains of Ganshin's valuables for Moscow?)

*As happens, a small concession inevitably entailed additional ones;
it was necessary to accept at least a partial swinish arrangement with
a barn and firewood.*

*That's it. The same story, not for the first time. Either squint,
grow blind, crack, or reflect what they show, damn it.*

*The breakdown of centuries gives birth to such faces; a time
that chose as its art subject Salomé, the fateful dancer, the kiss
on dead lips.*

*pale, refined nostrils, the sweat of sickly cold on transparent
temples tinged with blue*

*the smell of vinegar, a touch of melancholy, in which the spirits
are chilled to the bone somewhere between heaven and hell,
but not yet in purgatory, in the entranceway of a life not yet begun
and, maybe, of a death that has not taken place*

So, he said, shall we have some more tea?

10

*. . .during our meeting we contrived not to even ask each other
questions, which hung in the air like particles of steamy stuffiness that
didn't fall, however, as wet drops. It always seemed that we needed
more time to be ripe for questions. One really mustn't be like this, by
the way, after twenty years amidst shared superficial
interjections, conversations about pictures and mirrors, furniture
and books. I give you credit for your virtuosity, precisely virtuosity,
a special female brand of evasiveness. Although I was a fine one, too.
I should have begun, I know. I kept thinking that there was still time.
Alas, ultimately there wasn't enough.*

*Why didn't I stay for the night, at least? I can repeat all the
practical reasons; they'll be honest. But if you say that I ran (without
knowing myself from what)—it's possible I won't be able to dispute
that. Everything that had been between us—the slights and the things
left unsaid—already seemed so distant, as if in another birth,
in another life. But if I ran so as not to get hurt, then perhaps*

I achieved the opposite: now I feel that I won't find peace, not having explained things to you afterward, after our parting—and who knows, perhaps before another parting?

I evidently was confused, simply unprepared for such a meeting. I didn't connect the surname, which I knew only on paper, in any way with you. Accept my belated congratulations, incidentally, for all the years at one go. I omitted to offer them and probably with good reason. And don't take ignorance as an insult. It only confirms how fundamentally I was removed from local, and not only literary, life...

But why "literary"? Did the writer have any relationship to literature? He reread this section not for the first time, but now it suddenly occurred to him that a change of maiden name through marriage was not at all necessarily suggested here. Perhaps it was a pseudonym that became a last name? Long, long ago. A meeting after twenty years of not knowing anything about each other. And what if the addressee wasn't a woman at all? Did Milashevich keep the letter he received? Nothing seemed to confirm the contrary... But why did the handwriting seem so familiar?...

Now I recall that on route I already experienced an inexplicable nervousness. I hadn't even thought myself still capable of that. Was it just a presentiment of a meeting with memorable places? I don't know. Hardly. Such things hadn't bothered me before. But was it really a presentiment of meeting you? A convenient explanation; however, I'm wary of deception. There was something else...
No, first I'll finish saying everything that remained unsaid between us. I even seem to be delaying as I write. I have to break free. Not for the sake of self-justification; I have nothing for which to blame myself. There's little honor for a man in such a confession, but the choice wasn't made by me. She loved, and that means that she alone made the choice, alas. I was captivated by her concern, her selfless devotion. The disease played its part. At that time she cut off and sold her braid to get money. But what's there to say. She had something in her that was capable of capturing one's imagination for a while. This genuineness of feeling and a fantastic openheartedness,

*the sudden outbursts of tireless energy—and the just as sudden
prostration, the ability to sense the taste of oversalted food on someone
else's tongue, to intuit an unspoken thought, to soothe pain—
and compliance with another's suggestion. Everything here was capable of eliciting a superstitious delight. I can well understand that. But
I could detect an unhealthy basis beneath this. It wasn't really
a medical case; I'll put it like this: it was a condition of body and
spirit unlike that which is usually considered normal and healthy.
A late child brought to term with difficulty, the joy of her unfortunate
parents... But do I really need to start telling you that?...*

*You remember when I first brought her to our apartment, without
any idea of what would follow, relying more on you? Perhaps it was
foolish. Everything looked different then. We suited one another for a
while: she suited me—at least as a cover; I, perhaps, meant more to
her. But I wasn't seriously thinking about anything like that. We
weren't equal either in development or education—nor in anything.
By the way, she later turned out to be utterly sensitive, read
a great lot, in general displayed unexpected abilities... But why am
I saying all this? (I've decided to write as the writing itself dictates,
and I doubt that I'll try to whitewash—my determination will
disappear. This is one of those cases where you write not so much for
someone else as to gain an understanding of something for yourself.)
Yes, quite soon it became clear that we weren't fated to be together
long. True, at other times we recaptured moments when it seemed
to me that I loved her. But just moments. There was no happiness.
If it at least makes you happy to hear that now, what can I say? More
often than not I experienced awkwardness, an inability
to respond to feeling.*

*You have the right to smile and say—I even anticipate
this question and ask it myself: Maybe I'm just not capable of feeling
at all? I won't answer hastily. After all, you know me, too. No one
could ever call me indifferent, isn't that so? I had known strong
passions, true passions. I'd fallen in love and gotten carried away.
Ultimately she found something in me, sensed something; after all,
that's not so easy either.*

Of course, something joined us besides love. I meant a lot to her.

For her, I was like the prophet saying to the maiden: "Rise up and walk!" I did for her what her mother and father were incapable of doing; I delivered her from a nightmare. (This story, as it turns out, created a stir later; they even wrote about it.) It was as if I'd brought her out of a half-sleep into life, but you know how this life turned out for her from the very first. I deprived her of her usual support, but I didn't give her a new one, and at times I couldn't help feeling that I owed her something—that was there, too. There was also a feeling of guilt and the hope of changing something. She valued me, my mind … No, precisely my capacity for passion—that's what she discerned in me.

Above all I couldn't bear lies; at one time this also determined my relationship with you, and my whole life. Oppression, destitution, others' suffering—yes, all this stirred me to action. But maybe more than justice I wanted the maximum truth. This consuming passion didn't let me use my abilities toward a goal that was positive, simple, but private. Nature had endowed me generously. In exile I had the reputation of an encyclopedia and could easily pass as a professor, an expert on antiquities. An excess of demands got in the way. I had moments that I can legitimately call great; I say this not so as to boast—what kind of boasting can there be now! I just couldn't come out the winner. Alas. Always for the same reason. Nothing executed or attained brought me ultimate satisfaction; in a moment of triumph the anguish of incompleteness merely became sharper, I wanted to slip away as quickly as possible from each accomplished moment, so superfluous did it suddenly become. That's how it often is after the intoxication of love…

Ah, it was clear what the handwriting reminded him of: Maksim's was very similar. Forget that, then.

… suddenly you notice a pimple on your skin. Alas. You remember, in exile I asked them to send me perfume to alleviate the terrible smells. Not in justification, but so as to clarify things, I'll note that this fastidiousness wasn't just physical; as it turned out, I can't tolerate practical politics either. As early as Paris I didn't know

where to run from this behind-the-scenes kitchen, group games, intrigues, rivalry, allocation of funds and meal tickets.

We divorced almost immediately after going abroad. Yes, do you know that before that we'd had a child, a son? The delivery proved difficult, both of them were ill for a long time, and afterward couldn't get back on their feet. I was listed as on the run, and she wanted to follow me, but the boy was weak, and she left him for a short time with her old folks. That is, we thought that it would be for a short time; she planned to return soon. But then came the combination of circumstances, the war. The old folks died right before the war; she only found out about that much later. It seems someone wrote to her that the boy was healthy and settled; I don't know for a fact, by that time we weren't seeing each other anymore. I heard that she'd returned to Russia, but where and how did she find him? Is he alive? Whose name does he have? I don't even know—think what you like about that. To this day I haven't tried to find out either about him or about her. Her parents lived somewhere around here... but then, whom am I telling this?

So I wrote this and thought: What if behind my anxiety lurked the hope of accidently meeting one of them here? Senselessness, madness. Even to think about this is a no-no. People like me probably shouldn't have children at all. And given today's conditions, he'd hardly be overjoyed to be related to me. These times aren't for people like me. However, do times for such people as me ever exist? I couldn't even deceive myself with words for long; you're happier, I could be sure of this again. You know I did think about you sometimes. Both when I was still living with her, and afterward. It happened not in my best moments. In moments of weakness and uncertainty, of groundless embarrassment when, like a child, you long to close your eyes and hide quickly in your mother's warm skirt.

No, I don't want to seek anything, I don't want to hope for anything, I don't even fear anything—you know that this, too, isn't boastfulness. I was pathologically devoid of a sense of fear, and the years haven't cured me of this abnormality. Emerging unhurt from so many disasters, I got used to the feeling that nothing more could happen to me than what had already happened. In the end, any life is doomed to ruin; the thought of the impossibility of dying can frighten one more than the thought of death.

But then, what did this nervousness and flight mean anyway? Where did this need to write to you, to explain something, come from? It looked as if I could no longer have these feelings. I don't regret anything. Although the fates of at least three people turned out to be ruined: mine, yours, hers—and maybe even a fourth, about which I don't know anything. Don't laugh at what I'll tell you now: all the while we were having tea, I had this troubled sensation—it's manifested itself now and perhaps I'll finish what I'm saying, nonetheless...

X. SOMEONE ELSE'S SALIVA

Worlds are divided according to the skin's surface. When we're not given an intercourse of love, what do we know about each other?

> *sober and drunk*
> *sated and hungry*
> *man and woman*
> *different ages*
> *different nations*
> *different times*
> *life and death*

To see a convex reflection with someone else's eye: blood vessels on the white, the changing color of the iris and the pupil, like a little hole opened into an abyss, where stars teem.

You think: a slobbering idiot. You think he's not made like us. But inside I have the same complexity, and tender organs, and the secret life of juices. And I, too, am a subject of history, I especially. Because it's happening precisely to me, for my eyes, with white lashes, for my hearing, directed at the air, for the mind that stirs slowly and anxiously in the darkness.

Whoever has shifted his glance inside another person cannot be right.

Humor means understanding, and loftiness, and modesty before the Lord, the conjecture that we only touch something that it's better not to penetrate completely, and mercy to those who don't even want this conjecture.

*Knowing solitude well, we'll explain the solitude of others
and give consolation: it's the same for everyone.*

*Only that which is suitable for everyone is understandable to all.
What is too personal cannot be the same as ours—why do we need
it, then?*

*Let x be uniform within the boundaries of the system; then it can
serve as a basis of harmony. A disparity in x's leads to dissonance and
collisions.*

let the waves even everything out, like pebbles on the shore

*The possibility of understanding each other completely, without
leftovers and disagreements, makes everyone like Vas Vasich.*

1

During this visit, why was Anton so troubled by a new feeling? The
town, which he'd been used to since childhood, like his own clothing
or even his body, suddenly seemed cool and alien. Yes, just like an old
jacket, maybe, god knows which one, but comfortably worn, its folds
adjusted to your shoulders, elbows, sides, completely decent, but it
had simply hung for the winter on a hanger—and had become unrecognizable: the lining soaked in sweat and ripped in some places
makes the skin strangely cold, the pockets protrude, the sleeves are
uncomfortable, a trifle short, and the soiled collar not pleasant
against the neck. You have a different temperature and feel the eye of
a stranger assessing that which during the last visit was still accepted
without appraisal or comparison. The five-floor houses downtown,
the streets broken up by a trench (the constant promise of something, streets eternally dug up, dirt up to your ankles). The garbage
tossed out over the winter onto the street, not dried out yet, was
somehow different: coal cinders, rust, the plastic and rubber muck of
a changed civilization. An unknown carter from a commune was
wheeling crates with bottles on a cart, with the word WINE in large
letters on the label—something new in local production. A cart on
rubber wheels, that's progress—no, say what you will, that's

progress. And in a shining new store, with spacious sections done up in Dutch tile, the signs are, for some reason, in two languages: MIASO—MEAT. But why didn't he even want to make fun of the emptiness beneath these signs? Why didn't he feel like following the billboard promising a new attraction (pony rides) in the park? Pony rides, for Christ's sake! A fairy-tale childhood dream! But maybe we need this? At one time Anton had loved to listen to songs from the crude loudspeaker, a wheezing black plate; behind the cheerful voices he imagined young boys and girls in white sports outfits, in the wind, amidst the flags of a colorful parade; then for the first time he saw a television, and on the screen the choir that had sung the well-known song, a choir of bald fat men and ugly women with double chins; because of this disappointment, probably, to this day he hadn't bought a television for himself, even though he was always planning to. That too: now on top of all the roofs in Nechaisk crosspieces and dowels stuck up in the air, so that everyone could be tuned into public life and not feel like an orphan—you simply didn't have that. You still wanted to see Nechaisk in the smoke of childlike, young open-heartedness, when your parents so successfully fenced off the domesticated, educated little boy from too hurtful impressions. After the tenth grade Anton came here only on holidays, and then on days off, already equipped with the light, ironic, and comfortable philosophy of Simeon Kondratyevich. For some reason he suddenly stopped sensing the point and pleasure of this fuss in the houses behind the small front lots, in the small barns and gardens from which one could smell from far off the spring watering, in the lakefront courtyards, where they tar the fishing boats, although the word was that after two winter freezes only ruff, a small spotted European freshwater fish of the reich family, survived in the lakes; life where from morning people go to the starch factory, to the office, or to the construction site, past the stand with figures indicating milk delivery throughout the region, and in the evening, yes, by the way, from morning as well, and also at lunchtime, with a buzz of profound emotion and wisdom in their good-natured heads, they keep gripping each other by the buttons: "You're a human being and I'm a human being, right?" Right, but you've lost this wisdom, because you're now careful not to drink, for reasons of health; but you haven't acquired a new wisdom. Someone else's saliva, and there's no loving union with the world, that's all.

2

His parents' deserted house froze over the winter and suddenly became unfit to live in. The stove, which was very difficult to light, warmed only the circulating air, but not the dank flesh of the dwelling. Even the chilled smells decayed and rotted, as in an uncleaned cellar, and this hurt more painfully than the spoiling of things that you could only touch as you would a cold dead body, so as to cry over an irretrievable life. The cupboard, which had a secret storeroom behind it, a haven of cozy thoughts, magical rustling and shadows, now contained only mold and fly scum. The alarm clock that you could still wind up and listen to, to your heart's content, holding the shaking little body in your hands, observing how the ring turned around the back of its head. The spring bed on which, perhaps, your life began, nickle-plated knobs, the non-Euclidean space of an artist, where it had been so fascinating, without yet knowing anything about Milashevich, to try on the appearance achieved from varying parts, first with a martian forehead, then with a Neanderthal chin. The knobs had lost their luster, grown black, and no longer reflected anything. Where is a watercolor fresh with moisture? Where are the colored glasses of childhood that gave life to the simple surroundings? The house spirit had died, his tiny little corpse decaying somewhere, and not a single item could be moved now to the new apartment—it would never become acclimated.

3

Yes, a new apartment—by then that event had occurred. The house on Campanella Street suddenly was declared slated for demolition, and, moreover, urgently. O life! O triviality! O conflict, enmity and scores to settle, legal complaints and slops thrown in neighbors' pans! While the documents were still being processed, the tenants were quickly issued keys to work on various interior defects. Then the doctoral candidate did appreciate his neighbors' foresight: his own furniture could not be moved into the room with the smooth plastic floor, with straight walls and ceiling—well, perhaps comparatively straight. Even Anton's bookshelves were comprised of old planks fitted against the wooden walls—it was impossible to make them secure on concrete. And the main thing was that, when juxtaposed with the contemporary box of a house, everything became so dessicated and warped, such a provincial—yes, precisely provincial—squalidness manifested itself in everything, the old skin from which you've suddenly crawled out, that you look in embarrassment: it's time, it's high time to revamp your life. So as to slip away quickly without being noticed by his neighbors, Anton didn't even wait for the gas to be turned on, but got a cab and moved his simple bachelor's belongings, taking his books and the papers on which he was working before moving his shelves and his desk; he'd left everything unpacked in the meantime, and instead spent one night in the new house sleeping on a roll-away bed, inhaling the smell of oilpaint and the as yet vague novelty of it all. The house loomed high in the deserted outskirts—an ivory-colored tower (if you disregarded once again the streaked paint). From the window on the eighth floor there stretched before one a wide expanse of concrete stalagmites. The emptiness of the skies, a new silhouette of the earth! A little church that formerly had raised its divine domes above the people and their dwellings now looked like a knickknack seen from above. They say there used to be a cemetery here, then a scrap metal dump. If there had been any vegetation formerly, destroyed by construction, it was now transformed into concrete fungi or perhaps cactuses. Do we really know how this new landscape will tell upon our souls, thought Anton, staring through the naked window without a ventilation top, staring at the unfamiliar, as yet unassimilated space—this dwelling without the mysteries of a garret and an old stove, without sheds in the yard, without any pantry or porches? He decided that he'd choose his new furniture gradually, not buy a complete impersonal suite, but would naturally accumulate more and more things that fit him and his place. The unexpected impact of Nechaisk turned his train of thought in a new direction.

4

He arrived in town on Sunday morning so as to visit his parents' graves, but after leaving the house he glanced in on his father's school museum. They'd already told him to vacate the premises, which were needed for different purposes. The museum had been a relatively recent hobby of his late father's. It had begun from the chance discovery of some prehistoric fragments of pottery; as usual, samples of local soils and handicraft were added to them. As objects from olden times, there were also exhibited bast shoes worn quite recently by the workers at the local peat bogs, a watchman's truncheon, a wooden bathtub, and a trough cracked from the heat, which the gold fish returned to the old woman, after all*—that's how Anton and his father joked when once, in something of a hurry, Anton had dropped by the tiny little room with a dark window. It seemed to him that his father was a trifle embarrassed by his scholarly interest and his poor exhibits. That's why he said encouragingly that everyday objects even from our century's recent past are becoming ethnographic relics quicker than ever before. Milashevich had good reason to be interested in them as a museum topic. "Yes, I read your material," the old man faltered. "Maybe we can talk some time. I've got a reservist here, too—there's no place to put all this stuff." They never had their talk, and only now, for the first time, Anton went into the reservist—a closet without any windows, with bookshelves on three walls, cluttered like a storehouse of scrap.

5

In the light of the dusty pantry lamp, the semifamiliar objects that had disappeared from home, from life, as if forever, because of their uselessness, started to emerge from this clutter as from a soundless childhood dream: a tall, coal black iron with a wooden handle, whose

---

* GOLD FISH The reference is to the folktale "The Gold Fish," made famous by Aleksandr Pushkin's literary reworking of it. The tale illustrates how a querulous old woman exploits the ability of a gold fish to fulfill all wishes. Punished for her greed by losing all her magically acquired new possessions, the woman is left with her original dilapidated hut and old trough.

heaviness his hand still remembered (it had to be waved back and forth to retain its heat); a kerosene lamp, the glass broken, still emanating a sweetish evening smell that filled the room when the wick was unscrewed and the black flakes flew about in the air like insects, settling on the curtains and the white pillows; the oilcloth rug that once hung above the bed, with a yellow lion and a striped tiger on the bank of the dark blue pond with swans, where the cream-colored roses resembling cream puffs blossomed, with the red bellflowers, the flowers of dozing in the mornings, on the same stem. Once, during a visit on a school holiday, he made fun of the tackiness of this piece of handicraft, and on his next visit he no longer saw the rug; it had disappeared, to appear now, unexpectedly, as earlier had a ghastly money-box cat with the face of a mustached musketeer, with a luxuriant scarlet bow and painted lips, a paper squeaker called "mother-in-law's tongue" that produced a sound when someone breathed on it, and then retracted into a spiral, the remnant of a tricolor pencil; a garter for socks, a solitary galosh, Red Triangle brand—a specimen of footwear that was disappearing—and a little tag with "Stockings filé-de-perse" pinned onto the crumpled pelt of some unrecognizable little animal.

6

An album of amateur photos, some of them signed, also turned up: gray frozen faces, the clothes with tiny soft wrinkles looked as if they'd been washed many times and, at the same time, as if full of dirty dust. In one photo the Komsomol of Nechaisk for some reason formed a gymnastic pyramid: thickset bodies, heavy wide trousers, with the members at the bottom of the photo symmetrically supporting those at the top. Other shots showed people listening to the radio (a small box with two lamps at its temples), icons burning on Freedom Square—behind the bonfire you could see the familiar two-story houses, a tearoom, the monastery bell tower a little farther off. Below an incomprehensible latticed structure against the background of the pale sky there was an explanation in pencil—if one could call it an explanation: "Flight tower." Some papers had got stuck between the pages of the album: a wrapper from the cream soap Beauty's Secret, a press cutting about Australian aborigines who started to degenerate and go crazy without their sorcerers and superstitions, without the significance of primitive life, because they didn't find anything to replace it; a small lithographic icon with an accurate portrait of the familiar beauty on the wrapper, only this one was holding her long index finger to her lips as if urging silence; a sheet of checked notebook paper covered with his father's clear teacher's handwriting. The heading read: "An explanation of the museum." Lizavin started to read, and felt a twinge in his heart.

7

"I've read Antosha's article," his father wrote, "and at night I had a dream. I wanted to tell him about it, but it's probably impossible to explain. It's as if I'm groping my way in the pitch darkness, but I sense that this is happening in my parents' house. I don't know why. My fingers touch some objects, smooth, rough, and I can't tell what they are, but they're not just familiar to me, it's as if they're alive. As the only basis for guiding me, they can rescue me from bewilderment and fear. Feels like a cold washstand with a nipple, a mug with a candle inside it, the fringe of a tablecloth, a plate with a chipped edge (I remember dropping it). Then also something protruding, made of bone, rounded, I touch it and suddenly realize that it's my father's head... No, it's impossible to describe it. It's not a question of description, but of feeling. I woke up with the raw pain of anguish, guilt, and loss. I wanted to tell Antosha, but I didn't know how. Surely it's not possible that one can only understand it for oneself?"

8

My god, o my god, Anton Andreyevich thought, without wiping his tears. We didn't have time to talk. He, too. But it wasn't just me, just the laziness of a late-awakened interest, nor just the eternal fuss that postponed everything till later. His father himself, voluntarily or involuntarily, avoided frankness, as if embarrassed—he'd seemed talkative, simple-hearted, loquacious, particularly after a few drinks; but there was the feeling that he kept getting close to something, still wanted to say something; he'd hint, circle, digress, and at the last moment he'd close the blinds. Once, while sitting at table, he started recalling how, in about 1932, he took it into his head to learn bee keeping. "I already could get close to bees without a screen, they respected me and didn't touch me. Fine! Keep to yourself, don't be afraid of anything, of any forms." At this point Anton Andreyevich's mother for some reason sternly silenced him, he grew confused, changed the topic, and only after a delay of many years did the question occur to his son: "What was there to be afraid of?" Yes, this fear had a prehistory. Andrei Polikarpych left his native area, where the people knew his father, who was a rural priest. He hid out only briefly in the beehive garden, for he badly wanted to enroll in a teacher's technical training school, and in his application form he concealed his burdensome background, declaring he was an orphan, a teacher's son (which was true, in a way, since his father taught in a church school). He then hid out in Nechaisk, where only his wife discovered his secret, and not immediately, at that. Anton enrolled in a pedagogical institute with a reputation as the heir to a teachers' dynasty. Out of habitual, by then excessive, caution Anton's mother considered it prudent not to reveal anything superfluous, just in case, even then. She was always protecting him from something: from sickness, sharp metal, fire and water, from burdensome experiences, superfluous knowledge. We inherit the genes of our parents' fears, although the fears themselves lost their meaning long ago and perhaps never had any. We want peace of mind more than uneasy trustworthiness, habituated as we are to fearing our background and relationships; we would consider fair the actual realization of the principle "A son is not responsible for his father," and suddenly we'd realize what a loss that would entail. That's probably what his father suffered from—he, too. No longer seeing the possibility of returning to his parents' faith, the God to whom he'd prayed as an infant, he belatedly tried to feel his way toward—and to retain—some sort of support, even if only by means of objects that were solid but as vulnerable and perishable as paper flowers. Anton thought he could understand why his father tried to start his explanation of the museum with the feeling of a distressing dream—and didn't finish, didn't get to say everything. He probably would laugh it off or, as usual, would make something up whenever people asked him why he was collecting junk all over town, why he was trapping the smells of crackling birch firewood, oven fumes, wheel grease, and horse sweat in test tubes taken from a chemistry lab and in small bottles with the stoppers ground in them. And he felt more embarrassed at his son's interest, perhaps, than at some stranger's. Maybe he was waiting to have grandchildren—it's easier with grandchildren, they accept handmade rugs and songs from your bygone youth without sarcastic prejudices; there are no scores to settle with them, no arguments. He didn't get to have grandchildren; his son, an absurd bachelor in his thirties, a loner in space and time, didn't bring him that joy.

9

Lizavin came out into the street, blinded by the sun to the point of tears after the darkness of the storeroom. He made a definite decision that on his next visit he'd move his father's museum to his own place, and then, without remembering why, he found himself in the bell tower of the former monastery. The monastery was ancient, three hundred years old, but none of its original structure had survived. The latest bell tower and church had been renovated in the 1880s; they collected donations especially to replace the unattractive antiquity with small towers in a pseudo-Russian style, with traceries in red and white brick in the manner of cross-stitch embroidery. From here the town was visible very far—as far as the forest, the concrete columns of a glazed pottery plant with a brick-red date on the chimney: 197...—the last digit exceeded the limit of visibility, but it had no particular importance anyway because the structure remained as yet unfinished. On Market Square, under a layer of cobblestones that disappeared into the mud, perhaps there still remain the ashes of burned icons and, if one were to dig still deeper, planked footpaths, floorings, butt ends, and even pottery fragments and the ashes of bygone settlements submerged in the fossilized depths. Above the lake, among the bare trees of the town park with the ravens' nests, one could see the dais of a dance floor, with the floorboards that had collapsed during winter, the cradles of swings, their rusty paint peeled off, and somewhat farther a circle around which a hardworking pony used to run. On the footbridge some women were rinsing laundry in the cold water. The sky over the stretch of lake was vast, three times the size of an ordinary sky, the elongated clouds drifted across it like long, solemn fish outlined in a circuit of light. The wind whispered melodiously in one's ears, carrying from afar the women's voices, the caws of the ravens, the smells of moisture, sticky leaves, fresh earth and smoke—eternal smells, eternal sounds, and something pulsated and breathed in the air. Behind the lake there was the clatter of horses' hooves, the bare shores were overgrown, as in olden times, with a stubble of dense forest, a wooden jail rose above the precipice where a bonfire once burned to announce the arrival of an enemy, and people were sacrificed before the pagan idol. On a barely visible road some horsemen would unhurriedly canter to burn down the robbers' nest of the Nogtev-Zvenigorod princes. A layer of humus now covered the scorched area, the blood that had soaked into the earth fed the roots, giving color to the wild strawberries. Only in the breath of wind, in one's nostrils and memory, could one detect the smell of singed cornea, bewilderment, and fear. The cells of the elders who'd lived behind the lake had turned into rubble and moss; the forests had begun to thin out, the soil was divided into strips, the veins of the roads in the numb excrescences of hamlets swelled and thickened. An army of peasants, incited to rebellion, had passed through here once with a colorful red banner; the body of their leader, who'd been hanged in Totma, was brought and exhibited later in the Nechaisk square because the local peasants wouldn't believe in his death—and maybe they didn't completely believe in it even after seeing him, blackened, his face pecked out by birds. People here always lived according to their own local beliefs. Water and wind covered with sand and clay the idol that slipped down from the precipice; on the new layer of earth walked new people dressed in cloth peasant coats, bast sandals, overcoats, highboots and rubber galoshes, padded jackets and modern raincoats. Slowly, stretching and scratching, the epic hero, who'd lain for three and thirty years at the crossroads of provincial byways and had regained consciousness with the feeling of an adolescent who'd not yet managed to mature into adulthood, was awakening. A whiff of gasoline mingled with the smell of fish, pitch, manure, and tar—the wind was wafting it from the direction of the ravine, which had been transformed into a sand pit. A spring flood had washed away the slope here and opened up a burial ground with a lot of bodies; all the skulls there had extra holes in the forehead. The bones were immediately taken and, with the help of a steam shovel, buried in the forest, about four kilometers away, briefly giving rise in town to whispered talk about executions from olden times, but nobody confirmed anything definite, and the origin of the communal grave remained a mystery to the townspeople. Close to the cemetery behind the prefabricated five-story houses, the iron chimney of the boiler room steamed away. A soundless airplane pulled a thread out of the white cloud.

10

To tidy up the small mounds of the graves he had to borrow a spade and a rake from some acquaintances—he hadn't thought to bring the tools with him. His next visit—he'd do everything on his next visit: have a closer look at the office building, the former small cemetery church, and, most important, the wooden house, also an office building, adjoining it. The priest with calloused hands lived there in the old days, and maybe Milashevich had been there. The garden trees behind the office building had been uprooted, clearing a space for new graves they'd dug up and vacating unclaimed strips of land in a distant corner. Eternal memory doesn't exist, nor does eternal peace. Someone's ancestral continuity is severed, new ones demand room. The cemetery clearly reminded one of the march of time: today's is the last grave, and only for that reason the freshest among the others, but a year goes by, new losses are accumulated around it, and your small mound is already lost in the middle, like a memory, and you need to beat a path to it. People were bustling about everywhere, renovating fences with pretty silver paint, removing last year's grass, filling the saucers with seed for the birds, pouring water into milk bottles and jars to place plastic flowers in them, which could withstand all kinds of weather—the miraculous invention of the age, no worse than the earlier porcelain roses in the former crypts of the Zvenigorod princes, above which still hovered a lopsided, one-winged angel. The cemetery was crowded and somehow cheerful. It had been a long time since so many people had gathered there. Dressed up, some of them even wearing ties, although because of the mud they wore rubber highboots and fishermen's jackboots with turndown tops; the women seemed surrounded by a small cloud of perfume, their spouses rather by the aroma of alcohol, but one that was cheerfully festive, as in May. From the branches the birds gazed at the people with the eyes of the deceased.

11

At exactly that time the pensioner Bidiuk, a former accountant of the Regional Financial Division (RFD), was preparing to leave home; he'd already had his snack of thick sour milk and bread, the healthy fare of a solitary old man, had already drunk some elixir for the road from the two-liter jar with a layer of white mold called mushroom. He'd already peed, with difficulty, before leaving, squeezing out a few drops, and for the last time had cleaned with a clothes brush a green Tyrol hat with a moth-eaten bird's feather that was older than he. Bidiuk was a mysterious man who'd read all the books on counterespionage, and on the secret service, that one could find in the library, and he appeared to grasp the primary cause of many phenomena, which from a superficial view seemed to be elemental but in reality were governed by the purposeful force of events, whether they were the Colorado beetle or a lake's turning shallow. Now he was interested in something different, almost on a cosmic scale; he had a card index, and he copied extracts from newspapers and magazines, underlined something with varicolored pencils, drew diagrams with marks and small arrows, but as for the essence of what he was doing, he dropped significant hints that were none too clear, which in the old days could drive whomever he was speaking to crazy. Now perhaps they didn't make an impression on anybody; people of his age who were ready to suspect this perilous bore of having some secret knowledge had died, and people of the new generation weren't curious about him. Sometimes solitude would gnaw away at the retiree; he wanted to find a colleague in mind and spirit, but not in Nechaisk, that's for sure, among the ugly mugs that had grown blue from hard drinking and lewd, neighing laughter. You live in the oblast, he told Lizavin, whom he met on his way from the cemetery, you can't imagine. You can't imagine how hard it is for a man from the intelligentsia to live amidst this boorishness, stupidity, fistfighting, and cursing, among people who aren't even capable of stopping to think about why they're living. The savagery, depravity, and superstition of the era's obscurantism. In Sareyevo—do you know this village beyond the lake?—some sorcerers have turned up again. That is, they consider themselves sorcerers; they believe it themselves and people believe in them. And, encouraged by the silent attention of his interlocutor, Bidiuk started to tell him about some book he'd discovered that described a genuinely criminal incident of mass psychosis in that very same Sareyevo, at the beginning of the century, with, moreover, a certain girl who was really worthy of attention at the center of the cult. "What's her last name?" To his own surprise, Lizavin asked this stupidest of all possible questions and transferred his briefcase from one hand to the other; he listened to the annoying retiree with half an ear, thinking his own thoughts. Fortunately, Bidiuk didn't realize that. "Who wrote it? I don't remember by heart, but I can check. You know why they chose our area for their so-called secret meeting place? Only one of several, of course. First, precisely because it's out of the way, far removed, so to speak, from civilization." "Who are they?" Anton finally made an attempt to concentrate on the course of his thoughts. "Well, that's what I'm leading up to, Anton Andreyevich. Everything's all of a piece here. Clearly, they had a local resident whom they left here and visited from time to time. There was a minimum of eight such visits, I've counted them." Bidiuk glanced around to check whether some passerby could overhear them—and to his annoyance saw that one could: Kostia Andronov, nicknamed Trumpeter, the head of a radio repair shop and a longtime acquaintance of Lizavin's, was crossing over from Turgenev Street so as to intercept them. He was already waving his hand in greeting and calling Anton's name, so that further talk was now impossible for Bidiuk. He had no chance then to expound to the doctoral candidate the surprising facts and conclusions that explained so much in the life of Nechaisk and even in world history.

Trumpeter was with his new wife Klava; while introducing Anton to her, he called him an associate professor to impress her with his acquaintances.

"I didn't know that you'd gotten married," said Lizavin. Without realizing why, he felt an obstruction in his throat.

"Just about three months ago."

"And judging by appearance, I'd have said six already," the doctoral candidate joked, nodding at the woman's rounded stomach. The joke was a trifle risqué, but that was fine; for a man in his position it was allowed. Trumpeter even beamed with joy, pleased, and Klava smiled, although at the same time she lowered her head a trifle. She looked amazingly like her husband, as wide as he and already a little puffy.

"That's right," Trumpeter admitted. "We got married late. We had to wait for my divorce to go through."

Of course, the divorce. So he had seen her before. So stupid not to have understood at once that obstruction in his throat.

Anton successfully got out of their invitation to dinner of fresh Siberian dumplings, agreeing to come another time—he had to hurry to get the bus. But Klava herself suggested that her husband accompany his friend. "Maybe you can drop by The Lake and have some beer in honor of your meeting again?" As she went off, Kostia gazed after her, beaming with pride, as if to say: "What a woman, huh? Does anybody have a great broad like her? She understands everything. With her you can taste real life, a simple taste, when you're a simple man and your friend's a simple man, even if an associate professor."

"Zoika?" Trumpeter finally heard Lizavin's question. "What about Zoika? I told you, we got divorced. We saw each other in town maybe twice... no, three times. I took her things over to her, her spring coat, money."

"Money?" Lizavin asked again automatically, just so as not to say something else. Trumpeter took it his own way.

"Yes, I, too, was afraid that she wouldn't accept the money. It's always hard to understand what she wants. But she took it. She has no apartment of her own yet. She's renting. She was going to get a job in the hospital. As an orderly."

"An orderly?" (That meant she was living in town; she had an address and Kostia probably knew it.)

"I also told her she's crazy," Trumpeter readily agreed. "With her education she couldn't find another job? Eight, almost nine years of school. But she said they'd promised to enroll her in some special courses and give her a job that was time and a half. I'm afraid they'll cheat her. Even illiterate old women now don't go too readily to work as orderlies. So they found a stu..." he broke off. "Well, there's no point in talking with her. I'm no longer her adviser."

(It meant she'd talked with him. In spite of everything, she'd talked. Wasn't he surprised to hear her voice? He mustn't forget to ask for her address. Only not ask directly, of course, but somehow indirectly, in passing.)

"Maybe there's something I don't understand," Andronov shook his head and grinned at his own thoughts. "I'm a simple man. No, I wouldn't say a word about her. Perhaps we're just different. I can't even recall now why everything happened this way. Like in a dream, I swear by God. With Klavka, now, everything's clear, and she understands me..."

Two little boys, about six and eight years old, their rubber boots splashing water from the puddles, ran up to the two men.

"Uncle Kostia, Uncle Kostia!"

"I've got them, here they are," Andronov told them. He reached in his pocket for two tin whistles, which he handed over. The boys tested the lilting sound, then ran off, barely remembering to thank him.

"There's a guy who drives around on a cart here," he explained to Anton. "He collects rags, all kinds of used things. Boys bring him the stuff, and he pays them with these tin whistles. He gives adults jar lids, and whistles to the little kids. But he doesn't have enough to go around. When some of the kids run around whistling, the others get jealous. It's not fair. So they come to me: 'Uncle Kostia, Uncle Kostia!' They know I can make anything..."

13

Fiu-liu-liu, the whistles vied with one another in producing their simple music. The sun in the sky, dirt on the ground, fire in the stove, and smoke from the chimney. *Fiu-liu-liu.* Walking along, in boots, in the cold water of the glittering puddles, as if on the bright seas, with only the spray sparkling as patches of sunlight danced on the walls of the houses. The simple music lingered on the wind as naturally as if it had been produced by it. The reflections of a sunbeam emerged of their own accord from the fragments of bottles. Taking a shortcut, they walked through the yards of prefabricated five-floor buildings. On a bench by the last entrance sat a young woman in a close-fitting wasp-colored top, with a jacket thrown over her shoulders; from the open window a radio on the sill was playing music, and she swayed in rhythm to it; her shoe, which had slipped off her heel, also swaying on the tips of her toes. Her worn made-up face was pensive, her left eye blackened, the right one gazing blankly. The rigid planes of the houses, the striped sweater, the lips beneath the crooked lipstick, and above everything, the harsh blue sky. Enlarged. A pang of understanding. The oily black rainbow on the water may be beautiful to look at, but the mind poisons that beauty with corrosive knowledge about its properties. Yet...Do we need a lot from life? *Fiu-liu-liu. Fiu-liu-liu.* To return to the cave as evening approaches, tired, and to proudly tell your pregnant wife: I killed a big mammoth today, there'll be a lot of meat for us all now.

14

He recalled that sudden shift in mood, that inexplicable presentiment—and a new vulnerability to life and an unusually keen sensitivity of hearing—in the cafe, where there were no longer any tablecloths and the polished surface of the tables shone. Instead, a dais with a cluster of drums of various caliber as well as a jukebox had appeared. "Do you have any beer?" Anton asked the waitress, whom he hadn't met before, and she answered: "Sometimes." A strange Russian response, probably not quite clear to foreigners (had? have? will have?), but capable of giving them delight, because it points to the openness and the adventure that is our life, where you can't—and you shouldn't—be sure of anything; but maybe it signals the new perception of the world in our age, where a thinking based on probability has edged out dry mechanical definiteness. There's a provincial feeling in it that doesn't need a history without doubts and condenses life from *fantiki* and monuments, from an idea...and here she comes, bringing the beer—what did you think? Had? Have? Will have? Only a foreigner can ask that. Trumpeter even looked at Anton as at someone who'd made an incomprehensible joke. Great fellow. He'd grown ever fatter, balder, in the space of a year, tranquil, content, amazingly measured in his drinking. He probably shouldn't have asked him that crazy question about the execution. Why did he suddenly remember Maksim Sivers (though it's quite clear why) and this unexplained word? He'd become obsessed with finding out, as if there were no other topics of conversation. The smile disappeared from Kostia's lips, good natured and wet from the beer.

"Oh, you're talking about the army?" He'd had difficulty realizing what Lizavin was trying to find out from him. "Sure, we had all sorts of things there. We played the fool."

"Did anyone get beaten up?"

"What for?" Trumpeter grinned in good-natured recollection. "They'd just use a slipper on somebody's behind. Naked," he laughed. "For example, they'd call on a newcomer, asking, 'Are you literate?' 'Yeah.' 'Well, you'll keep track on a calendar how many days are left to my demo.' That means demobilization," he translated, just to be sure. "We liked to count the days. So, for example, whoever didn't do it, didn't mark the day, he'd be punished—as many times as days left before the demo. That's all it was, really—what else did you want to know? How Maksim ended up in the hospital? He did end up there and unexpectedly ran into some men and got beaten up without knowing what was going on."

Why mention this name, which was so unpleasant to Trumpeter? Why drag out of his tranquil memory the blood on the cement floor—the cold, wet floor—of the washroom? There was good reason for its having been relegated to the remote back streets of his memory, and, moreover, why go on about Marat? He barely grasped what it was about: "Ah, that unhappy psycho? I remember him." *Unhappy*—what a profound word! "Are you unhappy?" they'd warn any dissatisfied guy who used to keep running into them, asking for it, as Sivers did. Better not be unhappy—why be unhappy? we've got a sense of humor, the ability to forget, poetry. What else are you intent on looking for?

"What happened to him?"

"I just told you, he couldn't take it."

"Did he commit suicide?"

"No, they had to do it. Apparently he went crazy and had an automatic in his hands. They wanted to approach him in the guardroom, but he started shooting. It was lucky that a sentry reached him in time from the rear."

"But who wanted to approach him? What for?"

"I don't know. I wasn't there that time. There are always people who go crazy and lose it. Though one can do it nicely, be human. You know, I had an incident, too, when I was on sentry duty. It happened the night before the holidays—November—I was on duty and fell asleep. Suddenly our captain, Vasiukov, is waking me. 'What are you doing, you stupid fuck, you wanna be brought up on charges?' Yet I could smell the booze on him yards away. I got scared at first 'cause I was half-asleep. I'd played soccer together with Vasiukov—Sasha— on a team in our military district. He yelled for a while, then takes out a bottle: so, let's have a drink. We had a shot right from the bottle, and then he starts up again: military court, the brig—frig! I tell him, in that case, Sasha, I'll tell them you drink vodka with the sentry. What do you think his answer is? He tries to kiss me: 'Kostia, buddy, tell them, do! Let them kick me out of this fucking shit of a dump. I'm sick of it, can't take it any more, I'll get to be a total drunk.' You know, to put it simply, everybody's human..."

15

Outside, you could see the broken-down cupolas of the monastery above the small shed of the bus station. The sloping roof had become overgrown with weedlike grass. A military construction battalion was filing past any which way, coming from the sauna: faces steaming, a remnant of soap in a transparent plastic bag, towel in hand. People were crowding into the small old bus bound for Sareyevo. The driver got out, and used his shoulder to push the people closer together, so as to close the door. A visitor dressed in a storm jacket sat on a bench, studying a map of the region. A toothless old man with a twitching, unshaven cheek poked with his finger at the map and wheezed: "All in order, huh? Cuba's been put in order, right? Egypt's in order. There'll be order everywhere, am I right or not?" And off he went, for some reason glancing back in anger, as if ready to respond to any protest against his last rhetorical query: Did he and all mankind lack anything in order to attain universal harmony? Until quite recently the old man had been considered the town crazy and was called Fedia Kizilbash. Once a day, always at the same time, he'd come to the tearoom that subsequently became a restaurant, and still later the Lake Café. He'd come dressed in a padded jacket, belted with a piece of rope, the empty sheath that used to hold a sabre from the civil war dragging on the ground. They already knew him, a free mug of beer usually served as a way of getting rid of him—Kizilbash would drink it standing, spit with relish to express his contempt for everybody present, for their present life. Suddenly they found out that he really was a famous hero of his times, and not just some crazy leftover from that era. A journalist came from Leningrad and presented him with an ancient photograph where the young Kizilbash was standing, sword in sheath, beside a horse, in a Herculean helmet with a five-pointed star, but inexplicably naked up to the waist. People had him shaved and photographed again for the sake of history. As the only live, active participant of the revolution left in Nechaisk, he suddenly received benefits and a holiday allowance—the same that the highest administrators got—including Moscow smoked sausage. He could even travel free on public transportation within the district, if he so desired. But he had nowhere to go and no reason to do so; when suddenly a relative of his, almost a cousin, appeared from someplace, and started to look after him and to keep house for him (which hadn't happened before). Kizilbash seemed to be derailed from his craziness. Various doctoral candidates kept coming to talk to him, expressed surprised at the photograph: Why was he naked in it? "It's more comfortable to swordfight that way," Kizilbash wheezed. "And how could you tell friends from enemies, without uniforms?" "We couldn't." His relative, standing behind him, gestured with her finger at her temple as if to say: There's no sense in talking to him. Well, was he really so crazy? A fragment of undwindling spite and terror had got wedged in his twitching, turbid, languishing eyes. Maybe it was better not to remove it? Even now he dreams of swordfighting, shooting, and capital punishment. You won't get anything else out of him, and what's really concealed behind all that? It was sooner worth thinking about whether to invite the hero to stand on the platform when celebrating an anniversary to wave with his hand to the people . . . The Icarus, an intercity yellow bus of Hungarian make that had arrived from Stolbenets—a real beauty—braked so as not to knock down the invalid. Shouting obscenities, Kizilbash shook his fist threateningly at the driver and entered the Lake Café.

16

And yet another fate's hero got off the Icarus and made for the same place—a man called Sasha Kaif. But it wasn't clear what was his real name and what a nickname. Not that it was essential to find out. He had a rhythmical, prancing gait and was fat and effeminate. He wore a silver jacket that bore a drawing of a winged monkey, and had long greasy hair and an attempt at sideburns on his pimpled cheeks—a drummer and the leader of a rock band called Firebird. They'd contracted to play in the Lake Café in the evening, and they had to set up the equipment. As if on order, there was the man they needed, seated at a table: Trumpeter, the local radio specialist. He'd already helped them out once. In the corner behind the tall counter three local drunks met under a plaque on the wall that prohibited doing exactly what they were planning to do. As he passed, Sasha Kaif put a five-kopek coin in the jukebox and pressed a button without looking. He didn't need to do that: inside his own body there constantly sounded, without any payment, a light, clear mechanism with syncopation that made him twitch in time with his head and shoulders while walking, and tap with his heels when he stood and sat. His speech obeyed this rhythm, and a charm in the form of a transparent ball with a moving drop inside it on a chain swung left and right on his finger.

"Welcome, Your Majesty!" From his corner, Pankov, an authorized agent of the Industry Co-op, greeted the music. Only an uninformed man like Sasha Kaif could suspect him of being a drunk. What interested Pankov wasn't boozing, but the opportunity to talk, and for the

sake of doing that he'd entice with a free bottle people whom nothing else would induce to get together. And the group members were
pretty old for real boozing: Kizilbash, who'd stopped by the café
according to his old habit, as well as Bidiuk, who'd followed Lizavin
for some reason and now for his treat had taken out of his side pocket
the personal measuring glass with markings that he carried with him
for different occasions, for he didn't trust public utensils. Pankov
knew how to relish the particular pleasure he got from life, accompanying his every step with a game for himself: he always mentally
brought along with him a man from the past, even Ivan the Terrible
himself, and showing this unhappy czar the possibilities of his own
life, he amazed him at every step, and, most importantly, amazed
himself. He was delighted pressing a button for the electric light or
for a Moscow elevator, getting on an escalator or standing in front of
the automatic door of a bus. Or, say, they're walking down the street
and want a drink, but there's no rivulet, no well, and no puddle—
what can they do? Here's where he, Pankov, goes up to a roadside
column, presses something there—"Welcome, Your Majesty!"—mysterious and shrewd, like the prophet who cut water out of a rock.
This simple technique made life vividly colorful with miracles, which
children nowadays are no longer able to delight in, however hard the
new storytellers try to stimulate their feelings. Cars, the possibility of
movement from place to place at a speed inaccessible to the czar's
fleet horses, TV, finally. Was it possible to pine away in this life
instead of being delighted with the realized dreams of one's prede-
cessors? And what else is yet to come! Of late, Pankov's companion
had begun acquiring the traits of a foreign tourist whom one could
impress by a comparison of life today with its future prospects. The
figures of future plans, both city and district, delighted the representative of the Industry Co-op, ensuring his future hopes; yet right
now, when the simple spin of a copper coin produced music from
no one knows where, and not just any music, but dozens of fifes,
drums, and violins simultaneously, he couldn't contain an exclamation of pleasure and triumph: "Welcome, Your Majesty!"

17

Whose eye observed them all from a certain area? Whose ear listened to all the voices simultaneously? "What is this?" asked Lizavin, with his bent aluminum fork testing a lump of suspicious-looking suet camouflaged by a layer of biscuit. "What did you order?" the waitress asked, demonstrating her special school of logic. "A beefsteak." "That means it's a beefsteak, then!" The music from the box sounded familiar, only he couldn't remember where it was from. "I'll give you two thousand rubles per month," Sasha Kaif tried to tempt the radio specialist, pouring the drink locally called "wine" instead of beer into their glasses. "Restaurant food, a place to stay. Think about it." "No," Kostia insisted, "I'm fine where I am." Kostia, hopelessly old-fashioned in his sports sweater, with a stripe around the neck, with his ability to read notes and play the trumpet, was in bliss. Kaif looked at him with lazy condescension; he'd promised to help the old guy, but what the hell did he really need him for, the bald shithead, who still salivated over a tango and the march called "A Slavic Maid's Farewell." "Why, we'll have a fish plant according to this five-year plan," Pankov reminded his drinking buddies, licking the bones of a sea sprat. "It'll be just for the district and the region; we'll be exporting it. We'll have a million and a half just of the young fish alone." The music stopped, but the drummer's fat body continued to shake in the same pleasant rhythm, and his entire appearance invited one to join in: We're having fun, aren't we? One shouldn't drink wine after beer, of course, but perhaps it made sense to disinfect one's stomach a little after the dubious beefsteak? "It's okay. It's even healthy," a former accountant confirmed from his corner. "They put real wild strawberries into it, and they're good, because they contain more iron than anything." "Depends what you compare them with," Pankov countered, refusing to yield in erudition, and only Fedia Kizilbash was silent, his scornful yellow eye drilling the drinking buddies. What was he so dissatisfied with all the time? He must have seen everything there is to see in his life, but look at how we live now, and how well—there's no comparison. That means everything's fine. Pankov was no fool; he grasped something better than the others. "Yes," Lizavin backed him up, "it's important to be able to compare, that's the whole point. Let's say there was a homemade mural on the wall, and now there's this government-issue mosaic. Is it expensive?" "Six thousand," Pankov named the sum as he sat in his corner. "And what's in it? Is it an example of contemporary fashion? Nonsense! Why is there more taste in furniture suites and Picasso than in canaries, money boxes in the form of little cats, or in the masterpiece that I don't know called *The Lost Garden?* My father didn't save these little cats and swans for no purpose. You'll see, they'll soon start looking to pay good money for them, as they do with old icons." "Where did he save them?" Kaif showed some interest, unbuttoning his silver jacket and opening his shirt with the foreign texts on it: whoever knows the language, please read, there's no censorship. What's on it? Slogans of free love, results of Pennsylvania's baseball championship year before last? The letters, some of them illegible because of the stitches, bunched together not in the right order: SYV and FRE and EFO or FREE FOR SYV...well, you know!...This way you could form "FOR SYVERS..." "We've got them, we do," Pankov gloated. "And in three years we'll have twice as many—a half-million conventional units per person."

18

Once he was on the train, Anton recalled that he hadn't got ten her address, after all. Oh, Lord! All right. Fine, I'll ask him another time. Or I can get it from Information. If she's registered. Everything suddenly began to seem simpler. Everything will work out fine. Only he felt a little nauseated. He shouldn't have eaten that beefsteak and drunk heaven knows what. On the platform a boy buried his face in a man's knees, threw his arms about them, and wouldn't let go: "Daddy, don't go!" A carved image of pity and tenderness. Lizavin felt a tickle in his throat. I don't have that, but I will, I will. The man broke free and jumped onto the train footboard. The train began to move—toward that place where the unpacked bast boxes of a new life awaited Anton Andreyevich. A heavy-faced beggar, his scabby skull bare and painted with a green anti-inflammatory medication, rapped with his stage prop of a stick on the aisle. "He was collecting money to booze, of course, just look at that bloated mug," Anton thought. But now he was ready to give even to a fellow like him. The point wasn't whether he was begging for booze or food. So what if it was for booze. Since time immemorial, in Russia we've always given not so much for the sake of the beggar, but for the salvation of our own souls. The simplest mode of payoff. "Here you are, dear, here's a twenty-kopek piece for you." You won't need to go deeply into everything. Indeed, we don't see everything. What swarms inside there, beneath our skin, under our clothes. If you want, I can describe the vomit I passed by right now— describe it exactly, no worse than Leo Tolstoy did, with little bits of salad beet and yellow carrot, so that I'd get a reader to also...stop, stop...Let's take a deep breath. I shouldn't have had that beefsteak, however...It's gone...So what? Will we find the truth of life in such a description? And if so, what's it for? There exists a level of life that is the stuff of drawings and graffiti on the walls of public toilets; so let it be. But I'm not spoiling for a fight on account of the level of life I belong to, that's the difference between us. His thought suddenly returned to what he'd been focusing on earlier. Maksim—what did he look for? What did he want from me? Why did he need to have me read such personal, such morbid, such confessional notes? I managed to calm Ania down then and did so quite sincerely: no serious rivalry threatened her. But I grew confused myself. Everything became poisoned with the thought, the feeling of incompleteness; there was none of the previous joy. There's an oily gasoline rainbow in the puddles, life has an aluminum sound and aftertaste—a greasy fork with bent prongs and some suet on it, the wheeze of a radio speaker in a dance hall, the banal vulgarity of courting, the sloppiness of undressing somebody, anguished yearning without love, wretchedness, abstinence, and honesty where before one could get some pleasure. And all this because the woman with whom things were different had appeared once, and, it turns out, won't let go, although common sense, like an objective voice, keeps asking all the time, mocking him: Do you want this? Is this what you really want? Just try to see things clearly. What did you see in her, a woman who'd not graduated from high school? Only what you attributed to her, and you were prompted by Maksim, a doomed deriver of significance. No, it's amazing how a man may know everything about his foolishness, about being wrong, and yet in spite of that continue doing the same thing...Two girls twittering by the door were adjusting each other's collars with their small fingers. Through the unwashed window one could see the grass, green on the slopes. *Fiu-liu-liu*, the little fife sounded. Does Maksim realize that that can be happiness? Perhaps right now he understands better than I do. Because he lost it. And I'm going to have it. I outstayed my rival. Bah, that's nonsense. Anton became embarrassed at thinking that double thought. And he wouldn't think like that. A cargo flatcar traveling on the adjacent tracks drew level with the window, two figures were standing on the brake platform, one dressed in a padded jacket, feet planted wide apart, one hand holding onto an upright, the other cupping his girlfriend's breast. Neither noticed the passing spectators immediately, but once they did, they didn't alter their pose, just grinned wider, and the insolent fellow squeezed her breast harder with his hand, to the envy of the others.

19

A cloud appeared, a spring cloud, its color harmonizing with the first grass and the hazy trees, filled from within with a green radiance. The nonstop thunder and the noise of the downpour were deafening, like the crash of a waterfall. Buglebead threads dangled from the vizor of the railway station annex. Anton moved them apart with the back of his hand and went out into the rain that lessened with every step he took. The rain worms—the intestinal substance of the earth—had crawled out in droves onto the asphalt, trying to escape the water; they crawled lethargically, grew limp, and perished under the soles of people's shoes. The sun peered out. This kind of moisture dries quickly, like children's tears. Lizavin reached the square, still wearing the highboots that he'd put on for the Nechaisk mud, and here he remembered that to get to his new house he had to go on the other side of the railway tracks. In the distance a man in railroad overalls beckoned him for some reason—perhaps to fine him for walking along the tracks? Had he been in a different mood Anton would have thought exactly that, but that day he was feeling faith in life and didn't want to think badly of it. He approached the fellow and proved right to do so: the man offered toilet paper for sale, several rolls of Finnish toilet paper for only five rubles. As if he were a friend or family member. Everything was fine, everything fit together nicely: a new life with hot water, a toilet, and toilet paper, naturally. Everything was shaping up by itself. The doctoral candidate walked down the street, his ironed pants tucked into his boots for the moment, a garland of rolls, which didn't fit into his briefcase, hanging down his chest from a small rope around his neck, like the mark of distinction of a man who's been admitted into the corporation, like the chain of a doctor *honoris causa,* like a garland of Indian flowers around the neck of the guest of honor that had been stolen right there from the train cars. And his nausea vanished completely, as if it had never existed, and the signal light generously showed all three colors simultaneously—in the form of illumination—big deal!

This supercilious certainty of the inevitability of some form of success probably made the doctoral candidate carefree. Before, he wouldn't have pushed into a mysterious line at random. He suddenly saw a van pull up to a stall near an abandoned lot to unload, and he stopped, as if for no particular reason, but he was already third in line, and a dozen people joined him instantly; and it seemed a pity to abandon such a privileged position without even finding out what they'd brought. What if they had some scarce goods to sell. Why not? Lizavin laughed at himself. He had to get rid of that stupid fear of lines, that arrogant hostility to them. It's better not to get anything than to stand with everybody in line—was that the idea? Everybody wants to have food-stuffs and clothes like normal people, to be proud that they're no worse off—and what shall you offer instead? We're launched into life so as to gain a foothold in it, to produce a progeny and to sustain it by those means, not to perish fruitlessly, as some people do. What can you boast of, ultimately? Natural selection gives preference to happy people. Come back, come back here, and stand here with them. It's certainly desirable to be one of the first in line, but that's how it works out. Everything's coming right. He was walking along the street. He stood in line. Now they'll start selling something. Pillowcases, fake diamonds from Japan, or, someone here is saying, deodorized butter? We'll see. Around them was a rain-washed early evening landscape, as prominent as in a nightmare, of new prefabricated houses. The clay weighed down one's soles. The holes in the local ground were already full of everyday garbage—the waste even anticipated the people. One could see the first flowers on the edges of the uneven trenches, and in their hardiness there was a certain indifferent readiness to tolerate whatever turned up—be it mud, be it iron— and to transform it into a short-lived simple beauty. An obtrusive mishmash of rusty armature and crumpled coils of wire made one feel as if one were in a trap. Ahead of him for some reason there now proved to be five people instead of two. Like a primitive organism, the line could multiply by fission. An entire gypsy band was joining the black-haired woman with golden earrings. The gypsies were also modern, with plastic bags, tourist knapsacks...An attack of nausea surged in him again, then subsided. Sitting on a ridge of earth, three deaf-mutes were talking to each other in sign language. Overhead, a naked sky without any cover, a prophetic clarity to the point of horror, with every person transparent and intelligible. Fishlike lips kept opening in the air, which was too empty to breathe, the fingers of the deaf-mutes weaving their design with increasing speed, and now Lizavin could have answered them in their language. "I could understand her now, too," he suddenly thought. I understand everything at last, can explain everything. What is deodorized butter? *Deodorized* means without a smell. No, not imported, ours. Can't imagine what it's made from, but it really doesn't smell, I've tried it. It tastes of machine oil...A sharp pain in his stomach made Anton double up. Possibly that was what was making him slow-witted. It was as if somebody had hit him. Indeed, around him there was increasing turmoil; until now, deafened by the soundless clarity, he'd ignored it, but it was sucking him in. He stepped aside, and slipped on the clay. The garland around his neck pulled him down, his briefcase fell out of his hands. Something nudged him in the stomach. Whether it was a blow by someone or the consequence of the ill-starred beefsteak, or both, the doctoral candidate wasn't fated to learn for certain; the test, as the specialists said later, was not carried out correctly—a bright flash suddenly pierced him through all the way to his spine.

XI. Ormuzd and
Ariman

*Through the shimmering vapors, one could see a knight standing
upright in metal plate-like armor made of mud, with a Polish helmet.*

a horned head with human teeth

a twig protruded from an eye socket

a trunk, glassy eyes

slop gurgles in the cauldron, the smoke going into one's mouth

*To stay there, stay, and not want anything else. That's the pinnacle,
that's bliss.*

*Fear and triumph mingle during first coitus, when hope springs
in man and woman of amplifying their being into a totality.*

one's feet slide out from under one, disappearing into the ground

*our entire life was an involuntary resistance to this ease and
freedom.*

1

Dazzling weightless peace, a tense, helpless attention. The pain
existed separately in an airless space—primordial, sterilely white. It
pulled its hooks by jerks from an immobile, foreign body. From there,
from the space filled with suffering and muteness, one could see the
tubes poking out of his nose, sticking into his blood-stained wrists.
The vines of glass and rubber stretched through the void toward a
boundless structure made of a transparent, unearthly, iridescent substance. Something inside bubbled and gurgled, live vessels extended
somewhere upward, where the pendulum of an ancient cuckoo clock,

with a green house for the cuckoo, rocked and ticked. There, on the edge of the available tension, in the glitter of a needle firm as a ray, dwelled horror—separate, unfearful, mental. On the green velvet a bit of poplar down gleamed, looking like a headless insect, with inverted faces emerging and showing through behind it. His gaze recognized one of them, although it seemed to have been born just now and didn't remember any previous experience. A white kerchief was tied low, the cheeks shaded. The face was swelling, shielding the pipes, the glass, the light, the emptiness. Warm lips touched his forehead. He came to from this touch—light but horrible—because his fear returned with it, as if he were being pulled by a forceful suction out of a calm belly into pain, to unite his body with it.

2

You wore a suit, had a position—it doesn't matter what—but nonetheless, you were somebody, meant something, managed to accumulate a brainful of inimitable memories, occupied a place in the very center of the world, tried to control it. One could only be surprised at how this world sufficed for all the people aspiring to occupy a unique, central place in it. Suddenly something inside you went out of commission, or, let's say, they picked you up, as they explained later, after an unfortunate fall onto one of the dowels of the steel framework, which penetrated and damaged your inner organs; they made the incision to the left of your navel, connected you to the chemical system—and a helpless suffering piece of flesh regained consciousness instead of you. A tube called a catheter protrudes from your innermost place, young women are doing something with you that you don't want done, and the woman you were seeking, whom you thought about from a distance—from such a distance that she was partly losing her corporeality, aureoled by a mother-of-pearl mist—comes to take away your bedpan. Her mouth looked large in a face grown thin, in a kerchief that covered half her forehead, in a robe that tied from behind, fingers red and swollen from hard work, pupils dilated, tender, and silent. The appearance of this face was now connected with the onset of pain, and he wanted to return to peace, to unconsciousness, without saying a word, to close his eyes, and, as in

227

childhood, to pretend that he wasn't awake yet. However, his weakness gave him the right not to delve too deeply into the underlying causes of his own involuntary movements; only later would talking with the old man who was his neighbor reveal something to him; but in the meantime he should lie there, poor thing. We can even look around the ward without him: her replacement has already arrived and taken charge, Aunt Frosia, with a drunkard's red nose, always angry at the doctors, nurses, but most of all at the patients, who always want something, as if the rubles she charged them would be sufficient payment for her trouble.

"They lie there, worrying to death about themselves. What the hell," she unburdened herself as she dragged the mop along the floor. "My man was sick, but didn't want to check into no hospital. Better, he said, have a good time half a year, going full swing, than spend a year lying in shit. And he had a good time, all right, may the blood-sucking bastard rest in peace!"

3

The three ambulatory patients could choose not to listen to her if they didn't want to; they were leaving the ward. One of them was a solidly built guy with a coarse, pockmarked face, another, a pale, dropsical boy about twelve years old, the third bore an amazing resemblance to Lizavin's former neigbor Titko, even in his pyjamas— a double, a veritable double. Besides the newcomer, Anton, there was an old man with a toothless sunken mouth and a dim, lost gaze. Something happened to him, they said, after his operation. The operation itself was standard, the removal of an adenoma caused by age, nothing more serious. But apparently they forget to take his dentures out of his mouth in time, remembering them only in the operating room; finally they took them out, but lost them somewhere. And then, it seems, the woman in charge of the linen wasn't available to give him a shirt in time, to cover his nakedness. Evidently the old man saw something when he regained consciousness alone in the ward, without his teeth and without anything at all; doctors, however, are familiar with the phenomenon called "postoperative psychosis." In short, he started to scream, abrupt, senseless, and terrible screams, his crazy, shaking fingers writhing above his thorax, and only an orderly who happened to be nearby knew how to reassure him. She reached his bed before any doctors (actually, nobody seemed to be hurrying to get to him), started to stroke the poor thing's hand, her lips touching the white temple drenched in perspiration as she whispered something inaudible, senseless, and reassuring. And he calmed down and relaxed, his pupils gradually acquiring focus, like the lens of binoculars. She then found a nightshirt for him, even located his lost dentures (in the bin for dirty linen). Yet some psychological displacement, nevertheless, still remained. Fearing attacks—during which he might bite his tongue—they didn't leave his dentures in his mouth, but kept them in a night table far enough from the bed that he couldn't reach it. Yet the old man was a former doctor; his name was Iakov Ilyich Manin. Titko found out everything essential about him.

4

Yes, no double, but in fact Fyodor Fomich Titko himself, a public activist of ever increasing importance, now proved to be an outstanding patient in the same ward. Maybe somebody else might think that a person's position before he checked into the hospital wasn't important here. Not at all! The very disease that Titko had to show medical science, not yet written up and mysterious, was evidently connected with his successful public career, with his newly acquired life opportunities, so that even a discussion of it could only be assumed to take place at the highest level—that is, on the fourth floor of the main building of the hospital, where the special wards that not everybody knew about, usually called "deluxe," were located. In the morning before the doctors' rounds, personnel from a beauty parlor and masseuses would go in, special orderlies would bring in heavy bags, and after midnight a light would burn there and one could hear western music,* which suggested that on that floor diseases themselves

---

* WESTERN MUSIC During the height of the Cold War, when Soviets rejected popular Western music, especially rock, as decadent, only the politically privileged had (unacknowledged) access to it.

acquired a special, not so alarming quality. Anyone who managed to get there seemed to be guaranteed, in a sense, that his disease was not that dangerous. Titko had been promised a place in the deluxe, but either somebody else managed to get there instead of him out of turn, or they decided to milk him for more. His spouse, Elfrida Potapovna, appeared at the pertinent office every day, but Fyodor Fomich remained stuck in an ordinary ward without even being examined. Of course, in a hospital where beds were crowded together even in the corridors, a five-bed ward could be regarded as a temporary privilege, but Titko was nervous, suspecting that they'd made a fool of him. That he wouldn't tolerate, because his most significant acquisition was his knowledge of the system that defined rights and opportunities on every level of life; this was a scientific system, if you like, with every case prescribed an exact dose, a percentage of imported and domestic services—a system, not voluntarism, not crooked dealings and not a bloody mess, to put it in everyday language, and the most important thing in this system was the necessity and ability to distinguish your own kind from among all the rest, who resemble you only superficially, like a wolf among dogs, even the meat on their bones is different, and the smell and the habit of never taking into account whose turn is next. But times were changing and species were mixed; even the way people dressed was not a reliable indicator. That's why he was very cautious when first meeting people, just in case. He even examined now with new interest his former neighbor—a slippery quiet person who'd not only contrived to get into the best regional clinic, but ended up being treated on the level of worldwide medical standards, using the newest equipment, an artificial kidney, with the participation of Feinberg himself, to whom even those at the top, they said, had to seek access. And at first he suspected old Manin, who for some reason or other didn't tell anyone about his medical profession, practically of being there incognito. A doctor in a hospital was, after all, one of the guys, like a salesman in a store. After the operation, his suspicions, of course, disappeared. To get even a minimal benefit from his forced proximity, Titko sometimes tried to put his dentures into his mouth and tortured him with medical questions, but got little sense out of him. Titko would sit,

wheezing uneasily, his eye only appearing to be covered by his piglike
lid with its tow-haired stubble of eyelashes, but in reality it was the
squinting eye of a former rifleman who continued to assess jealously
the people around him.

5

Igor Bogatyryov from Moscow was, as his last name of "bogatyr"*
dictated, an athlete, a master of some form of wrestling or boxing,
maybe even a member of the national team. He traveled abroad. He
had an appearance that said it all, and a coarse mouth adjusted to
saying the word "shit"; everything about him was fairly clear, if one
discounted the incident that brought him to the hospital. He was
brought in with a knife wound in his stomach. A militia investigator
visited the ward twice, but the guy from Moscow told him only that
he'd been attacked from the rear (he emphasized that, not without
the injured pride of a wrestler or maybe a boxer). He meant to say:
otherwise I'd have let them have it; there were three of them, he
thought, but he couldn't make out their faces. Since they didn't steal
anything from him, including even the two hundred rubles that happened to be in his pocket, the motive for the crime remained unclear.
It was also puzzling why an athlete had gone to the region on the
other side of the river when he was supposed to be waiting for his
connecting flight at the airport. He was already getting calls from
Moscow, and, judging by the phone calls, one could tell that he'd left
the airport on his own initiative, undermining the group's efforts in
some important competition. His career as an athlete seemed to be
over now, and not only on medical grounds. Titko sniffed out a fall
here, and the fact that the man was falling from such a height
gratified his sense of justice. Moreover, the guy from Moscow had
permitted himself a rudeness when Fyodor Fomich had hinted mean-
ingfully at the special, elevated nature of his disease. "You got hem-
orrhoids?" he asked, and instantly made an enemy of Fyodor Fomich.
At that time Bogatyryov was already able to walk and hadn't lost his
physical strength, so that Titko allowed himself to mention only in

* See note on p. 47.

his absence some people who received money and privileges without being of any benefit to society.

6

The one who was immediately obvious, with no questions asked, was Kolia Iazik, a stutterer from the country. The guy got into the ward maybe only as an old-timer of the hospital. Kolia had been maimed around nine years ago, when he'd saved his younger brother from falling under a truck that was about to run him over, and since then he'd been wandering from one medical institution to another, not out of hope, but rather out of medical curiosity; they tried to patch up one or another part of his system, reviving and frustrating his hopes for some decisive operation. He recalled his inadvertent selflessness reluctantly. "I s-simply d-didn't have time to think about it," he explained, stuttering. "If I'd have thought a bit, I d-definitely wouldn't have done it." Kolia was most upset not because of the disease itself—in winter small ice crusts froze on his feet and his bones ached as if he had rheumatism—but because of his damaged bladder, the bad smell, and being teased. He was forever hungry and Fyodor Fomich gave him his hospital food because Fyodor himself ate only food brought from home, and he justified Kolia's stay in the ward by the different services for which he used him, as, for example, running down to the newsstand for the papers.

7

When Kolia passed Lizavin, wafting a smell of urine at him, Anton experienced a distress for which he couldn't find the right words. It wasn't just pity for the poor fellow with a maimed body and a mangled destiny, for a stinker from an orphanage who'd learned to take care of himself any way he could, seeking protection from the powerful and even trying to please them. Once Fyodor Fomich started to say all kinds of things about the boy's brother: "You got maimed on his account," he said, "and he doesn't even help you." Iazik readily picked up on it: "If the truck were going by now, I'd push him under it myself." The little brother he'd saved was already graduating from a special technical school; he was seventeen, and Kolia twenty—Kolia only looked as if he were twelve years old. That day Titko found a book called *Sexual Hygiene* under his pillow and, roaring with laughter, read the title out loud. Iazik screamed in an unfamiliar voice "Put it back!" and even brandished his small cane, but didn't hit Titko (how could he!), having a hysterical fit instead. He wept clumsily, like a teenager, howling as he did so. "Okay," Titko said in conciliatory tones. "I'm putting it back now, see?—and I'm not saying a word. It's something necessary. You should try it with Zinka, the orderly." Old Manin moved restlessly and made mooing noises, as if asking for his dentures so as to have his say, and it was impossible to interfere, to speak up. Anton could only close his eyes and withdraw from the craziness of it all. He had already realized whom the retired captain called Zinka; he obviously didn't recognize her in her get up—and thank God. To close his eyes, to desire nothing. He didn't know when exactly she appeared in the doorway; first there was a draft of air, he could hear voices in the corridor, and Igor Bogatyryov came in to say that Iazik was being summoned by a doctor. "But you'll certainly have strong competition," Titko was finishing his thought as Iazik left the ward, and he addressed himself indirectly to the athlete now. "Broads go for men who are strong. On whose account do you think Zinka keeps looking in on us all the time? Here," and right then, suddenly opening his eyes, Lizavin met her gaze; she was staring from the doorway directly at him, and from the unexpectedness of it he lowered his lids for a second, as if he'd unexpectedly encountered the light. Just for the blink of an eye—quite literally, for as long as it took to blink. Then Iazik blocked her off, wafting the smell of urine his way (*A childhood smell is sweet to the nose*). "So what," he forced the words out, stopping for a moment. "I've already h-had my h-hands on h-her tits." Manin was in torment on his bed; the small crumpled rag of his lower lip moved amidst the spittle, while in the doorway, as if in the next frame of a film, there now stood a visitor with a bunch of expensive greenhouse tulips; her blond hair tumbled onto her cheeks, reminiscent of shots in fashion magazines, where it's sufficient just to outline the oval of a face and one can draw in the nose, lips, and eyes oneself, for they're perfectly paradigmatic. Igor Bogatyryov made his way to the door...

8

O, how suddenly his heart ached, as if from a sense of error, of inaccuracy or guilt. She could misunderstand something—he had to
explain, to correct it as soon as possible. They hadn't exchanged a
word with each other yet; after all, that was something she, as always,
didn't need, and he hadn't completely recovered so as to even look at
her, to express what he'd wanted to express recently from a distance.
Why did it prove to be so hard? He finally seemed to regain full consciousness—all he had to do was wait for her to return to the ward.
Wasn't he really afraid of Titko's swinish glance? He waited, listening intently to the voices and footsteps in the corridor, and was still
waiting when Iazik returned, crushed by the news that he was being
discharged from the hospital. The poor thing had hoped to be operated on, but the doctor explained that he still wasn't strong enough
for an operation. "Go for walks, get some strength out of doors."
"I'm strong enough," Kolia insisted. He didn't want to let go. "I'm
like a sick cat, you know? They're the greatest survivors." But in his
heart he already sensed that it was no use asking to stay, he had to
leave for a few months, say good-bye to a full stomach, to feed himself in the artel of invalids that produced clothespins for linen. Those
clothespins always hurt his fingers with their wide nails—white, as if
after a sauna, when the steam has softened them. Lizavin waited; he
winced when Bogatyryov came in, slamming the door, and, as if it
were a broom, picked up the bunch of flowers that had been tossed
onto his bed. "Already bringing me flowers, huh?" He showed them
without addressing anybody in particular. "As if to put on the grave of
the deceased." "Maybe you should go to the chief doctor?" Titko
advised lazily. "Say to him, what's going on? You promised me..."
Manin, suffering from his inability to get a word out, was dying to
take part in the conversation, but they didn't pay any attention to him.
"I can s-say," Iazik tried to put on a show of bravery, "If you d-don't
operate, I'll throw up right on your t-table." "She came to check,"
Igor grinned to himself, his hard mouth twisting. "To sniff out
whether I'm still worth anything." Titko finally took pity on the old
man and gave him his dentures. "Well, what is it?" Lizavin waited, listening to their voices. "Did you see her?" the athlete asked. "That's not

just a woman, but a prize for the winner." "Not that way, you can't do that—" the old man tried to get through, evidently something in his mouth had got lodged wrong and he had to speak hastily, with an effort, swallowing after every other word. "What are you talking about, when it's forbidden...this is something else here..." "Do you mean *this*?" Fyodor Fomich anticipated him, rubbing his fingers together to indicate money. "No, not that." Manin got excited, and so became even more incomprehensible. A disappointed Titko deftly removed the old man's useless dentures. "That's just what I'm saying, there's nothing he can do. And throwing up—what nonsense! They'll just make our Zinka clean it up." "We'll see," Bogatyryov grinned wryly. "Maybe it's still early to bring me flowers, eh?"

9

The shadows of late twilight had thickened in the ward when Lizavin realized that he had to wait twenty-four hours for her, until the next shift of nurses, and he fell into a doze. The tops of the ancient limes outside shone an unnatural electric green, illuminated by the lights above, from the fourth floor. Here, on the second floor, Fyodor Fomich experienced pain in his heart; he had to swallow some medication in earnest and to breathe carefully, drawing a half-breath so as not to feel the stabbing pain more acutely. The battle for the right to demonstrate the exceptional nature of his disease and organism at a higher level, and to relax there, threatened to turn into an ordinary attack. He experienced his sickness as a slug of anguish that prevented him from breathing. Why, o Lord, what for? How much effort, how much sweat and blood he'd had to expend so as to get on in life, to get what others have, including the opportunity, during projects that didn't pay, to eat caviar of both colors, to drink cognac—sometimes even a French brand—which isn't so harmful to his weak kidneys, but at the same time makes you aware that inside your body you have the equivalent of fifty rubles a week, and even more, if you calculate it per month...O Lord! Why did other people's stomachs digest everything quite normally, while delicacies left your stomach undigested, without any alteration at all—the caviar didn't even change color. Not that this tortured him, but it didn't bring any physical pleasure either; that is,

235

he didn't even salivate and produce other juices of authentic pleasure. It proved morally offensive. It was as if delicacies weren't for
you. A turnover with cabbage you could eat and fully digest and enjoy,
but delicacies—forget it. That is, you're a peasant, low-class through
and through, always were, and don't try to become somebody different. Why, Lord? It's not fair. Others eat and shit to their hearts' content and have managed to get a deluxe room, and in what respect are
they better? I know them, as do you, even longer. They haven't seen
what I have, and haven't suffered as much, have they? They skimmed
the surface without getting their soles dirty, but from where did I
have to clamber out? O Lord, what can I say? For you it's not a matter of sounds, you can see through it all without that; I can understand that and I acknowledge it sincerely...Lord, it's exactly with
words, for others, that you can't express a lot of things, whereas without a sound, like right now, with the soul, you yourself know I've
never refused to talk to you. I used to go to church with my grand-
mother—I remember the words even now: "Our Father, who art in
Heaven"—and as for the priest who caught cold in the punishment
cell, he wasn't a priest at all according to us, by our standards he
wasn't a priest at all, he didn't wear a cross, and nobody can steal the
remnants of seed husks from cows (by the way, that's state property).
You, Lord, are the highest instance, the guiding instance, so to speak,
and you know whom you have to govern, and I'm not the one who
arranged this life, and not the one who created people the way they
are. That is, I'm not anything. I say that without any criticism; if
something happens, I won't refuse to take responsibility for it, but
haven't they insulted me? And yet I've tried to treat people decently,
I've tried to behave as an educated person with a conscience would.
Perhaps that's why I've suffered—because of being too kind. If I had
the power, I'd arrange my whole life and everyone else's according to
fairness. All I'm asking for is fairness, o Lord!

10

In the morning Iakov Ilyich suddenly asked the doctor who looked in
for permission to smoke a cigarette. He and Anton were the only two
left in the ward. Iazik has been discharged and Titko had been moved

up to the fourth floor (the prayer that the world couldn't hear had helped). The athlete hadn't come back to the ward after breakfast. Emptiness, the silence of a Sunday, birds' twittering outside. Doctor Feinberg visited the ward; he wasn't the doctor on duty, but for some reason he wanted to examine Manin. For a long time, eyes half-closed, he listened to Manin's pulse rate, felt for it in various parts of the patient's body; under the doctor's boneless fingers the pulse was like a live, naked body that betrayed the deep secrets beneath the skin. Legends circulated about Feinberg that not only had he sewn the severed fingers of a hand back on in such a way that they worked as if they were normal, but once sewed together a man who'd been cut in two with a circular saw, and kept him alive for twelve days—and he could have lasted longer if the poor fellow's liver hadn't been destroyed by cirrhosis from alcoholism.

"Let me have one for the end, colleague," Manin said. "Or at least a half."

"Strange talk, colleague," the doctor raised an eyebrow ironically. "You yourself realize what you're asking. And what does 'for the end' mean?"

"It's precisely because I realize," Manin replied, half closing his lids, yellow and thin, like a bird's.

"You seem not to recognize me, Iakov Ilyich," Feinberg said. "I did my doctor's internship under you in Kolobov's hospital. Of course, you can't remember—one day they brought in a girl who'd poisoned herself with the essence of vinegar because her partner at a dance invited her friend instead of her. You certainly knew how to tell her off, the fool! She seemed to grasp what you were saying, but a week later she made another attempt, and this one succeeded. Remember? I was surprised what an effect it had on you. We went out onto the porch, you were smoking, and you suddenly started elaborating a literary plot: how a suicide attempt gets punished by making the hero live his life once again from the very beginning—the same life until the very moment of the attempted suicide. I always remembered that. Particularly your words that self-respect, a duty to restrain yourself, to bear up despite everything, isn't just a personal duty, but the imperative of a Higher Force. What happened to you? You yourself know that you don't have anything seriously wrong with you." He touched Manin's shoulder and went out, leaving the old man with the dentures in his mouth, as if to confirm that there was nothing to worry about—and he personally had nothing to do with that silly humiliating make-believe of the old man's imminent death.

11

With his dentures in place, Iakov Ilyich's face didn't look so old and pitiful at all, as if it recalled its former intelligence and significance. Scored with a multitude of distinct, amazingly clear wrinkles, this face made clear that a human being gains value precisely with age, like an old object that has managed to survive hard times, enriched by its markings.

"I'd heard of him," he talked slowly now, either addressing his neighbor or simply enjoying the opportunity to speak out loud. A tear was running down his temple. "A phenomenal doctor. Phenomenal not just as a surgeon and diagnostician, but in how he conducts himself, how he finds it possible to do his job amidst the squabbles and chaos of this place. That's all fine. But I was also talking about that— why didn't he understand? We're so proud of our coolheadedness. Indeed, why does a man who's condemned to death need a dinner with wine and coffee at the end? It's ridiculous. What's the difference whether you've eaten or not...or even understood...something at the very end, if in half an hour it won't matter at all? Well, even if in five hours, in a day...it's still the very end. It doesn't matter. That's precisely the trick. In five years or in five minutes—you can't allow this small chink. I've been through a lot of things. Prison, war. I could have been killed many times over. Simply killed. But I wasn't afraid of that. I was afraid of something else. Always. Of humiliation. The loss of self. I thought: before the last moment...at least to have time to smoke a cigarette. He didn't get it, he's simply not experienced it yet. Why this 'at the end'? Who's mocking us?" Manin swallowed something and fell silent, and from his bed across the room Lizavin saw that Iakov Ilyich was weeping: no, it appears he hadn't yet completely recovered from his earlier displacement. "I yelled disgustingly, didn't I?" The old man gave a final sob and suddenly turned to Anton.

238

"Though you didn't hear, I don't think. They hadn't brought you in yet. It was probably disgusting. And I shit under myself, too." He controlled a spasm once again. "It's impossible to explain to anybody from the other shore. I almost didn't exist anymore, that's what's so terrible and shameful... How can I convey that to you? Maybe I need to, so that you'll know... The main part of me had already come apart; it was transforming into something sticky, indifferent. Horror and at the same time the shameful, treacherous temptation to let yourself go completely... No, our words from here aren't adequate. If it hadn't been for that girl... amazing... something extraordinary comes from her touch... Even from her coming closer to you... I'll try to say it somehow. It's important. It affects us all. A clash of indescribable forces takes place. Now, every moment, all the time. We participate without suspecting anything. Everything's connected. The astonishing skill of doctors, their fantastic technique... but it penetrates through a chink—an insignificant, boorish one—through us..."

12

He had a dream or saw the following as he drowsed lightly: from under the clouds the setting sun hit the eyes with the furious, savage, excessive light of electric theater lamps, when everything becomes black and white, like painted lips in a deathly pale face. The leaves were illuminated like a negative: white flatness from the glare, with black-and-green shadows. The park and the city are below, beneath his feet; the air fills bodies with a sense of anxiety and flight. How painfully it brings us together and pulls us apart again! I didn't even have time when I was awake to tell you what I wanted to say, what I was thinking about all this time. I got weak. Yes, I probably wasn't strong to begin with, nature didn't give me so much. At times I tried to keep up with everything, still hoping to come through. And suddenly something knocks your feet out from under you, like a clown in a circus, and if you don't understand this the first time, there'll be more where that came from. And what you lost hurts, and that's why you feel at last that it's really happening. It doesn't mean that before I was insensible, but I had inside my being a kind of anesthetic element. I could even endure toothache for weeks; doctors would get outraged afterward.

And now there's no anesthesia. And again it seems to me that I didn't live normally. What was the matter with me? I'd lost myself, that's what it was. But not the way a man who loves somebody loses himself, dissolving in love and realizing himself in the process. Now I'm able to experience you as if you were a feminine part of my own soul, that's why I even see you and this light. But then it was something else. I succumbed to something else. The old man found the right words for me. I know what I was afraid of, even if only for a short moment. And I proved to be imperfect—that's what it was called once. I'm weak now, and therefore more honest than usual. But we really don't know ourselves completely, that's our hope. This unhappy boy (for some reason, when I smell his urine smell, I keep seeing the child's face on the *fantik*), I can imagine him being terrible, if only given the opportunity and the strength...Milashevich has something on this subject, too...but there was something within him that made him throw himself under the wheels of the truck before he could think. Does that mean that anything can happen to any one of us? to me? and you, too? One probably shouldn't think like that—that's exactly what terrified the old man. What did this unhappy man say about you?...No, no, I know I shouldn't ask like that, I don't have the right to, and you won't answer...Once again you're unrecognizable, as in my dream, an unfamiliar bag over your shoulder, the trees and the city below. You don't answer, as if you're waiting for somebody else. That's irrelevant. And there's nothing to be done, and the only life you have is passing by, irreparably. It's separating us, separating us again. But why irreparably? Here the old man found the words, managed to recover. He was strong, superhumanly strong, there's no comparing us two, and she wasn't silent either, as you were. It's hard, nonetheless; if you only knew. *To compare with oneself this muteness spilled in the air...* Where did so much pain come from?—and this unbearable music...and the light behind the half-open door...

13

The lamps are lit on the desks of the nurses on night duty; semi-darkness in the corridors, which are crammed full of beds with sweaty, groaning bodies snoring in their sleep; the smell of misery, medication, and patients' excretions fills the air. And on the floors above, the bright incandescence of lights; sounds can't carry through the ancient walls and doors made from stained oak beams, after a hundred years still fit for a Stradivarius. Once old Bogolepskii himself, the founder of the hospital, sat here on the fourth floor past midnight, reading a German journal; here in his youth Manin attended feasts of a scholarly nature, and there was a grand piano in the corner that people would sometimes play; right now one could also hear music. It's not flowing out through the wide-open windows, but is confined indoors, like a thickened light trapped by the leaves of the huge lindens. Painted mouths look black; the perspiration of zealous enjoyment squeezes out of pores and expands into thick drops on the upper lip. Bodies shake in time to the music, also not in time, for that's not the main thing. We create our own music. We're having a good time, right? Wandering smiles, frozen faces, eyelids half-closed in self-oblivion, but the gaze tries to catch others' expression as if to say "I'm no worse off than you, I don't think." It's not so simple to play the role of happy people as you push aside a fear of life. Heels stamp on the ceiling of the floor below. Bottles from the orphans' feast show green in the shaft of light. The illuminated windows float through the night above diseases and deaths, above pain, defeat, and misfortune. We're all temporary, they say, but everyone has a particular, special temporariness. There, beneath us, they may die even today, but in the meantime we'll have a look and, then, who knows? There's no absolute proof that the end is equally inevitable for everyone. Right now that's only a statistical fact, a conclusion based on the experience of the people who lived before us. But there were no people like me before in the world! Ultimately somewhere there exists a floor higher than the fourth, there's still hope—who knows? The air is full of the small wings of night moths, damp down invades the nostrils, and the humid darkness thickens with fumes.

14

"Well, what now?" Frosia the orderly proclaimed as she disrupted their morning sleep with the clang of her pail. It wasn't even seven yet, and the old woman's little nose was already red, her expression jovial, as if she'd already had something to drink. "You two just lying there? Go ahead, go on. That student of yours has run himself into trouble." She poked with her mop at Bogatyryov's bed, which hadn't been occupied all night. "They're trying to bring him to in the reanimation room right now. Who knows how it'll turn out. Know who he got caught with—God almighty!—with our Zoika. He got caught in the bushes behind the boiler house, you know, near the fence. Venia, who works in the morgue, lives right there alongside the hospital. He comes out in the morning, looks, and this guy's there in just his undershorts, and she, Zoika, that is, is right there with him. Well, they either jumped with fright or maybe he went too hard at it with her—his stitches are still new and they burst, they say, from the strain. Pah!" Aunt Frosia spat and started to move her mop with pleasure over her own spittle. "He sure picked the right person for who to break the fast. You couldn't keep her out of any of the men's wards here. Both reeked of wine. He didn't spend the night here, did he, huh? What?" she finally asked.

"A doctor, call the doctor, quick," Anton repeated.

"A doctor—what for?" The orderly didn't understand. "The doctors are already making a fuss. Slept the whole night with her, they say."

"A doctor, hurry, get a move on, please," Lizavin urged, having difficulty restraining himself from screaming.

"Ahh, ah-ah!" the old man yelled. His eyes were staring wide, his hands shaking, twisted above his chest. A sticky, deathly moisture exuded from his pores, the window frame was swimming, and headless insects began filling the air that was impossible to breathe.

XII. ZETA OMEGA ETA

1

By the opening in the hospital fence, as arranged. Hospital-issue pyjamas, the color faded, in a shoulderbag with the letters SPORT. The air feels the fullness of her body under the light dress. Below, beneath the embankment of the ravine, the tops of the poplars are stirring. Far behind them, like a mirage in a haze, a block of new prefabricated buildings shimmers. To the right of the trees, where the branches thin out, a dump was gradually forming and expanding in the empty hollow. Either from the quiver in the air or from a turn of the head some precious splinters flashed here and there, as if something live were moving in the substance that had served its time

———

a flash of the childlike feeling that the time which passes doesn't vanish but accumulates at a distance, like a visible stagnant locale from which one hears the voices of the departed, even, it seems, forgotten voices; after looking there closely you'll see their faces (but it's impossible to get close to them); sometimes a slow small complete turn, so that after glancing in the other direction you could see the person who hadn't yet reached you and hear in advance what he would ask as he approached. Do you know what your name means? Yes, my father told me. In Greek. It's written like this. Do you want me to show you? With a small red twig in big letters in the snow. It wouldn't come out in small letters, the frozen snow crust would crumble. Thin ice crusts. Zeta, omega, eta. The neighbors' faces are glued to the windows. How easily one can breathe—just right for getting scared. Of what? One just can't explain it in words. We understand ourselves thanks to others. I came here without suspecting what I was looking for. Though, no, I was close to understanding, and here I reached complete understanding. If that were possible for me. Do you know Anton well? I didn't know him at all. I think he took part in my dad's amateur talent activities. If I'm not confusing him with someone else. He seemed like an adult then. Later he left, probably to study. But why are you asking? Oh, just. Keep him in mind. He's a man you can rely on. He knows that life is impossible without yielding to incompleteness, and it doesn't lose stability because of that

---

only in the huge alien city, in a house where his portraits hung and another woman moved about, did you feel that you'd lost your way, and there was nobody at your side who'd take you by the hand, like that nice tender bearded man whose voice made you feel warm, like a warm yarn, whose touch stopped your trembling, whose words were so clever and explained so much about both of you—why did you have to distinguish something else through them, like a thin web against the skin? The lines of the pattern were displaced; there's no transparency again—a crossroads amidst blank stone walls, a road past the opaque windows, other people's doors. Over there by the post office, an old woman slipped and fell in the street and couldn't get back on her feet. The smell of pure spirit that's not burned, mixed with the scent of cheap perfume. Thank you, dear. In the creaky, loud voice typical of those who are hard of hearing. A monstrous head with a warm kerchief wound around it, rheumatic rubber boots on her feet. A hooked nose above a crudely painted mouth. Did you hurt yourself much? I'll see you home. Oh, *merci*—this time she thanked her in French. I don't live far from here. They made for a ramshackle building, two stories high, with a rickety staircase and a damp smell of cat. A piece of bast matting stuck out from the tattered padding on the door. A heavy smoke-gray cat jumped from somewhere on the lintel onto its owner's shoulder, making her start. Come on, Apollo, can't you see we've got a visitor. The bed in the small room is covered with a gray army blanket. A table without a tablecloth, a small icon in one corner, in another, a female dummy without a head, but for some reason with men's pants in a huge size attached to its lower body. Together with the dull tailor's mirror the dummy indicated the owner's former profession—a profession from olden times, incidentally, even before the bombardment of 1943, when Roksana Vikentyevna suffered a contusion and something in her mind was dislodged. Although the only visible signs of this shift were perhaps the pants on the dummy and also an incomprehensible passion for keys; she'd already collected several very heavy bunches of them for purposes clear to her alone. Her pension sufficed for the purchase of cheap Polish cigarettes, but the old woman had the reputation of a witch doctor or even a sorceress; she sold ointment for rheumatism, and when she took her Apollo—a castrated cat feared even by dogs and neighbors, who attributed numerous outrages to him—for walks on a leash, wearing her incredible hat, with her hooked nose, she looked like an out and out witch. Possibly thanks to her notoriety she managed to retain her apartment, which could be regarded as a two-room unit: behind the veneer wall there was also a closet with a folding cot. "Stay and live here if you have no place, I can see that you're not pushy or crude." Everything about this old woman—her appearance, actions, and speech—consisted of various parts that on first glance seemed incompatible: her SPORT shoulderbag, the beak-shaped hat, curses, French, the men's pants on the female dummy. "I'm not just from the nobility, I'm from the family of the princes Ganetskii." Some slop boiling on the small kerosene stove smelled of boot polish. The insistent drone of a loud-speaker. Roksana Vikentyevna, does this really work? The ointment, you mean? It depends. It's worked for some, probably. At least I never heard that anybody died from it. There was a disdainful humor in her loud, creaky voice. For my own needs I have a small coil pipe for making bootleg vodka, but don't tell anybody that, they'll inform on me. I make a distinction between people who have moral rules and those who don't. When you get a job I'll have you pay ten rubles for living here. It's not too much? Why would I offend you by making you a parasite?

———

what was good about work in the hospital was the freedom from an imposed rhythm. Her own rhythm didn't make her tired. Plus the promise of a position and a half and the possibility of making more money, for example by giving blood, or, even more profitably, marrow, although they say that the latter's painful. Well, there were no problems with money, except when people would insist on slipping rubles into the pocket of her robe, but then she could buy candy for Kostia Iazik; he liked sweets, like a kid. The air and smell in the place reminded her of Grandma Vera, of sorrow and pity, life's fears, shivering in the night and the touch that brought relief, the noise of the drip from the tap in the kitchen, death and shock, guilt before a person dear and, as it turns out, close to her, with whom sooner or later time and space had to bring her closer. Just a little longer, so as to let your inner feelings ripen when you see and remember more and more clearly the voice, gestures, the warmth of his fingers, words, the merging, the weight of a recovered completeness. And beneath the half-closed eyelids—the dear, suffering face...why the hospital tubes in his nose?—as if it's in a dream, and the dream's terrible, but it proves not to be a dream. Here in the hospital everything was so hard, so real: misery, pity, pain, tenderness

———

and the fulfillment of the meeting she'd dreamed about was so horrifyingly real, it was so hard to look at the dear shaken body with tubes in the nose and bloodstained wrists. At the door Roksana Vikentyevna lifted her hooked nose like a little animal with a keen scent. What's the matter with you? You smell somehow different. To see those temples covered with beads of perspiration from suffering, those lips with the coagulated white crusts, to think of the eyelids covering the eyes so as not to look at anyone. The night is imprinted on the cheek with the hem of a pillow. Thoughts are disordered, like hair after a sleepless night. "Zoia?" In the other room the old woman is awake, worrying. "Zoia, what's that knocking sound from your room? Stop it, please. There it is, even louder. No, don't try to tell me. Are you doing it on purpose? I can hear it." And suddenly Zoia heard it herself—a loud, regular sound. It was impossible to tell where it came from. The air trembled in time to it, the windowpanes rattled, as if from the force of the wind, and, laying her hand to her chest, she finally realized that it was her own heart

———

she's already grabbed the bag and pants, and will have to explain. To awaken Roksana Vikentyevna after her all-night vigil was impossible;

she didn't pay much attention to what time of day it was. And what's the sense of it now. The fresh juice of the blades of grass that she's chewed becomes saliva on her lips. When you stand like that for a long time you start feeling that you're a property of the place. Ants are clambering up her leg as if it were a tree trunk. It's pointless to continue standing, but you delay leaving. Where would you go? A beetle reached the top of a blade of grass. What for?—he's got no wings. Just because the way led upward. Now he even can't turn around to go back. He'll either have to drop to the ground or wait till a gust of wind carries away his light little body God knows where

———

it wasn't just the old woman—everyone else felt it too, even Kolia Iazik, the poor stutterer. In the dark corner under the stairs where by the end of the day the public telephone was filled to the brim with conversations about sicknesses, food, apprehensions, news from the city, and home concerns. She didn't immediately understand when she saw Kolia trying to extract something from the telephone. Once he was calm again, Kolia explained that it was simple to open up the phone, then to join the wires, just like that, so that it would work without a coin, then to plug the coin slot with a piece of cardboard, and the coins would pile up on it without dropping. A technician he knew had taught him how to do it. He'd leave with his booty and head for the telephone booths at the hospital gates; over there you could always find someone who needed to change money for the necessary two-kopek coins. His legitimate profit was always the one-kopek difference during this exchange. He wasn't simple; although he came from the country, he was pretty shrewd and he was no worse than the others at getting what he needed. Only she shouldn't have touched him the way one does a little boy; that was a mistake. At first his fingers touched her bosom accidently, but then they seized hold of it convulsively, painfully, desperately, like the paw of a wounded little beast. His frozen grimace only attempted to pass itself off as a smirk—an insolent smirk, not characteristic of him. Okay, he mumbled, okay then, while saliva appeared on his childish lips, anguish in his eyes, and his trembling prevented him from getting through her inconvenient robe to her live body. She felt sorry for everybody, felt guilty before everybody, and it was impossible to untangle it all

Bogatyryov intercepted her in the street on her way to the laboratory building. A heavy box with vials weighed her hand down; it was unbearable to stand there and it was hard to look at his coarse, assured face. "Only pants," he urged her. "I've got a shirt. I'll pay you three times over—I've got money here, it's being kept for me, but I can't get it today. You hear me? It's a question of life and death, do get them. Size fifty-two. But any size will do. Buy them. Or do you have somebody? Otherwise I'll leave in pyjamas." His hospital pants are turned up to his ankles, showing his socks and a strip of his smooth leg. Strong muscles, a firm body that gets cut during the operation. No, no. The orderly from the morgue almost knocked them down with his gurney. The rubber tires made no sound, but the loosened iron parts rattled. "Hey, want a ride?" He exposed his bristling red lip. They'd sewn it on right here, in the hospital; his drunken brother-in-law bit it off while kissing him; to this day the nurses remembered how he'd appeared, past midnight, his mouth all bloody, looking for the surgeon on duty. They started looking for the piece that was bitten off, and it proved to be home, in the pocket of some other clothes, for some reason, and they had to go get it. Thank God it wasn't far. They found it all covered with garbage, with tobacco flakes, but it was fine, the lip adhered, though in the form of a small flat cake all covered with hair, and the words that emerged from between it were like sticky viscous stuffing. "Okay, I'll get you another time." Bogatyryov was pale—so big and coarse, yet weak as compared to the hairy orderly who allowed himself the pleasure of philosophizing as he moved on. The process of production is a stream. Fulfillment of the plan is at one hundred percent. He checked the area around him with the dim look of a man to whom the entire hospital seemed an interim technical structure between the city and the sixteenth building. Better the city not think about or know how in the various cells here human bodies are getting ripe for burial, while he makes the rounds with his gurney to collect the final product, to give it that final perfection, freezing it a little, painting the lips, shaving it and rouging the cheeks, and, if necessary, decking it out in a wig at the relatives' request. A master of his profession, he spent a great deal of money on drink and either because of his wealth or because of his awareness that he was irreplaceable he took a lot of liberties, sincerely convinced that all the efforts and labors of the earth's inhabitants, including doctors, could ultimately be used to personally ensure his condition: a cheerful, simple, and drunken haze. "Kings can do whatever they want, kings can do everything," he'd shout as he'd move away, and wherever the spray from his mouth fell, the grass turned yellow and dried up. That's what she was afraid of, not for herself; and also there was the strange thought that the presence of the pants on the dummy—the mysterious caprice of the confused old woman, which coincided with the patient's request— was getting an explanation, justification, and significance, which it had only been waiting for.

2

The shadow lengthened as it crept along the slope, using the convenient ledges of the ground in order to traverse the asphalt path below, to disappear under the trees, where one could hear women's screeching and drunken voices, along the grass, cigarette butts, shards from broken bottles, and the routes of the hardy urban ants, to spill and merge with the shadows of the city park. The geometrical columns behind the trees were growing heavier in the bright light of the sunset, like rows of cemetery stones. The red letters over the building of the Swallow Café, which had been turned into an evening restaurant now, were lit up before dusk fell. The doorman at the entrance was taking the measure of a girl who, with her first salary in her handbag, couldn't understand at all why they wouldn't let her into the restaurant alone in the evening. But I want to have something to eat. Huh, still a teenager, and already has wants. The blackheads on the doorman's face were moving like something live, and a blush of comprehension and shame flooded the girl's soft, innocent cheeks. On the opposite side of the street a guy was hanging around the liquor store, dressed in a white shirt and baggy pants that clearly belonged to somebody else. The ones she'd managed to get for him. An hour earlier he'd stood like that across from the the marriage registry office, waiting for arrival of the young couple, who certainly hadn't invited him to their wedding. He'd observed the arrival of one couple after another before having the sense to call the bride's home. The voice of the paralytic who couldn't attend the wedding ceremony kept trying at length to pin down who was calling, but learning that it was a school friend, proudly informed him that they'd managed to transfer the ceremony to the new Wedding Palace that had opened that very day. The bridegroom, a powerful man, had managed to arrange it, but they'd asked that no one tell any outsiders, for some crazy guy could cause a scene, and they didn't want that. The guy now standing near the restaurant didn't understand himself what he—the uninvited—was still waiting for. He tried to recall the name of the movie or the book they'd studied in some high school class or other. Someone in it was also too late to prevent a wedding, and the bride who got married against her will now couldn't go back on her word. Well, this bride could and would, even her signature in the registry office wouldn't mean that much— only she was getting married because she wanted to. Although not out of love, but these words were already ridiculous words. It was also ridiculous to be waiting for something, but he was. A wedding motorcade pulled up at the restaurant. Six black cars decorated with ribbons, balloons, and good-luck charms. A bride in a virginal-white dress stepped out and looked around. It was impossible to read the expression on her face from a distance, but the former wrestler didn't need to. Suddenly Igor understood everything—it was so clear, it was amazing he'd never understood it earlier. He made his way back to the hospital, staggering like a drunk. The tramlike sound of thunder approached. The sun disappeared and the wind picked up. There was a sprinkling from the small cloud as if from an atomizer, creating pimples on one's skin and specks on the asphalt. The tin roofs of the garages were soon covered with the exhalation of cool perspiration. The street lamps, washed clean and transparent, came on. He walked in their diffused light as in a golden reservoir, with the unnatural gait of a diver for whom it's hard to walk precisely because of his weightlessness, and he didn't recognize right away the stupid girl who was wearing an open dress instead of her usual hospital robe with the strings that tie from the back. He'd completely forgotten about her, he didn't think she'd be waiting, and he remembered only when he was already at the hospital gates. Just in case, he walked around, along the fence. "Excuse me," he said in English. "An unexpected hitch."

She didn't react, just stood there, huddled, cold, sending out clear signals—and how clear the whole mess now seemed to him: the wretched lapwing who'd waited so long for him just for the sake of the cheap pants, but, of course, not only for their sake, you could tell by the little bitch's eyes. Pathetic little bitch who'd looked for a chance to visit the men's ward one more time (as that swinish snout of a guy had put it—he knew how to call them all by their real name). But at least you could still feel sorry for her. He undressed her with his gaze, as was his habit. Perhaps he was looking for something sordid now, the way a pig probably seeks dirt to get rid of an itch.

"So, we can't get into the building now, it's closed, right? Okay, they won't discover I'm missing till morning—today's a day off. I know the kind of order they keep. So? Why the silence? Do you have a place?"

The glittering rings of branches wound around the street lamps. A staircase smelling of cats and damp. Quietly, so as not to make the floor creak. The door opened soundlessly. Behind it, as in a delirium, you could see a bright white tablecloth; a bottle and three long goblets reflected the candles in a triple candlestick; a hook-nosed old woman with a black painted mouth rose to greet them.

3

No, she didn't rise, but roused herself, as someone does when regaining consciousness after a dream—an anxiety dream—with gratitude for being awakened.

"Ah, Lord, at last!" she croaked plaintively. "I was really getting worried! I didn't know what to think. I was at my wits' end." By the end of the last phrase, however, she managed to control her voice, modulating it smoothly, like a bridled horse, to a genteel though no less creaky tone; she smiled at the young man with her black mouth, and held out her hand—not to be shaken, but kissed. "I'm Princess Ganetskaia." She was wearing something inconceivable, either a housecoat or a dressing gown with flowers. "You may call me Roksana Vikentyevna."

"Bogatyryov." Out of initial embarrassment he touched his lips to the hand smelling of vaseline. "Fuck it" more or less sums up the essence of his thoughts—although extremely approximately and in abbreviated form; these thoughts contained the simple conjecture that he was meeting the old mother or relative of this (roughly speaking) idiot, who explained her completely; that this was a trap of sorts prepared for him; that nevertheless there was nowhere to go and really no purpose in leaving—there was even an aura of gaiety, and the bottle on the table corresponded to his dominant desire of the moment; no, you could laugh until you burst. Now, now. "You can call me Igor."

"I'm pleased to meet you," said the princess. "And this is Apollo. To those he knows, he's simply Pusia. And this..." She was about to point to the dummy, but stopped short and made a dismissive gesture. "Don't pay any attention to him."

The dummy had a chest without nipples, but then, it also lacked a head; its lower parts were now wrapped in a temporary gray duster resembling a skirt—Roksana Vikentyevna seemed to be embarrassed by the absence beneath its torso, as if it were something indecent. Nevertheless, he moved closer to the table, behind which a triple tailor's mirror was spread out like a screen—possibly so as to hide the unattractiveness of the apartment from the guest.

"Please sit down," the hostess bustled about. "You can't imagine how worried I've been. I'll explain in a second. She's also surprised, don't think she's not." Roksana Vikentyevna addressed her guest and spoke about Zoia in the third person (but with that inflection with which one speaks about people on their name day or, if you like, about a bride who's being visited by matchmakers). "Today happens to be the anniversary of my illness. I suffered a contusion in 1943. And two years later, on exactly the same day, I was reading a very beautiful novel in French and suddenly realized that I hadn't understood anything—what it was about, what the title was, nothing. And it didn't matter. Because at the very same moment I discovered something else more important. But I can't deny that I was extremely upset. And now every year since then I'm afraid of this week, of this moon. But this year everything is surprisingly calm, it's unbelievable—no symptoms. Since she came here. She can corroborate it. A minimal amount of alcohol. And suddenly today I wake up and look," she glanced over her shoulder at the dummy, "he's without his pants—pardon me, without his trousers.

I was almost at my wits' end. But then I got hold of myself and tried to put it all together logically. You know I've sensed it for a long time, you shouldn't think any different" (with a smile at Zoia). "People like me sometimes understand more than you imagine. I thought: he couldn't do it himself, he's got no hands, it's ridiculous to suppose that. A stranger wouldn't be able to get into my apartment. That means she did it. And she wouldn't do that for no reason. Right? And if a girl like that needs to bring men's trousers to the hospital, that means I should provide her with a bottle of wine by evening before the store closes, since perhaps she's got no time to buy it herself. Logical, right?"

"Mmm...yeah," Bogatyryov was forced to agree wryly, although in contrast to Zoia he couldn't appreciate the real magnificence of this logic. He simply didn't understand anything about the pants and the dummy.

"What a relief that I wasn't wrong, and here you are! But why are we just sitting here? Open the bottle, please. Try to imagine, this is Tokay, real Hungarian Tokay, you can never tell what they'll bring to the sticks. There's no tea, but Tokay's for the asking...Well, here's to you...to getting acquainted!" the princess touched the rim of the goblet restrainedly with her lips. "She's got nobody, you know. Who apart from me would worry about her? You may smoke if you wish. Do you smoke?"

"I used to," he said, patting the pockets of the borrowed trousers.

"Did you give it up?"

"I was forbidden to smoke. The regimen."

"Regimen's right," the princess creaked respectfully. Zoia was unaccustomed to, and couldn't understand, a certain respectful shyness in her. "But you don't have to look for any, I have some. Here you are."

"Not my trousers," Igor explained his futile gesture with a grin. They weren't really having fun, and instead were succumbing to fatigue and emptiness. Roksana Vikentyevna finally got a light from the candle her guest lifted toward her.

"Don't be embarrassed about your clothes," she interpreted his words in her own way. "I don't judge people by their clothes. I've worn heaven knows what myself. She, now, she walks barefoot as if she's wearing size thirty-two shoes with high heels, and when she wears high-heeled shoes she walks as if barefoot. I used to have that same kind of walk. Yes, that's hard to believe. But I'll show you a photograph. Nice face, slender waist, soft voice. What combines into making each of us a person. And you, pardon, what do you do? Or, as they say nowadays, what's your specialty?"

"Wrestling," he said and felt that he had to explain. "I'm a wrestler."

"O Lord! Forgive me my stupidity, but in what sense?"

"In all senses." He himself didn't understand why he was getting involved in explanations in which he was deprived of the possibility of using his customary language. He filled his goblet with wine and drank it down in one gulp. "Well, over a broad...so more or less... I tried to fight over a woman..."

"Ah," the princess said in relief, but she seemed disconcerted by the goblet drained in one gulp. "So, your business is to fight, ours is to make a choice."

"To tell the truth, I didn't really need her that badly. I know her quite well." To find the right words was like picking seeds out of manure, and that resulted in a somewhat different significance. "My pride was piqued. We parted pretty much without making any promises. I didn't invite her to come to Moscow, but when I arrived at the airport here, I thought: Why not call her..."

An unexpected intervention interrupted their conversation: the width of cloth slipped off the dummy, revealing the lower absence that made it resemble an invalidlike stump—the absence more indecent than nakedness. Roksana Vikentyevna was about to cover it again, then gave a dismissive wave of her hand, as if to say: Okay, it's too late to cover it now, let it lie there.

"It's so...Pardon...I didn't understand completely. Whom did you call, you said?"

"A girl I know...I had a girl. And suddenly I hear she's getting married. The point's not that she's getting married, though, but to whom. They make the choice. Well, she certainly did! A prize for a winner. I know them all inside out. I'm a local boy. I used to belong to the gang on the other side of the river."

"You've got me thoroughly confused," the princess said plaintively, her fingers touching her temples. "What did you need trousers for?"

"I asked her to get me the trousers just for today." Igor frowned at her lack of comprehension. Why was he going into these explanations? Certainly not for the old woman and not for this girl whom he couldn't figure out, who sat there, reclining in the depths of the chair, her swollen eyelids half-closed. He took the bottle, poured some more wine, and drank it down. "Are they yours?" he finally realized.

"No, his," the old woman indicated the dummy, wrinkling her brow painfully. The dummy almost bowed in confirmation and seemed to nod, even though it had no head. The candles in the dull candlestick were gathering a distorted circle around them. In every part of the mirror you could see the tablecloth, bottle, goblets, sardines drowsing in oil. "Listen," Roksana Vikentyevna suddenly had a brainwave. "Let me get out some of my homemade 'monopoly' vodka. It's more effective and easier on the head."

The cat, which had been sitting behind her shoulder, dug its claws deeper into the back of the chair to keep its balance. The mirrors, in their crooked distortion, carried the three people at table into the murky semidarkness, like minor doubles who were being served food in the kitchen.

"I'll have some with you," the old woman said, cheering up. She glanced at Zoia, who seemed to have dozed off where she sat. "Ssh, quiet now! Lord, how you confused me! And I thought, I'd already decided: it's starting again."

"It only came to me today," Igor shook his head. "Just today it all fit together. I called just her, right? So how could they have known that I was coming? By chance, maybe? They were lying in wait for me. I know all of them, particularly this guy. Scum with money. They have their own accounts to settle with me. And they're envious of me. I'm a Moscow resident, I travel abroad, I've got all the glad rags I need. And all that sort of thing."

"Glad rags means clothes," for some reason Roksana Vikentyevna translated for Zoia, who was asleep.

"I'm a wrestler, fuck it! A master of sports! We'll get you without any master skills, without any rules, simple style."

"And in your... that is, in, as you say... wrestling—are there any rules?" The old woman gave a start.

"What do you mean? Of course there are."

"But you say you took money with you?"

"What's money got to do with anything? I took some. For no special purpose. I just had it on me."

"A lot?"

"Two hundred."

"Yes, nowadays that's no big deal."

"What big deal! I'm telling you, I had no special purpose. If I'd needed to, I could have brought more."

"You know, you can really drive one crazy. So, how do you like my 'monopoly?' It's more comfortable drinking from a glass, right? I use these goblets for her. They're also mine, but from the old days. The candlestick, too. They took everything away from me. And now I'm expropriating. I'm today's proletariat, I have the right."

As she spoke, Roksana Vikentyevna speared a sardine on her fork and gave it to the cat, which was still sitting behind her on the back of the chair. It didn't like something about her movement or her words, for it gave the old woman a light tap on the cheek with its paw and jumped over onto the dummy's shoulder. The dummy swayed, but didn't fall. "He's displeased," the princess grinned with her black mouth. "He, of course, is sinless, since he's castrated. But then, he's smarter than a lot of others." She glanced at the dummy as if seeking reconciliation. "It's fine for him, too, he's got no head. Everybody does what he can. You, you poor things, have to fight each other. Whereas I'm familiar with the idea."

"What idea?"

"Oh! You want me to tell you just like that! The idea of not being afraid of anything. Whether you remember the rules or couldn't help yourself—you'll find the key anyway. I also was...I'll show you the photos in a minute. Or even without a photo...just look at her. What combines to make us individuals?" she repeated her perplexed question. "Elegance, trepidation, high heels, size thirty-two shoes, on the one hand, and an indecent old woman, on the other? Life. That's what it is. When it hits your brain as it should, maybe I'll tell you then. Or are you far enough along already? Okay, for her sake. She felt sorry for you, and I can, too. Only don't tell anybody."

"Word of honor," Bogatyryov said.

"Oh, Lord," the old woman exclaimed, making a wry face, "a peasant and a lout in every word. How could I think?...A peasant and a lout. Okay, even if you tell anyone, they won't understand anyway. Here..." She leaned down with difficulty somewhere under the table, keeping an eye open on what was happening above the tablecloth so as to be sure that he wasn't spying on her, and took out a heavy bunch of keys in different sizes and shapes. "These aren't all of them, of course. Get it?"

"No," the wrestler admitted honestly. "What do you need them for?"

"We'll see up there," Roksana Vikentyevna pointed to the ceiling with her finger, yellow from smoking. "I'll never make it there, given my record. I don't think it likely others will either. Except for Apollo. But the rest will stand at the locked gates, waiting to be questioned. Name, patronymic, how you lived, what your sins were till such and such a year? Till this fellow with the keys lets them in. But I'll make do without him. I won't even introduce myself to anyone. Understand?"

"No."

"See how many there are?" The princess shook the cluttered key ring out in front of her uncomprehending guest. "And I've got more. We've even started duplicating some of them—I can't keep inventing new ones indefinitely. Perhaps some key will fit..."

Her eyes with the dark round outline lent the old woman the look of an alien twilight bird. Bogatyryov finally understood what she meant and he burst out laughing. Indecently, irrepressibly, louder and louder...Roksana Vikentyevna didn't get offended at all; on the contrary, she joined in.

"Go on, laugh, and I'll laugh along with you. Maybe we need to laugh more than anything else. I'll tell you: it's only a step from the ridiculous to the sublime. You think that's already been said? You're mistaken. It's been said: 'from the sublime to the ridiculous'—and that's a completely different thing. It's exactly the opposite."

Reflections stirred in the leafs of the mirror as they surrounded the table, multiplied the small lakes of melted wax on their gently dripping edges. Bottle glass that looked blackish and green in the light. The color of antiquity, of the moon and moss under the moon. Faces pale and exhausted, like the candles. Unable to withstand the weariness, eyelids drooped for just a short second, but when the cockerel in places unseen crowed the third time, day was breaking outside the curtained windows. The old woman had vanished. The candles had dripped down, and sinuous whitish wisps still curled upward from the small sunken wicks.

4

The freshness of the morning air, tenuous, vulnerable, like the freshness of a still-wet transfer—an imprudent movement, a sound, a word could spoil something in it.

"You, well, *excusez-moi*," he started to mutter when they came outside into the street. "Forgive me..."

She raised her fingers to her lips, beseeching silence.

Birds' voices sounded intermittently, painfully. The moon had lingered overlong in the west—friable, porous, devoid of light—a rough shape with a third of it gnawed off. They climbed uphill in silence. At the opening in the fence they paused to catch their breath. Behind the boiler house one could see the black pieces of coal and the rusty pieces of iron on the well-defined grass. The humid morning light lent everything a monstrous clarity and brightness. She passed him a bag with pyjamas and turned around to let him change his clothes. Only quietly, quietly, mustn't scratch or tear it... Now, why not be more careful? Fear mounted, rose from behind the messy garbage where a mug with a dirty stubble, its red lip sneering, appeared. "Aha!" it cried out. "AND WHAT ARE YOU DOING HERE?..." The screeching, rickety wheels of his gurney hung in the air; a thick, viscous mumbling goo of words overgrown with wool, raucous laughter, and whoops. The wool was visible on the bricks, on the black grass, the air started to waver. To get hold of him as soon as possible, to drag him away. He started up awkwardly, then doubled up, holding his stomach. Tiny plant lice, like black dots, were quickly, quickly gnawing through a thin shroud with everything that was on it, leaving holes in many places at once.

XIII. A Beautiful Woman's Smile, or a Promise Fulfilled

I fell asleep in the fresh evening. Shadows were playing in the lush foliage. The air was painted with the colored glass of the terrace.

I awoke in the cold morning and couldn't understand the change in the weather. Outside it was light, the branches were naked, and the small cobweb of warm sleep was still scattered in my memory.

I half-closed my eyes, then opened them again. Life settled on the line separating the leaves.

For us everything has a direction, from our unique birth to our unique death; for the latter, everything is a play with material.

An elusive substance stirs, lives, trickles through the fingers—just try to retain it, discern it, ponder it.

1

Why, in fact, beat around the bush without making up my mind to accept what's been so clear for so long: the golden-haired little boy on the *fantiki*, the cherub who mortally wounded Ganshin, the unwitting cause of guilt and unhappiness, was her son, the son of the woman to whom the provincial madman devoted his life, his thoughts, and of the man to whom in his story many years ago, with such unexpected astuteness, he gave a nickname instead of his real name. In the textured design of this plot taken from life, not even the place of exile—which Milashevich, according to the regulations then in effect, probably could have either chosen from those offered him,

259

or managed to arrange through effort—was accidental. That's where she was from; there, in Nechaisk, the old Paradizovs were still living in their old age, he a village teacher, who escaped to the city from the Sareyevo sorcerers, with his bustling spouse, who was scared her whole life long. But even if Simeon Kondratyich first turned up there by chance, he subsequently kept his focus on Nechaisk, maintaining relations with the old folk, sending them presents—Ganshin's caramels—and calling on them sometimes to drink tea with strawberries and cream in their cozy house, details of which he later depicted in his provincial idyll: all these embroidered napkins, runners, small pillows for people's backs (because he himself never had such a house—and, besides, who'd embroider all this for him? Aleksandra Flegontovna? That I can't imagine, simply can't imagine! . . . Maybe he'd have to do it himself, like Gogol's governor). He understood and appreciated their shy yearning for peace, he was filled with sincere and tender sympathy for them, but at the same time he kept them under observation—imperceptibly, in an indirect way, from afar, first from Stolbenets, then from the capital, knowing that the woman he'd lost, who'd disappeared somewhere, sooner or later would let them know where she was and perhaps even would come herself. At some point he became certain that she'd finally return and, moreover, come back to him, and he'd already prepared and sorted out the words for their meeting, was already sketching in his mind, in his soul, and on paper a world where she would have a fine life (a world, but hardly a well-organized home). Fine, so what if it took time for this to ripen, grow clearer, and take shape, so what if his thoughts kept changing and if for a while he refused to wait and tried to find a certain external stability, a position; he attempted to find a foothold in the capital as a writer, and having found a niche in the literary world, to gauge, to grasp the rights and the possibilities of getting settled in the provinces—without suspecting yet that written words could acquire an unexpected power, that he could be offered a choice between the lack of responsibility that is customary for a loquacious era lacking in modesty and the necessity of answering for what he'd said. He still tried to negotiate without foregoing his self-respect and principles for a long time, still stayed in the unheated hotel room with

cheap furniture where, like his hero, in the mornings he'd stir porridge in a saucepan, hugging his aching stomach with his left hand,
and then he'd put a proper collar, a dickey, and cuffs on under his
jacket, adjust his only tie, then still without a patch, and would leave,
to play almost one and the same performance in the next publishing
house—moreover, a decent publishing house; that is, where they
could have heard about the scandal connected with his name, and if
they hadn't, he himself would start with a preface, he'd begin the
unnecessary explanation, one so suspect that it was only a question of
the time needed to find the proper words to refuse him and to return
the opus to its author. Maybe it was the same funny story each time,
about the joker who, standing on the deck of a Volga steamer one
clear, peaceful day, thought of a challenge, a bet on an epidemic of
seasickness: he was the first to lean over the handrail in an attack of
simulated vomiting, and then watched with interest as that set off
uncontrollable convulsions that passed down the rail from one neighbor to another: from an impressionable high school girl to her
mother, then, carrying over the bow of the steamer, to the opposite
side and the stern, and came back to the instigator, who, with a psy-
chologist's pleasure, was reflecting, inter alia, on the infectiousness
of ideas that are accessible to everyone—but the next moment he
caught at the knot of his tie and leaned over the handrail again, this
time to be really sick. This is a strange story (the author published it
afterward separately as a small book), and even stranger is the idea of
offering precisely this story for publication, after everything that hap
pened. But it's possible that he himself was pressing them not to publish, that he was almost happy at the misunderstanding that was
pushing him out of generally accepted literary life, because he already
knew something that belonged to him alone: the little boy was already
with his grandparents—a pledge of her return—and he rushed to get
closer to him, from a distance of readiness to watch what would happen next, to watch, wait, to court her return.

2

Who's listening in on our wishes? It's terrible to be misunderstood.
Better to desire nothing else. Was he waiting for the old couple's

death? But he didn't want it, didn't press, and he certainly couldn't foresee that, like Philemon and Baucis, they'd be granted the rare happiness of dying on the same day. The question also is, however, at what price is this happiness granted? Isn't there behind it an accident, a fire, god knows what?—the intrigue of *fantiki* connections reminds one to be cautious. However that may be, he found out about it and hurried to get there; nobody knows what claims he asserted, nobody knows what papers he drew up (they've possibly survived somewhere to this day), but maybe he managed without any formalities and just took the boy away to Ganshin's estate. There was nowhere else to take him; he himself was living there at the time and had no other lodging, just as he had neither a definite position or profession, nor a stable salary—all his life he didn't have his feet firmly planted on the ground; those aren't the people to be responsible for taking care of a child. Here, for a short period, at least, he could settle him in comfortably, even have him live well. Why didn't he tell Angel immediately and simply who the boy was, where he was from? Why did he decide to make up a story about an unknown orphan, an adopted child? Because of the urge to mystify? Because he felt obliged to keep someone else's secret? Because of his instinctive incapacity to tell the truth immediately and simply? Because of the impossibility of giving away something too intimately personal—his wounded feelings, his expectations and hopes, which so far had fed only on his imagination? Because of the need to construct around himself all the time a defense of words, fabrications, jokes, to hide the tracks, get people confused, as if he was afraid to be caught in something, as happened once, before the investigation? And maybe he partly had the salutary notion of giving the folk-loving Maecenas cause for genial laughter later, at the price of guilt complexes? If only he'd been able to sense in time, if he'd been able to foresee his poor friend's lamentable, long-concealed weakness, a weakness that a chance temptation exposed and awakened, a temptation that unexpectedly became something more significant—love! Remote as he was from Platonism, he'd not even supposed such a dirty trick from this direction; when suddenly the dangerous ambiguity of the situation became apparent, he experienced something like panic and lurched ahead perhaps too hastily, awkwardly, without finding in time the only words that were necessary: the small inaccuracy proved disastrous. No, come on now, of course he could hardly blame himself in that ill-starred death so like a suicide, and that even was a suicide, except that there was no choice of weapon. He could just as justifiably blame himself for the simultaneous outbreak of the war—he wanted some shock or other, a displacement, and was already impatiently courting it, hastening it: anything, if she would only come back, and who knows into what unforeseen landslide a grain of sand that had been dislodged earlier could expand? Following a small chain of determining causes, you'll reach the origin of the world, but you still won't explain anything. We don't know what landslides were concealed beneath the layer on which they intended to build. There was a disappointment in the last unhappy, illicit feeling, a shameful mockery of fate, the wall caved in, the dangerous fruit without a name ripened, the pods snapped like a spring coil, the hard seeds flying in all directions, breaking the greenhouse glass. But, nevertheless, maybe the clever critic Phenomenov wasn't completely wrong to detect in Milashevich's prose an amenability to amorphous temptation from which those times suffered, a readiness to disregard strictness even for the sake of a happiness cherished for someone.

3

Where did he get up the little boy? Milashevich definitely didn't keep him at his place, there's no hint of that in his writings, and it's hard to imagine how a bachelor who'd not settled down could afford to take care of the child for many years, a child, incidentally, who'd already tasted certain pleasures, eaten chicken croquettes at Ganshin's, slept on lacy bed linen, and who could hardly understand by what right this man was in charge of his life, why he'd almost forced him to leave a life of comfort and affection. How old could he have been then?—seven? eight?—and he was still growing; one could suppose that he had less than ideal relations with the man whom he certainly didn't regard as his father. *A child can call us all to account.* Maybe that's related to him? Here we already see a nervous, complicated, confused character, of the kind that becomes a real misfortune for a family: we see a little boy in the standard gray jacket worn at Levinson's liberal orphanage; it's most likely he, it was the most natural thing for a man like Milashevich to place the boy in a progressive and well-designed boarding house, where school regimentation was abolished, where children of different ages freely formed groups according to their interests so as to cultivate each other, where equality was maintained in everything, beginning with clothes... What happened next is hard to tell as yet: on the *fantiki* the little boy with golden hair remains unchanged; there's no one older who resembles him, as if Simeon Kondratyich didn't see him growing up—although he must have kept track of him, even if from a distance, like a man in love whose feelings aren't requited, for the boy was a pledge of her return, a pledge of the meeting he dreamed about and cherished. Just a little longer, just a bit—he knew what he was waiting for, even though the war interfered and delayed the day—he'd learned patience and knew how not to look at his watch; the war also had to be dealt with, he had to get through it for something to come to fruition. He already knew how to make all of them happy, he hoped, he was sure that she'd stay with him, for he knew some things better than she did herself.

4

Now it's emerging, it's surfacing from the remote depths, a barely distinguishable, intermittent, wordless melody, and the face of the girl is taking shape from the incomplete lines—she's not yet turned into a beautiful woman with refined features and light hair: a late child, a gift from God, the unexpected joy of her unfortunate parents, a child who survived by a miracle, kept warm in the dough, protected by the fearful mother's breath. The blue veins show delicately translucent beneath her skin—as thin as tissue paper. It's said of such people that they're not long for this world, but a certain strength fed her from within, and Efim Pianykh, a terrible peasant horse doctor and sorcerer, guessed this strength and used it for his own purposes; the head of the Sareyevo sorcerers, he could stop the flow of blood with a glance and his ear could detect the voices of internal organs and by them identify diseases and foretell a person's fate. This name had been mentioned in an essay by a Petersburg journalist and an agent of the court; Pianykh was involved in a case of violent attempted kidnapping of a certain P., who'd escaped from his power over her. The girl had been in a mysterious state of paralysis since the country sorcerer had volunteered to have a look at the teacher's sick daughter; but it was also he who had spread the rumor about her amazing ability to foretell events and to find things that had been lost. Usually immobile and silent, at his command she would stand up and utter words that Efim could immediately interpret—always correctly. A cult was virtually being formed around her when her mortally frightened parents managed to remove her secretly to the city. However, this time Pianykh didn't even try to stop them, perhaps the opportunity to transfer the center of his activity to a more prominent place even suited him. The enlightened author of the essay justly and bitterly wrote about the sickness of the times, which, unable to understand and cope with its vital problems, proved overly inclined to believe in forces that defied human reason, overly receptive to hysterical prophets and epileptic miracle workers, inspired charlatans and sectarians, the seekers of unprecedented revelations—in remote areas things well known in the capitals were being interpreted in their own peculiar way; it must be that history has periods that favor some fads, since they favor precisely these and not some other tendencies. Why a susceptibility precisely to those as opposed to other tendencies emerges was a separate question; the author raised the optional question of whether it was the simple caprice of independent development or the influence of periodic cosmic forces that contributes to the intensification of certain inclinations and abilities. For, after all, one also needs abilities, one needs suitable pliant material. The author had no doubts that the entire story indicated nothing more than psychological suggestion, behavior under hypnosis—that is, things that belonged to positive medicine—which was confirmed by the fact of P.'s sudden recovery, achieved not even by a doctor, but simply by an enlightened man, a visiting student; it was also he who persuaded the parents to send the girl to the capital, where she would be safe from superstitious attempts on her life. The criminal part of the story actually started when Pianykh succeeded in catching up with the fugitive and finding her in Petersburg. Rumors of his unusual gifts must have had some basis, and he'd have taken the girl away if the same protector, the student who by that time had become her fiancé, hadn't succeeded in standing up for her; the fiancé's surname was given in the essay: Bogdanov.

5

We now know some things perhaps even better than the author who was attracted to this story only as one of several trial cases that characterized the spiritual state of society; perhaps he conflated two figures into one. The first was a chance visitor—always chance, everywhere a visitor—a sober mocker who sufficiently possessed, however, the strength of his convictions to say to the girl, like the prophet, "Rise and walk!" Later, inspired by this success, as if by an adventure, he volunteered to take her away, to hide her from further dangers, perhaps even having developed in this regard some detailed plans, in which he himself believed for a while, but only for a while, because he himself was an eternal fugitive who was forced to hide all the time; it looks as if then, too, he was making his way secretly from his place of exile, and to have a girl travel with him in the role of acquaintance or even beloved was a convenient cover. One can even imagine their flight to the railway station, not to Stolbenets, however, but to the godforsaken areas where the tracks divided, veering off to the side, away from the highway, through the estate of Ganshin, who was given to concealing fugitives... Perhaps that's the extent of the details one can know; Milashevich writes nothing about this, of course, other than just one or two sheets that may be considered relevant. *Whispers and rumors multiply around the house. How does one stop them from getting inside? How can one hide from this hope, entreaty, demand, and threat?* Perhaps he sketched the idea for the plot of the ancient story that he hadn't yet made his own—but he set it aside. No, it's no accident that you won't find Shurochka in any of his stories (except for that same memorable and understandable exception, and even there nothing is made explicit except for the name); he was afraid of reminding anyone of her, so that no one would find out about her, even twenty years later, but that's already an idle supposition; it would have been simpler, after all, to leave Stolbenets. The Petersburg episodes, where the student-protector is already a different person, aren't much clearer: the clash right on the street with the thickset fellow (he was picturesquely depicted in the courtroom as all overgrown with graying hair, with piercing deep-set eyes, indifferent and evasive in his responses). The scenes flash by as if taken from different places in a film: the woman's hat fell on the roadway, her hairpins tumbled out, her light brown braids came undone (those braids that she later cut to feed herself and the sick man), the student's green, peaked cap was trampled in the mud, his glasses crunched underfoot, and the man, completely helpless because of his shortsightedness, held onto the wall by touch alone, without realizing yet that somebody had come to his aid in time, for he couldn't make out the buttons of the uniform; probably then, at the police station, while explaining what had happened (but not frankly, still hiding the tracks, like a hare, and shielding someone), he for the first time called Shurochka his bride, which only became true some time later—clumsy, shortsighted, in love, he'd felt it his duty and vocation to keep, protect, and defend this woman, who'd run away from home neither with him nor to him, and had awak-ened as if after a semisleep in a world that immediately proved very fearful; there, in the semisleep, the immobility, the nightmare, remained perhaps the only understandable support, a simple-hearted belief of which she now had been cured; who could give her a new support?—only he, to whom she'd suddenly been given like a mira-cle; the other man had disappeared, and all *he* could do was explain to her why. For the first time in his life he recognized in her the sim-ple-heartedness of his childhood dreams, and the childhood hurts of the provinces, and that ability to feel for others, from which per-haps subsequently derived his view of the world and even his vege-tarianism. *Take shelter in the silence, even let your watch not tick. You can't run eternally.* He probably decided to take her farther away, even if only to Moscow; she'd gradually recovered and blossomed, and that's where the eternal visitor found or met them by chance, without at all intending what happened subsequently; what followed was not decided by him.

6

Perhaps, perhaps...We probably fill the spaces between the *fantiki* willy-nilly with the meaning that we've sensed in our own lives; what can you do? We understand others through ourselves, just as we understand ourselves thanks to others, for only through each of us does the way to some common depths get discovered—isn't that the reason we sometimes have the feeling as if we've already lived once in some alien but recognizable incarnation? There, in the depths, all our rivalries and thrashing about, betrayal and even murders from jealousy serve, possibly, the selection and continuation of life in general; but something is rooted there that can't be explained so simply, a hopeless expectation, a faithfulness in spite of common sense and even in spite of death itself, as if there's only one fulfillment in the world for you that is capable of crowning the sense of completeness. No worldwide elemental forces, no wars and revolutions shake this feeling, but it's as if they work on it. Somewhere on the surface the wind of history revitalizes the pattern of ripples—that's where our life resides, where one finds all the divine variety of events and encounters, business affairs and conversations, gains and losses; there, the invasion of a newcomer is incidental, sickness and ambush are accidental, there, people are scattered aside like chips in a storm—but what holds immutable is that they are attracted to each other through all this, through space and time, even if for the time being only in thought (which doesn't yield even to death), and then what possibilities lie ahead? We can err in the details, but few visions, illuminated for a moment, are directly accessible to the eye. Here's an overcrowded train car, stuffy and bespattered with spittle, sunflower husks, obscenity, and raucous laughter; some deserters have squeezed a woman into a corner; she herself removes the gold earrings from her ears, intentionally slowly, so as to gain time, an additional minute is gained while someone tests them with his teeth, and help has already arrived, in time. We can also see one of them: a pockmarked soldier in English puttees, his eyes so irritated that they resemble raw meat, with nostrils of unusually keen sensitivity; the fellow traveler of the woman who was hurrying to get to Stolbenets through Petrograd,* let's assume with a certain mandate, but, most importantly, to find her former husband, who maybe even then was still regarded as her husband (they could easily have foregone a formal divorce). Did she know that he was waiting for her, the selfless crank she'd left for another man?—because she hadn't appreciated him fully yet, because he still nurtured a feeling of gratitude to the other man, a loving delight, a hope that the other man would do something for her, would help her to cope at last with such a hard life, change that life or cancel it out... She probably knew; whether he wrote to her or she found out some other way, she knew that this incomprehensible man, capable of sometimes frightening one, wasn't just waiting for her (for he had a little something that the other man lacked: he loved her), he was preparing for the meeting, and he had with him a pledge of her return: her son.

7

Who's listening in on our wishes...Does that mean she'd seen the boy? So, so...But, having discerned so much in the prehistory, here again we come up against a blind spot—the film is spoiled through overexposure to light. A snowflake has coagulated in the November air, the ice floes of the strewn field try to coincide, to join together once more with their jagged edges, the roofs and the bell tower shiver with chill; an old man with a gray beard is groping with his foot for a galosh that has got bogged down in the mud, and the ravens under the turbulent heavens are a parody of a tragic chorus; she's wearing a light coat, inappropriate for the local weather, the knuckles of her fingers white from cold or tension, the raft made from old gates on the bank of the puddle can't hold more than three people, and he extends his hand to her: "Careful, don't stumble,"—just as before, whether in reality or in a dream, and the little helmsman is waiting for them. The saliva of zeal and delighted curiosity is flowing from his flabby lip—he's the only one of the three who doesn't understand in what dramatic action he's a participant...

* See note on p. 101.

8

a day when for the first time he obtained passage

the night when people were up to their waists in wine and drank their fill from the puddle

the air is extracted from winy fumes; just breathing makes one's head spin

'What have you been given such happiness for?...

Well, let's go one step farther: even this has been fulfilled, and is it worth asking about the cost!—without a cost such as that, maybe there wouldn't have been complete fulfillment, when even words become superfluous and the hands of the clock aren't necessary; former time is over, the brain cells have been replenished...

9

And yet, and yet. How can one present this union? It already seemed possible to see the two of them together, having found peace after storms, having gotten older, perhaps even sad, as by the stove they reread the pages that they remembered by heart anyway—but where's the third member, the former little boy, who'd grown up and matured? Why don't we see him with them? Surely he hadn't died right after being found? No, that would have been reflected somehow on the *fantiki*, because the feeling that these sheets of paper were connected with life even more than we'd imagined until now was growing stronger and more certain—more than the diary, the notebook, the draft of transformed plots, where reality joined with fantasy, where unnamed personae were themselves and Milashevich at the same time; here there seemed to be yet another life code of his, which emerged either inadvertently or deliberately, as if the man who'd written it had both wanted, and yet been afraid, to understand.

10

You've forgotten the word sesame,* *and in its place you try to
remember something that means the same. Kunzhut?* ‡ *Hemp?
It doesn't open. But it will open for a passerby who'll simply mention
the word in passing during a conversation.*

*I wrote this knowing that I would burn it, but for some reason
I corrected a word, found something more precise. As if it makes any
difference whether the paper burns with this word or any other.*

Do we really give birth only to bodies?

*it's like the charge of electricity in a cloud, even if there's no
lightning*

11

Guessing at barely visible landmarks in the darkness, having filled the
emptiness in some places with a sighted touch, we're groping our way
out of the blind spot—here's the light again. The green yard of the former estate is flooded with sunlight, a table for the samovar has been set
under an apple tree, the museum objects have been taken outside for
packing and loading, somewhere further off the carts and horses are
waiting, the movers are wrapping armchairs, the remains of mirrors,
and the gramophone in a bast mat, covering up with wooden boards
the Flemish office furniture and Danzig secretaire with the clock without hands, and the museum keeper relieved of his duties in the meantime is drinking tea with the man who came to take the treasures of the
province to the capital, because it was more proper to concentrate in
one place all the refined products of human thought, having leveled the
rest of the area—all this had one purpose, the triumph of the province
on a scale that a modest sage might only dream about. It all came
together: the former rival, so brilliant at one time, now broken, disappointed, dragging with him, like fate, an odor of vinegar or anguish,
could now witness his triumph. But then why, why didn't Simeon

* Pun on "sesame" as both magic word and plant.
‡ A kindred plant.

Kondratyich want to show him the completeness of his triumph? Out of nobleness, out of his penchant for secretiveness and allusions? For the sake of some other game? Just so as not to worry needlessly about her and himself, not to disturb the peace that had been attained? Or, maybe, out of a lack of confidence—in her or in himself? All right, let's say we accept any version, let's say he managed not to make a single slip in the course of the entire conversation, even managed not to invite the new arrival (and what a new arrival! it wasn't Semeka, after all) to the house where he'd be bound to see her (he was living with her at the museum, in one of the buildings on the same estate, where else?), let's say . . . the weather played a role here, inclining one to sit outside—but she, what about her! How could she have not shown herself, not come outside, even by chance? She wasn't locked in, after all. She could have made her presence heard. She couldn't not have heard him arrive, not have guessed—not with her keenness. Or hadn't she wanted to? . . .

12

Lord . . . why go on playing hide-and-seek!—especially with oneself. As if we're afraid of telling everything, and we keep sidetracking and coming back, just so as not to see what's already been revealed: the poor woman couldn't come out to see the guest and even to make her presence known, because from the moment she'd returned she'd been lying sick, mute, immobile, as she'd been when the bearded sorcerer from Sareyevo had shaken her with his gaze. There was no point even in reading the medical books in the library, though one could read them; as if without them we couldn't understand, couldn't imagine what this new shock to a fearful soul was capable of turning into, only at first assuming the deceptive form of a fever after the meeting in the cold November wind. Maybe the only thing we don't know well yet is what kind of shock it was: she was prepared for the meeting as such, a misunderstanding about his arrest could have disturbed her but briefly. But nevertheless . . . after so many years . . . to see how time had left its mark on people whom she hardly recognized now . . . and did she recognize her son? He couldn't even remember her . . . they just looked similar. No, it was impossible to tell properly, because subsequently the boy wasn't with them, that's the point; as before, there wasn't even the slightest hint of his living together with them, of his staying in the house where now there was not only Milashevich, but also the woman who fell sick after their meeting...Oh God, nothing now could dispel this sorrowful sight, on the contrary, little things increasingly confirmed it, like crystals that cluster around a new thread in a solution that's reached its saturation point. They're already forming a design; a soft, clear, mournful ringing sound is born of their touch. What is this music about? About the woman who was lying in the house behind the cotton curtain among the boxes with seedlings, amidst the fragrance of flowers—a beautiful woman who didn't age, restored to the garden of peace? About how the suffering man crazily in love with her constructed around her a world where clocks didn't need hands, where the only measure of time consisted of summer, fall, winter, and spring, a children's merry-go-round; one had only to transfer the *fantiki* from one place to another. *Just a little more, just a bit, and it'll come together, come to pass, be resolved.* The expectation was now transferred onto her son, who should have come and set her on her feet, who somewhere, unseen by us and by them, too, was growing up, turning into a youth and then a man. *How I hope, how I wait...* but who keeps on laughing there all this time, unable to stop? What's yawning ahead, like a cave-in—and what's in the air there?

XIV. A Life Plan

This stink persists even in the midst of the meadows. O you people, how much of the earth you've managed to befoul!

Suddenly it occurred to him to glance at his own sole. Oh, my God! It was he who'd stepped into something and was carrying it around, spreading it over the flowering stretch of meadow.

Let x be uniform within the boundaries of the system; then it can serve as a basis of harmony. A disparity in x's leads to dissonance and collisions.

1

A cast-iron balloon on a cable, the bludgeon of the age of machines: with a sweeping swing of their arms, they struck the cheekbone of the house with it—a house that was no longer alive, however. They crushed what was already a corpse: the eye sockets were empty, broken glasses crunched underfoot, the doors had been removed, the tin plate stripped off the roof for someone's household needs. The walls around the kitchen had been dismantled even earlier by firemen's hooks. In the corners of the ceiling an inveterate cobweb was uncovered, invisible while they'd lived there; soot from the fire outlined it in greasy coal. Layers of torn wallpaper were exposed; you papered the room yourself with the top two layers and had already forgotten the former design of honey-yellow vases, and now from a distance you recognized even the memorable splotches, the traces of a squashed bedbug, a microscopic indentation made by the thumbtack from which some year's wall calendar had hung. Under the wallpaper, a layer of newspapers with photographs from times past. Layers of life, short geological periods, layers of paper, dust, soot, stove white-washing, moist breath, smells that permeated the walls, soaked into

274

their crumbly pores. How many layers of cornea peel off us, how many layers of cells, hair, and nails come off—in bodily terms we're no longer the same as we were several years ago, and only memory unites us with our previous selves. The layers die away, to be replaced by new ones, that's exactly what a sign of life is. An indifferent bludgeon strikes the cheekbone, bricks shatter into dust, clouds of lime and wood dust hover in the air, for a moment smells are released which remind one that within these walls more time and experiences had been lived through than one had realized. The smell of encounters with one's neighbors in the kitchen, of burned fish, the bitter taste of guilt and loss in one's saliva, the patter of a dripping tap, an unexpected light, the acridness of an overboiled kettle...and the lump in one's throat has been swallowed. None of the idlers who were staring from a distance twitched their nostrils.

2

The dusty whirlwind tossed a piece of crumpled paper at Anton Andreyevich's shoes. Carefully, holding his hand to the stitches in his side, Anton Andreyevich bent down to pick it up. It was a fragment of a typed document, but in the corner, in two colors of ink—red and green—the name "F. F. Titko" was artistically traced by hand. The document represented Fyodor Fomich's personal five-year plan; red check marks opposite the points that designated the acquisition of an apartment (2 rooms, 32.5 sq. m.) and the purchase of a Malva brand furniture suite indicated a mission accomplished. The plan also projected writing a work entitled "A Refutation of Bourgeois Perspectives on..."—the ellipses at the end presupposed that the title would become more precise by the set deadline. "Look at the Eiffel Tower in Paris and say that our Ostankino tower in Moscow is taller" was beside the next point, and then, right at the edge of the fragment, "For Elfrida".... An aftertaste of copper made his saliva run, as that day when the orderly Frosia, her red wrinkled nose shining, popped into the ward to share her delight: "Remember the big-bellied guy, you know, who was here in the ward with you and then left for the deluxe—well, his wife was run over by a trolley bus." In the reanimation ward behind the glass dividers, an old man in a state of shock, attached by wires and tubes to a cold apparatus, continued to breathe, unable either to die or to recover; Feinberg the magician, in spite of everything, incorruptibly maintained the man's life by means of unbelievable scientific achievements—out of professional conscientiousness, on account of the Hippocratic oath, of course... there was no choice; since we have to resist death, since we're obliged to serve life and only life, you can't cut it short intentionally. Who'll take that responsibility on himself? So he's alive—to everyone's surprise he's still living, with his dissected thorax, and the enormous efforts of the human mind merely extend and multiply his suffering. But surely not indefinitely? After all, as yet there are no immortals, are there? Let's hope not.

3

Anton Andreyevich had asked the few people who visited him in the hospital not to worry about when he'd be checking out, and he purposely didn't specify the date. He had to deal with himself: his confusion and loneliness, the lightness of the air and of walking. Why had he ordered the cab driver to first drive him to the old house? Was it to inquire on the way about the things that he'd not had time to move before his stint in the hospital? (Some guess!) The dust settled. What did Anton experience then? All his feelings were colored, perhaps, by weakness. He'd overestimated his strength. He went back to the cab, which was waiting for him. For a long time the driver couldn't find the new street. In a short time the block had grown up a little and changed, the identical houses didn't have numbers on them, the new tenants distinguished between them somehow—by some signs—but they couldn't even name the nearest street. The wasteland capable of provoking the most depressing memories had vanished, been leveled. The asphalt that had just been laid was torn up and intersected by a trench. The eternal promise, recalled Anton Andreyevich, as he got out of the car so as to cover the last stretch on foot. But what space! How freely the wind can blow! The boys had set up a place for playing soccer on the street. The goalkeeper took off his sandal so that it wouldn't fly off together with the ball, kicked it with his bare foot, then put the sandal back on. Good, Anton approved. And even the elevator exceeded his expectations by working. During his absence the door to his apartment had been covered with yellow imitation leather; it looked very attractive, with a design of a small rhombus made up of buttons and shoelaces. Anton Andreyevich merely shook his head at the unexpected conscientiousness of the craftsmen, so atypical of the contemporary way of doing things. He'd only had an oral agreement with them, but he hadn't paid anything in advance and now felt indebted to them, not just financially, but morally, too—all this restored some of his faith. (He hadn't left them his keys, either, but that simple fact didn't occur to him immediately; a lively music with a strong beat that grew louder and louder was driving all thoughts out of his head.) The key didn't fit into the lock. Finally he managed to insert the thinnest one, but now it wouldn't turn. Anton tried to press against the door with his shoulder—it gave suddenly, and he almost fell on top of the man who was coming out to see who was trying to force the door open. A dumbbell in his hand. Completely naked. A fat effeminate chest, folds on his stomach. The dilated, dazed pupils of his eyes stared at Anton Andreyevich as the music now pounded for real, and Lizavin recognized as real the swollen face with slovenly sideburns.

"Come in, Boria," said Kaif.

4

"Sorry!" Lizavin recovered. "I got the address wrong. For God's sake, forgive me. The floor, the number...how could I...the buildings all look alike. How funny and sad..." Indeed, a sense of hilarity—albeit a somewhat hysterical one—started to stir within him. "I'm always doing something like this. It's a good job I'm at least doing it with someone I know...once again, sorry..."

"Do come in, Boria.
My home is your home." *

Pronouncing these words in English and without listening to his apologies, Kaif moved back inside the entrance hall, twitching in rhythm, pulling him in like a piston that can't leave any empty space.

---

* In the original, the lines are spoken in English, but appear in Russian transliteration.

The dumbbell in his hand proved to be a black rattle—or what's the name of the instrument? Maraca, I believe. His white stomach hung loosely over his flesh-colored swimming trunks, which made him appear a naked and, moreover, sexless creature with a fat jiggly chest. His lifeless eyes stilled. The hollow clicking rhythm of the rattle, in addition to the music from the tape player in the other room, bewitched them, forcing them to accommodate their gait and speech to it.

GUEST: No, no, really, I should go.
My apartment's here, you know?
It's hilarious! Don't you think?
While going home, I've landed here,
At a friend's. Well, one thing's clear—
To each his own, but... Still the same,
We're back again at the oldest game.
Place things cheek to cheek; and now
That's what they do with houses, too,
Like honeycombs made by machines,
Cell-like apartments, through and through,
Interchangeable one and all.
What's the difference if they pall.

HOST: Boria, Boria, you're a prof,
An academic and a scholar.
I don't get anything of this,
But, then, ignorance is bliss.

GUEST: Actually, I'm not your Boria,
But, then, what's the difference.
Here, too, you happen to be right.

HOST: Just now I had a little bit
To make me fly... a touch.
You want some? It's about to hit.
Maracas, maracas.

GUEST: So that is why your pupils look
Just like plastic beads.
I don't need it. As it is,
I've got a buzz, am dizzy, see,
As if I've sniffed some grass.
(So, Simeon Kondratyich,
You get what grass I mean?)
You reach your high while others booze.
Let's get this straight.
To get blissed and vacanteyed
This is what you choose?

HOST: At the door the horse hoof stomps
Maracas, maracas,
The spilled and swollen lamp
Is enveloping us.

GUEST: The senseless, powerful beat of
Maracas, maracas,
Seems a dangerous force.
It levels, subjugates,
And also unites us.
Side by side, hand in hand,
Our tread will sound throughout the ages
'We're spat out from the pods as shoots
Of a new life in history's pages.
For hunting, for war
We'll become united
Beat the drums, the bowl of brass!

HOST: Maracas, maracas!

GUEST: The felons tap dance; through the dance
They recognize their sort.
By grouping in a special way, they
Can safely take a snort.
The first idea that's cited
To get them all excited.

279

How could this speed incite
Our own times. Is it right?

HOST: The face is twisted sideways,
Eastward shifts the eye,
And vacuous as the moon
Appears the side. Oh, my!
Reach for the bottle, drink instead,
Get that beauty out of your head.

GUEST: No, my capacity now's not much,
The stitches in my stomach hurt...
Listen, let's change the beat a touch.

HOST: I see Glück,* which means true joy,
Someone once explained that to me:
Stitches sprout blooms on slender stems,
Real beauties blossom on walls gloomy—
Their colors vary, they're all sorts,
And they're all yours; you touch by hand,
Know true delight, and float off to wonderland.

GUEST: A spinning wheel 'neath the beauties lurks.
Above the tape player looms,
Like the sun, a cuckoo clock,
With embossed-paper blooms.
To the wall is nailed a pair of small
Bast shoes, and a kerosene lamp,
With its glass broken, as I recall,
From my father's museum; as luck
Would have it, the music's stuck.
There's no sound of it now at all.
Just a snapping hollow beat
Resounds in my enlightened brain.
Comprehension dawns: quite a feat.

---

* GLÜCK Here Kharitonov indulges in bilingual wordplay. In German, Glück means "joy,"
while in the jargon of Russia's youth and drug culture, "gliuki" means "hallucination."

Did I place the target in your sights?
Did I uncover my father's treasure?
Is all this taken from his place?
Nothing now can be proved, for good measure?
That right, Kaif? Now I have no rights?
And no hopes either to lodge a claim?
I didn't save Father's heritage,
Abandoned it, let it go down the drain.
The school museum's tossed on the dump,
Thrown on the scrap heap; it'll be pulped,
And should I be saying "thanks" to the thief,
That he stole it in time, saved it? Good grief!
I see, by your eyes, you've regained your mind,
Goddamn, we briefly became two of a kind.
Not to speak of the soul, of course,
But things...the lay-out of the apartment...
And even this church from the window, see...
The wall-paper, too...the floor...Let me...

xv. A Psychiatry Textbook

Now, now, that's enough, stop! Stop making me laugh. You've certainly let yourself go!—even in verse, suddenly. Let's finally catch our breath, drop the rhythm, and return, so to speak, to prose. Or, as philosophers say, to reality. It's seemed to us for some time that the room where we see Anton Andreyevich isn't the same one. The bright lamp continued to spotlight the papers on the table and the face above them. The eyes needed some time to get accustomed to it. It obviously wasn't the same dwelling. But it wasn't a prefabricated-building apartment with a level, though low, ceiling, and without a ventilation pane in the windows, either. No, the ceiling was comparatively high, but it was all veneer, painted over with oil paint, and it was impossible to call it even; the window had a ventilation pane and double frames, old-fashioned ones, and on the wide windowsill (the kind they don't make nowadays) stood a fleshy flower in a pot. It's difficult to tell about the walls; they're almost completely covered with books on simple shelves without any fitted glass. Despite the crampedness, there's a coziness to it all that's definitely not in today's style. One could even call it "compact," and that compactness, incidentally, has certain obvious advantages. For example, without leaving one's chair one can reach a book on a shelf just by stretching one's arm, take the sugar bowl from the small cupboard, the kettle from under the table—very handy. One can get the books without leaving the couch squeezed in between the bookshelves. In general, one can save on many movements and on walking. Also time spent on cleaning the room. There's no room here for superfluous things; willy-nilly, one's way of life becomes more expedient. No, if one really thinks about it, a life like this has its own advantages and charm.

2

Well, thank god. Now, some time later, he can philosophize a little, even with humor, if you please. Then, however, in initial shock, he was in no mood for humor. Even Kaif gradually recovered, and after grasping the situation, started to pull on his pants and to speak more sensibly; he still seemed somewhat stupefied, however, rambling like a drunk who hadn't succeeded in getting as drunk as he wanted to, "So that means these are yours... Yikes! Well, there was no problem with them, they were transferred according to the law... I'm completely legal... here... wait a minute ... This has nothing to do with me. Sure, go ahead and look, just don't try to get at me. I did it all legally." And he kept trying to find the papers to show them, moving a small dirty syringe from place to place (although, if one recalls, he ultimately didn't show him anything). But who cares about the papers? Could Anton Andreyevich show anything either? No. The papers had been filled out for him, but he hadn't actually received them; his registration form for an apartment existed only in principle, as a verbal promise, and they promised to clear up as soon as possible what had happened in his absence—whether bungling or machinations. In all the relevant institutions and offices they made noises, though genuinely, called somewhere, settled him for the time being in a comfortable room in a dorm—the equivalent of a room in a hotel with all the amenities, and all at public cost. True, it was on the outskirts of town, but then they themselves suggested that for the time being, until the court case, he should move closer to the downtown area, into a separate, though quite small, room. He had no reason even to write complaints to the highest authorities—the lower ones were so cooperative. And all his things appeared to be in order according to the official list of items, and if subsequently he couldn't find some of his small items, which had been unpacked ahead of time, let's face it, no move is possible without losing some things. One couldn't find fault in the officials with whom Lizavin was dealing then no one was to blame for his affair and they still had to determine the guilty party, but in the meantime some rearrangements took place in the relevant department: someone left his position altogether, and someone well informed about his case was on leave. Apologizing to Lizavin, they asked him to wait a day or two more, to be patient, and to call then. The housing union gave him a loan, and various public organizations got involved. Sometimes he felt a pang of conscience about having created so much work for strangers. But from the day Anton Andreyevich got settled in the temporary apartment that was close to the center of the city, however, the tone of the conversations with him started to turn sour somehow. A kind of skin was drying up over the polite phrases that became more and more indifferent, then perplexed and politely bored. So, what does he want them to do if he's got himself into a mess, the clod? Who promised him anything, and what did they promise? Does he at least remember the man's name? Ah, only his face and the number of his office? But the faces have changed, the numbers have been hung elsewhere, and for some reason the papers cannot be found. Maybe there were no papers? By contrast, the next person he talked to started to shake a whole pile of papers in his face: see, hundreds of people who had been placed on a waiting list are crowded into communal apartments, six people living in twelve square meters, including a newly married couple—should they be denied because of him? Does he have a right to claim greater benefits than they, having a whole room to himself, albeit a small one? Was it fair, was it Soviet for a man without a family to demand anything beyond the housing that had been given to him, even if it wasn't in a new house? Didn't it have running water, gas, and even central heating? As experienced people, they knew that the pressure of such arguments had an immediate effect on bearded intellectuals like him. Particularly when an intellectual is weakened by sickness and inclined to appreciate as a gift every little detail of life that a healthy man is so used to that he no longer notices it; in this state you still remember that happiness and the essence of life are not at all in the size of a room and the presence of a bathroom. And when will you realize that the apartment assigned to you is certainly not occupied by a man with many children who's on the waiting list! You know very well when—

when you've already left the office, maybe even when you're already on the street, in the public garden with flowers, with birds singing, even if they *are* sparrows, in childlike voices, like the sound of leaves. The best arguments always come as an afterthought, but it was too late to go back! As Kaif said, you can't undo what's done. One should give the office clerks their due; they're familiar with the lofty science; they know, among other things, that one shouldn't lead people who feel done wrong, who register complaints, up a blind alley of despair, one should above all give them hope and continue to give them as much hope as possible, and then offer them a glimpse of a solution— however wretched—but still a solution! The person will stand firmly on his feet, then go on, swaying a little, his original fit of rage imperceptibly cooling. Time itself completes that task. Decisiveness should be nurtured, its temperature maintained, and if you lose control of it, the next thing you know, it's disintegrated, like tin buttons on uniforms that have lain around too long. One's approach to things has changed physically, and it remains only to explain to oneself mentally that everything in the world is relative—gains as well as losses.

3

In short, did he back down? Did he give up? Did he let them twist him around their little finger? Well, let's face it! It's all ridiculous, stupid, and, if it comes to that, even outrageous. One is already sick of that impracticality on the part of the so-called sublime types from the intelligentsia. Well, you see, it's not their business to get involved in squabbles about the everyday aspects of life, to struggle, to try to get somewhere, to fight for their own interests. That's why they yield ground bit by bit to rogues, leave them apartments, positions, significant posts, and the pages of journals, while they themselves huddle together in tiny rooms, make what little money they do at mindless work... but the lousiest thing is that they look for philosophical grounds for their insolvency. They even seek some higher meaning in it. Losers, weaklings, sluggards—let's call things by their real names! Although one could apply even worse words. Particularly because these people yield not only their own positions, but our common ones. And that's why we make do as we can, eating schnitzels from kerosene and ducks from sewage water, why we buy deodorized butter, breathe the devil knows what instead of air, listen to the devil knows whose lectures, read the devil knows what in our press; a dirty aluminum fork with bent prongs bangs against the side of a plate in the state canteen, and we call that our culture, our life, and don't notice that this food, both physical and spiritual, is gradually changing the very structure of our being.

4

There, at least Lizavin made it possible to unburden ourselves. We've found what's called a scapegoat. We can't speak into a mirror. As if we don't know how it happens. Something envelops and paralyzes your will like a viscous dream, leaving only one desire—to hide in the kennel you've acquired, quietly, meekly, so that not a single dog will pay attention to you... What was good about working in the library was the opportunity to be on his own: in the chink between the cabinets of the card catalogs which was considered the office of the researcher, who had at his disposal a gas range and a kettle, Anton Andreyevich really felt free and protected as never before. You continue being surprised, he thought once again as he sorted out his notes at home in the evening, along what routes, through coincidences, accretions, crossroads, and failures, a man nonetheless arrives at what he was inclined toward from the outset, according to his nature, at what he was perhaps created for— and finally you feel good. Well, Simeon Kondratyich? No, joking aside, what if one were to learn, as you advocate, not to compare, not to look at oneself from the viewpoint of others? It's not important where one lives and what one wears; a wise man understands the world without leaving his house... Well?... What are you laughing at?

Milashevich squinted from the photo on the desk: the bridge of his pince-nez was tied with narrow tape, a sad smile on his large mouth.

"Me?... No, nothing."

"I think we understand each other now as never before. Did I learn anything from our common experience?"

"What do you consider experience, Anton Andreyevich? They force a man to live in a kennel, give him a bowl of swill, and he's glad to assure them—and he's sure himself—that he's living in heaven?"

"Well, that's some talk! First, why speak of 'a kennel'? My place now is better than the one I had before—speaking quite objectively, it really is. I don't need any wood for heating, there are radiators, it's warm in the toilet. Only two families share the kitchen. My neighbor's a drunk, but he's peaceful, even likable..."

"Really. So you live like a hermit, a monk, an eccentric bachelor who's let himself go? And at your age?"

"Not at all, Simeon Kondratyich! Can't you see? Look at my place and at me—we're well looked after, not neglected. You can sense the presence of a woman, can't you? See, she gave me this shirt recently, a few days ago. The curtains on the windows are new, and what about this thing in the chamber pot... Well, what do you think?"

"What's her name?"

"The woman's? Liusia. Imagine, she's my former student. She didn't finish her studies because of some practical circumstances and she's working in a bookstore now. That's where we met, where else? It was also a strange meeting. It all depends on the person... exactly. She says she fell in love with me a long time ago while still at the institute. And I saw her, administered exams to her, yet didn't notice anything. She's nice all around... and something about her moved me: can't tell whether its her thinness or her vulnerable appearance..."

"Does she look like her?"

"Especially when I saw her on the street," Lizavin continued, not hearing the question, "in pants—you know how young girls have started wearing them now—in a tight-fitting blouse, so thin. It was moving... that's exactly what it was, moving. I don't know how to put it any other way. And her elegance is moving, as is her desire to please. Only a woman knows how difficult that is, particularly with her salary... the daily effort to keep up her appearance and her shape and to conceal her weakness during her monthlies. For some reason I feel sorry for all of them ... particularly women. They're kinder than we are. She'll see a little dog or a child and right away she's smiling. It's true. What's more important in life? And she cooks well..."

"Why have you become so talkative, Anton Andreyevich? Wait a minute. I want to ask you about *her*."

"Ah...No, I didn't find her, after all. The address they gave me at the hospital turned out to be wrong. Nobody lives there—I went to see. The tattered door's locked, a big cat looking from the lintel with eyes this big—awful, I've never seen cats like that. They say some old woman used to live there, but she ended up in a psychiatric hospital...in a house of sorrow, as they used to call it in the old days. The people in the information office say there was no one like that registered in that apartment. Maybe she left again...I don't know. I don't know anything about her, everything's uncertain...I feel bad for her, too, of course."

"Were you that disturbed by what happened with her and that athlete? Maybe it's not true."

"I didn't check it out and I don't intend to. It's not for me to judge. And I don't. People are different, it's hard to understand one another. And maybe there's no need to. In fact, I didn't really know her well. I just didn't see something clearly. From one perspective you see one thing, from another, something else. Possibly, one of us recovered. Although I'm not sure...Wait just a moment..."

"What are you doing?"

"Nothing. Just a moment."

He bent down, pulled a flat bottle of cognac from the bottom drawer, unscrewed the top, filled it, and drank the contents. He immediately repeated the action, then screwed the top back on. Simeon Kondratyich squinted reproachfully from the desk, even seemed to stretch in an effort to follow the bottle with his gaze till it was back in the drawer, but, unable to see over the edge, fell face down. Lizavin picked him up, dusted him off a bit with his fingers, and deferentially replaced him.

"I'm sorry, I didn't mean to. I accidently banged it."

"That's all right, it was my fault. That means you still drink at times. That's what I was afraid of. You shouldn't...You look..."

"Come on, does this show I'm drinking? You saw yourself. Just a tiny bit. For my health—it's even good for me. To calm my nerves a little."

"Why, what happened to you?"

"Nothing, really. Nothing at all. I probably overdid things a little. I overestimated my strength. One really should know one's limits, what one can do, and live according to them, not someone else's. My needs are basically very simple. Philistine, if you want. I like to lie on this couch, to read detective stories or science fiction...no, really. As for something else... I don't know. Maybe, nobody ever has that. You know, there are some silhouette films in which they beat a man on the head with a cudgel, hammer him into the ground, flatten him with an asphalt roller, tie him up in a knot...and the next morning...just as in that song of yours ..."

But next morning there she was, smiling,
Beneath her little window, as of old,

Milashevich reminded him without enthusiasm.

"Yes, that's it! It's wonderful. I discovered the complete lyrics just recently:

Once a beautiful girl
Entered the sea to play.
But the keel of a big submarine
Cut her in half right away.
A sea reptile gobbled up her innards
And instantly spat them out.
But next morning there she was, smiling.

"Wonderful! There's a kind of philosophical wisdom here. Place something right beside something else and they'll grow into each other. Life goes on. In spite of everything. Here's a *fantik* for the finale—what do you think, Simeon Kondratyevich? For the end of any chapter, if not for the end of the book. The ending of a book is more conventional. In reality, nothing actually ends, you're right. Only individual people perish in a disaster, but sooner or later they'll have to die anyway, the only question is postponement. People who perished a hundred years ago wouldn't be alive today anyway, so it's strange to grieve over them. We shouldn't exaggerate historical upheavals. There have been cases, however, of an entire nation completely disappearing, but even that was the end for them alone, others survived. I'd like to know one thing, though: Who keeps laughing in your corner all the time and can't stop? Do *you* know?"

"I don't like all this, Anton Andreyevich," Milashevich said quietly.

"What? The laughter?"

"If you call that laughter."

"Yes, sometimes it makes your skin crawl. But, you know, our constant humor, I feel, doesn't spring from living well. One needs to laugh sometimes so as to dispel fear, to make a misfortune seem minor. So as to enable one to go on living."

"In some sense laughter resists death itself," the philosopher reminded him, with that expression people have on their face when raising their finger significantly. "If only it had such a possibility."

"Yes...But why does it make your skin crawl? By the way, there's good reason, obviously, that religion has complicated relations with laughter. They knew what they were doing when they drove out the old Russian jesters with sticks. Christ, they say, never laughed."

"And in this regard, Anton Andreyevich, also note that for some reason it doesn't suit a woman to be funny, to make faces, play the buffoon—that's all for men. There's something unnatural about a female clown, isn't there? Just as there is about a woman who's drunk."

"What is this...I didn't hear you talk like this before."

"We hear only what we're capable of hearing. Everybody gets the kind of conversation he deserves. Imagine an interlocutor who all his life responds only to the extent of the questions he's asked."

"I do what I can, Simeon Kondratyich. I've already told you: anything more is beyond my abilities."

"My dear man, what do you mean, 'beyond'? We discover ourselves and our abilities through effort, through doing and seeking."

"Perhaps. But I've had enough. I need to get well. To put my nerves back in order a little and the rest of it...You know, as time passed, I even started to confuse things somehow. Recently I was asked in a polyclinic how old I am, and imagine, I had to think about it! I quickly started subtracting the numbers, but to do that I first had to ask what year it is. It sounded funny, but it fitted my image. You know, the image of a man who's not of this world. It even elicits empathy. Though I don't know what the doctors thought. Sometimes it can get even worse, you know. I'm right to be afraid."

"Of what?"

"Nothing. Just...Mainly of idiosyncrasies in my own thinking. If I were to be completely honest, I stopped agitating about the apartment not only for reasons I can explain. I started being frightened of my own dreams. And I don't mean the nightmares...Sometimes they're almost harmless, but suddenly the air would be punctuated by a scream and Iakov Ilyich's fingers would be over his thorax: *a-a-ah!*"

"Come, now, Anton Andreyevich!"

"It's all right, everything's fine. I won't go on about it. Just a moment..."

He turned Simeon Kondratyevich so that he faced the wall, as if he couldn't guess what was going on behind his back by the sound of the drawer being pulled open and the splash of liquor being poured. So that when Anton turned him back as before, the philosopher's face expressed not so much reproach as an air of injury.

"Really, you're behaving like a child. It's your business, do what you want. But you did say 'just a little.'"

"And have I had a lot? It's all right. I needed it now. Now I've started, maybe I'll get it all out. In general something in my feelings started to frighten me inexplicably. The senselessness of certain words, concerns, actions, movements. Not only mine, but other people's, too. You rush to cross the street in front of the radiator of a car, yet you left home too early and are even looking for ways to fill in time. You buy a thing you don't need, you go stand in line...well, better not talk about lines. It's better if I tell you about one impression. You know, for the first time I finally visited the district where Ganshin's estate is located. For the first time—you have a right to be puzzled. I know all the areas around there well; actually, I'd been all over them. But this—I only had a general sense of the location. Since childhood that locale was regarded as forbidden to us. My mother, of course, didn't explain why, and it was better not to ask; she didn't like us to talk about it: You can't go in that direction even to pick mushrooms, and that's that. With no explanations. But, of course, we knew anyway:

there was a concentration camp there. Sometimes there was talk of somebody escaping from it. In general, people had a fear of that zone, and maybe it unconsciously played a role. Besides, I knew that the estate had burned down. And there was no convenient way of getting there. It's far from the bus route, closer to the railroad, two stops beyond Stolbenets... but why am I telling you this! Just to explain why I didn't go there before. So I especially took not the suburban electric train, but a regular passenger train. I get out. By the section where the tracks divide, there are some buildings and the track walker's hut, but seemingly no other dwellings in the vicinity. I asked the track walker for directions to the estate, and, strangely enough, he understood immediately and showed me, although he gave me an enigmatic look, which I understood only afterward. As it turns out, a deserted narrow-gauge road led there through the forest. The rusty, half-dismantled rails and rotted railroad ties were overgrown with grass. Then the rails stopped, and one could see only the remains of a ruined bridge across a stream. Then suddenly a fallen column with a sign: STOP! RESTRICTED AREA! WE SHOOT WITHOUT WARNING! The same one, from my childhood fears... The forest ended, ceding to a green meadow and a hill. On the hill... How can I describe the first impression to you? Among the greenery were columns, sort of, and some piles of something that was unclear from a distance. It proved to be the remains of a pediment, a wooden two-floor hut added on to it. And, in addition, the ruins of a brick wall, a small piece, but with an iron gate that was closed, Simeon Kondratyich. And above all this, the sky, thick, naked... At the bottom of the slope of the hill a man in officer's riding breeches, but wearing old working shoes, was digging something. Not just any old pit, but a huge trench. He'd fill a wheelbarrow, cart it along some wooden planks, then empty it in a low-lying area. I went up to him to talk. 'Do you live here?' I said. He muttered something not very cordial, but I understood that he was definitely a resident. 'What are you digging?' I say. He glanced at me over his shoulder. 'A Caspian Sea,' he says. 'Why?' He snubbed me. Not a sociable fellow, I thought. Fine, then, I can take a look around myself. I'd already started walking away when he said, 'If you came without a spade, ask up there, they'll give you one.' Quite something, don't you think? Well, I went up there, toward the gate. It wasn't just closed, but the lock on it was rusty and you couldn't get it off. I walked around the wall. There really was a brick ruin and, the main thing, everywhere piles, mountains of soil. Some had already sprouted grass, others seemed fresh. I managed to get around them. I see people beside the structures nearby; one of them seems to be observing me. But I'm in no hurry to approach him. For I'd seen another structure. The remains of a latticed wooden tower, the wide tier of the foundation made from crossbeams and planks, and I recognized it from a photo I'd seen. Some of the remains were rotting in the ground. A small flight of steps led upstairs. Carefully, I climbed up them. The view was sweeping and impressive. The fellow was digging below, and as I looked closely I see—God damn it!—his huge trench really does have the exact outlines of the Caspian Sea. I went down, and the fellow was already waiting for me below. But he doesn't say anything, as if he's waiting for me to speak first. And this whole atmosphere starts to affect me. It was lucky I had cigarettes on me: say what you will, they really help in making contact. You take them out, offer them—'Do you smoke?'—light the match, and the conversation's already started. 'I see the digging here is going full guns?' I start the ball rolling. 'Yes,' he says, 'they keep on coming.' 'And this fellow, too?' I indicate below. 'No,' he says, 'he's ours. A former colonel.' 'He's really dug a Caspian Sea.' I grin, just in case, as if to say that I have a sense of humor. 'Yes,' he says, 'he's trying for the second year now and doing everything himself, doesn't let anyone help. As for me, heaven knows, this is good therapy through hard work. Maybe we'll put in a stream afterward, fill it with water, and breed fish for general use...As you can guess, it's already started to reach us bit by bit.' 'And this,' I point to the area around us, 'Was it also the work of your folk?' 'No, the people who come here do that. We don't allow our own people into the cellars. There may still be cave-ins underground; we're responsible for the patients. And they're not interested in treasures, they have enough of their own things...'"

Milashevich suddenly gave a laugh.

"That's some twist you've given it, Anton Andreyevich! I kept thinking all the time: How will you finish the story? You've really got literary talent."

"Why literary? Do you mean I invent things? Well, you know, you're hardly the person to take a dig at me for that. I still had doubts whether it was just my imagination: a wall that had collapsed and ancient cellars underground, and it turns out that for many years people kept coming there to look for treasure, and sometimes so many came at once that the local personnel established some rules, and, by the way, collected taxes for their own use from those who came to search. They were even expecting to get the usual fee from me, ten rubles, as I understand. There's no other reason for a normal person to come here. And there's no point in the local people's looking in another place; for them a fragment of the wall with a locked gate is enough. But maybe they absent themselves for a while; you can't tell them apart that easily. This feeling started to dog me, Simeon Kondratyevich. You look at a man sitting in the library, his book open at a page of reproductions. The presentation of the banner, I don't remember who painted it. He's sitting, head propped on his fist, and looking. Then suddenly he starts writing in his notebook. He'll sit and look some more, then will write down another thought. An art critic, probably...No, I can't explain it. On the bus you'll peer over somebody's shoulder at a newspaper, trying to figure out precisely what item is engrossing him like that; you try to follow the ray. On the front lines of the struggle for peace. What idea shifts from these lines into the brain? How is it compatible with yesterday's idea, which has already become invalid? A delicate construction is restructured every day in the brain of a newspaper reader, Simeon Kondratyevich, all the time you have to make your mental organization correspond to new words. In the process, life is as if bifurcated: one part of it has its own half of the mind, the other part has the newspaper half, but they're marvelously compatible. Amazingly expedient ordinary schizophrenia. I already know the terminology, you know. See, I got hold of a textbook. And on every page, Simeon Kondratyich, on every page I find some familiar symptoms. I had no idea earlier that everyone has them."

"Now, now," Milashevich said, and it sounded like: "Don't get carried away."

"I assure you," Anton said, flipping through the book to the places where he'd earlier inserted bookmarks. "Here—'Breaches in perception of life's mutability.' Everything seems dead, immobile, and therefore alien. Isn't this about Angel Ganshin? Or, look, an example taken from Kretschmer* about a surrogate for happiness. About a clerk who contends that he lives better than any minister. Isn't this Pankov?"

"You're indiscriminately throwing different things into one pile," Milashevich shook his head again. "First, that's not a sickness yet. Read the section alongside it; the right name for that is right there. Second, what you call ordinary schizophrenia may be really essential for the existence of society as a totality. Society seeks stability and equilibrium. For that, it's necessary that every day, every hour, individuals ensure, as you put it, that their mental equipment corresponds to general formulas. Truth, as we've already realized, is not important. One can base common life on doubtful and even false knowledge. On a belief that will safeguard harmony, even with death. On a myth that will suit everyone better than anything else."

"Moreover, there's still the question of what is truth."

"Exactly. It's more accurate to speak of a will to truth, of seeking it, of aspirations to get closer to it."

"Yes, and that immediately brings us to Bidiuk," Anton joined in. "Now there's someone who seeks the underlying cause of all the world's mysteries and historical events. And he's finally found it. He recently revealed his conjecture to me. Amazingly sweeping, it encompasses everything. What do you think it is? It's visitors from other planets, of course. Are we about to deny a passion for seeking here? And what a passion!"

"Why do you say that so sarcastically? Don't you believe in it?"

"Simeon Kondratyich!"

"Wait, this idea will be acknowledged. I don't say corroborated, that's not necessary, but you won't be able to refute it completely."

"Oh, yes!" Lizavin agreed.

"Well, then. And if the majority's convinced that it's expedient, then we'll see who'll come out crazy and a candidate for isolation.

---

* ERICH KRETSCHMER (1888-1964) Psychiatrist and professor in Marburg and Teubingen who philosophized about the relationship between body types and character traits.

I formulated the following somewhere: 'Craziness should be uniform within the boundaries of a system. A disparity...' I don't remember what's next."

"'A disparity leads to dissonance and collisions...' Do you mean, then, that for you x is the point of craziness?"

"Why not? Try to expose where it's vulnerable, ruminate on it, set it up. What's important is a generally accepted, common system of values, an equilibrium of internal and external, of desire and realization... Why are you looking at me as if at a photo?"

"I'm trying to catch your eye. And you're avoiding mine. I don't have any idea how you look in profile."

"What profile! It didn't even come out in the photo."

"One completely stops understanding anything with you, Simeon Kondratyich. I just told you about the place I visited, really visited, but now that I've told you, I'm beginning to have doubts myself: Did I imagine it all? Did you ever have a feeling like that? You're either dreaming or reading something that somebody made up—and suddenly it becomes painfully real and you can actually touch the bump on your head. I still didn't get to finish saying the most important thing, Simeon Kondratyich. I dream only my own dreams. I've already seen this wall, and the flight tower, the inscription carved with a knife on the wood, the orphanage or prison, Iona's ark... and among the children someone like my Kolia Iazik, with a white face... everything gets confused. There, on the estate, the children's prison gave way to a prison for adults; they added a simple wire fence to Ganshin's wall and adapted the remains of the tower into a lookout for guards. Whose visions do I plug into and see, Simeon Kondratyich? Smoky air, a burned forest, exhausted naked people standing in pits among crosses, holding each other's hands... Makarii's followers. My mother told me once about the hunger during those times. She was a girl then, and two men came after her in a field. It was a good thing that a peasant she knew happened by and frightened them off, and later he gave her a talking-to: 'Why are you walking alone? Do you want to end up in a cauldron?' The cauldron... Did you know about that? And I seem to be present everywhere, but I don't see myself..."

"I sometimes tried to imagine you," Milashevich said suddenly.

"A man who would read me one day. Who'd sit over the papers, going through them...the cells of my soul, my life, my brain. And, you know...I imagined you approximately the way you are: with a beard, in a shirt made of a material I'm not familiar with. Only I thought you'd wear glasses."

"Really, Simeon Kondratyich, you can drive a person simply crazy. You'll soon be saying that I'm a product of your imagination, along with our conversation and all the rest."

"How can you say that! Why? I really did imagine our conversation, and it turned out something like the one we're having now, more or less."

"You weren't far wrong as regards the glasses. I had to go to the doctor's recently, and he prescribed them. 'You should have started wearing glasses a long time ago,' he says. What else did you dream about me?"

"You look as if I've offended you, Anton Andreyevich. I didn't mean...If you want, think the opposite, that you invented me yourself. Go ahead. I don't hold onto my authorship. It's funny, in fact. Maybe somebody is inventing both of us right now—don't you have that strange suspicion from time to time? Somebody's writing your life, moving a crummy pen over paper; we drip off the nib, are given form by the letters. Right now, as we're speaking. Or as we read. And we're right to worry about what he'll do with us. But the point is that not only are we dependent on him, but he also needs us for some reason. Our creations create us. He who's inventing us now—or thinks he is—maybe at that moment starts to suspect that his life is also written by somebody. Somebody invisible is looking expectantly at him with hope and a prayer. If you only knew, Anton Andreyevich, how dependent we all are on each other. I'm real, if you're real—can't you get that into your head?"

"You seem to want to confirm, Simeon Kondratyich, that my mind is really vulnerable. Of course, my head is already buzzing a little, but that's not the point..."

"Drop it, Anton Andreyevich, I'm talking more seriously now than I've ever talked before. This textbook of yours is helpful, of course, but don't get confused. Keep in mind that besides subjective feelings there are objective symptoms. I remind you of that as a man who once studied medicine."

"For instance?"

"Look in the book. At least the handwriting changes. Sometimes so much that it's impossible to recognize it."

"Yes, yes, as happens with drunks."

"Or because of drugs. You're absolutely right."

"It's just like in this notebook of yours . . . I'm still squeamish about examining it."

"A natural feeling. But let me finish. It seemed to me just now that you acquired this textbook, too, so as to escape something, not to complete yet another thought. Do you remember how you put it, speaking about me once? 'That's how a sly character from a fairy tale marked his neighbors' houses with crosses to conceal the one that mattered.'"

"I don't understand."

"Why didn't it occur to you to look for *her* there?"

"Where?"

"There . . . in the house of grief, as you called it."

"Well, really! . . . I think I'll finish the little bottle now, Simeon Kondratyich, and you'll stop making the comments you've been allowed."

"Wait! By all that's holy! I haven't finished. I unexpectedly got sidetracked. So, I'm asking you. If I could, I'd go down on my knees."

"All right. Why not? I'm aware that this importunate idea of her came from the same textbook. A splinter. And once you can't get it out, you shouldn't pay any attention to it. Why specifically I? There *is* someone else. He'll be out soon, maybe they'll find each other. Everything will work out right."

"But why did he want you to read his notebook?"

"I don't know. I don't owe anybody anything."

"Anton Andreyevich, you have no idea how much depends on you, precisely on you! Every feeling, every life, every thought, even if not ingrained in one's memory, breeds a charge, that's a fact, and it also can be sustained somewhere for an instant or for centuries, unnoticed, and influence even the living, gradually weakening until it disappears. But for something like lightning to occur, you always need somebody else who's able to understand, to perceive, and to hear it. One of our thinkers, a provincial, too, by origin, kept exhorting us to animate people from a small particle of earthly dust. In all seriousness. A strange perversion of an idea. Do we give birth only to bodies? Don't the departed, those gone, in repose still continue their existence in an equal capacity, owing to our sense of life? That sense never really dies. Quite recently I was dead, voiceless, didn't exist where anybody was concerned. You animated me through your effort, your trepidation, the warmth of your own life. And I'm not the only one. Just go a little farther... you're not eternal either; think about it, you're also dependent on someone, on someone's thoughts, someone's love, someone's memory. Finally, while we're both still visible and able to see...

XVI. A NOTEBOOK WITHOUT A COVER

*if we draw a molecule, it is structured like the planetary system
Or an atom I forgot Not important Let's imagine that invisible
planets are swarming with life the way ours does Skies with rainbows
and heavenly bodies and tiny ants We can't suspect about each
other's existence because of incommensurability It's impossible to
understand to feel the self only in the clearance of a huge substance
Each of us contains a Universe and the blood contains more than
animal memory and fish infusoria crystals and the ancient salt liquid
of the world ocean and the embryo of future worlds Everything
together and it's impossible to get away from it The key was here
I can't understand The smaller the nucleus the stronger the forces
that's the law I'm not to blame You grab hold of one thing and
the other's escaped The smaller it is the more difficult it is to predict
I went back to correct to explain but first to finish writing on the
small sheets of paper I didn't have any more I chose the last beautiful women on earth I want to explain carefully I won't even give
the name and you can burn it later so as not to cause any harm
because the nuclei themselves are stirring here and are summoning
up another life one should keep track of everything one should correct
it It's difficult to remember The nuclei pour from here to there the
blood rustles The throat's dried up there's no water in the well
just dirt at the bottom of it dissolve the ink with saliva if necessary,
there's no saliva left either There's nothing here with which
to moisten a pencil don't take it amiss I kept this notebook finally
in case I'd have to explain to you and that's what's come about
No one's to blame I'm not reproaching you although what does your
nice face need a trunk and these flat eyes for She couldn't bear it
Life ended in a second darkened as if becoming charred with the skin*

in necrotic knots and veins There are black holes in the air as in
muslin There is nothing to breathe with Don't be angry I left
with a coffin amidst coffins Otherwise I wouldn't have been able
to get out Later I didn't know how hard it was for Him and I went
over came again to see the coffin it was for her and it was said Here
appeared her beloved Our first prophet The cauldron is boiling
the Eucharist is available to everyone It's hard to do it singly but if
they were to merge to become intertwined to spill into the pit How
I wanted to be with them I saw delight and a consummation but one
has to have earned it A child didn't let its Mother do it and I realized
that I won't be able to do it I wasn't completely there not alone
in my own right there remained you and everything that's here
I was needed Nobody was guarding the way back I returned to
finish taking care of things to await the moment and now I can't do
anything My feet are like cotton I have no voice or fear The nuclei
stir the cold is icy there's nothing with which to get warm but if
I were to roll some grass in a piece of paper The letters enter the body
along with the smoke make it warm the fingers can write you'll
understand I've remembered now to whom and for what I see you're
looking out of the circle And you me It's a little bit small should
be bigger but there won't be enough paper there's none left huge
fingers but I understand With whom did I think of competing
in argumentation But not for my own sake And now we need to take
care of it one can't allow holes in the air The universe can get cold
A terrible ugly emptiness between stars a pile of stones Energy needed
all the time

XVII. An Ark, or A Stone Will Come in Handy Yet

"But you knew that he's certainly not the son of the Sun."
"That's how you see it now. But then belief in him wasn't just the truth. It enabled victories in battle, it took and gave life."

Delusion, drunkenness, sickness. But prior to this delusion, to this madness—what did we know about life?

There is no truth without delusion

it's like the charge of electricity in a cloud, even if there's no lightning

1

When did it happen? Probably not at once, not instantly; something was shifting in the mind of this inconceivable man or in his soul (we're speaking, after all, about a spiritual malaise, when a mind is profoundly shaken, on top of the shocks of the times and exacerbated by them). Something definitely wavered in his soul even then, on the raft made from the old gates, amidst a mythical puddle, in the instant that once drew close to us in the transparent curve of time, so that in greater and greater detail we can closely examine the dismantled crossroads and see again the dammed up lowlands, small benches along fences, pale, crumpled, cautious spots in the windows, see knuckles white with tension or cold and the lifeless face of a woman, but now we peer with particular intentness at another face striking in its resemblance to the portraits on the *fantiki*, waxen in the light of the dismal November weather: a dribble of saliva stretches from his half-opened lips. As for him, he definitely didn't recognize anybody and didn't even understand that he had been recognized throughout his life (or guessed correctly, on the basis of the resemblance). Did he know anything definite at all about his origins? Did he consider any one of the men who meddled in his life as his father? Did he wonder about that at all?—in any case, not then, in his moment of triumph, when a new era did indeed begin for him, and not only because for the first time he gained possession of the river crossing to which he'd not had access before—the undersized, weak favorite of adults, but a social outcast among the residents of Levinson's boarding school. The ravens are cawing in the turbulent heavens, a parody of a tragic chorus, but no words have been uttered yet—it's not the right time, and perhaps not the right place; some things haven't come together properly, and not only because one of the people on the raft is under arrest and owing to a misunderstanding will be locked up in jail... he's still delighted how everything came true, was realized; he's returning in the darkness through the mud, along the roadway in the light of a lantern, his head spinning; the air is extracted from winy fumes, with the hubbub and shouts, black streams flowing along the gutters. He's not grasped the change yet, but something has already been shaken in his brain—or will be shaken the following day, when he finds out that the little boy is no longer in Stolbenets, that the family reunion will have to be delayed, and in the meantime he's got to take care of the woman who's already sick, already in a fever, to provide a new explanation for her, a new promise, new words, and to fill the little trunk with words, listening to them stir and form structures, so that there won't be another slipup; he'd become convinced of their bewitching power. *Just a little more, just a bit...*

2

For the little boy was recognized not just by her; that day other eyes gazed at him with a special feeling, inflamed eyes, damaged by German poisonous gas, so that they resembled raw meat. The pockmarked housepainter and artist in English puttees was delighted to recognize the features that he had first seen on a picture and then reproduced so many times; they seemed not to have changed during all these years—impervious to time, they were a living fulfillment, a hope, an opportunity—for him too, for him too. Perhaps it was he, Iona, who drove the former mercenary owners off the raft and gave the pole to an orphan dressed in the quilted jacket of Levinson's boarding school, and the boy, fearful of the consequences, later tried to stay closer to his unexpected protector; he'd flinch slightly when the big hand patted him on the head and he'd accept a present in his little palm—a sticky caramel, a sweet rosy juice painting lips that were bright without it, as in the picture; maybe he spent that first night somewhere at Bosoi's, in the house in the trade settlement area or in some temporary place, on a greatcoat spread on the ground while a soldier was shattering the bottles in Sotnikov's storehouses with a buttstock, his hand shading his face from the fire... It's difficult to see what Milashevich didn't see; we'll never know at what time and how—was it by ordinary cart? by horse, seated behind the rider?—the little boy traveled the fifty versts along a bumpy forest road, leaving Stolbenets for Nechaisk together with a newfound protector and defender, a man of the new order and strength who was now fully convinced that the people of the former order were hopeless, doomed, the poison of the former way of life having ineradicably eaten into them; you couldn't change them, you couldn't establish anything like the dream you'd once envisioned—you could only cancel out the past, making room for a new life; it had to be segregated right now, isolated from the infection all around them; Iona was going to Nechaisk to found an ark for the people who deserved it.

3

The moment is near, close at hand!
An abyss of water all around.
Let's equip an ark that'll serve
For the new age of a future life.
But why should one save and sustain
Foul creatures in pairs, once again?
And into blameless offspring
Its baneful poison pour?
Fire for the world's protection

Should cleanse it of infection.
By burning every seam we'll strive
To let no parasites survive.
Spoilage, though, we cannot stop,
The body pulls us to the earth.
We're doomed already, one and all,
To turn to dust beside the wall.
But along the waves our ark
Will ascend toward the heavens,
And a chorus of children's song
Will burst over the mountain tops.
I see a marvelous face among
Those of other youths:
Forehead tender like a petal,
Curly the soft, fair locks.
The scent of childhood is sweet,
The voice of childhood an aural treat.
You remain as young as ever,
Never crossing over the mark.
Your ascent toward happiness will begin
Here among orphans in the ark.
Your fate I glorify and sing,
And the thoughts within that head,
The hump between the shoulderblades—
The embryo of future wings.

4

Without question these were his verses, the verses of Iona Sverbeyev, they were linked with the ones that had been published as parts of a single narrative poem, which every poet probably writes his whole life—with those, for example, where he dauntlessly agreed to fertilize by himself the soil of the future, only first he wanted to clear and make a place for a new infancy:

We're to rot through with the earth
You're to soar beneath the sun.

Iona seems not to have found the words for his bright vision—
something like that isn't susceptible to words. Maybe he tried to paint
it, but where are those pictures? We can only guess what he still
wanted to accomplish in the location of Nechaisk. Did he himself
know? And what did he mean when years later in the former
Ganshin's estate he tried to construct the flight tower? Maybe by then
he remembered only vaguely and didn't consider that his concern;
others will build the future according to their way of thinking, of
those who'd live in it—his was only a preliminary job. He was more
modest and maybe more sensible than others, without having pretensions either to a world scale, or even a national scale—he was just
more energetic, more impatient, and more serious. The Nechaisk
republic that the smoke of papers burned in the archive enveloped in
such an unnecessary mystery was just a name for an orphanage that
was founded within the walls of a former monastery that by then was
deserted; the rest of the town in the meantime had to provide food,
utensils, clothes, and all the necessities for its carefree life—what
happened outside the walls was secondary for Bosoi, he was only
concerned with increasing the number of inhabitants of the happy
ark and with its steady expansion until it finally would coincide with
the entire population of Nechaisk (and maybe even more, but that
was other people's business); his myopic, irritated eyes were not
interested in details, they were fixed on a distant point beyond those
who were doomed in any case, and if he sometimes took them into
account, he did so without any special hostility, maybe even with the
sympathy of understanding—for he didn't single himself out from
their general fate (and having started his verses addressing "you," he
subsequently treated himself as a member of the rest); simply, his
turn would come later, like that of the sweeper, who has to sweep
the square before a public celebration and then leave for good. There
were people besides him who could take care of the details; that winter there was more than enough work for the former cemetery priest's
hands, which were worn from the spade; Sverbeyev had no reason to
surround this work with writing—there was nothing of interest here
for descendants, only the sand of Goat Ravine preserved the residual
traces, and for a long time afterward immigrants from other regions

continued to settle into the Nechaisk houses that had remained empty. One could all too easily submit the papers on the basis of others that looked like them; if they were still preserved somewhere, they could only have provided supplementary information about how and why Iona had to leave Nechaisk, transferring his ark elsewhere. But that came later, and now another music is breaking through the thickness to reach us; it's more important for us to bring it to light, to become firmly convinced in the feeling that for a long time yet after Nechaisk the boy stayed with Iona—his joy, his hope, and his promise.

5

How he jumped—fearful, baited, always the very last—how he sensed protection and his new position! That could be about him, as could Sverbeyev's poems. A cherub with teeth ruined by too many sweets, the new blood in the veins of the old world, the first in the ark of the future—he, who in the boarding school and outside it had to endure the superiority of others who were stronger and taller because he was invariably weaker and smaller, so he could snap, could take revenge only secretly—a small child who attracted so much love but who brought misfortune to all who loved him (only children were repelled by that which elicited tenderness in adults: a too-vivid beauty, lips always damp with saliva, the ways of a little animal always expecting someone's touch—in the form of either a caress or a blow, ready in advance to bend down, displaying his little hump, and this expectation, this weakness would bring on the caress or blow—and maybe he actually provoked the infliction of an injury sometimes so as to complain later to his defender—he always had protectors—and to observe the reprisal with satisfaction); now he had a superiority and strength—the superiority of a physical disability, the strength of misfortune. Lord! What's to be done if so many things in our history smack of misfortune and illness? There's no hiding from it; the obviousness of an individual bodily defect allows us, of course, to call everything else health—a blessed opportunity, a merciful right; but one shouldn't delude oneself too much—who doesn't get bent out of shape when time is contorted? Who'll call himself untouched by anything? And what's to be done if an unlucky vision has already stuck and doesn't want to disappear (the little boy arrested in his growth with a scarcely visible small bump on his back?)—and all the words about the best of intentions, hope, and an idea that had gotten sidetracked about willful creations, about guilt, error, love, expectation, horror, pain, and attempts to escape from the truth are already waiting to be linked not with historical abstractness, but with this figure that has condensed as from a dream, and the ever new details add contours to it. A museum exhibition without a fixed venue: a measuring ruler with notches. Iona installed it in his orphanage, and any boy who measured below a certain mark got an extra portion of sweets. But sooner or later all the children outgrew it, became like adults, with cheeks, damaged hair, breath poisoned with tobacco; time, alas, continued along its course, and there was no place to get a genuinely new and unprecedented being; everything in life, after all, consisted of the same available molecules. Only one boy continued to console him with hope, didn't disappoint his expectations . . . We see the shell-shocked man's trembling fingers on the curly head, and see them carefully touch the bud of tender wings that haven't yet unfurled; confused nostrils inhale the smell of sickness without understanding it, lips muttering verses that stir in his mind—the creator of violent prophesies, he hasn't yet noticed that he's become ridiculous, superfluous, and dangerous, that his turn of mind no longer coincides with the tendency of the times. But by then the boy also will leave the man who's lost his strength, who's an invalid, who's lost touch with all real actions; he'll find a new protector and a new future that's uniquely his—gradually growing up, but hardly growing much taller, only the boots with hidden heels and the tall hat making him a little taller . . .

COMR. KARL

THE PROVINCE PLENIPOTENTIARY

IN BATTLE . . .

—that's all we needed, wasn't it?—the final outburst, his name on the tattered form, to suddenly close the circuit.

6

All that would be fine, but the name is careless. And with such a height!* Didn't it erupt onto the paper like the sigh of a loving man who's received news from afar about his child, admired him, worried about him, sought ways of helping him, of guarding him against danger amidst political changes? His name was acquired, for sure, adopted instead of his own during the period of general renaming, at somebody's ideological prompting or out of his own diligence. Time revealed and accentuated in him an unexpected nuance, almost a hint, but it was probably impossible to go back on his word, it would be misunderstood, and Milashevich was anxious at home in Stolbenets; he was rewriting for himself the rapturous poems of the poet who shared the same love, and sometimes he couldn't control himself from addressing the boy on paper—without uttering his name, instantly breaking off and not completing his thoughts, fearful of consequences, because one can't always speak about things that are so dear. *How I hope, how I await, admiring from afar.* One could go through it again as if following the tracks, the lines, one's nose glued to the smell, like the keen dog Hammer and Sickle. One could look for his name in real lists from the province, to match them by their marks, to confirm something, to get more precise information, make corrections—but would these really add much? Milashevich himself didn't see his little boy for many years; he lived more in his soul or mind, unchanging, beautiful, inspiring countless dreams on the *fantiki* about a blessed perpetual childhood, about the malleable makeup of the mind, capable of seizing from the empty air an essential idea and of changing in happy accord with it, about time arrested and erased. Yes, the papers in addition to everything else were like the accessories in a magic act: on them one could transform life for the sake of those one loved, for the sake of that motionless, voiceless woman who received such a shock then on the raft—perhaps not just from the meeting or because of recognizing him. He couldn't leave her for long, he couldn't immediately go after the boy and bring him back—to whom? and how? with what words?

---

* The word for dwarf in Russian is *karlik*.

One still had to prepare something, perhaps first to combine something on the *fantiki*, and until then only to promise a final return, a last meeting, postponing it from one year to the next—there was no reason, after all, to count the years.

7

A little more, just a bit, and it'll come together, come to pass, be resolved. Something continued to be displaced in his mind or in his soul, but even Semeka hadn't noticed anything yet, only a strange embarrassment wafted his way from the joker's words and his smile. The sick woman lay behind the partition, in the musty air of the cramped apartment, while he surrounded her with something resembling a flowery paradise, jotting down words on the backs of the *fantiki*, where a fair-haired beautiful woman embroidered, watered flowerbeds, poured tea from a decorated teapot, the feminine symbol of the Stolbenets or Nechaisk coat of arms. Now one can see behind all this a mad, doomed attempt to save, to protect his beloved from a universal human fate; till the very end he refused to recognize not defeat, but a collapse, and maybe not only because of pride he insisted that he was happy, that he experienced happiness in all its unbearable fullness.

8

Lines crossed and met, white roots interweaved beneath the earth in the fearful summer of cholera, drought, and fires. As the peat bogs near Sareyevo burned, the air was replaced with darkness. Flies and mosquitoes vanished, and a lot of small white moths appeared instead. Their density made breathing even harder; they stuck to glass and sweaty skin, disintegrated in one's fingers like fatty meal, and left sores on one's tongue. The puddle at the crossing of the three low-lying streets dried up, never to reappear, and the Stolbenets lake receded far from the shores, leaving around it a stinking swamp with a hardened but unreliable crust. Coated with silt, objects that had lost their shape protruded from the layer of mud at the bottom; a knight in metal plate-like armor made of mud, with a Polish helmet—it was difficult to distinguish him from a distance through the wavering vapors in which memories nobody recognized suddenly emerged and dissolved like phantoms. The air, dried out by the sun, was fatal to them, and after barely enduring it for a second, the Pole disintegrated before they could even try to reach him—who he was and where he could have been taken alive in this area remained an eternal mystery— and was there nevertheless some truth in the legend about Koltunov, who'd long ago disappeared from the stone? In his place now stood the last plaster figure, with both sides lopped off: the same inevitable fate, alas, befell the companion-in-arms to the right as had met the one leaning in the opposite direction; the reason was the same for all of them, and even the one that remained couldn't count on a long life: the same *fantik* could be applied to any year. *There must have been a defect inside the body. A cavity, a crack. Most likely, in the head. Then it spread farther…Water will find its own way; it doesn't care through whom it flows…*And just as always, the eternal Vas Vasich, the town fool who didn't turn gray, continued to accompany the coffins with the deceased, only now they were transported in piles on carts and buried outside the town limits, and the barriers prevented the people who accompanied the deceased from going any farther: because of the epidemic all entrances and exits were closed, and soldiers provided with gas masks for breathing amidst the smoke stood at the barriers. But for Vas Vasich smoke was nothing; tears flowed from his faded eyes, but his mouth smiled in its customary triumph: Here I am, accompanying everyone, yet I'm still walking, still alive.

9

Well, now even the poems about the ark could fit in a new place— though the scale would have to be smaller: no longer the monastery orphanage or Ganshin's former estate; from the familiar lines, one could reconstruct a corner in the house where the invalid, retired but not transformed into a drunkard, lived out the short time left to him, wearing a greatcoat burned through on the back, his face pock- marked, his pupils reluctant to accept things that were all too obvious. Milashevich probably called on his former acquaintance to speak with him and to ask him some questions—they certainly had things to talk about. *Where are those eyes looking? Past me, past me.*

311

Pangs of a feeling that had not completely evaporated could be deduced from the sheets of paper. *Light through the unwashed windows—as through a bottle of badly refined home-distilled vodka. In the small pens behind the temporary partitions living flesh was densely stirring; the flesh swayed, touching other flesh, tumbled out onto the street, grew, spread, dried, decayed, aged, lost its warmth, and was transported to the gully.* One could settle into the last ark here all the people who weren't recognized and settled in other places; it's a little crowded, but room will be found for everyone, for the doctor's attendant, who to prove his skill keeps a small bag of teeth extracted from the townsfolk, and for the various livestock, the piglets and she-goats, which somebody must be keeping in the larder (strong-smelling rivulets are leaking out from under the door, and one has to step over them when going through the passages), and maybe also for the cockroaches that encircled the wall lamp like a monogram, but certainly also for two more people who never appeared on the *fantiki*: Katka, her profession unknown, and her one-year-old son whose name we don't know.

10

A small body like a bladder is sprouting from the protruding little stomach with the sweet little knot in the place where it once was connected with the maternal being—maybe that's about him? Maybe Simeon Kondratyich had time to see the last person to whom Iona became attached, for whose sake he was ready to delay the realization of the prophecy:

> *Fire for the world's protection*
> *Should cleanse it of infection.*

He could definitely have been reminded of these verses later in court as a threat of arson uttered aloud; transferred to a new time, the words of anger against those who were alive acquired then an impermissible, even dangerous sense. And what could Sverbeyev reply to that? He himself took his own words seriously and he warned others honestly, knowing that in any case he wouldn't be heard, that even those who were warned wouldn't be able to change anything in their inexorable fate; how could he not exhort them to repent and to offer up a last prayer? He wasn't a doctor who prescribes drugs merely out of duty, knowing their futility—the only believer among all the locals who kept icons, the only one capable of taking faith seriously, no matter what it may be called. He was ready to endure his own life and that of others only for the sake of the child to whom he'd grown attached with the tenderness of an old man; in this ark, swarming with scum, he was called upon to protect the little boy from his own mother: Katka's lover (or husband) was supposed to return, after a three-year stint, from the province prison, and she feared for her life.

11

Close, close, almost there now. Calamitous times breed a lot of phantomlike fears; people are prone to them and are ready to multiply them, as if the phantoms help to chase away real horrors. On streets gray with dust, people were staggering and falling as if drunk—others looked at them calmly, merely making the usual distinction that if they're lying quietly, hunger's the cause, if they're twitching, it's from cholera. From the windows emanated the smell of carbolic acid. A sound like a quiet, monotonous howl didn't subside day or night—no one noticed it, as if it were the soundless background of existence. But something did disturb people's thoughts and offered them temptation; the eyes of the plaster hero on the stone exuded a moisture that paved dirty furrows on his dusty cheeks. Where did it come from? After so many months of drought? What pores had it been stored in? Disturbance and temptation. They'd already observed a woman in Stolpie who tried to catch a drop in a vial—not a plain drop, far from a plain drop! Whispers throughout the town ascribed a significant and ominous aura to everything. They finally had to pull down this figure, too, with its absurd amputated stumps on both sides, but they'd got used to seeing in it an image of the late Peresheikin—to take responsibility for that was risky, it could lead to any number of things. From an airplane they discovered in the nearby forests two settlements that weren't indicated on any maps. Supposedly, a sect fleeing from the authorities had settled somewhere there; the people worshipped a miracle-working body in a grave, not the relics but the actual body; some specified more precisely that it was a woman's body, and this woman was alive, radiant in her beauty, but lay as if in a dream, voiceless, because she'd recognized the futility of vibrating the air; she lay, impervious to time, her features unchanging with the years, privately knowing the secret word for salvation from misfortune, but the time to utter it had not yet come. And they also said: the authorities took her away from some people and concealed her somewhere, but the time of her return was near, the exhausted inhabitants of the starving villages were drawn to the empty coffin where in her name a preacher from among the former priests preached of a consolation soon to come...

12

It was coming together... it was. Just a little more. There was no need to resist any longer, Anton Andreyevich; there was good reason that the small icon looked so much like the beautiful woman on the *fantiki*. *Whispers and rumors multiply around the house. How does one stop them from getting inside? How can one hide from this hope, entreaty, demand, and threat?* No, it's not the plot of reminiscences about the distant past, it also cropped up at another time—almost a diary entry. Did anyone recognize her? Was the rumor born of its own accord? An incorrigible, absurd joker, he could have contributed to this rumor with a careless word—for example, while explaining the source of his political perspicacity—he was capable of doing that! They tricked the fool! And afterward he himself attempted to flee from those whispers to a remote estate where, quite handily, a museum was being arranged, and maybe he went even farther, as far as Nechaisk (along the highway paved under Catherine the Great) loading his scanty belongings on a ramshackle wagon or on a low wide sled: bundles of clothes, crockery and simple utensils, seeds in little bags, and maybe also small pots for seedlings and a small trunk full of *fantiki* with a lid pasted over. Maybe it's true that for a time he lived in the priest's house by the cemetery, but not for long; it wasn't any more peaceful in Nechaisk, on the contrary, and both of them, steadfastly attached to each other by expectation, couldn't run very far from the dangerous area or didn't want to. *One can't run forever*—through the years, that's the melody of his entire life. But there was no chance to hide, time was ticking away implacably, and we're already prepared to see how into the house that drew (dangerous, and the next moment, hostile) rumor like a magnet, at last, after a long absence, came the province's plenipotentiary in battle...—long-awaited, desired—his short legs in boots with built-in inner heels climbing up the steps of the rotten porch with a hunchback's gait...everything was realized, the last lines were coming together.

13

No, we can't see his face yet, only the ribbed snout of a gas mask with its round, flat, glass eyes—the mask of an authorized agent, which might have seemed to him a mark of distinguished service, of belonging to those who had a right to different air; he was ready to put it on when it wasn't necessary, was as vain about it as a child, as a provincial is vain about pinning to his chest a chance badge,* the sense of which he doesn't quite understand, poor thing, reveling in the feeling of having acquired a power not yet fully discovered. Maybe he even thought up the notepad with a title and inscribed with the owner's name himself, just as for questionnaires he had invented an origin and the details of a glorious past and had placed the order at the printer's, but his ascent up the wrungs was taking place all those years, even if in areas inaccessible to direct scrutiny, even if at first he merely helped the tax inspector uncover hidden profits, peering into pans in other people's kitchens or noting down people who were buying sturgeon in the store. But there he proved his competence and even his irreplaceability in general in delicate matters, subtle cases where a man who looked different couldn't get anywhere— he was still the same, scarcely any taller, with a small, hardly noticeable hump, with a sweet little face predisposing one to compassion and kindness...He finally removed the gas mask, revealing his smile—a grin that wasn't entirely conscious; teeth spoiled by sweets betrayed time's inner work, and perhaps the curls had thinned

---

* BADGE Soviets produced numerous metal badges or pins celebrating various political programs, groups, figures, etc. Such badges were worn by adults as well as children.

out...there was a smell of Holofernes cream for enhancing hair growth...We're ready to see how the obviously shaken old man emaciated from lack of food gets up to greet him, his pince-nez swinging on its lace, a trembling hand trying to find support against the back of a chair, his large mouth twisted...Maybe he also tried to say something to him, to hold him back, not to let him come behind the cotton curtain, that wasn't the way he'd imagined this meeting and this arrival and his boy—a caricature of how he was supposed to look—but how could he not let him in! With him, an inexorable materialized truth was entering their house and their life, neither delusion nor love, neither God nor eternity, neither heaven nor hell existed for it, only the stagnant air of a poverty-stricken dwelling without napkins and embroidered pillows, only the smell of sickness and unattractive flowers in pots, and a woman, half-raised on the bed covered with a blanket quilted from scraps of cloth, the eternal beautiful woman with fair hair, in a dress from a former era, awakened from her living dream, as if suddenly singed by a draught that blew, in a burst, into the room, creating an instant change. Her delicate skin darkened and wrinkled; the man who entered saw a strange old woman with sickly nodes of veins, yellow-violet tumors on her numb feet; and the holes with charred edges widened in the blackened, burned air...

14

It's impossible to make out anything more. But there's no need to. And we'll never completely hear her words. Did she make a move toward him? Did she say everything that she'd kept for him for so long, repeating it only in her dream?—so as to then fall back onto the pillow plumped up by thoughtful hands, not to open her eyes thereafter? Let's think that in the end she eased for her little boy the task whose meaning he probably didn't understand anyway (as it wasn't given him to understand his own life, no matter how long it lasted). The only thing he left was a scrap of paper found in the small trunk—but how did it get there? Was it dropped accidently and picked up by the hand of the hopelessly loving man? Or could it even have been stolen as a keepsake? Or left for somebody else, but not passed on?

Merinov Fedot
Zagrebelnyi Ivan
Gubanov Ilya
Vikulov Prov

They cheated the fool for all he was worth

*Only in the village of Sareyevo did saboteurs try to conceal four rich peasants to avoid paying taxes**

15

Well, you know!...This is already resembling hysterical laughter. One shouldn't do this. One shouldn't search for this meaning, too. As if it must necessarily exist. As if we're equipped to understand logic and connections where only the direction of a general flow reigns—all we know is where it leads to: this music, a melody of destruction and loss, has been in our ears for a long time. It looks as if Simeon Kondratyich, despite the ban, managed to leave the town altogether with a coffin, to conceal himself somehow in the cart with its sorrowful burden, but maybe they just let him pass like that, without noticing him immediately, and there was no purpose in turning back a fugitive. The barriers guarded the city more from those who tried to get into it from the villages where there was no bread left, to get closer to alms, to rumors about bread rations and about the concealed miracle worker, to a railway station, to the trains that passed through it; only a madman would leave the town for the burned empty spaces—he wouldn't be allowed to come back. But he had no intention of coming back; he knew where he was going from the freshly filled grave or from the widened gully where that month they'd just poured more sand on the graves, leaving room for the next row; there was no one to dig an individual grave for everybody and not enough time to do it...Here's a man walking along, body bowed as if against the wind, staggering from weakness, slowly, as in a reservoir, his lungs singed from the smoky mournful air, through the charred dead trees, through the sour smell of misfortune and burning, through the ashy color of indifference. An ominous

* Kharitonov puns here on the word "kulak," which means both "fist" and "rich peasant."

goat dogged his steps; dirty fleece on its hollow sides, a horned head with human teeth, a crazed yellow gleam in its eyes, and the manner of a beast of prey; it kept at a distance, neither coming closer nor dropping back, and stopped whenever the man stopped, as if waiting to see whether he would fall.

a look that rips at the skin

the subject of history—meat on bones

the sacrum sticks out pitifully under the skin, and the entire skeleton is visible ahead of time: that's the way he'll lie, the vertebrae bent, as he collapses, the skull separate

how much time one had to eat, to ingest, to accomplish with hard inner work in order to become so big and so perfect

a twig protruded from an eye socket

Can one see a tree and not be happy?

The tree lived and only one half of it was green, the second half was paralyzed, like a person who'd suffered a stroke

Here already there's greenery, a hill in the forest like an island, with living air above, and a familiar voice welcomes the newcomer: "Here her beloved has come."

16

Did the ancient elder Makarii think before his end or his transfiguration—a tiny little old man with a tremor in his fingers and a barely audible voice, overgrown with moss while he was still alive, who left behind him neither pupils nor writings, only the breath of a fleeting life, only the quiver of a thought and a few words that melted in the air—did he think that this spiritual tremor that sank into the void between the stars would suddenly find, by the will of chance, a response across centuries in a kindred mind, would find ground and take root, that his word, an outcry of feeling, similar to an interjection, would be transferred onto paper, amplified, interpreted, and would have an effect on life, fate, the death of others? Could Milashevich, a solitary, careless, although cautious, thinker, suppose the appearance of a sect of Makarites when he gave the name of the apocryphal elder to his unremarkable hero, endowing him with the traits of a cemetery priest, an amateur gardener, with whom he exchanged seeds, experience, and maybe some ideas? Maybe he heard about the apocrypha from the priest; but maybe, on the contrary, he himself pointed out the craziness of the strange heretical thought to this natural freethinker with calloused peasant hands and the sparse beard of a Mordvinian, to the man who'd become disillusioned with the church before he was banished from it, to the seeker with a scholarly turn of mind who, under a pseudonym, had published two pamphlets: about the soothing and healing properties of certain herbs that he'd tried out on himself, and also about the special sensitivity to vodka of people with an admixture of Mordvinian blood. But, be that as it may, it was no accident that all this meshed together; the name of the elder who'd vanished long ago and the solid figure of his contemporary in the dusty highboots, gray cassock, and hat faded from the rain, the fantasy of ancient ideas, the shocks of new experience, and the provincial thinker's search—from Milashevich's precipitous lines there emerged a living fate, incarnated, and at the same time one of the possibilities of his own thought pushed to the limit, of that very thought that had reason to resist an attempt at direct words.

17

The new Makarii's ideas were linked with his experience of the church, where people came—as he knew—not necessarily out of genuine belief, but from timidity, weakness, and cautious habit, so as to have something to lean on outside of themselves: but he also knew how unreliable this support was, based on allusions and promises that weren't subject to verification. Not satisfied with such a half-hope, some people are ready to go the full stretch themselves; in ancient times there lived in these parts self-immolators, those who buried themselves in the ground, those who walled up each other with earth and stones, and with children in their arms, singing psalms, they slowly and patiently, through the torture and pain, left the earthly valley for the bliss of the

other world. The new Makarii knew, however, that this is too frightening and beyond the strength of those who are weak, for whose sake
Milashevich and he, his spiritual double or selfproclaimed apostle,
tried to do something. The way of a quiet transformation suggested by
the elder was closer to what was needed, but one had to interpret his
experience only in an allegorical way; for direct imitation one needed
holiness, which also isn't accessible to everybody. The new Makarii listened to everything. Along with the times he understood and accepted
the rightness of those who didn't overly trust in the bliss of the other
world, who were ready to promise full realization of it right here. He
stopped reading the burial service for the dead, closed the evasively
dishonest church, and at first tried to find the words for those whom
he would have to bury later; he closed their eyes, smoothed out the
spasm of suffering on their faces, and was glad to see them pacified.
He carefully read the writings of his contemporary, who taught him to
think about the resurrection of the dead, and he singled out his appeal
to make a burial place the center of life, triumphs, and religious rites
(but at the same time he had no intention of returning to the cemetery
cathedral). He even went to Moscow to look at and stand near a new,
unprecedented sacred place. Wasn't it Simeon Kondratyich who
advised him to include in the list of names of the dead to be remembered in church a prayer for the well-being of the German Fige? Wasn't
it Fyodor Ivanovich himself who gave him money for the trip and was
remembered in prayer out of gratitude? Several hasty words pronounced at the shrine with the body had a result that exceeded all
expectations; but the capital seemed not to understand itself too well
and was incapable of going any further, while he, collecting ideas like
pollen from various flowers, transformed those ideas into a united
faith. Was there much left to add? Maybe just his own experiences with
soothing herbs capable of bringing bliss. *A religion for the people…*

18

No, there's no need to rearrange anything anymore, Anton
Andreyevich; everything seems to be right, it all seems to have come
together. An empty grave rises on a wooden platform in the midst of
the forest settlement, among the dugouts and cabins covered with a

dry bark to give them protection not from the rain but from the sun, among cemetery crosses that resemble dead trees. A bonfire from the last religious rite is burning in the clearing. The welcome broth is gurgling in the cauldron. The half-naked exhausted people look at the man who's finally come: their rotted clothing has grown into their dirty bodies; only by the beards can one distinguish the men from the women—by the little folds of skin in the place of nipples; their faces are covered in green spots. But the light of inner delight, of imminent joy, flares in their eyes. There's nothing more to wait for. A sweet steam rises over the cauldron, the smell makes them dizzy. Rejoice, you long-suffering people who have endured so much for so long—everybody will have a chance to drink from this, and you will know a moment of bliss that will make your past life worth it, and this moment will become an eternity. Our whole life was an involuntary resistance to this ease and freedom. The search is frightening, thought is excruciating, every belief threatens to become a delusion, and we lack the personal strength to deny ourselves, squeezed as each of us is into a miserable, perishable shell, to join the radiance of the sun, spilled like juice, or of the night stars. Here we will help each other, will make contact with our hands and bodies, fear and triumph will merge as in sexual intercourse, which resuscitates men's and women's hopes of being complemented by each other. It's as if an uneven mirror that until now has given only distorted surface reflections is dissolving and allowing us to pass through into the depths, where nobody has been before; there's only the vegetable simplicity of life, only the movement of tentacles, the sweetness of slime, the freedom of spreading roots. To stay there, to stay and not want anything else—that's the ultimate, that's bliss...if only you were here...

19

What effort enabled him to wake up? What mother suddenly recalled the child who could not be left without her?

> "I'd be glad to, I'd like to, but I can't."
> "Then go. Do as you want."
> "Can I really?"
> It's so easy. Like leaving a dream.

20

He realized that he was still alive because he remembered everything, only he didn't recognize the place. Empty bast shoes lay on the ground, as did foot wrappings brown from sweat, like somebody's hide, cast off in the course of a transformation. The tiniest of creatures, smaller than ants, small black dots, were quickly carrying off something bit by bit, returning to the earth what had come out of it. He knew what he'd come back to town for, as if he had no doubts that he could enter it, because there was no longer any reason for barriers to guard it; everything came completely true, a shaven-headed house robber left the district prison, and his unfaithful mistress, drenched in sweat from fear, strangled her baby with a pillow in the night, and there was nobody anymore for whose sake to guard the doomed den. He didn't know that, and he was going to his house, to his small trunk, as if he had no doubts that it would remain untouched by any fire. Along the roadway, along the smoking site of the fire, the wind carried sheets of paper salvaged from Ganshin's burned-down factory; a beautiful woman was smiling from the *fantiki*, her hand gently bent, while water flowed from her watering can. He kept retrieving the sheets, shaking the ash from them, and putting them in the pocket of his Tolstoy peasant shirt—this was the last of his supply, at home he had only one more notebook left, saved for the most important explanation. But first he had to draw the lines of the life plot to an end, to record the flashes of decisive feelings and thoughts—not for himself, certainly not for himself, he had to warn someone about the mortally serious thing he'd finally realized—and which he'd been horrified at—he had to leave someone a key to the fragments of a shattered idea; he still recalled for whom it would be as he filled in the last *fantiki* with the remainder of the ink. His mind was already shaken, but his handwriting was still recognizable as he wrote, looking for the right words, and if they were to burn, let them: even if we didn't have those sheets now, the shadows of his words would linger in the air, particles of breath, the ashes of a burned-out life, and our minds would try to restore them, to condense them from the elusive, yet authentic, substance. He still remembered whom he was writing to when, in the handwriting of semidelirium, in ink, then with a pencil stub, he produced the uneven lines, without punctuation, in the cherished notebook, perhaps trying to urge on, to refresh a mind growing turbid with the smoke of a joy-bearing herb, but something new, like a familiar face, was already peeping out from the letters—he had to finish telling it all to someone anyway, to release it into space if necessary, without even entertaining any hope—this was the last act of service available to him.

21

like a thin layer of skin over a wound, the ground is healing

the humus of oblivion

children smiling as they step over you with their innocent heels

a chicken leg is amusement for a child

the slap of a fish bubble underfoot

how flimsy is this substance, flesh and mucus, how vulnerable to a spike, how any blow with it can crush and squash it

something else, which cannot even be touched, turns out to be firm and permanent

do we really only give birth to a body

a pile of stones, darkness and the cold of the universe, terror and emptiness

only a creator of beauty and meaning brings beauty and meaning into the world

for some reason this is necessary, but only for us

someone is relying on us no less than we rely on him

XVIII. ON THE AIR, or THE NAME OF A FLOWER

The flower on the window sill was yellowed and dried up. The icicles suspended from the window trim oozed, emanating a limpid light. The snow would disappear soon, and the remains of the metal machinery—levers, springs, and headlights—mixed with the fragments of skulls and bones would be exposed in the devastated cemetery: a broken light bulb rolled into an empty eye socket, a battery with the remains of its nutritious liquid is drying up under some ribs, an exhaust pipe sticks up toward the sky. And immediately the tall weeds will cover them, small trees will propagate themselves, the tenant on the eighth floor will look at the picturesque greenery. "But not me. And it's a good thing I won't," Anton thought listlessly. A state of sickly apathy had descended on him again, as it frequently did of late. Serious effort, both mental and physical, came hard to him. All he wanted to do was lie on the couch and finish reading a fantastic tale. The story told of catastrophe, which took place in full view of everyone, but so slowly and gradually that nobody was aware of it until the last minute, because no one was disposed to be aware of it. He couldn't take more serious reading. It wasn't just mental tiredness—he seemed to have become weak willed. Even to get up once he was lying down was difficult—something wasn't right with his balance: the floor under his feet had acquired an uncomfortable slope; he had to adapt to it, first by holding onto the wall, onto objects on the way, or to move faster right away, as on a bicycle. He should go to the doctor, but he wasn't sure that it was only a question of inner sensations. From time to time Anton noticed that chairs seemed to slowly move, to slide along the floor by themselves, and plates constantly seemed to move to the edge of the table. He had to put pieces of plywood under the legs of the table. Maybe the foundation of the house was sinking and getting warped? After a day spent at home Lizavin managed to get so used to this slope that when he went outdoors he felt uncomfortable—he tottered like a sailor who after the constant rolling of the ship totters when he steps on solid ground.

2

With a box under his arm and his glasses on his nose, Anton imperceptibly fell asleep. He dreamed about a Moscow escalator. He stepped onto it to go up from the basement. Past the palace columns and arches entwined in ivy. Once the sky was overhead, the incline of the escalator grew less and less noticeable—holding onto the handrail, he rode past the slow buildings that seemed like the houses in Nechaisk, and the people on the level below seemed to be familiar; their eyes, full of a puzzling silent pity, followed Anton. He gave a frivolous wave of his hand to them—as if to say, I'm off—but nobody responded; there was anxiety and sadness in this silence. There, below, as if from a high bridge, he recognized his mother; she also was looking at him in tense silence. He could jump off to join her— it wasn't so awful, but as if she'd guessed his intention, she roused herself, her whole demeanor sending out the message: Don't, don't do it. You stepped on the escalator—stay on it, you've got to go to the very end, with no detours. Where? What for? It's so far and you can't see the end. Maybe *she* is standing somewhere among the people staring at him. Maybe he'll see her once he reaches the end? Suddenly there are cries: "He's jumped off, he's jumped off!" Someone fell from a height, far below. If one leaned over the rubber railing, one could make out something terrible below, although terrible only mentally, for in reality there was only a blob, facilitated by distance. Where were you looking, scum? What were you thinking of? How's it possible to drink so much?...

3

Lizavin came to. He was lying on the couch. On the other side of the wall Seryozha's wife was swearing at him. "You should know when to stop every now and then, you fucking bum!" The sound that accompanies a pillow being beaten lent the words emphasis. "I know... I always know..." his neighbor responded with patient dignity, and in stages, during the intervals between the pounding of the pillow. "What do you know...you shit...you miserable drunk?" his wife asked, sustaining the same measured rhythm. "Don't call me...a drunk...A drunk drinks...he drinks anything without looking. And I look to see." "Ah, you do, do you? And what do you...damn you... like so...and so...what do you look at?" "Urine. I look at my urine. As soon as the urine's black...it means 'Stop, that's enough.' That's popular wisdom." "Wisdom, hah?" the woman had suspended the rhythm while listening to this explanation, but now compensated for it by doubling the rate of her beating. "And who did you bring instead of Sashka? Just look...go on...look, you sot. Is this Sashka? Is it?" The gist of the conflict between the spouses gradually became clear to him: the neighbor, it turns out, usually went to kindergarten to pick up Sasha, but, being drunk, he took some other boy, who, one gathers, was quietly observing what was going on around him. "All right, why the fuss," Seryozha tried to cut through things, peaceably, like a man who knows he's at fault. "Big deal! We have to take him back there tomorrow anyway. We'll exchange him." "Tomorrow's Saturday," his wife reminded him. Her hands were evidently busy with buttons now, she was putting on her coat and noisily looking for something; she finally left, slamming the door so hard that all the windows of the house resonated. I should get up, Lizavin thought. Either his recent dream or the episode on the other side of the wall filled him with a strange anguish. Liusia was supposed to arrive soon. They were planning to celebrate his birthday in the evening. He had to get out of this frame of mind. There was something I wanted to do, to make a decision...Or did I only imagine it? I don't want anything else. Not even to think...Ah, Lizavin recalled what it was. Should I finally marry Liusia?

The woman brought him an expensive present: a Spidola radio made in Riga. Anton even felt awkward, but then he recalled what he was planning to say today, and everything became simpler. He turned on the radio right away to try it out, started to adjust the tuning knob, and unexpectedly cheered up. "We've started living like normal people," he said suddenly. The woman looked at him the way one looks at a favorite child whom one's managed to please; she tried so hard, she wanted so much to please him, but she wasn't sure whether she had or whether she'd accidentally made her unpredictable lord and master angry. Her shyness was touching...God, how much quiet, self-sacrificing love shone in her gaze! Her eyes had a new moist luster...she'd grown prettier...No, she's simply pretty in general because she loves him.

"Well, let's have a drink, shall we?" Lizavin grinned.

The woman shook her head.

"What's the matter? Did I say anything wrong?"

"No. I just don't drink."

"Since when?"

"Since then. I wouldn't say no to a bit of wine. But I don't drink vodka."

"Why?" Lizavin asked once again, then suddenly understood. Looking at her face, he understood by her moist eyes and embarrassed glow. "Ah...Why are you being like this about it? You won't even tell me. I hope this has something to do with me? Am I right?"

"What are you talking about?" she blushed. "How can you think that?"

"Why are you being like this?" Anton repeated, and shook his head; once again everything got settled by itself, without words and decisions on his part.

"But I don't need anything," she said.

"Come, now. That's not right. Whom do you take me for?...Listen, you move in with me for good, all right? It's a bit cramped, of course. Look, let's advertise for an exchange. We'll get a large efficiency instead, maybe even a one-bedroom apartment."

"A one-bedroom," she seconded him.

"See? Everything will be fine." Anton looked around his room as if estimating its value. "By the way, I keep forgetting to ask you, what's the name of this flower?"

"This one?"

"Yes. As you can see, it's completely dried up. I need to throw it away."

"It's an ordinary century plant."

"Yes, that's right. Strange, I actually knew that. I knew the word and the flower, but I couldn't put them together."

"What's wrong?"

"Nothing," Anton said. "Two rooms, imagine! I'll pay a bit more if necessary."

5

Just a minute, just a second, just close your eyes, think about the other woman, and visualize her. Otherwise it won't work. What can you do? There's no love, but there's compassion, tenderness, and the wisdom of the blind body, and the deviousness of the poor mind. Now it's fine. An eyeless fish reaches out into the darkness with its seeking little lips. One needs to have another person exist, made like one's other half, who'll complement one. That's for starters. A merciful body, in which you seek a haven from weakness and anguish, and hold onto for support. All over town in the cells of their apartments men were hiding in women's merciful bosoms, recapturing their mothers' breasts with their lips. People burrow into each other in the hope of recovering a lost completeness, but they rarely realize they're doing so, thinking more about vanity, pleasure, compromise, pain…Life's ruse…and it's taken its toll. Nothing in it ever ends, men just feel that it does; a woman's better at understanding infinity…A drunken voice could be heard outside, a motorcycle roared past, and somewhere a dog started to bark.

6

In the morning Liusia left his apartment to go to work. Without knocking, as if he were the landlord, Sashka from the apartment next door appeared with a cat in his arms. Although he didn't come in from outdoors, he brought with him a smell of freshness—the smell of watermelon, water from melted snow, the smell of laundry that had dried outside in frosty weather. The cat immediately found a spot for itself on the couch. It was impossible not to admire the expediency of its movements. Having climbed onto a chair and kneeled on it, Sashka asked for some paper to draw on. The lamp illuminated his cheek, with its crust of dried snot, his tender pink lips, and his small grubby fist with bright marigolds. Looking at the boy, Lizavin experienced astounded gratitude to the force that had allowed him to be born and grow up the way he was, given his family, this house, and this backyard, where the profound idiot Albert strolled, a small paper tube shoved up his nostril—among drunken profanities, fights, and obscenities, filth didn't seem to stick to him. In spite of everything, life managed, if only for the time being, to protect its creation, providing him, like a tender seed, with a protective cover. But will it suffice for long? In such an environment it will corrode—how can one save those limpid eyes, those sturdy trusting eyelashes, the fuzz on the rosy cheeks? Yet for all that, it's a miracle, a boon. Sasha knew that he was loved here. Frightened and cunning at home, in Anton's room he behaved with regal confidence. Once he got the paper, he started to draw an airplane. He put a marksman on the plane. He put a bow in the marksman's hands.

"You know, Anton," he told his host as he worked, "Vovka, who lives in the hut, found a nuclear bomb in the yard. It's true. He showed it to me himself."

"Really? And what does it look like?"

"Like a pumice stone," Sasha said.

"I should throw out the century plant," Anton remembered. "Why did it die?" Useless thought. But a splinter, a splinter had stuck in his chest, and his dream about falling, and an inexplicable feeling—it was as if something had come to him out of the empty air, inaudibly, without words. For some reason he picked up the radio he'd received as a gift and started to turn the tuning knob.

"Anton," Sasha was talking to himself. "You know, America turns out to be not like our territory—it was discovered..."

What did Lizavin want to hear now? Why did he turn the tuning knob without keeping it on a music station? It was as if he was looking for something specific. No, nothing. He was checking the sound of what was on the air. The crackle of tearing paper, a wheeze, the gurgling of drowned men, machine gun-like noises of flatulence, the periods and dashes of an incomprehensible Morse code. The working people of the district... *hrrr...shsh...ppk...pppk...shenrechten sivers.** No, that's in my brain, he thought. I'm starting to rave. At whose death does a century plant die? At any moment, at random, right now, somebody is dying every second, perishing, jumping from rubber handrails, from a windowsill on the eleventh floor, and is hurtling toward the asphalt, bombs are falling onto the beds of sleeping inhabitants, without any radio we're pierced with shouts and voices that are absolutely clear now: Sivers. No, it wasn't a fantasy, he didn't imagine it, you knew it from somewhere: Maksim Sivers. Committed suicide. A crack is spreading on the white wall, a glass that's moved is teetering on the edge of the table...

7

A shot in slow motion, a prolonged moment of explosion, when everything flies upside down, but the change of position in every film in each frame is so imperceptible that we continue to talk, to move, to put our affairs in order, to command armies, to produce offspring—and only from time to time, briefly surprised at the discomfort of our position, we change the slant, restore the balance, we adapt, insert small pieces of wood, finish a phrase, without understanding that everything has already happened, everything's already happened, and somebody who's the most sensitive and vulnerable, outdistancing us, is falling from a height...

8

"It's me. Me," Anton muttered soundlessly and senselessly, for some reason pulling out the drawers of the closet, examining them as if he were sizing them up to see whether he could put something in them. His actions were senseless, like his muttering, and he was aware of

---

* To an uncomprehending Russian ear, the sound of the German words "schon... rechten Sie...wer s..."

that. "I've known it for a long time. I felt it—and allowed it. Now there's nobody except for me to do it. That's what he wanted to tell me. He had nobody to rely on anymore. He wanted to pass it on to me. Now there's only me. Maybe it's not too late to find it. He kept delaying so there'd be more likelihood of hearing: there's no one with that name here. Behind the door that they open with a trihedral key. It would be good to hear, but he had to look anyway. There's still hope. There's hope while someone tries to revive it. And there's nobody except you to do it. There's no meaning besides that which you yourself can create. We're doomed to hope; we have to live in such a way as if it depends on us to start from the very beginning. Because as soon as you let yourself feel otherwise, someone is betrayed—he's already hurtling, falling irrevocably, and you're not there at his side to hold him back and free yourself from blame. Maybe only this feeling of connection is what's called fate. You're free to accept it or not, but someone's waiting for you anyway. Only for you..."

"I know," the boy philosophized. "Seaweeds came from water, all kinds of little crawfish, tadpoles, and fish came from seaweed, lizards from them, animals from lizards, monkeys from the animal, man from the monkey..."

And what's the shaving gear for? Doesn't that look like another escape? Someone will be waiting for you here as well, with a fetus in her belly...

"Anton," Sasha said. "And from us?"

"What from us?"

"What will come from us?"

"Difficult question. I don't know. Something probably will."

The sun had emerged from behind the clouds and now shone through the window. Specks of dust teemed in the wide ray, moving up, down, sideways—the usual specks of dust, impossible to keep track of, but now they belonged to the ray, were structured by it, shone in it. What a light, what pain, and what clarity!

"And is it true that Kashchei* is not that immortal?" the boy

---

* KASHCHEI In Russian folklore, Kashchei (or Koshchei) the Deathless is a cruel, seemingly imperishable old man whose death is hidden in an egg.

continued the discussion. "He's got death in a needle. Not in our needle, not my mother's. Our needles are the ordinary kind. It's in a different one."

His hair smelled of the sweet smoke of a camp fire, of a misty meadow over a clean river. Light filled the air, penetrated the curtains, dissolved the outlines of objects, and the haphazard particles tautened and shifted, subject to an invisible force.